Maggie Mason is a pseudonym of author Mary Wood. Mary began her career by self-publishing on Kindle, where many of her sagas reached number one in genre. She was spotted by Pan Macmillan and to date has written many books for them under her own name, with more to come.

Mary continues to be proud to write for Pan Macmillan, but is now equally proud and thrilled to take up a second career with Sphere under the name of Maggie Mason.

Born the thirteenth child of fifteen children, Mary describes her childhood as poor, but rich in love. She was educated at St Peter's RC School in Hinckley and at Hinckley College for Further Education, where she was taught shorthand and typing.

Mary retired from working for the National Probation Service in 2009, when she took up full-time writing, something she'd always dreamed of doing. She follows in the footsteps of her great-grandmother, Dora Langlois, who was an acclaimed author, playwright and actress in the late nineteenth–early twentieth century.

It was her work with the Probation Service that gives Mary's writing its grittiness, her need to tell it how it is, which takes her readers on an emotional journey to the heart of issues.

MAGGIE MASON

The
Halfpenny
Girls

sphere

SPHERE

First published in Great Britain in 2021 by Sphere

1 3 5 7 9 10 8 6 4 2

A CIP catalogue record for this book is available from the British Library.

ISBN 978-0-7515-8072-3

Typeset in Bembo by Hewer Text UK Ltd, Edinburgh
Printed and bound in Great Britain by Clays Ltd, Elcograf S.p.A.

Papers used by Sphere are from well-managed forests
and other responsible sources.

Sphere
An imprint of
Little, Brown Book Group
Carmelite House
50 Victoria Embankment
London
EC4Y 0DZ

An Hachette UK Company
www.hachette.co.uk

www.littlebrown.co.uk

To the loving memory of Marg Seaman, Alice Flood, Edith Walker and Ada Leadbeater, who live on in the memory of their grandchildren; Bob Coltman, whose memory is cherished by his daughter; and Averil Moore, remembered and cherished by her daughter.

And to Jackie and Clive Pennells, a golden couple.

All enriched this book by lending their Christian names to characters. Thank you. I hope I have done you proud.

ONE

1937

Marg

'Oh, Alice!' Marg's heart filled with pity as Alice came towards her. One of Alice's eyes was swollen and her cheek looked bruised.

Before Marg could react further, Edith stepped out of her house across the road at the top end of Whittaker Avenue, in Blackpool – a street lined with terraced houses with their living room doors leading straight onto the pavement.

Edith called a greeting as she ran over to them, just as Alice reached Marg.

Another day working in the packing department of Bradshaw's biscuit factory loomed for them, but though the work was repetitive and back-breaking, their hours of labour were some of their happiest. Released from their cares at home and all that weighed them down, they enjoyed the banter that went back and forth amongst the women they worked alongside.

Marg linked arms with Alice and Edith. Friends since baby-hood, they'd been born on this street within days of each other and would celebrate their twentieth birthdays this September.

Alice, the shortest of the three, had a dainty figure, a mound of blonde curls framing her pretty face, and huge liquid-blue eyes that were the first thing everyone noticed. Though her looks were often spoilt by a black eye or bruised cheek – even a split lip on one occasion.

Edith, the tallest by an inch, had strong, beautiful features and hazel, expressive eyes, which gave her a striking presence. Her jet-black hair added to this as she wore it rolled off her face and falling in waves down her back.

Beside them, Marg felt the least attractive, with her face dotted with freckles and her mousy-coloured hair that had a mind of its own – more prone to frizz than curls, and sometimes untameable.

Sighing, Marg leant towards Alice and asked the question that she had no need to. 'Your da?'

Alice nodded and a tear plopped onto her cheek.

Snuggling her in closer, Marg felt the pity of Alice's life. Her da was changed beyond recognition from the jolly man Marg remembered as a kid. He'd always had time for them. If they were playing in the street, he'd pick them up in turn and twirl them round with his hands held high, making them scream with a mixture of laughter and fear at being dropped – which he sometimes pretended to do.

Then a fateful day five years ago changed him: an accident in the rock factory where he worked left him in a coma for months. Unbeknown to him, his beloved wife, and ma to Alice and her three younger brothers, fell ill with cancer. She had passed away by the time Alice's da came to. This saw the

2

dawning of a change in him: the fun-loving man was no more and the anger that seemed to constantly burn in him erupted over the slightest provocation.

Marg felt at a loss as to what to say to Alice, but was saved from worrying about it as a cry from her own front door had her turning her head to see her gran standing on their step. Running back to her, she took her hands.

'I'm hungry, Marg.'

'Stay inside, Gran. You've had your breakfast. Porridge, remember? I made you a nice bowlful and you ate the lot.'

'Did I, lass?'

'You did, Gran. Now, go inside.'

'I tried to calm her, Marg.'

'I know, Jackie.' Marg's adored younger sister appeared at the open door.

Marg smiled. 'It's all right, lass. Have you got everything you need ready for school?'

'Aye, I'm ready. And I've washed the pots. Gran was asleep in front of the fire while I did them.'

'Is Ma not up yet, lass?'

'Naw, I took her a mug of tea up. She looks awful, Marg.' Jackie's expression held despair.

'Look, lass, you're not to worry. I'll sort it. I'll ask Ada Arkwright to look after Ma and Gran for the day. I've got a bit extra coming in this week from the overtime I did on Saturday. It'll be enough to pay her. You're not to concern yourself. You just concentrate on getting that school certificate — that's the most important thing in your life, Jackie. You leave the worrying to me, eh?'

'I can chip in, Marg. Mr Fairweather gave me a bit extra for staying on last night and helping him to pack all the grocery boxes for his round today.'

'That's good, as I had earmarked some of my overtime money for paying your tutor – I owe him two weeks as it is.'

Marg's one ambition in life was to give Jackie a good start. She'd never known a cleverer kid. And no matter what it took, she was determined that Jackie would make something of herself and not end up in a dead-end job like herself.

To ensure her sister got her school certificate with honours – something she would need to be considered for college – Marg had approached her old headmaster, Mr Grimshaw, and asked him to give Jackie extra lessons after school. He'd agreed to tutor her two evenings for two shillings a week. This was a lot to find out of her average weekly pay of thirty-two shillings. After that and the twelve shillings for rent, ten shillings for food, five for a bag of coal, which she bought every week, stockpiling in the summer to cover the bitter cold of the winter, she only had a few bob left to feed the gas meter. The rest went to the tally man, to buying the books Jackie needed and to paying for help to look after her ma and her gran, who'd lost her marbles.

Like most others around here, they couldn't afford the doctor often and relied on Ada Arkwright's services for anything medical. A Red Cross worker during the Great War, she delivered all the babies in the area and saw to most folk's ailments for a quarter of what the doctor charged, often accepting a favour for payment, such as knitting her a new cardigan. But Marg had no favours to offer, and so had to find the two shillings she charged for a day's care.

4

'Marg! Come on, lass. We're going to be late!'

'Sorry, Edith, you two go on. Clock me in, will you? I'll not be a moment. I'll knock on the side door so listen out for me and make sure that Moaning Minnie don't notice anything. Mind, she's always too busy making eyes at the boss.'

Edith laughed at this as she turned away, taking Alice's arm.

But for all her bravado, Marg's heart dropped to see her two friends carry on on their way to work without her, and though she'd made a joke, she really didn't want to get on the wrong side of Mrs Roberts, the floor manager, known behind her back as Moaning Minnie.

Sixty if she was a day, Moaning Minnie painted her face like a youngster experimenting with make-up. Eyes heavy with bright blue shadow, ashes clogged with mascara, and her bleached blonde hair frizzed to rival Marg's. She was a tartar to them, docking them a full half hour for being just a few minutes late, and lording over them, picking up on the minutest of mistakes that would get through but for her beady eye. Then bawling out the culprit and making them repack the whole tin. This meant a setback if you were on piece work.

Shaking these thoughts off, Marg concentrated on helping Gran. 'Eeh, love, let's get you settled back by the fire.'

'I'll find you a biscuit, Gran, how would that be?'

'No, ta, Jackie, love. I've had me breakfast. Marg made me some porridge, didn't you, Marg?'

'I did, Gran.' Marg smiled at Jackie. 'Pop along to Ada's, lass, ask her to come as soon as she can, eh?'

As Marg tucked a blanket around Gran's knees, it seemed to her that her troubles were piled high, and coping with everything was weighing her down.

Gran had been this way for over a year now, not knowing from one minute to the next what was happening, and it felt as though they were losing a piece of her each day.

She'd moved in with them when their da had died six years earlier. A lovely da, who Marg still grieved for. He'd had a weak heart, then one day he just keeled over and was gone. Her ma had never been the same since. Always ailing, she suffered with her breathing, and often had days when she was so weak she couldn't get out of bed.

These times escalated Marg's problems as she just had to go to work. The only alternative was to fall back on the meagre parish relief, and she didn't want to do that. As it was, she ended up borrowing from her uncle more often than she wanted to and more than she could pay back.

Her da's brother, Uncle Eric, was nothing like her da had been. The local money lender, bookmaker and pawnbroker, Eric went from house to house collecting his debts, or some item of value that he'd hold until the borrower could pay – or sell off if they couldn't.

He'd jot down everything Marg borrowed, licking the tip of his pencil before writing in his grubby little book. But then sometimes, out of the blue, he would let her off her payments, saying, 'Your slate's clean, till the next time.' Then he'd smile a funny smile and say, 'Your uncle's always here for you, you know that, Marg.'

Marg had mixed feelings about her uncle. Mostly, she didn't like him, though she couldn't have said why – apart from his bullying ways with folk who couldn't pay, and his preying on the poor, he always treated her with respect and spoke kindly to her. It rankled her that he wasn't like that with Jackie. He

6

wasn't unkind to her, but, well, *indifferent* is how she'd describe his attitude where Jackie was concerned.

With Gran settled, Marg was about to leave when the sound of her ma knocking on her bedroom floor made her dash upstairs.

'Ma, Ma, are you all right?'

Ma dropped the old walking stick she kept by her bed and looked up at Marg. The sound of her ma wheezing and the sight of her leaning over the side of the bed hurt Marg's heart. 'Ma? Eeh, Ma . . . Don't worry, Ada'll be here in a mo. She'll help you. She always gets you going again with a bowl of hot water and Friars' Balsam, don't she?'

Lifting her ma's frail, thin body, Marg held her gently in her arms. Fear trembled through her at the feel of Ma's struggle to draw her breath in. 'You'll be all right, Ma. Try to calm down and breathe slowly. That's it. By, you've been right for days. I thought you were having a good patch.'

'I – I was, lass. Don't . . . worry about me. Get – get off to work.'

'All right, Ma.' Propping her up against the mound of pillows, she kissed her sweat-soaked forehead. 'I love you, Ma. We'll get through, I promise. There's a bit of overtime going at the factory and not many want to do it. I've asked for as much of it as they can give me.'

'You're . . . a good lass.'

'I wish I could do more, Ma. Anyroad, I've got to get going. I've got the tea all ready for tonight: I've peeled the spuds and put them in a saucepan of water and I've got a casserole on low in the oven. It'll take all day so don't worry about it. I'll soon get everything going when I get in. Oh, and there's a couple of hard-boiled eggs in a dish on the cold slab. You and Gran can have them for your dinner with some doorsteps off that loaf that's left, and there's a nice bit of dripping an' all. Make you both a sandwich, eh?'

'Ta, love. Now, off you go. You'll be getting the – the sack.'

Hugging her ma once more, Marg skipped down the stairs.

Ada met her as she got to the bottom. 'Now, Margaret, this shows you that what I've always said is right.'

Ada always used her full name when she was on what she called 'official business'. It was a name Marg loved as it was her da's mother's name, and she'd loved her Granny Margaret.

'You're going to have to put your gran in an asylum, lass, and think about sending your ma to a sanatorium – both would be better off. You know that this can't go on. I can't always come to your aid. I've got Mrs Coop about to drop her fourth nipper and Mr Herald on his last legs. I'll have to go if I'm fetched to either of them.'

'I know, Ada. Get Ma on her feet and she'll cope with Gran. But neither of them are leaving this house until they have to – God, I hope the day never comes. But no matter what, I couldn't put them away. I couldn't.'

'Well, you get yourself to work, lass. Your gran looks peaceful there. Look, she's snoring, bless her. I'll see to your ma first.'

'Ta, Ada. I'll pay you at the end of the week.'

Hugging Jackie before she left and telling her not to be late for school, Marg took off and ran all the way to the factory on Mansfield Road, a three-minute sprint instead of her usual five-minute walk.

Her first tap had Edith opening the door. Marg sidled in.

'Moaning Minnie's been on the prowl, Marg. I told her you were in the loo, so hurry yourself.'

'I will, ta, lass. I'll nip into the cloakroom and leave me jacket. You get back to the line.'

The line referred to the women picking the biscuits as they came down the conveyor belt. Today, they were packing fancy biscuit barrels that would be on the shelves for Christmas – the snow scene they depicted was at odds with this being July.

Each tin had to contain four custard creams, which were placed inside the corrugated paper that was shaped into pockets. Once they'd done this, the tins would go to the next belt to be packed with chocolate digestives, then on again to have rich tea added and, finally, shortbread biscuits.

As Marg took her place next to Edith's side, Edith grinned. 'Eeh, Marg, you're like a cat with nine lives, but you must be coming to the end of them soon. Moaning Minnie's on to you, I'm sure of it.'

'I know, and I worry about you and Alice – if you're caught clocking in for me, you could get the sack too. Oh, I don't know, life's so complicated.'

'Maybe you should listen to what Ada's always telling you?'

'No, never. Gran stays with me. Anyroad, I'm hoping she won't play up in the mornings again. You just never know with her. I'll nip home during dinner break and make sure they're both all right.'

When at last one o'clock came, Marg scooted out of the factory gate. She'd no time to eat the oven-bottom bun that had been part of a batch she'd baked over the weekend, but she didn't care. She just needed to put her mind at rest.

It was as she was about to cross Talbot Road that she met Betty, Edith's mum, and felt a sense of dread wash over her as Betty called out in a slurred voice, 'Hel-yo, lash.'

Marg groaned. A known drunk, Betty was the last person Marg needed to see, even though the encounter made her troubles seem like nothing to what Edith, and Alice too, had to put up with.

'Hello, Betty, love. I can't stop, I've only got a short time to get to me ma and gran.'

'Have you got a couple of bob to shpare, Marg, lass? I'm dying for a fag.'

As Betty wobbled towards her, her sour, alcohol-fuelled breath wafted over Marg.

'No . . . where will I get a couple of bob from, eh? Anyroad, you only need fivepence to get five fags, and if you're think-ing of another drink, you've had enough, Betty. See you later, love.'

'I'll jush have to sell me body then, won't I?' Betty shouted as Marg carried on making her way home.

Marg wanted to shout back that no one would pay for her body the state it was in, but she just laughed and ran on her way.

The laugh didn't touch her inner self, though, as she thought of how mortified Edith was when her ma got like this, and how it usually meant that she had to go around the town paying folk back for what her ma had borrowed. Marg had told her time and again not to because knowing Edith would pay, the locals never refused Betty credit, but Edith needed to keep her pride – well, as much as she was able to with a ma like Betty.

When Marg turned into her street, the sight of her gran sitting outside on a kitchen chair cheered her. 'Hello, Gran. Enjoying the sunshine, eh?'

'Do you know me, lass?'

'Aye, I know you. You're a lovely lady who I love very much.'

'Oh?'

'It's Marg, Gran.'

'Our Marg?'

'Aye, the very one.'

'Why didn't you say so? Hello, Marg. Were you a good lass at school today?'

Marg sighed. 'I was, Gran, but I've to get back there before the whistle goes. Is Ma about?'

'Me ma? Where?'

'Never mind, Gran. You go back to your daydreaming.'

As Marg stepped inside, her ma greeted her: 'Marg! Hello, lass, I didn't expect you home.'

'Are you all right, Ma?'

'Aye, Ada got me going again, ta, lass, but you shouldn't have left work.'

A whiff of stale tobacco gave Marg a feeling of despair. 'Ma! You've been smoking! How did you get a fag? Who gave it to you?'

'Oh, don't take on, Marg. I told you, it clears me lungs. It really helps me. I need me fags.'

'But how did you get them?'

'Your Uncle Eric called round. He brought me a packet.'

A voice from outside shouted, 'That's not all he brought her, I heard . . .'

'You shut up with your silly waffle!'

Ma had gone red in the face at Gran calling this out, but she laughed a nervous laugh. 'Me ma can be a silly old cow with her sayings. She's just not your old gran anymore, is she? Anyroad, lass, get back to the factory afore you lose your job.'

Just before Marg left, she asked how long Ada had stayed. Once again, Gran piped up: 'She left when that uncle of yours came, and I've been out here since – I want to come in, Marg.'

'I'll get her in. You get going. Go on, lass.'

As Marg went, she heard her ma telling Gran off in a joking way. 'You don't miss much for all your brain's addled, Ma. Come on, let's get you inside and out of trouble.'

Her gran's reply shocked Marg: 'Well, having fun and games with that Eric – it'll get you nowhere, you know. That kind only take, they never give, you mark my words.'

Though Marg tried to shake it off, the feeling that her gran had planted in her head wouldn't leave her all afternoon.

No, Ma wouldn't . . . would she?

TWO

Edith

Edith sighed. Waiting outside the factory gates was a familiar and embarrassing sight – her ma screaming and shouting at Bob Butcher, the local policeman.

Poor Bob was trying to hold on to her, but she didn't want to be held.

'Kick him one, Betty!'

This coming from Phyllis Smart, who was anything but smart and who was another who liked the drink, mortified Edith as many of her fellow workers laughed out loud.

'Oh, Ma, what've you been up to now?'

'I wanted a fag, Edith. Old Flanagan at the pub knows I'll pay him, it's this idiot. He shays he's going to arresht me! Gerroff me, Bob, I'm warning you.'

'I'm sorry, Bob. I'll take care of her.'

'See that you do, Edith. She's that far from trying my patience and being up in front of the magistrates. If it weren't for you and your da ... well, she'd be down the line by now.'

'Ta, Bob.'

'And have a word with that brother of yours an' all. He's following in his ma's footsteps and they ain't good ones to tread.'

'Our Albert? Why, what's he done?'

'He got into a fight again, only the lad weren't half his size and he gave him a right pasting. I've cautioned him, but next time he'll be in line for a spell in borstal, that'll sort him out.'

Edith gasped. She couldn't bear that, though she knew in her heart that her brother deserved to be punished. He was getting too much to handle of late, and at sixteen going on seventeen was a big lad – almost the size of a grown man. She'd suffered a few blows from him when he'd lost his temper. 'I'll have a word. Ta, Bob.'

'I'll help you with your ma, Edith.'

'Ta, Marg. But you've enough on your own plate as it is.'

'Don't let her near me, mean cow. She could've given me enough to buy a couple of fags with, but she refused.'

Marg looked taken aback. Edith didn't know what to make of this – Marg hadn't said anything to her about her ma.

'I – I don't have any money, Edith.'

'I know you've not, Marg, but you didn't say anything about having seen me ma.'

'I thought it best not to say, it only worries you and makes you want to go to her. Anyroad, she seemed to be making her way home when I saw her.'

Alice surprised them both then by taking Betty gently by the hand. 'Let's get home, Betty, love, we don't want to give this lot a show. They'll rag Edith to pieces and she doesn't deserve that.'

'Naw, she don't, lash.' Then in a much louder voice, Betty shouted, 'And just let me catch any of you ragging my Edith.'

Edith cringed.

'Let's go, Betty. You don't want to make things worse.'

'All right, Alice, lash. You're a good 'un. Alwaysh were. I've no time for that Marg. Mean cow.'

'Huh, you don't say that when I bring you one of my meat pies. I always make an extra one for you, as I know how you like them, Betty.'

'Aye, yoush right there. I could jusht eat one of them now – or a scabby cat. I'm starving.'

'I was going to call in at the chippy for our supper tonight, Ma, but now I'll have to go to the pub and pay for them fags you nicked.'

'I didn't nick them. I had them on me shlate.'

'Oh, Ma . . . What am I going to do with you, eh?'

'Dance with me, thatsh what.'

Edith laughed out loud. 'I'll dance with you one of these days – and it'll be at the prison Christmas party. Come on.'

They were all laughing by the time they got home. Trying to support her ma, Edith, with the help of Alice – as Betty still wouldn't let Marg near to her – had a merry dance as they jigged around. Marg was in stitches.

When they managed to get Betty inside, she collapsed on the sofa and was out like a light.

'You had fun and games with your ma again, Edith, lass?'

This from her da was accompanied by a fit of coughing.

'Take your time, Da. I'll talk to you in a mo. I'll just see Marg and Alice out.'

'I'm to get fish and chips an' all tonight, Edith. I'll call for you in about half an hour.'

'All right. See you then, Alice. I can offer a bit to the land-lord of the pub and pay him the rest at the weekend.' Turning to Marg, Edith told her, 'I'll see you later, Marg, lass, and don't worry about what me ma said.'

When the girls had gone, Edith leant on the front door. Her da looked up at her, his expression full of sadness. 'It's all my fault, Edith, lass.'

'No, Dad, how could you help getting ill, eh? You worked years down that pit in Burnley. We hardly saw you as kids when you stayed with your ma during your work-ing week.'

Coughing again, her da leant forward. His bones stuck out through his shirt, he had so little flesh covering them. Edith feared for him every day. She couldn't bear the thought of losing him. He brought love, kindness and patience, to balance the unpredictable moods and behaviour of her ma and brother Albert that she had to deal with. Especially Albert, who thought of her as no more than a skivvy for him – or, at least, that's what it felt like.

Albert worked in the rock factory and earned a reasonable amount – about a third of what she did, although it was good for his age. But he rarely tipped up any money to help with the family budget.

What little miner's pension her da received just about covered the rent, but with her ma's antics, as she tried to get her daily quota of drink and fags, it often didn't as Da was a soft touch where Ma was concerned. She regularly took his last penny to see to her cravings.

But for all her faults, her ma had a lovely soul – until someone crossed her when she was drunk. Then she became a monster.

'I'll get the pot on, Da. Have you had a brew today?'

'Naw, lass. Your ma went out this morning and I felt too weak to do anything.'

'Oh, Da, I'm sorry. I won't be a mo. Has Albert shown his face yet?'

'He looked in after work and said he had to go and see that Eric. Is Albert gambling, Edith?'

'Naw . . . well, I don't think so. I think he's a runner for Eric Porter.'

'He needs to be careful; he could get into a lot of trouble. What does he do with the money he earns, I'd like to know?'

Her da started another fit of coughing. He spat something into his handkerchief and the fear that lay in Edith came to the surface. When she'd done the washing at the weekend, she'd found her da's soiled hanky had splatters of blood on it.

Lying to try to soothe her da, she told him, 'Oh, he tips up something to me now and again. And it ain't too bad for a lad of his age. Don't worry about him, Da. He'll turn out all right. He's just finding his feet.'

This prompted her da to tell her about his youth and how he was a boxer as a lad. 'I were Albert's age at the time.'

This was a story Edith had heard so many times she could repeat it word for word, but she never tired of it. It gave her an insight into how strong her da used to be. She listened as he told her how he had been the pit champion and had gone on to be the county champion. And marvelled at how strong

17

his voice was as he told of his conquests. It was as if visiting the past gave him the strength he had then.

A sigh escaped Edith as she thought of her da's medals, his lovely belt and the cup he'd won, all of which used to be displayed in the cabinet. Her ma had long pawned them.

Edith glanced at her ma, slumped in a drunken sleep, and her sigh deepened. For all her antics, and there were many, her ma loved her. Every now and then, she'd try to stay sober, and she was a different person during those times. Edith would come home to a nice clean house, her da smiling and well cared for, wearing clean clothes and looking smart, and the smell of something good cooking on the stove. How she wished life could be like that all of the time.

Sipping her tea while listening to her da, a kind of peace came over Edith. She stretched out her legs, felt the weary strain of them and her aching feet, but didn't let this deter her from enjoying this moment with him. The door bursting open spoilt it.

'Where's Ma?'

Edith sat up straight and looked into her brother's angry face.

'Shush, son, your ma's sleeping.'

'I'll give her sleeping, Da! She's embarrassed me again with Eric Porter! She only owes him more than I can earn. I'll kill her!'

'No, son. Your ma can't help it. You should be helping her, not bullying her.'

'I'll help her all right. She's left me short now. Porter owed me two quid, but he only paid me five bob! Five measly bob for all I've done for him this week! He said I had to pay off me ma's debts.'

As he went by Ma, he kicked out at her. Ma cried out in pain.

'Don't you dare hurt Ma, Albert!'

'Oh, and what're you going to do about it, Edith, eh?'

'I'll tell Bob Butcher, that's what. He's already asking after you. Assaulting your ma's a criminal offence.'

'What does Bob want with you, son? What are you getting up to?'

'Sommat and nowt, Da. Eric Porter'll sort him.'

This frightened Edith as she realised that the pasting Albert had given to someone smaller than him was probably at the orders of Eric Porter. She'd heard a lot of bad things about Marg's uncle. He'd had kids beaten to show an example to their parents. She couldn't believe that Albert could stoop that low.

Bawling him out would do no good, though. 'I'll pay some of it back when I get me wages, Albert. I'll offer Porter a weekly sum and ask him not to dock your money. I'll pour you a brew now. Will you sit on the step with me and drink it, eh?'

'Aye, all right, sis.'

This answer gave Edith a feeling of relief. She knew how to handle Albert, but it wasn't often easy as he made her so angry.

When they sat down, she gave him his tea. 'Try not to show your temper in front of Da, Albert, love. He's getting to be very ill and I'm afraid for him.'

Albert shrugged. The gesture told of his hurt. Beneath it all, she knew he loved his da and had always looked up to him.

'Bob Butcher said you beat up a lad much smaller than you, Albert. What was all that about?'

'Just leave it, will you, sis? It's me own business, I knaw what I'm doing.'

'But you're only sixteen, and I worry about you. Bob said that if you get into any more trouble, he'll take you in and you'll end up in borstal.'

Albert stood up. 'Huh, let him try. Porter'll sort him out. He's very pleased with how I'm working at the moment and won't stand for me being taken off the streets. He likes that I can handle meself.'

Albert said this with such pride that Edith felt herself despairing. 'Well, I've got to go to the chippy. Have you got some money to tip up? I'm going to be short with having to pay for some fags Ma put on tick at the pub.'

'Naw, I told you. Porter didn't give me much and I need some fags meself.'

This shocked Edith. 'You're not smoking, are you? Oh, Albert, I just don't know what to do with you anymore. You used to be a good lad, now you're full of anger and getting into all sorts.'

His face came close to hers, his eyes glared. 'If you don't want more of what I gave you last time you interfered, I'd shut your gob and stop getting on at me.'

A shiver went through Edith as he turned and marched away. Getting up, her rarely felt temper rose. 'Well, I ain't getting you no supper then, so you can go and stew!'

He turned and put a finger up to her before walking away. His swagger incensed her so much she felt like running after him and giving him a thump. But she was afraid to. She knew he was much stronger and wouldn't baulk at giving her a hiding.

As she turned to go in a tear fell onto her cheek. What had happened to her lovely family? How she longed for the time when her da was fit and healthy, her ma was happy and never touched a drop, and Albert was an angelic little lad she adored.

Somehow, she couldn't accept that those days were gone forever and made her mind up to work hard to bring them back again.

THREE

Alice

'You lazy good-for-nothing! I come home after a day's graft and there's naw tea ready!'

'I had nothing in to prepare afore I went to work, Da. I'm going to the chippy, I won't be long. I just wanted to see that the boys were in from school.'

Her da plonked himself down on the sofa and put his head in his hands.

'Are you in pain, Da?'

'Bloody shurrup, will you? You've always got sommat to say. God knaws who you take after 'cause it ain't your ma.'

Alice cringed. The headaches her da suffered could come on so suddenly they knocked him off his feet. Her heart went out to him, but she felt at a loss as to what to do. If she offered sympathy, he lost his temper with her; if she carried on and ignored him, he called her an uncaring bitch. And always he compared her unfavourably to her lovely ma.

Alice thought about her ma. She remembered her tinkling laughter and her da catching hold of her and twirling her around, his love for Ma shining from his eyes. The memory reminded her of how pitiful her da's life was and helped her to understand him a bit better.

He still worked at the rock factory and was good at his job. He had a lot of time off, but they tolerated it as they felt they owed him a debt after his courageous act of saving the boss's son's life, which had caused his condition and put him in hospital.

On the whole they were good to him, but his pay reflected the few hours he could put in and so money was short, with her brothers – three growing lads – to care for too.

Harry, the eldest at almost sixteen, Billy, twelve, and Joey, just ten, were out in the street kicking a ball. The younger two had visions of playing for the Tangerines, or the Seasiders, as Blackpool Football Club was called.

Billy had dreams of being another Stanley Matthews – his footballing hero, who played for Stoke City. For Joey it was George Percival, a Manchester City player, though he was another of Billy's favourites really – Joey just did everything that Billy did.

They were both avid collectors of football cards and hounded anyone they saw smoking Woodbine cigarettes, as the cards were given away with every packet; each card showed a photo of a player on the front and gave some information about him on the back. Billy had recently been given one of Stanley Matthews, and it was his prized possession, but they were always in a frenzied swaps game as they sought desperately to get a card each of their hero.

Alice smiled as she reflected on this because she too had joined the hunt, pestering anyone who smoked the brand at the factory. So far she hadn't been successful, but she had found some of what the boys called 'valuable swaps'.

Harry loved football too, but had other hobbies he loved more – reading was his main one.

Alice loved her brothers. Many a time, it was caring for them that kept her going. They were all good-natured and kind and gave her very little trouble. She would lay her life down for them.

'Where's the bloody lads? Can't you send one of them for the chips while you make a brew? I'm dying for a drink.'

'Harry can make a brew. I promised Edith that I'd go to the chippy with her.'

'Bloody Edith, and that other one, Marg – they're all you care about.'

'They're not, Da, I care about you and the boys much more.'

'Ha! That'll be the day. If you did, you'd have used the money you have for chips on buying some spuds and a bit of meat. It'd cost you half as much and give us a good feed. You're just bloody lazy and always have been.'

As his voice rose, Alice flew out of the door. 'Harry! Harry, lad, come here. Quick!'

'What's up, Alice? Is the house on fire?'

Despite feeling anxious, Alice laughed at him. 'No, but I need you to make a brew for Da while I go to the chippy.'

'Me? But . . . you knaw I always upset him as I don't make it how he likes it.'

Alice could see his fear. She knew the feeling only too well. Unsure what to do as she so wanted to walk to the chippy with Edith, she hesitated. But then decided she just couldn't face going back inside. Maybe, if she had his supper all hot and ready to eat, her da would calm down.

'I'll go to the chippy, Alice. You make the tea, eh?'

She looked into her brother's blue eyes, so very like her own and showing the same fear she felt, and her heart melted. 'All right, here you are.' Giving him the money he'd need, she told him, 'Bring a bag of scraps for Billy and Joey, a portion of chips between me and you and one for Da. And ask Alf if he'll throw in a meat pie – tell him I'll come and clean his fryers on Saturday for him if he can.'

'Is that for Da?'

'Aye, Da'll enjoy that. I'll whip up some gravy while you're gone, I've still got some of the meat juices from Sunday. Hurry, now, there's a good 'un. Oh, and tap on Edith's door and tell her I won't be coming. Ta, lad.'

Harry kissed her cheek. She knew he felt guilty for letting her face their da, as he put his hand up and touched her puffy eye. 'He can't help it, sis.'

'I knaw. We'll sort it, don't worry, lad.'

'What the hell's going on around here? You're nothing but a useless lump. The kettle ain't even on the boil!' Her da stood as she went back into the house, his arm raised.

'Naw, Da! I've already got one black eye off you today. I'll get everything sorted if you just leave me alone.'

'By, you may look like your ma, but you ain't a patch on her. I wish it had been you who had died and not her.'

Alice gasped in pain at his words, but said nothing. Skirting the table to avoid him, she grabbed the kettle off the hob and ran outside to the pump.

'Don't tell me you ain't even filled the bloody thing!'

Alice despaired. It didn't matter what she did, she just couldn't do right. She felt like shouting back that if he'd just mend the tap, they'd have running water again. It dripped constantly unless he twisted it so tightly to the off position, but then she hadn't the strength to undo it. Harry was able to, but he had more leverage as he was taller than her, even though she was three years older.

In those three years between them her ma had given birth to two more girls, Lillian and Ethel, but both had died in their first year. They were buried in the Layton Cemetery where her ma was, and she often picked daisies and buttercups to put on their little graves when she visited. Sighing, Alice thought for the umpteenth time that she'd have loved for them to live. How nice it would have been to have sisters.

But then, Edith and Marg were like sisters to her, and she wondered what she'd ever do without them.

Ada appeared in her back garden next door and shouted over the fence, 'He not mended that tap yet, lass?'

Alice gave a frightened look towards the back door of her house.

'And is that a black eye you've got again? I'll bloody swing for him one of these days if he don't leave you young 'uns alone. You tell him from me that I'll be round to sort him out if I see you like that again. Hang on, I'll fetch sommat for it.'

'Naw, it's all right, Ada, ta. It's nothing. I banged it on the cupboard door. Ma always used to say as I was the clumsy one.'

'Ah, your ma was a lovely lass. I did all I could to save her.'

'You made her comfortable, Ada, I remember that. She used to call out for you sometimes in the night.'

'Did she, lass? Why didn't you fetch me? I'd have come no matter what the time.'

Aye, and you'd have wanted payment for your trouble an' all, when I didn't have two pennies to rub together.

'I know, Ada, but I was only a lass and was afraid of the dark. I used to sit with her and managed to soothe her.'

'Bloody get in here and stop gossiping with that cow, will you?' Da appeared at the door. 'Bugger off, Ada. You knaw nothing except how to fleece them who can't afford what you charge for your bloody witchcraft. Keeps you in clover, don't it?'

Ada ran indoors. For all her bravado, when it came to it she was just as scared of Da as Alice was.

As Alice went inside, her da shoved her so hard she went hurtling into the edge of the table. The air left her lungs as pain shot through her. The kettle crashed to the floor, spilling the water like a lake over the red tiles.

Da's hand clutched the collar of her blouse, tightening it around her neck, strangling her as he dragged her to an upright position. With the sight of his fist raised, tears ran down her face. 'Naw, Da, please, don't.'

'Leave her alone, Da! Stop!'

'It's all right, Billy. Billy, no!'

Billy held a cricket bat high above his shoulders. Not heeding her, he brought it down and cracked it across Da's back.

'Stop, Billy!'

Da staggered. Alice's screams mingled with those of Joey, who appeared at the door just before Marg. In a flash, Marg foiled Billy as he was about to strike again by grabbing him by the scruff of his neck and dragging him outside.

Before Alice could do anything, Edith appeared at the door, rushed forward and pushed Da. Da crashed to the floor.

The moans coming from him told of his pain. Alice looked down, fearful of seeing him injured. His cries tore at her heart as she saw him clutch his head in his hands.

'Da. Oh, Da.' Kneeling beside him, Alice took him in her arms. 'Da. Come on, let's get you to the sofa.'

He let her help him as if he were a baby, his clothes wet from the puddle the dropped kettle had left. Grabbing a towel off the fender, Alice wrapped it around his waist and guided him to the sofa.

'I – I'm sorry, Alice. I had to do something, he looked like he was going to come back at you again.'

'It's all right, Edith, I knaw why you did it, love.'

'Eeh, Alice, this can't go on. He might well kill you one day.'

Behind Edith, Alice could see Harry cowering in the doorway. Poor lad had taken his share of beatings and the impact of them had left him a frightened shivering wreck whenever Da started. Somehow this reaction seemed to rile Da more, whereas with the fearless Billy, he wasn't half so brutal.

Ignoring the terror in Harry's eyes, Alice tried to control her shaking body and asked, 'Harry, lad, did you get the chips?'

'Aye, and the pie an' all. Alf said he'd be glad of your help on Saturday.'

Noticing her shaking, Marg asked, 'Eeh, Alice, are you all right? . . . Aw, Alice, love.'

Alice nodded her head. Marg's eyes never left Da.

'I'll be fine, ta, love. Thanks for your help, both of you. We'll get our tea now. Will you tell Billy and Joey to come in and get theirs? Tell them they can sit on the step to eat it and that they'll be all right. Especially our Billy. Tell him not to be scared.'

'Aye, I will. Oh, Alice, I don't know what to say.'

Alice tried to smile at Marg. She followed them out of the door. It was Edith touching her arm and rubbing it up and down in a soothing gesture that undid her. Her tears overflowed once more.

Her friends held her in a hug and it felt good. Until Marg said in a loud, angry voice, 'Just scream if he comes near you again, Alice, and me and Edith'll come to help you, lass.'

Alice leant backwards and peered around the door as fear gripped her, but her da hadn't moved from where he was sitting holding his head.

She turned back to the girls and in a low voice told them, 'I promise you I'll scream out. But go now or he might start again. He needs his tea and his chips. And yours'll be getting cold, Edith.'

Marg shook her head. 'Look, love, I've had me tea so I'll stay and help you, just in case. I'll fill the kettle and get it on for you, Alice. Then I'll get the mop in and dry the floor. You get the supper dished up.'

'Ta, Marg. But you go, Edith, love, I'll be all right now. Da's quietened down.'

When Marg left, the tea she'd made seemed to soothe Da's pain and he tucked into his supper. He didn't speak, but kept his head down. Harry sat at the table with her, his eyes darting back and forward from his tea to Da, looking to all the world like a nervous animal ready to flit. He was eating as if there was no tomorrow, shovelling his food in his mouth quickly.

29

Stretching her hand across the table and patting his, Alice was rewarded with a smile, though Harry's lips quivered as if he wanted to cry. She knew he was thinking that he should have helped her. She nodded reassuringly at him and indicated to him to follow her and bring the rest of his chips outside.

The late evening sun still had plenty of warmth in it as they leant against the wall of their house. The street was buzzing with folk – some sitting on chairs they'd brought out from their kitchens, and some on steps or just leaning, arms folded, against their doors. All were engaged in a good gossip, and laugher rang out.

To an onlooker, it would seem like a happy bunch of neighbours, but Alice knew that, when closed, most of the doors in this street hid problems and unhappiness. Though to balance that, most houses held love too.

They were good neighbours despite their individual difficulties. They pulled together at times of crisis and helped each other out. Yes, there were some like Ada, who only offered their services to others if they could get something in return, but there were those like Marg and her ma who would give you their last penny if you needed it more than they did. And Edith and her da, who welcomed everyone and would help you out if they could.

'What did you want, Alice?'

'Just to tell you, Harry, that it's all right to be scared. It doesn't mean that you're a coward.'

'I'm not like our Billy, though, am I? He's fearless when he sees others being hurt.'

She looked over to where Billy and Joey were now back to kicking their ball from one to the other as if nothing had happened. 'Billy hasn't had to put up with as much as you. You've always been Da's scapegoat and punchbag. There's only so much a body can take – it's natural to want to save your own skin.'

'I don't know. It ain't so much that I'm scared as I freeze. It's like I can't take it and me head starts to scream. All I want to do is to run.'

'Is anything else troubling you, Harry?'

'Naw. I'm all right.'

But Alice knew he wasn't. This brother of hers was visibly going through a lot of changes in his life as the wispy hair around his face told of. He'd almost got a full moustache – had it been that he was dark instead of fair, he would have had to shave before now. And goodness knew what other problems he might have in the growing-up stakes; she had no experience of what it was like for a lad to transition into a man. Everything that happened to Harry was something she could learn from to help Billy when he reached the same age, but Harry had no one he could turn to. Da never spoke a civil word to the lad.

'Are you still friends with Albert?'

'Naw, he's a bully. He doesn't bother with me. We used to be good mates as kids but not anymore. I've a good friend in Kev from school. He's lucky is Kev. He's got a kind da who cares about him.'

'Well, couldn't you talk to Ken's da about anything that's bothering you?'

'There's nothing bothering me, other than how Da acts. I knaw it's because he's in a lot of pain, but he frightens me. I'm scared of what one of his outbursts will do one of these days.'

31

Alice didn't know what to say to this. There were no words of reassurance that she could offer. She had the same fears herself and prayed every night for some help for her da. She hadn't forgotten what a nice man he was until five long years ago. She longed to have him back.

FOUR

Marg

It was a week later that Marg's uncle called round as she came in from work. The evening was still warm, if windy and over-cast. She'd made him, Gran and Ma a cup of tea. Gran had been full of questions about what she'd done at school that day. Not having the patience after a long week of grafting in the factory, Marg had humoured her rather than trying to make her see reality.

As she gave her uncle his tea, he handed her a crisp pound note. 'Here, Marg, darling, this is a gift from your old uncle. Take your friends out on the town and have a good time, eh? I'll sit in with your ma and gran. We're going to listen to that new wireless I brought.' He patted a rolled-up magazine protruding from his jacket pocket. 'I've got a *Radio Times* here. It says there'll be a report on the King and Queen's visit to Wales, and then music hall coming from Morecambe.'

Marg immediately feared what she thought might be the real motive for her uncle wanting a night in with her ma, but reasoned that nothing would happen while Jackie was around, surely? And besides, a Friday night out with Edith and Alice was too tempting to resist. Taking the quid, she pocketed it. 'Ta, Uncle Eric.' She turned back to the stove and switched off the gas flame from under the bubbling saucepan keeping her meal hot. 'Ma, I'll leave me tea a mo and nip to see if the girls are able to come out tonight.'

'All right, lass. It's only a piece of fish and some mash, though I made a nice parsley sauce that needs warming separately. Me and Gran had ours at dinnertime as Uncle Eric's going to bring some fish and chips round for me later.'

'And a bottle of beer to swill it down with. Might even bring you two if you're good.'

Marg saw her ma blush.

'You can bring me a bottle of stout. I like a stout, lad.'

'All right, Gran. Stout it is. I knaw you like your stout and I never leave you out, do I? But I tell you, it'll put hairs on your chest one of these days.' He laughed at his own joke and then added, 'Aye, and'll make you sleep as usual.'

'Well, you'll never see them if it does, and I'm better off asleep, I don't have to listen to your waffle then.'

Uncle Eric laughed out loud, but judging by Gran's expression, she hadn't meant what she'd said to be funny.

Marg hurried out, leaving them to it, and skipped across the road. As she banged on Edith's door, Edith's da's weak voice called, 'It's open.'

'Hello, Mr Foreman, is Edith in?'

'She's gone to the lav out back, lass. Sit down a mo, she won't be long. How's that gran of yours? I sat outside earlier and she was there – she kept calling me Arthur, and wanted to know when I got back from the war.' Mr Foreman laughed at this, but then went into a fit of coughing.

'She's all right in herself. But her mind's away with the fairies. She's happy, though, and that's the main thing.'

'And is your ma keeping all right? I haven't seen her in a while.'

'She's much the same. She's having a good run at the moment and hasn't had a bad breathing attack. I get scared when she does.'

'I can relate to that. It's a horrible feeling, and she has me sympathy.'

Betty came in from the kitchen, eyes puffed up, boozy fumes preceding her. Marg wondered how she'd greet her – she soon found out.

'Oh, it's Miss Meany Pants. What d'you want then?'

'Am I not forgiven yet, Betty? I told you, I hadn't got any money on me when you asked or I'd have given it to you gladly.'

'Don't talk like that, Betty, lass. Marg's a good girl, and she's our Edith's best mate.'

'Well, a neighbour is supposed to help another when they're in need. This one nearly got me arrested!'

Marg gave up. Betty was determined to think the worst of her. Mr Foreman didn't leave it, though, and surprised her as he shouted, 'Will you listen to the lass when she says she didn't have any cash on her! What's the matter with you, eh? Booze addled your brain, 'cause it's addled everything else? Have you looked at yourself lately, lass?'

Betty sniffed, then got out her hanky and wiped her eyes, before sitting down on the nearest chair and putting her face into her hands.

'Aw, come on, lass, I didn't mean it. You're still me beauty, but you'd no need to talk to Marg like you did.'

'I'm sorry, Marg. I get me knickers in a twist over sommat and I can't get me head straight.'

Marg jumped up, went to Betty and held her in her arms, while trying not to retch at the stench of stale body odour, tobacco fumes and alcohol. 'I tell you what, Betty. You get a good swill down and a change of clothes, and I'll buy you enough fags for a week.'

Betty's face lit up. 'And a bottle of gin, love?'

'Ha, Betty, you'll try all the tricks in the book. Fags it is and that's me offer.'

'I reckon that's a good deal, Betty, love. I'd take the lass's offer if I were you.'

Betty smiled at her husband, revealing a mouthful of brown-stained teeth. 'All right. But you're to go to the shop now, mind. Eeh, it'll be lovely to have a pack a day.'

Mr Foreman surprised Marg then. He was usually one to give in to Betty, but he spoke quite firmly to her: 'And that's how you'll have them, not all at once, as Marg'll give me a pack each day for you, won't you, Marg?'

When Betty left, Mr Foreman said, 'You can't afford that, lass, and why should you? I've got fourpence here. Go and get her a pack of ten and leave it at that.'

'Naw, I'll keep me word. Betty was good to me when I was a nipper after me da died. Anyroad, me uncle's given me a quid. I can afford to buy her seven packs of five – that'll only be one and fourpence.'

'Well, that's very kind of you. But drop them in to me at a pack a day, otherwise she'll smoke the lot, or our Albert'll have them.'

They were quiet for a minute, then Mr Foreman said, 'I know he's your uncle, Marg, but I reckon Eric Porter's a bad lot. I'm sorry to say that, but I worry what he's getting our Albert into.'

'I know. I worry about what he does, but he is me uncle. Though I am confused about how I feel about him. How him and me da were brothers I'll never know.'

'Well, I can understand that, the blood of the family is a strong bond. But eeh, I wish our Albert weren't mixed up with him.'

Marg didn't know what to say to that, but was luckily saved from needing to reply as Edith came through the door. 'By, I thought you'd fallen down the hole, lass!'

'Ha, naw, I was talking to Ida over the fence. I didn't know you were here.'

'I'd have thought you saw enough of her at work.'

'Ida's all right. She has her ways, but we can't fault her as a neighbour, can we, Da?'

'Naw, you're right there, lass. Ida's one of the best neighbours you could have.'

'Anyroad, I came to ask if you can come out tonight: go down the town and have some fun. My treat ... well, me uncle's.' Marg told Edith about her windfall. 'I thought me, you and Alice can enjoy some fun.'

'What's come over him, then? Anyroad, I don't want anything to do with his money, it'll be ill-gotten.'

'Aw, Edith, go on. We can't alter anything by not taking it so we may as well enjoy it, eh? We can go to the Tower and have a sherry or two.'

'Now then, Marg, don't get carried away. I don't mind our lass going out for some fun, but I don't want drink involved. We have enough of that in our house.'

'Sorry, Mr Foreman. Teetotal it is then, but please come, Edith.'

'Oh, all right. Will you manage, Da?'

'Aye, lass, I'll be fine. Your ma won't be going out. She's had her fill and slept it off – well, almost. She must be still a bit drunk as Marg here's been able to persuade her to have a wash and put clean clothes on.'

Mr Foreman had a lovely smile; Marg felt sorry that he was dogged by illness. But then she thought about how he'd checked Betty just now – it was surprising that he hadn't curbed her antics years ago as she obviously listens to him when he gets cross.

'What? How did that come about? I've been trying to persuade her all week!'

Edith laughed when Marg relayed what happened. 'Well, I'd better go and gather her dirty clothes before she puts them back on. I'll call for you about eightish, Marg. And ta, love, it'll be grand to go out on the town, sherry or not.'

'Now, now, Edith, lass, it's for your own good that I caution you.'

'I knaw, Da. I'm only joking.'

Marg said her goodbyes and almost ran down to Alice's. The boys were in the street as usual. 'Hi, lads, is Alice in?'

'Aye,' Harry nodded.

Harry's dour expression gave Marg a sad feeling. He used to be a jolly soul, but that had changed lately.

Alice was over the moon, and to give Marg another surprise, her da agreed that she should go.

'What about me eye, though?'

They were stood on the step when Alice whispered this.

'You can hardly see it now. Come over to mine and I'll put some pan stick on it, that'll cover the small mark you've got left.'

'Ta, Marg. My, a night on the town – we haven't done that for an age . . . What're you going to wear?'

'Me purple satin blouse and me pencil-slim black skirt. You know, the one I bought off Ruby Clarke for the price of a gin. I tell you, I got a real bargain.' Marg laughed as she told Alice how she'd also used bribery to persuade Betty to have a wash.

Alice giggled. 'She's a one that Betty. Poor Edith gets so embarrassed by her antics, when most of us just find them funny – not that we'd like to be in the same position. And Ruby Clarke's no better. Anyroad, you'll look lovely. I've only got that short-sleeved lemon jumper and me slimline grey skirt. Did Edith say what she'd wear?'

'Naw, we didn't talk about it. But that outfit'll be grand on you. You'll look really nice, Alice.'

When they walked down the street an hour and a half later, they were giggling like children. They'd all been in Marg's bedroom putting on their make-up. Marg was an expert at applying it, using a picture of Rita Hayworth that she had on her bedroom wall as a guide. All three admired the film star, and Edith had even copied the hairstyle Rita had. She'd parted her hair in the middle and clipped back the sides, letting its full length fall over her ears. The effect was stunning. Elegant is how Marg would describe Edith in her plain green frock, fitted to the waist and flaring to her calves, with little puffed sleeves.

Marg felt good too, as Edith had brought a hairband with her. She said it was called an Alice band: 'So, you'll have our Alice keeping you neat and tidy.'

This made them giggle, but then, they were in such high spirits that they laughed at every little thing.

Edith said she'd always thought wearing one would suit Marg – it did make a lot of difference, and she loved the look of her hair being scraped back, taming the frizz and showing off her large dark eyes. And as Marg had thought, Alice looked lovely in her jumper and skirt – cute was the word she'd use.

Gran had made them laugh as she'd asked if she could come. 'I ain't been down to Blackpool for a long time. We girls used to have hijinks with some of the visitors. They had plenty of money, you knaw, and some notion that our sea held healing properties.' She'd tutted loudly, and then giggled at whatever had come into her mind. Marg was glad when she didn't share it as her gran had taken to saying odd things that made her blush lately.

Uncle Eric had arrived just as they were leaving and, for a moment, Marg felt like changing her mind. She found herself battling constantly with what she feared was going on – not being able to believe it one moment, and then feeling sick the next.

She asked herself, if it *was* happening, did her mum only give in to him so he would let Marg off with her debts? The thought didn't sit well with her.

When they got to the end of the street to turn into Talbot Road, they met Jackie coming out of the corner shop. This was the first time Marg had seen her tonight as Jackie went straight from school to work in the shop on a Friday evening. 'Hello, lass, you finished now?'

'Aye, I'm whacked out, Marg.'

Marg opened her arms to her sister and hugged her close. 'I know the feeling, lass. You're a good 'un, but don't neglect your studies, even if you are tired. One day you'll not have to slave with your hands, but make your fortune with your knowledge.'

'Ha, that's just what I do feel like, a blooming slave. I've to go to me tutor now.'

They giggled as Marg added, 'You'll be fine. Keep at it as I expect you to one day keep me in clover.'

Marg knew that though it was sometimes hard for Jackie, she loved learning and often said how grateful she was to Marg for making it possible for her to study.

'Is that why you push me so hard, so that I can make you rich? You're me blooming slave driver!'

'Go on with you, lass.' As they'd reached the corner shop Marg had a sudden thought. 'Hold on a mo, Jackie. I've to nip in here for some fags for Betty – come in with me and get yourself a treat: a bar of chocolate or something. That'll keep you going till you get home for your tea.'

Jackie giggled. 'Ta, Marg.' Then added, 'I like your hair, it suits you. Anyroad, where are you all off to, dressed up to the nines? You all look lovely.'

'We're going to paint the town red, lass. So, you like this band in me hair, then? It was Edith's idea.' She made Jackie giggle as she told her the joke that they'd shared over the band having the same name as Alice.

'Anyroad, I love it and it's grand for taming out frizz. I'll tell you what, I'll buy you one while I'm down town. Bound to be a stall open, there always are.'

When they came out of the shop, Jackie looked like the cat who'd got the cream with her treasured bar of chocolate, and was already ripping the silver paper off it. Marg hugged her again. 'Right, we'll get going. You keep them fags in your satchel, lass, drop one pack off at Betty's when you get home later, and put the rest under me bed – don't let Ma see them.' Kissing Jackie's cheek, she said, 'See you tomorrow, me lovely lass. Enjoy your lesson.'

Waving Jackie off, Marg suddenly felt at odds with going out again. She already had her suspicions about what might be happening, and now she was worried Jackie might see or hear something.

Just as she was about to tell the girls she was going home, Alice said, 'You know what I'd love to do? Go to The Regent. Cary Grant's on, starring in *The Awful Truth*. Phyllis at work was telling me about it; said she drooled over Cary Grant so much that she dreamt about him . . . Ha, I can't tell you about her dream, though, she made me blush.'

Marg forgot her worries and thoughts of returning home at this and put her tuppence worth in. 'You don't have to, knowing Phyllis. She'll get herself into trouble one of these days and find herself caught out. But I like the idea of the flicks. We might get there in the middle of the B film, but as long as we see the whole of the main one. What do you reckon, Edith?'

'Great idea. We can cut through Cookson Street and we're there! Best foot forward, lasses!'

'Then I think we should go to the Tower Ballroom?'

Both Edith and Alice agreed with this suggestion from Marg.

When they came out of the cinema, Marg understood Phyllis's fantasies. 'That Cary Grant's a smasher, ain't he?'

They were starry-eyed as they made their way to the seafront and found that, as Marg had thought, all the stalls along the Golden Mile were open.

The noise that met them as they walked down Church Street and past the Winter Gardens was a mixture of gramophone records and stallholders shouting their wares, against a backdrop of breaking waves on the sandy shore. The familiar smell of fish and chips wafted over them, mixed with the tang of seafood from Robert's Oyster Bar and tatties baking on open-griddle fires.

The feelings that always assailed Marg when she turned towards the famous Blackpool Tower gripped her now: joy, excitement and a love for her home town.

FIVE

Alice

Bendy, the contortionist who ran the coconut shy and performed an act of tying himself in knots on the pavement to attract customers if trade was slow, called out to Alice as they neared.

Alice quickened her steps. 'Come on, let's just carry on. I don't want to hear his tales again.'

'Ha! About your ma nearly marrying him, Alice?'

'Shut up, Marg. Eeh, imagine having Bendy for a da?' Alice laughed, but the fleeting thought came to her that it might not have been so bad. Bendy was a good sort and always cheerful, like her own da used to be.

For a moment her mind took her to being fifteen again. Da had turned the corner into Whittaker Avenue. Alice, not yet a woman, but no longer feeling like a child, leant against the wall of their house.

'By, my lovely Alice, what a sight to meet any da as he comes home from work.'

'Da!' she'd shouted, running to him. Da had dropped his

satchel carrying his snap tin. His arms opened; his face lit with a smile.

The hug had felt good – comforting, reassuring. She'd snuggled into him. He'd smelt like Da – fresh sweat from a day's labour, a tinge of the Brylcreem that he used to smooth his hair.

'What's me lass been up to, then, eh?'

'Oh, not much, Da. I have a stomach ache.'

'Aye, well, you should welcome that, me lovely lass. That says you're growing into a woman. And a fine one you'll be. Come on, I can see your ma and I need to hug her an' all.'

When they'd reached the house, Da had said, 'We'll go for a walk after tea, Alice. Best thing for tummy aches.' He ruffled her hair. Then, as always, grabbed Ma and lifted her. Ma had glowed, her laughter ringing out. 'Put me down, George!'

'Aw, me lass, I love you. I missed you all day.'

Alice had gone inside as her parents' lips had met. She'd found it embarrassing and had hoped the neighbours hadn't seen them.

Walking with her da had made Alice proud – such a handsome man, kind and known by everyone. They never got far without someone wanting a chat, but all the while her da had made her giggle at his antics, and had pointed out different birds, wild animals and flowers.

'One day, Alice, we'll have a garden. A lawn to sit out on and a tree for the birds. Aye, and flowers, lots of lovely flowers. Won't that be grand, eh?'

'Alice, Alice . . . are you with us or not?'

'What? Oh . . . sorry, Edith. I went inside my head for a moment. Aye, I'm with you.'

As she said this, Alice allowed the excitement of all that was going on around seep into her. She let go of her memories and clutched Edith's arm. 'Oh, I love the prom on a summer's night. It makes me feel like a kid again. I want to go on everything and run onto the sand in bare feet to paddle in the sea.'

Marg agreed, 'Me too. Come on, let's all pick what we want to have a go on, we've got some money to spend!'

'Naw, Marg, you've been generous enough. We'll just go into the Tower as we planned, then you'll have some left over to see you through the week.'

'Aye, I agree with Alice. Just going to the Tower Ballroom will be magic.' Edith's face lit up with the same feeling of anticipation Alice felt.

'Right, let's get there, then, and with eyes front so we don't get tempted on the way.'

They giggled as Marg surged forward, tugging them along with her, though Alice found it wasn't easy passing by the different stalls without thinking of her da. There was the candyfloss stall, the target stall where you had to shoot tins off a shelf to win a teddy, the 'win a goldfish' stall where you had to land a ping-pong ball in a goldfish bowl – this one especially, as she remembered him winning the fish when he'd brought her down to the prom one afternoon. She'd watched the man fish it out of a huge tank and place it in the round bowl for her. She'd clutched the bowl all the way home, not letting her da take it from her. When they'd reached home, a nurse had met them with the words, 'You have a son, Mr Brett.' It was hard to imagine that she had been almost four at the time, as the memory was so vivid to her.

She'd been taken into the front room where Ma lay in a bed, her cheeks all rosy and her eyes seeming to bulge. But it was her smile that Alice remembered most: it stretched from one ear to the other. And then her da showing her Harry, who lay snuggled up in the drawer that had been taken from the large dresser.

Alice had felt a surge of love for him. She remembered the feeling now; couldn't forget it as it had stayed with her. But as the little girl that she was then had looked at her brother for the first time, she'd told her da she wanted him to have her most treasured possession. When Harry had finally opened his eyes and become alert, he'd stared and stared at the shiny golden fish as it had swum around in endless circles. Ma had said it was the perfect gift for a baby.

The warmth that had filled Alice then filled her now.

'My, that's a grin and a half.'

'Aye. I'm just having the best of times, Marg, ta ever so much.' With this she leant over and kissed Marg's cheek.

'Eeh, you daft apeth!'

Edith did the same on Marg's other cheek. 'Me too. Ta, Marg, lass.'

Marg looked from one to the other. 'You soppy mares. Come on, we've more fun to have yet. Only I'll just stop here a mo and buy one of them Alice bands for Jackie.'

As had happened on the few occasions Alice had been here before, her mind filled with wonderment at the magic of the Tower Ballroom, the magnificent arena-like layout with theatre boxes and balconies lining its walls. The opulence of the gold gilt, the elaborate carvings and the arched beams of the ceiling. And the magnificent paintings between each ceiling arch — beautiful depictions of angels fluttering in a blue sky. Each wearing a different coloured floating gown.

Reginald Dixon, the handsome radio star, sat at the white Wurlitzer, his fingers deftly playing 'Alexander's Ragtime Band', dancers energetically twirling and kicking their feet. The women were dressed in wonderful frocks of all shades, and the men in dark evening suits.

When this came to an end, the music tempo slowed with 'Let Me Call You Sweetheart' and the couples went into a waltz.

'May I have this dance?' The gentleman requesting this of Edith was taller than her, and handsome in a rakish way. His black hair flopped to one side and his moustache curled a little at the ends in an old-fashioned style. His smile was impish and his expression held an appeal. Edith passed her handbag to Marg and glided onto the dance floor with him. They looked magnificent as they waltzed around, and the gentleman bent Edith till her back was arched and then twirled her round.

Alice and Marg gazed on in envy until a voice suddenly interrupted their wonderment. 'Instead of watching, why don't we join them?'

Alice turned to look at the most beautiful face she'd ever laid eyes on. As their gazes met — his eyes the deepest blue she had ever seen — she felt a tingling shoot through her. 'Ta, I'd like that.'

'You're a Blackpool lass? That makes a change. Most of those I dance with are visitors.'

'Oh, aye, born and bred.'

Seeming to be dancing on air, Alice answered his questions. She wanted to lie and make up a much more glamorous – and, she thought, *more acceptable* – life than the one she truly had, but telling him that she worked in the biscuit factory and lived on Whittaker Avenue didn't seem to put him off.

'I live not far from there, and work at the hospital. In fact, this is the last dance for me as I'm due on the night shift in an hour.'

'Oh? How on earth do you manage that? I'm a morning person – up like a lark, but flop into bed in the evening. I'd never be able to stay awake all night.'

'You would, you get used to it. I've slept most of today, but I couldn't resist coming here this evening when my friend suggested it. That's him over there dancing with your friend. His name is Philip Bradshaw.'

'Oh? Our boss's son? I – I didn't realise. I get a glance of him sometimes, but he don't look the same tonight.'

'Well, I don't think he recognised you girls either. I'm Gerald, by the way.'

'I'm Alice.' A shyness came over Alice as Gerald smiled down at her. She suddenly felt clumsy and dowdy against his elegance, and his posh voice made hers sound common. But as she thought this, something else occurred to her: were these two just amusing themselves with girls who were obviously of a lower class to them? This thought made her feel even more uncomfortable. 'I – I should get back to me mate, I've left her on her own.'

'Oh? Must you?'

'Aye, well, there's three of us together, and now one is left alone. Excuse me.' She couldn't escape fast enough, though felt strangely bereft after coming out of Gerald's arms.

'Eeh, Marg, guess who Edith's dancing with? Only the son of our boss!'

'What? Oh, aye, I thought I'd seen him somewhere before. By, that's a turn-up. Who was that you were with?'

Telling her, Alice added, 'I think we are a source of amusement to them.'

'Whether that's true or not, I wish I'd have been chosen. What did it feel like gliding around in the arms of a gentleman?'

Alice blushed, but answered truthfully. 'Grand. I forgot meself for a mo; I was taken into the film we saw, with Doctor Melford becoming Cary Grant.'

They giggled.

'A doctor, eh? Who'd have thought. Here you are, love, I bought you a drink of orange juice.'

'A drink as well? It feels like we're rich!'

'We are, Alice, lass. Rich in friendship and rich in a lot more an' all – me sis, ma and gran for starters, but then, the crowning treasure, you and Edith, the best friends a girl could have.'

'Aye, the halfpenny girls. We've always been known as that since Edith's da once said, "You three may not have a halfpenny between you, but you have sommat that money can't buy – friendship". The name stuck and stands as a reminder that riches ain't all material things.'

'No, but they'd help, not that I reckon they're in our lot to have.'

The music ceased, and Alice glanced over and saw Philip guiding Edith back to them. She winked at Marg and whispered, 'You never know.'

This set them giggling again, but they stopped as they

heard Philip say, 'Thank you, Edith, that was a pleasure. And don't work too hard tomorrow, my father's a hard taskmaster.'

As soon as he'd gone, Alice nudged Edith. 'Oh, you knew who he was, then? And yet you carried on dancing?'

'Aye, I did. He told me after he asked about me. He said, "Don't be embarrassed, but your boss is my father – I'm Philip Bradshaw." I nearly died as it wasn't until then that I recognised him; we only see him at a distance usually. But he was charming and didn't seem to be taking the rise out of me. Anyroad, you can shout, Alice, a doctor no less!'

'Aye, I was that embarrassed when he told me, I ended the dance.'

'You daft apeth, you should have enjoyed it while it lasted. I did. Took me out of meself for once and made me feel different.'

'I felt that an' all.'

'Count yourselves lucky, I felt like a wallflower.'

Marg was laughing as she said this. Edith sat down and joined in. 'The ugly sisters got to go to the ball, but not Cinderella!'

Alice hit her playfully for the insult and they all collapsed in laughter.

To Alice it seemed that all her cares lifted off her shoulders. She looked across the room. Gerald was nowhere to be seen. A small dent appeared in her expectations of this wonderful evening and suddenly her troubles came flooding back into her. 'Shall we head home?'

'Oh? Is that it, now that you two have had your fun!'

'Oh, I didn't mean—'

'Aw, I was only joking. We should go, it'll take us a while to walk home.'

Marg stood and they linked arms with her.

They hadn't gone far along the prom when Albert came sauntering towards them with a small sack over his shoulder. When he spotted them, his demeanour became more urgent. 'Hey, Alice, you'd better get home. There's been a rumpus at your house.'

'Oh God, what's going on?'

'Your da, beating the living daylights out of poor Harry.'

'No! No . . .' Alice stared at Albert, unable to grasp what he was saying.

'Had all the neighbours out, it did. I would have helped Harry, only I was due to get here, and with Eric Porter being at your house, Marg, I daren't hang around for fear of losing me job.'

'What about Harry? Oh God, is he hurt bad?

'I don't knaw for sure. I think Eric Porter sorted your da out, though. I saw him go towards your house – probably knifed him. Eric likes to cut folk who annoy him. Anyroad, as I turned onto Talbot Road the police and an ambulance came tearing around the corner. Going like the clappers they were with their bells ringing.'

'Ambulance?' Alice couldn't take it all in. 'But who's gone to hospital . . . Harry? Da? Are the others all right?'

'I don't knaw. I told you, I didn't hang around, but I saw Joey run into Marg's. I never saw Billy, though. But then, you know Billy, he'd be trying to protect Harry and be giving your da what for.'

Alice's legs went weak. She clung on to Edith and Marg.

'What's up, lad? What's that you're telling Alice?' Bendy came over from his coconut shy.

'Aw, there's been some trouble at Alice's.'

'By, Alice, lass, I'm sorry. Is there owt I can do?'

'I – I just need to get home.'

'I can help with that. Our Simon's running his cab up and down the prom, he'll be back by in a mo. I could get him to take you wherever you want to go, on the house, lass, as I used to love your ma. I would have married her—'

'Aye, I know.' Alice could have screamed at him, but she kept her voice steady. 'Another time, eh? I've just got to get home, Bendy. How long will Simon be?' Alice kept her voice steady though she was knotted with fear.

'Naw more than a minute. By, you look like your ma, lass. You're the spitting image.'

Alice nodded and looked along the promenade, eager to see Simon's red car coming along.

Edith touched her arm. 'It'll be all right, love. Our Albert's only speculating, he didn't see it all.'

'I know, but I also know me da and know it could have happened how Albert's told it.'

'So, what are you going to do, love?'

'I'll get Simon to take me home, and if they've taken any of me family to hospital, I'll ask him to take me there. Oh, I wish he'd hurry up!'

'We'll come with you. I just hope me ma's all right. She's one for wading in, as weak as she is.'

'Don't worry, Marg, your Uncle Eric would have seen that she and your gran were all right, I'm sure. I'm glad you didn't have a go, Albert. For once, you did the sensible thing ... Ah, there's Simon coming.'

As Edith said this, Bendy hurried to the edge of the pavement and flagged Simon down. Not as generous-natured as Bendy, Simon wanted to know who was going to pay for the journey. Bendy told him that he would, but Alice was glad to hear Marg say that she had enough for it as she didn't want to be beholden to Bendy.

When they arrived in Whittaker Avenue the neighbours were out in force, the women with folded arms, the men in groups smoking. They all stopped to stare as Simon's car pulled up. Marg was out first and ran into her house. Alice stood by the open car door, hardly daring to ask anyone anything, but she didn't have to as Billy came racing over to her and flung himself at her. 'Alice! Oh, Alice, Da's near killed our Harry. They've taken him to the hospital.'

'Oh no! Where's Da? And our Joey? Are they all right?'

'The cops have taken Da, and I don't care if he's all right or not. He got a good blow from me on his back and then on his chin from Mr Porter. He was out cold for a minute. I felt like spitting on him.'

'Billy! You shouldn't talk like that, lad. Where's Joey?'

'He's asleep on our sofa, Alice, love.' Marg was back by her side. 'It's as Albert said, Joey ran into ours when your da kicked off. Me gran's asleep in the chair, but not sure where me ma is. Probably upstairs. Joey'll be all right with us. What are you going to do, lass?'

'I'm going up to the hospital. I don't care that it's out of visiting hours, I'll make them let me see Harry. Oh, Marg, Edith, I'm scared.'

'Don't be, Alice, love, everything might not be as bad as it sounds. I'll come with you.'

'Ta, Edith.'

'I would an' all but Gran needs me, and I bet me ma's in a state. I haven't seen her or Jackie. She'll have gone to her bed as she were whacked out, and Uncle Eric seems to have made himself scarce, but I can look after Joey and Billy for you.'

'That'd be grand, ta, Marg. I'll be fine with Edith.'

'Aye, I'll look after her. Will you look in on me da, Marg, make him a pot of tea or something? He must be in shock over it all and I doubt me ma's capable.'

'I will, Edith, love. Here, Simon, will that cover you taking them up to the Vic?'

Simon took the couple of shillings from Marg and told Alice and Edith to get in as he wasn't hanging around.

Alice only just had time to tell Marg, 'I'll pay you back, Marg. I will. Ta, love, you're a real pal.'

As they sat in the back of the car, Alice felt Edith take her hand. This was a comfort to her, as was the fact Edith hadn't offered her own thoughts on the matter or suggested Alice do all she could to have her da sent down.

That was the last thing she wanted, as she clung on to her memories and her staunch belief that none of what her da did was his fault.

SIX

Alice

Watching the empty streets, the darkened housés and the patterns the street lights made on the car windows, Alice wouldn't let her mind think about what might happen next. She just concentrated on Harry, willing him to be strong – not just now, but in the future. His increasing nervousness and fear of Da was a worry to her.

The night sister didn't object to Alice seeing Harry, but wouldn't let Edith in. 'Be as quiet as you can, lass, but try to calm your brother.'

'Is he going to be all right, Sister?'

'He has fractured ribs, which are very painful, a broken arm and cuts to his face and head.'

Alice swallowed her tears. She had to stay strong.

'I'm sorry, lass, this must all be awful for you. Harry told us that you don't have a mum and that you're the one who takes care of them.'

'Yes. At least, I try.'

'Well, I don't know your situation, but I would say that you do a good job, lass. Harry obviously loves you very much and has been calling for you. That's why I am going against all the rules and letting you see him – that, and because I'm worried about his mental condition. Harry's body will heal, but what this has done to his mind, I cannot say. Your father should be someone you rely on to care for you, not someone who beats the living life out of you.'

Alice didn't know what to say. She didn't feel as though she could tell the nurse her theory about her da's outbursts, but she was so angry. Angry because whatever ailed her father, he should still have tried to exercise control and fight the urges he got to take things out on the ones who loved him. Because despite it all, they did. She'd seen to that over the years, telling her brothers to remember how Da used to be, to remember how brave he was to have saved another man, knowing that he would be hurt, or likely killed.

Harry wasn't screaming out or physically fighting anyone off, as she'd imagined after the sister had said she needed to calm him, but to her, the sight of his distress manifesting in his silent terror was much worse.

She understood what the sister was worried about – while seeming to be asleep, Harry was trembling all over. Sweat pooled out on his face.

Touching his arm gently had him sitting bolt upright, his eyes wide and staring, then moaning with the pain the action had caused.

'Harry, it's all right, lad, it's Alice.'

'Alice?'

'Yes, love. Lie down, gently . . . that's right. Eeh, lad, don't be scared. No one in here will hurt you.' She stroked his hair,

57

then lifted the glass of water on his bedside. 'Here, take a drink, love. All this sweating will make you thirsty.'

'I – I don't want to go home, Alice.'

'Harry, love, please don't fret. Have a few sips then we'll talk, eh?'

As Harry drank the sister said, 'I'll leave you to it, lass. I can see you're just what the lad needs, but please try to keep the noise down so as not to disturb the other patients.'

'Ta, Sister.'

The sister hesitated and then shook her head. 'I don't know your story, lass, but it seems to me you have a lot on your plate. I'll get the ward orderly to make you a cup of tea.'

'That'd be very welcome, Sister, ta. Can me brother have one an' all? He's a one for tea is Harry.'

'Aye, I don't think it will do him any harm. Just ask if you need anything else.'

When she'd gone, Alice felt at a loss. She had no words of reassurance to give to her brother. 'Are you in a lot of pain, Harry?'

'Aye. Agony . . . Why, sis? Why does Da take it out on us?'

'Lie back against the pillow, love. Let's get you comfy. You'll enjoy a brew, I'm sure.'

'Alice! I want to knaw why?'

'I haven't got an answer, Harry.' She helped him lower himself, seeing the pain in his grimace, but also noticing something she hadn't done before – that Harry was strong, and, yes, courageous. He must be in terrible pain and yet he was bearing it. He wasn't bemoaning his injuries, only his hurt over his da's actions.

'Harry, love, I can only say what I always do, that I think something happened to our da – in his mind. Something he can't control.'

'Will he ever get better?'

'I don't know. But I do know that when we're hurting like you are now, you need your loved ones to stand by you, no matter what. How would you feel if I hadn't been here when you needed me, eh? That's because you need more love when you are hurting. I want to make you better and to give you comfort. Da needs that from us too, even though he hurts us. We have to believe that he can't help it.'

A cough behind her made her turn. For a moment she had the impression that she was seeing a vision, as the young doctor she'd danced with came through the curtains. He looked beautiful to her in his white coat, his blond hair curled just like her own. His concerned eyes held a twinkle and were just as blue as hers. And his expression gave her the feeling that he was her saviour.

Mentally telling herself she was being silly, she felt her cheeks blush.

'Sorry to disturb you. I – I knew your voice when I heard it.'

Alice could only nod her head.

'Forgive me, but I also heard what you said just now and I was fascinated by it. I was with a patient in the next bed.'

Alice still couldn't speak, and she wasn't sure what she'd said that had fascinated him.

He gave a little laugh, which, like his voice, was soft and sort of soothing. 'You must think me mad, first asking you to dance when I don't know you and now wanting to know

59

more about your father. But you spoke as if he cannot help having violent outbursts and, well, I treated your father here – the police brought him in to make sure he was all right to take to the cell – and I got the same impression that you have. He spoke of having an all-consuming head pain. And I—'

'Was he hurt bad? Did Mr Porter cut him?'

'No. He wasn't too bad, Alice. Why, did someone go for him with a knife?'

'I don't know. It was just something someone told me had happened.'

'Oh, I see. No, he wasn't cut, just bruised. Whoever had restrained him hit him very hard in the face as his eye was badly swollen, but he also had many severe bruises on his back. He wouldn't say how he got those, or name anyone who had restrained him.'

The orderly came in with the tea then. A welcome sight to Alice, but she helped Harry to have a sip of his first.

Harry hadn't taken his eyes off the doctor. He winced as she sat him forward, but tried to smile when she showed her concern.

'You have a very brave brother, Alice. One of the bravest lads I've known. He hardly cried out when I tended to him, and yet his injuries are extremely painful ones. We have given him some painkillers but, he . . .' His gaze went from her to Harry, 'You can have more if you need them, Harry. We don't give them unless the patient asks for them, but we do have something stronger. Would you like something to help you sleep?'

'Naw, ta, Doctor. I have nightmares. I'd rather stay awake.'

'Not always the solution, Harry. We need someone to help you tackle the fears that you have.'

'Like, kill me da for me?'

'Oh, Harry, please try to remember what I told you. We're nothing if we break the family up.'

'I can't take any more, sis, I can't.'

'Don't upset yourself, Harry. From what I've seen, you're made of strong stuff. It's just your pain making you weak. If your sister can take whatever it is that you're all going through, then I'm sure you can and will be there to support her.'

This seemed to get through to Harry as he reached for her hand. 'I will, sis. I'm sorry. I won't leave you.'

'I know, lad. You just feel angry and hurt – in your head and heart, as well as your body. But keep telling yourself that Da can't help it.'

'That's what fascinates me and prompted me to interrupt you, Alice. Why do you say your father can't help what he does? Did this come on suddenly – his moods, I mean?'

As she sipped her tea and helped Harry to drink his, she told Gerald what had happened to their father and how he suffered headaches on a regular basis. When she explained about his violence, she tried to make him understand why he was like that, but she couldn't stop a tear plopping onto her cheek as she thought of the hopelessness of it all and how, after what had happened tonight, she may not be able to save her da from himself.

'And does he hit you?'

Harry jumped in. 'Aye, he does. That's why I hate him, not for what he does to me, but for how he treats Alice.'

'My God, Alice!'

'Eeh, Harry, lad. Shush. It's all right.'

The concern Gerald showed sparked a hope in Alice that he hadn't just been making fun of her when he'd asked her to dance.

'Look, don't get your hopes up, but from what your father described I suspect I know what might trigger his violence. Well, what I'm trying to say is . . . that I may be able to help. My father is a brain surgeon, doing pioneering work and having some successes.' He smiled then and said, 'And he's a talker too. He never stops when he is engrossed in a case or when he makes a discovery. Anyway, one of the conditions he has told me about – and in great depth – is how an injury can put pressure on the brain, how fluid can build up and cause the patient, who may have previously been a placid person, to become violent. Apparently, it all depends on which area of the brain is affected by the pressure . . .'

Alice felt unsure. It all seemed confusing to her, and yet, as he spoke she could see that Gerald understood and wasn't condemning her da.

'I'm losing you, aren't I? Sorry, but it's just that I think my father may be able to help yours.'

'Really?' A great surge of hope filled Alice.

'Well, if nothing else, I've made you smile, and that's a sight to see.'

Again, Alice blushed. To hide how he was affecting her she turned to Harry. 'Did you hear that, lad? There may be something we can do for Da. By, it'd be grand to have our old da back, wouldn't it?'

Harry nodded, spilling the tears that had brimmed in his eyes. Wiping her own away with her hanky, she offered it to him. Lifting his good arm caused him pain, so she wiped his face for him. 'Oh, Harry, I feel that hopeful, lad.'

'I do an' all, Alice. It'd make all me pain worth it if that were to happen.'

Alice leant over and kissed his forehead.

'Gerroff! Eeh, Alice, you're like a mother hen at times.'

She laughed at this quietly, even though she wanted to put her head back and let rip as the feeling of hope inside her was for Harry too. This was a different Harry, one that behaved just as a lad going on sixteen would – embarrassed by his sister and fighting back.

She looked over at Gerald and couldn't stop herself giving him a huge smile. He looked taken aback for a moment. 'I – I, well, I'll leave you now, but . . . well, I'll be in touch when I've spoken to my father. I have your address on file. May I call to let you know what he says, or . . . well, you may prefer that I write to you?'

'No, I'd like you to call. You'll have to take us as you find us. And if you call on a weekday, I'll be at the biscuit factory like I told you.'

'Sunday? I will need to sleep tomorrow. I come to the end of my nightshifts in the morning – till the next time – but I'm usually like a wet week for at least twenty-four hours when they end. I can have a word with my father at breakfast on Sunday and call after that.'

'Aye, that'll be fine . . . One thing, though, Doctor. If your da can help mine, how much will it cost? Me da used to pay into a mutual aid fund, but that all went on paying for his care when he was in a coma.'

'Oh, how long was he in a coma for?'

'I don't know exactly, but it was a long time. Me ma was very sick too, but there was nothing in the fund to pay for her care.'

'I'm sorry. You've been through a lot as a family. I read in the notes that your mother was deceased.'

His gentle voice and concerned look almost brought her to tears. As if sensing this, he brightened and became the professional doctor he was. 'Look, I have to go. Don't worry about the financial side of things. I'll ask Sister to see that the almoner comes to assess your situation with regards to Harry's treatment, but there are charitable organisations who offer help in cases like your father's. The almoner will be able to advise you. But remember, if medical help is an essential need, the patient is always treated, no matter what.'

'Ta, Doctor.'

He held her gaze for a few seconds. In his she saw something she couldn't discern – or dare not – for her own heart was telling her things she knew couldn't be true.

'Well, I'll see you on Sunday.'

'Aye, I'll get a good rest tomorrow knowing that you've given hope where there was none.'

'I – I . . . hope you don't mind me saying, but you have a special way with you, Alice. We could do with someone like you – or, I should say, *more* people like you in our profession.'

When he'd gone, Alice felt how she had when she'd left his arms on the dance floor earlier – as if her world had dimmed a little.

'Do you knaw him, sis?'

'Naw . . .' She told Harry how they'd met earlier.

'Ha, I reckon he has a fancy for you.'

'Shush, Harry. And don't be daft. He's above our station in life, lad, he'd never look at the likes of me.'

'He was right, though, you do have sommat special. A way of making folk see things in a better way, and of making them feel better.'

'Ta, little brother.'

'Ha … Ouch!' The pain the laugh had caused Harry was etched on his face, but his expression soon brightened again. 'Not so little now, sis.'

'Naw, you're taller than me. And, Harry, you are strong and brave. Don't ever be afraid of anything. Always think about how you can make the thing that's frightening you better, eh?'

'How can I make Da better? He hates me.'

'He doesn't. Look, try not to be afraid around him, it gets on his nerves. I'm not saying that anything Da does is your fault, or mine, but we could be extra careful not to upset him. That don't mean pussyfooting around him, as that makes him angry quicker than anything, but do the things he expects of us, like polishing our boots – you know he expects you to see that all of our shoes are shining, but you leave it and leave it till he gets angry. Not doing that sort of thing is how we can help matters.'

'Aye, I knaw. Sometimes I find meself not doing them to spite him.'

'Oh, Harry, it ain't something you can get back at him for. Look, lad, you're going to be out of action for a while. Now, supposing I took that as your fault and did things to spite you, eh? How would you feel? 'Cause you've got to think, just because you can't see Da's pain, it don't mean it ain't there. A broken arm in plaster'll get you sympathy, but a broken bit inside your head won't.'

'I never thought of it like that, sis. You know, you've a way of looking at things that makes it all easier to understand. You're the best sis anyone could have.'

'Ha, you're the one being all soppy now!'

Harry smiled. His smile held pain, but it was a smile, and that was enough for Alice.

'I'll see you tomorrow. And Harry, focus on the good that's come out of tonight, eh?'

'Aye. I'll pray that doctor can help us, and sis, I'll be a better lad when I get home, I promise. I'll help you more and I'll do the chores Da expects of me. And I'll look for a job. They'll release me from school once I do.'

'Well, they will at the end of term anyroad. You having your birthday at the back end of August meant you started later than most, so you were always going to have to stay on longer. Anyroad, we'll talk about it when you get home, eh? Good night and sleep tight and—'

'I knaw . . . Don't let the bed bugs bite!'

They both giggled. Harry grimaced again, but his pain didn't stop him from raising his hand to wave and then blowing her a kiss. She winked at him. 'You're going soft, lad!'

And with this, she left him, feeling uplifted in her heart that, though tonight had been one of her worst experiences, the future held hope.

SEVEN

Marg

Marg was mortified when she went upstairs and found her ma struggling to catch her breath. The living room stank of smoke and alcohol, which, given her mother's bad health, made Marg angry.

'Ma! Eeh, Ma, you're your own worst enemy. I wish you'd think of me and Jackie when you go down this road. You know smoking and drinking makes you worse.'

'Aye . . . lass . . . I do, but I don't drink often. I – I wanted to keep Eric happy.' Ma struggled to speak between coughs.

'Is it worth keeping him happy when you become this ill?'

'I didn't want . . . him moaning about giving you a night out . . . Just seeing the look on your face when you got a chance to . . . was worth keeping him happy.'

'Oh, Ma, now you make me feel bad. Yes, I loved my night out, but not at the price of this! You had choices, Ma. You didn't have to smoke or drink as much. Anyroad, I'll send Billy for Ada while I make him and Joey a mug of cocoa, and then I'll get Gran into bed.'

'Eeh, I'm sorry . . . I – I . . .'

'Don't try to talk, Ma. Ada won't be long.' Marg left her ma's bedroom and called out to Billy as she made her way downstairs.

Billy appeared at the bottom of the stairs. 'I was just standing outside by the wall a mo, Marg.'

Marg could see the tear stains on his cheeks and the silver line where he'd hurriedly wiped his sleeve over his face and his snotty nose. She didn't comment, just asked him to run to Ada's.

Checking the kettle was on the boil and glancing at Joey huddled on the sofa, his knees under his chin, his thumb in his mouth but his eyes open and staring, she told him, 'I'll make you a nice hot drink, eh, lad? How would that be?'

He nodded his head. For all the world she wanted to go to him and scoop him up, but though small for his age, she knew that at ten years old he'd not welcome being made a baby of. That didn't stop her heart aching to cuddle him.

'Has me gran gone to her room, Joey?'

Another nod. 'All right. I won't be a mo, I'll just check on her.'

Going through to the front room, which had been converted into a bedroom for Gran, complete with an ancient commode that Uncle Eric had found on a market stall, Marg saw that her gran was out for the count. Her snores rattled around the room, tainting it with alcohol fumes as she released the breath through flapping lips.

Smiling, Marg was glad of this. She knew Gran would sleep all night now; she always did when she'd had a couple of stouts. Otherwise she would ring the bell that stood by her bed and make a sound that could wake the street, and have Marg out of bed two or three times a night.

Marg smiled at the thought, *Maybe a couple of stouts every night would be a good investment for me!*

But then she remembered that such nights were also accompanied by a stinking wet bed the next morning and a mortified Gran. 'No. Not worth it,' she muttered to herself as she put Gran's shoes under her bed and picked up the discarded frock that she had somehow managed to get out of.

Ada came through the front door as Marg went back into the living room. 'Eh, what a carry-on! Never known the like. I've had me head out of the curtain looking for poor Alice to return for the last fifteen minutes.'

Marg gestured with her head towards the sofa.

With clamped lips and an expression of concern, Ada nodded, then spoke gently to Joey. 'Eeh, lad, everything's going to be all right. You'll see.' Joey didn't react. Ada tutted. 'Well, I'll go on up.'

Marg heard Ada greet her ma. 'Vera Porter, what have you been up to, eh? You never learn, always liked a tipple if there was one going ... Eeh, you could rival Betty Foreman when you take it in your mind to do so. But it's a good job you don't try too often, it never did do you any good. You could never take it. Now look at you!'

'Shurrup, Ada, you were naw saint, lass. I helped carry you back from the club many a night when we were lasses.'

'Aye, but we're forty-odd-year-olds now, and you have young 'uns and an old 'un who need you. Not to mention lung disease, lass. Them nights were good fun but should be memories now. You shouldn't even have the odd one these days.'

'Give over preaching . . . Ada, and help me . . . lass.'

'I will, love.'

Marg was walking back to the kitchen when Ada called down. 'Marg, let me have most of that boiling water you've got on the go, will you? Put it in that enamel bowl you keep for your ma. Oh, and fetch the Balsam up.'

'Aye, all right. There's plenty in the kettle, I only need enough for some cocoa for the lads.'

When she took the water and Friars' Balsam up, Ada said, 'You're a good lass. Did you have a fun night till this happened? You deserved one.'

'We did.' She told Ada about the film. A giggle from downstairs warmed her heart. 'See you in a mo, Ada.'

When she got downstairs, Billy sat beside Joey and both lads were laughing. 'Tell us some more about the film, Marg.'

'Aye, let me get your cocoa then.'

This done, she relayed the scene where Cary Grant takes great pleasure in his ex-wife's discomfort as her new partner swings her around the dance floor in a showy way. 'He's enjoying it so much that he pays the orchestra to play the tune again, and earns a look that could kill from his ex-wife.' Warming to her appreciative audience, Marg skipped around imitating the dance and the looks Cary received. It gladdened her heart to hear the boys laughing.

'Eeh, Marg, you're a great mimic, lass. You should be on the stage yourself!'

Ada had helped Ma downstairs. Ma was holding her sides, but then started to cough even more than she had before. Marg ran to help her.

'She's all right, lass. I've brought her down as she wants to pee.'

Ma didn't look all right, but Marg left her to Ada, who could manage her a lot better than she could, and turned her attention back to the lads. They were still giggling.

'I'll tell you what, next time I've got a penny to spare I'll take you both to the flicks, lads.'

'Ooh, ta, Marg. I'd love that.' Joey's face beamed.

'They have a Saturday matinée for the kids, you know,' Ada told them as she came back inside.

'We're not kids, Mrs Arkwright!'

'Oh no, sorry. I was being silly. Of course you're not.'

Ada's wink at Marg told of how this had amused her.

'Drink your cocoa while it's still hot, lads.'

'Ta, Marg. It's lovely!'

'Not as good as our Alice's, though, Billy.'

'Naw, lad, no one can beat anything our Alice does in your eyes, can they?'

Billy raised his eyes at Marg, who giggled as she knew full well that Alice's cocoa wasn't liked by either of them.

The exchange made Marg want to cuddle them both – fourteen-year-old Billy acting like a father to little Joey, and going along with him so as not to upset him and ten-year-old Joey afraid of all that was going on but wanting to be loyal to his sister.

They'd come through this all right, she was certain of that. But whether Marg would come through the ups and downs of her own life, she didn't know.

EIGHT

Edith

Joy surged through Edith when she caught sight of Alice coming towards her with a smile on her face. It propelled her to run along the hospital corridor to meet her. 'Eh, Alice, is the news better than you thought?'

'A lot better, Edith, love.'

As she listened to Alice and all the hope she held, Edith cheered. 'By, that's good news. And to think your da may get help an' all? You've always said his ways were down to his head-aches, and everyone knows what a changed man he is.' She tucked her arm into Alice's. 'There's a lot to be happy about, then? But poor Harry, this could affect him for a long time.'

'Well, I've made him see a few of the things he does to trigger Da, and he realises that he can help matters. Also, he heard what Doctor Melford said so he feels, like me, that at last something might be done to help us all.'

'But you don't trigger him, do you?'

'Aye, I do. My tiredness means I haven't always got things how they should be. Harry said he'll help me more, though.

And I'm going to talk to Billy and Joey an' all. I've been too soft, trying to carry the burden of running the home and doing my job at the biscuit factory with hardly any help.'

Edith could relate to this. It happened a lot in her life too. She tucked her arm through Alice's. 'Don't come into the factory tomorrow, love. I'll tell Moaning Minnie what happened and that you've got to come here to see Harry.'

'Ta, love. At least it's only overtime so they can't force me to work. I needed the money, though.'

'It'll work out. Anyroad, there's something you're not saying. Come on, I can see it in your face.'

'Aw, you're going to think me daft.'

'Ha, no changes there then – I do already.' It was good to hear Alice's lovely laugh.

But this changed and their conversation came to an end when they opened the hospital doors and looked towards where they expected Simon's car to be and saw the empty parking spot. Edith was exasperated. 'Oh no. He's gone! He's a pig. He said he'd wait.'

'He did say he wouldn't wait long, though. Never mind, love, we can walk.'

By the time they got home they were both exhausted. Marg met them – she was standing against the wall of her house, lit by the street light and the light that flooded through her open door. 'Am I pleased to see you both! I was worried out of my mind. How's Harry?'

When Alice told her he was all right and that she had other good news, Marg clapped her hands. 'Hold on to it for a mo, love. The lads are asleep on the sofa, and Ma and Gran are away to their beds. I'll make us all a hot cocoa. It's still warm out here so we can sit against the wall and you can tell me everything. Eeh, what a night, eh?'

'Have you seen me da come back, Marg?'

'Naw, Alice, love. I've been in and out for this past hour and not seen him, and there's not been a light on in yours all night.'

'Oh no. That means the police have kept him in the cells. He'll be in a terrible state.'

'Is he worth worrying over, lass?'

'He is, Marg, he's me da, and anyroad, you know this ain't how he really is. Don't talk like that.'

'I'm sorry, love.'

'Aye, Marg, that wasn't a good thing to say, but you're not to know Alice's news. I'll go and see if me ma and da are all right. You tell Marg all about it while I'm gone, Alice. I'll be back in a mo to have me cocoa.'

In her own home, Edith found her da asleep in the chair. She nipped upstairs and found her ma in bed snoring away. This gave her comfort, especially as she didn't detect a strong smell of alcohol.

Downstairs once more, she shook her da's shoulder, his rattling chest filling her with fear. 'Da, Da, I'm back.'

'Is that you, Edith, lass?'

'Aye. You should have gone to your bed, I have me key.'

'Old habits, lass. Though I've given up waiting for our Albert. Marg said that you saw him. What was he doing?'

'We did, but I don't know what he was up to.'

Her da sighed. 'Well, how's things?'

She sat on the floor at her da's knee, on the rug that had long seen better days, as she told him what she knew and how they'd had to walk back.

'You shouldn't have paid him till he got you back here, he's a crafty sod that Simon. He'd think of earning more money and wouldn't care about leaving you stranded. But it's good news over George Brett – he used to be a lovely bloke who would help anyone out and adored his wife and kids. I remember once when I was working away and your ma fell sick. George took you and Albert into his home, and his lovely wife cared for Betty. You knaw, not many men would take kids in, let alone be the one to suggest it.'

'I remember that, Da. Ma had sickness and diarrhoea.'

'That's right, and you kids came down with it an' all. And still George insisted you were cared for in his home.'

'He made us laugh a lot as kids. We all loved him.'

'Aye, he was well loved around here. Many folk remember how he was and all talk of the pity of what happened to him.'

'It's a tragedy, Da. Alice and the lads have suffered.'

'You have an' all, lass, with how your ma is, and now Albert. I wish I could protect you.' His fit of coughing and the red patch on his hanky terrified Edith. Without her da, she just didn't know how she could go on.

'Shall I make you a brew, Da?'

'In a minute. Put another of them logs on the fire and sit here a while, lass.'

Though Edith was sweltering, she knew her da felt the cold, so did as he said. 'Da, do you think if you went to the doctor's—'

'Naw, lass, we haven't the money for that. I'll be all right. I have me good days and they're all I can hope for.'

'But there might be something they can do. Who'd have thought there was an inkling of hope for Alice's da?'

'They can't give me new lungs, Edith. What I want to happen is to see you settled with a nice bloke who I can trust to look after you when I'm gone. With you going out tonight I was hoping you'd meet someone.'

'Ha, Da, you old romantic. No fella will take me on.'

'Lass, you're beautiful, inside and out. You'll make a lovely wife and mother. I'm right proud of you.'

Tears pricked Edith's eyes as they became quiet. Her da was everything to her and had been all her life.

When she heard him snore, she got up and tiptoed out of the room, closing the door softly behind her.

Skipping across the street, her spirits lifted to hear Alice and Marg giggling. 'Your cocoa's on the side next to the kettle, love.'

'Ta, Marg. It'll be welcome, I tell you. What a night, eh?'

The pavement slab struck cold through Edith's thin skirt as she squatted down after fetching her cocoa. She shivered.

'It is turning chillier now, but you soon get used to it and you'll warm after you have a couple of sips, I've only just made it.'

'Ta, Marg. It's . . . well, everything gets to you, doesn't it?'

'It does, but all you can do is pack up your troubles in an old kit bag and smile . . .' she added in a sing-song voice.

They all joined in with Marg's singing until the next-door neighbour's upstairs window opened and she shouted,

'Shut that racket or you'll get me piddle pot emptied all over you.'

This sent them into a fit of giggles, but had them running inside Marg's house just in case. They didn't trust Mabel Jones not to carry out her threat.

Tears were running down their faces once they got inside, but after they'd controlled their laughter they went into an impromptu huddle.

'We're all right, lasses, as long as we have each other.'

'We are, Marg.' Edith looked at them both as they released each other. 'Hey, remember, we're the Halfpenny Girls! And always will be.' She took Marg and Alice's hands. 'I love you both. You're like sisters to me and I'd do anything for you.'

As they came into her arms, Edith thought, *If only I could do something to put all our lives right. Because we've all got such a lot to contend with.*

When she entered her home, having helped Alice take the boys back to hers, Edith was overwhelmed by a sense of hope-lessness at their situations. Da was no longer sitting in his chair, and she guessed he'd gone up to bed. She felt disap-pointed as she would have liked to have chatted some more with him, and she'd had it in her head to offer to help him to have a wash. She so wanted to make his life better, though doubted he'd take kindly to her actually washing him. It might have helped him if she could have brought a bowl of warm water to stand on a chair next to his, and his facecloth and shaving gear.

As she prepared herself for bed, Philip came back into her mind. She hugged herself as she revisited the nice feeling she'd had when dancing with him, refusing to give in to the niggling voice that said she was stupid to dream.

Dreams didn't hurt anyone. And they wouldn't lift her feet off the ground. She knew her place in life – though her dream did give her hope.

The front door crashing open brought her down to earth. 'What happened, Edith? Is Alice's da dead? Is Harry all right?' Albert shouted as he made his way inside.

'No, and yes. Harry will be all right.' She told him about Harry's injury.

'Poor Harry. I like him – a bit of a softie, but a nice lad. Have you got a cup of tea going? I'm dying of thirst.'

About to protest, Edith thought better of it. Now wasn't the time to rile Albert, so she smiled and said, 'Soon will have, love. And I've a lot to tell you so I'll join you, even though I have had cocoa at Marg's.'

As they sat together sipping their tea, Edith told Albert all that had happened, even feeling lulled into mentioning Philip.

'Don't get ideas, Edith, love. Them sort only want us for what they can get out of us. He'll be setting his sights on bedding you. Well, just let him try and—'

'No, Albert. Don't talk like that, he's a gentleman. I liked him.'

'Just watch yourself, that's all, and tell me if he tries owt.'

This wasn't said in temper, but in a caring way, and Edith thought for the umpteenth time what a complex character this brother of hers was. He brought to mind the poem she knew as a child:

There was a little girl,
Who had a little curl,
Right in the middle of her forehead.
When she was good,
She was very, very good,
But when she was bad she was horrid.

For Albert, she could substitute 'boy', but the sentiment was him exactly. She'd take the good and enjoy it, and cope somehow with the bad. Or, rather, manage it. She needed to do that, but how?

'Well, I'm off to bed, sis.'

He surprised Edith then by leaning over and kissing her cheek. As he walked out the room, Edith was left with a warm glow.

She'd not give thought to Albert's bad traits tonight; she'd enjoy the small amount of comfort she'd been given, and let herself think about Philip.

Life had its moments.

NINE

Alice

When Sunday came, Alice woke with a feeling of excitement tickling her belly. The sun shone through her bedroom window, though all was quiet in the house. She listened for her da, who was usually the first up, but she couldn't hear him.

Dressing quickly, she ran down the stairs and out into the yard, hoping to find the lav empty, then felt relief when it was.

When she was back in the kitchen, there was still no sound from upstairs. This worried her, but then, when her da had come home yesterday morning, he was exhausted. He'd hardly spoken except to ask how Harry was. He'd hung his head in his hands as she'd told him.

'Don't worry, Da, he doesn't blame you and said he's going to be a better lad when he comes home.'

To this her dad had shook his head as if in despair and gone up to his room. They hadn't heard anything from him until the evening, when he'd hardly touched the supper of egg and chips that she'd cooked for him, and even then he was very quiet.

Although nervous at telling him about Gerald, who she addressed as Doctor Melford, Alice had taken a deep breath and begun by saying, 'None of this is your fault, Da, it's a condition that you have. And it was caused by the accident.'

He'd looked up. She'd not been able to read his expression, but hadn't felt intimidated by it, and so had gone on to tell him what the doctor had said.

It was one of the best conversations she'd ever had with her da. No temper. No putting her down and, most importantly, no objection to the doctor coming, except to say they'd never be able to afford to have anything done for him, even if something could be.

This Alice had taken as him not wanting to raise his hopes, but to her it was everything. She also told him the almoner would apply to a charity she knew well, and she had every hope that they would pay towards the operation if they thought it would improve the family's life. She'd said that Mr Melford – Doctor Melford's father – would only say he could do something if he thought it possible, and if he did, he would also back her in her bid to get the money.

To this, her da said, 'Well, it does affect us all, and to knaw it ain't me own fault would mean a lot to me. I just hope they can do sommat. Ta, Alice.'

All of this increased the hope Alice had felt on Friday night: hope for their future, especially for her beloved brothers.

As she busied herself getting the kettle on, Alice worried about what the outcome of his arrest had been, as her da hadn't said and she hadn't liked to ask.

Her plan was to try to keep this new footing they'd found with each other, and to do something that fear had prevented her from ever doing before – taking a cup of tea up to her da.

Her heart clanged in her chest as she climbed the stairs. And yet, she didn't have that feeling of being afraid of waking a sleeping wild animal, just a realisation that him not being down before her meant that he really wasn't well this time. She needed to show him with this small gesture that he was loved and that she cared.

To her knock on his bedroom door, he growled, 'What?'

'I've a cup of tea here for you, Da.'

There was a long silence.

'Da?'

'All right, leave it there on the landing.'

He hadn't bawled her out, and his reply hadn't been said in anger. This pleased her as she placed the tea on the floor outside his door, then told him where it was. To this, he said, 'Ta, Alice.'

It was as if he'd said, 'I love you, Alice,' such was her joy. She couldn't remember the last time he'd spoken to her in a nice way. 'You're welcome, Da. And I've some bacon bits. I'll fry them up for your breakfast.'

There was no reply to this, just a grunt. But still, that wasn't a 'bugger off' or worse, which she might have got.

Skipping downstairs, she scurried around tidying the living room. She'd put a bit of polish around later; she didn't want Gerald to think of their house as dirty. But as she looked around now, she saw how shabby it was. The brown sofa and matching chair had seen better days, and the table was scratched. The sideboard was a nice piece, though, and always polished up well.

She thought of taking Gerald into the front room, but that wasn't a lot better and was hardly ever used, so unless she opened all the windows, which her da would never consent to, it would smell musty.

Sighing, she resigned herself to freshening up the living room. 'That will have to do.'

Once the smell of the bacon bits frying reached Billy and Joey, they appeared as if by magic.

'Will there be some for us, Alice?'

'There will, Billy. The butcher heard what happened and called me in as I passed by yesterday on my way back from the hospital. He gave me these and a bit of scrag end, saying he was sorry about it all. I couldn't believe how much he gave me.'

'That's 'cause he's sweet on you.'

'Billy, you daft apeth!'

She laughed out loud at the thought of the lovely but over-weight Mr Roden, who was forty if he was a day, being sweet on her. 'More like he's just a kind man who wanted to do something to say how sorry he was for what happened. Anyroad, you're not to tell Da or he'll throw them back at him, you know how he is about charity.'

She wondered whether this meant he wouldn't accept charity when it came to his operation, but he hadn't said as much, so she dismissed it. With him, it was his pride, and that wouldn't be affected by an organisation helping him to get better, but by folk he knew thinking his family were deprived.

'And I want you lads to go into his shop and thank Mr Roden on your way home from school tomorrow. And ask if there's anything you can do for him. That way if Da finds out, we can tell him that you earned it.'

'Aw, sis, I hate the smell of the butcher's shop, all them dead animals hanging up.'

'I'll do it, Billy, I don't mind. I like Mr Roden and we should thank him.'

'Oh, all right then. I'll come with you, Joey, but if there's any of that mopping of the blood . . . ugh! I couldn't stomach it.'

Alice laughed. 'We all have to do things we don't like in life, lad. Now, go and get dressed, the pair of you, and I'll have a drop of tea and a doorstep bacon butty ready for when you come down.'

As she sat munching her own butty, the lads having eaten theirs and run outside to play footie, Alice watched her da eating his and looking as though he was really enjoying it. It warmed her heart.

But then her world soared as he looked at her and asked, 'Does this doctor really think he can help me, lass? And . . . well, him thinking that me . . . well, you know . . . does he reckon he can stop me . . . going into a temper?'

Alice was amazed. It was as if a light had turned on inside her da and he could see for the first time the hurt his condition was causing them all.

'He doesn't know for sure, Da, but it's something to hang on to, ain't it?'

'It is. You take after your ma in so many ways, Alice. She always looked on the bright side – her favourite saying was "Tomorrow's another day, things will be better then, lad."'

A shadow passed over his face.

'It is, Da, and it'll be a good one, I'm sure of it.'

'Aye, maybe . . . Do you and the lads remember how it used to be when your ma was alive and before me accident?'

'Aye, Da, we do. Even Joey, though he was only five. We often talk about it.' She gave a small laugh. 'Joey remembers running along the street to meet you when you turned the corner, and how you would pick him up and swing him around – you were always doing that. Me, Marg and Edith remember how you did that to us when we were young 'uns, and how we used to scream when you pretended to drop us.'

A smile crossed his face, something Alice hadn't seen much of. It changed his features and put the twinkle back in his eyes.

'Do Harry and Billy have a memory?'

'Aye, our memories are what's kept us all going. Harry remembers much the same as me, Billy and Joey do, about how playful you were. How you used to play footie with them and take us to Stanley Park and the beach to have picnics.'

To her surprise, Alice saw her da wipe a tear from his eye. 'It'll all work out, Da. They say every cloud has a silver lining. Well, this has been a bad cloud, but it might be a turning point for us all. Harry'll come out of hospital to a different home. We can make it so, if only we can get the help you need.'

'Aye, lass.'

'Your paper's here, Da. Shall I make you another brew and you can sit in peace then?'

He looked up. His eyes were red with unshed tears. 'Ta, lass.'

He didn't have to say more. To Alice, a bright light had come on, and it filled her with happiness.

Just after eleven, Joey ran inside to tell her a car had turned into the street. Stepping onto the front step, Alice smiled to see all the kids following or running alongside the open-top car.

She could see the laughter in what, to her, was Gerald's beautiful face.

As he drew nearer, Marg and Edith came out of their front doors for a nosey, but they weren't the only ones: curtains fluttered and front doors opened. A car coming into their road was an unusual event.

'He's here, then, Alice! Good luck.'

'Ta, Marg.'

'Fingers crossed, lass.'

'Aye, Edith, fingers crossed.'

The car stopped in front of her. 'Hello there. You found us all right, then?'

'Yes. Hello again. I only live a short distance away on Newton Drive. How are you, and how's your father?'

'We're both all right. Thank you for coming.'

Billy and Joey stood close to her now. 'These are my brothers, Billy and Joey. This is the doctor I told you about.'

'Hello, mister. Is me brother Harry all right?'

'He is, Joey. He should be home with you in a couple of days, but you're to take care of him, as he must rest for a while.'

'I will, I just want him home.'

Gerald ruffled Joey's hair. 'Good lad. I'll make sure he's home soon.'

'Come this way, Gerald . . . You stay out here, lads, I'll tell you everything later.'

Once inside, Alice's nerves took over and she found herself telling Gerald, in a stilted voice, to please sit down and she'd make him a brew.

He must have picked up on this as he gently made her feel at ease. 'Alice, there's no need to be formal. We're friends, aren't we?'

'Aye . . .' Her nerves were replaced with a feeling of shyness as she looked away from his gaze.

Taking a seat, Gerald looked around. 'Your home is lovely, as it is just that – a home. My beautiful, eccentric mother has decorated our house as if it is a princess's palace, or a film star's exotic paradise – there's nothing homely about it like this. And my father goes along with it. They are two brilliant minds, but products of the aftermath of the Great War, when everything frivolous was admired. They and their friends are bohemian in their tastes and away-from-work lifestyles. I like this, it is welcoming.'

The film Alice had seen with Edith and Marg came to her mind – the elaborate settings of the ballroom and the homes of the characters, and how it all took you to another world. But she couldn't imagine living in such a place, nor did it seem to be the kind of home a family of doctors would live in, and yet, she liked the sound of it. 'It sounds very nice, sort of happy and carefree.'

'Oh, it's that all right. Anyway, is your father in?'

'Yes, he is, but he wanted to stay in his room until I could tell him whether the news is good or bad. You see, you've given him hope, and I reckon that he can't take the disappointment if you say nothing can be done – at least, not in front of you he can't. Anyroad, I've the kettle boiling, so I'll just go and make the brew.'

A feeling of pride lifted Alice as Gerald had sounded sincere in his praise about her home, but still she found she was shaking as she went into her small kitchen and lifted the kettle from the hob, where it was impatiently splattering water and steam from its lid.

The action of making tea helped to calm her, as did the opportunity to show she knew how such things should be done. She placed the pot on the tray she'd prepared and, checking it over, thought it looked grand, with the pristine white cloth that had tiny pink rosebuds and elegant green stems, which her ma had told her had been embroidered by her gran. The cloth provided a lovely background to her ma's best china cups, which hadn't been used since she'd passed away. They were adorned with the same little rose pattern.

A picture of her ma came to mind. *Eeh, Ma, I've hope for Da now. Please make it good news.*

'Ah, that's very welcome, thanks, Alice. I've been on duty after all. They called me in for an emergency so I haven't had time to stop for breakfast.'

'Oh, can I get you something?' Though this had been asked lightly, Alice prayed he'd say no. She could only offer him a slice of bread – the rest of the loaf she had to keep for supper. She had the scrag end on the go for dinner, but the lads would be hungry again by teatime.

'No, thanks. Mother is cooking Sunday lunch and we're all expected to eat every morsel or there's trouble!'

She joined in with his laughter at this and felt herself relax once more, until Gerald became serious.

'Well, Alice, my father has said he will examine your father to see if there is anything he can do, which is all I can tell you for now. Except to say that when I shared your father's symptoms, he, like me, suspects that your father could be suffering from pressure on the brain that could be caused by a leak of CSF, which is the fluid around your brain and your spinal cord. If that is so, then he can operate, drain and repair so that it doesn't build up again. He is amongst the top pioneering professors on the subject of brain injuries. However, we can't be sure until your father is examined as there are certain other conditions that give similar symptoms, but are more complicated.'

'Oh? More serious, you mean?'

'Yes . . . Look, you mustn't get worried, but there is always the possibility that this could be a tumour.'

Alice gasped.

Gerald stood and came over to her. He sat on the arm of her chair. His nearness sent a trembling through her that she couldn't understand, but it made her totally aware of the warmth from his body, the smell of his aftershave, mingled with the freshly washed smell of his shirt.

When he touched her shoulder the feeling intensified, tightening her throat.

'Please, Alice, don't fret about the worst scenario, but hope for the best one, and please don't tell your father of that possibility as some men can object to even finding out, preferring to be left ignorant of what is really wrong with them.'

She looked up into his concerned face. Their eyes met. His expression registered a look of shock. He stood. 'Alice, I – I, well ... are you all right now? Shall I carry on telling you everything?'

'Yes. Ta, Gerald. I was shaken by the possibilities, but I'm all right now.'

'I know, all such news is hard to take, my dear, but hang on to the positives. I know you can do that, Alice. You did for your brother. You enabled him to see that your father couldn't help what he'd done. Call on that strength and way of looking at things to help you now – to help your father. As you were right: whatever this is, the poor man cannot help or control his reaction to anything that triggers his temper to flare.'

Alice nodded, unsure if she had any strength. It seemed that her hopes had been dashed.

'Listen to me, Alice. You were amazing, I so admired how you handled everything. You were calm, you looked at every angle of the situation and you had solutions, when most people faced with what you were faced with would be screaming abuse at the man who'd done that to your brother.'

'Well, I do feel like that when one of them is hurt, but I always make myself remember what Da was like before the accident, and before losing Ma.'

'Yes, and that is what he can be like again if my father can help him. And it will have been you who saved him as it was overhearing you that encouraged me to investigate his case.'

'Ta, Gerald, that makes me feel better. I do so want him helped and to be happy again. What will happen next?'

'I will go back home and tell my father that yours does want his help – he already knows that the almoner is working towards getting the funding, so he will schedule an appointment for a consultation with your father. That will come in the post. Then it is in the hands of the gods, as they say.'

'If . . . well, if it is a tumour . . .'

'Oh, Alice, I'm sorry. My father will try to operate, if he thinks he can, but there is a massive risk. But having said that, there has been many very successful operations. It all depends on the tumour itself – where it is, the size it is, and if there is evidence of it being "live" or, in other words, still growing, or if it is dead but just causing pressure.'

'I see.'

'I know it is a lot to take in, but all in all, what my father is offering – as one of, if not the top surgeon in the country – is the very best chance your father has of recovery, of not being in pain and of not being on a short fuse.'

'I understand and I am very grateful. Can I have a minute to explain things to Da?'

'Yes, but I have to ask you again not to mention the possibility of this being a tumour, only that it is likely to be fluid on the brain.'

As Alice went up to her father, she prayed he'd take the news well and agree to seeing Gerald's da as soon as was possible. But at the same time, she prayed fervently that what ailed her father wouldn't turn out to be a tumour.

TEN

Marg

As soon as the car had left the street, Marg called for Edith and together they went to Alice's house.

'Mmm, something smells good, Alice.'

'That's me scrag end, Marg. I've got it in the oven with some tatties, carrots and onions, and I'm slow-cooking it in gravy.'

'Ha! Not only has a posh, very handsome bloke called on you, but you have a good cut of meat for Sunday dinner – lucky you!'

'You daft apeth. I told you, it's scrag end, not topside of beef! And I told you yesterday where I got it from.'

'Aye, from another of your conquests.'

Alice hit out with the oven cloth she'd picked up, but Marg ducked in time and they all laughed.

'Anyroad, Alice, what did the doctor say? Can they help your da?'

Alice told them what had been said and how Gerald was going to bring Harry home on Tuesday night if he was discharged.

'Gerald! Ooh, first name, eh?'

'Yes, we started off like that on the dance floor and it comes naturally now. I tell you, Marg, Gerald's so nice and ordinary, and so easy to talk to.'

'You're sweet on him, aren't you?'

'Ha! I told you that the night me and Alice came back from the hospital,' Edith chimed in with. 'I could see it in her face. She's fallen hook, line and sinker.'

'Oh, Edith, stop it, and you, Marg. Gerald's helping us out, that's all.'

'Oh no, it's not, lass. Doctors are not far off being toffs and they don't usually call on us for anything like this, they'd send a letter. I'm telling you, he's got his eye on you.'

'As if. Now stop being so daft. I've to get on and get the table laid. Me da will be down in a minute and he likes everything done.'

'What did you say the other night as we walked home from the hospital, Alice?'

'What, Edith?'

'Aye, I know, you've forgotten already . . . Well, you said you were going to get the lads to help you more. That's something they can do. Call them in, it won't hurt them. And put them on a rota so they know what their jobs are and know to come in and do them.'

'Aw, I don't like to. They've been through a lot these last few days. I'll start that next week.'

'All right, but don't carry on making a rod for your back, 'cause if you do, there's them who'll beat you with it.'

'I know, Edith, I promise you. Now buzz off, the pair of you. There's no more gossip and I've got to get on.'

When they got outside, Marg called the lads over. She could tell they'd sussed that she wasn't best pleased with them. They stood in front of her, Billy with a slightly stubborn expression on his face and Joey looking as if he might cry. 'Look, lads, you haven't done anything wrong, but I want to ask you to promise me and Edith that you'll help Alice more in the future.'

'What to do?'

'Everything and anything, Joey. She's not your skivvy. She works full-time at the factory and full-time at home, it ain't fair.'

The lads hung their heads.

Edith nudged her gently. 'Leave it to Alice, eh, Marg?'

'Aye, all right, but by, you lads should think on. Alice deserves some life and a bit of rest now and again.'

They both nodded and went indoors.

'You're lucky they're both nice polite lads, Marg. Any other lads would have given you a load of abuse.'

'I know. I just feel so sorry for Alice, but I'm scared to help her myself in case her da starts. I was on tenterhooks in there and always am.'

'Me an' all. I was listening out for his footsteps. Eeh, I hope he can be made well. I feel so sorry for Alice.'

'Aye. Anyroad, I've to go in and see to getting dinner. Not that it'll be much – I've a Lancashire hotpot on the go, but without the meat. I just couldn't run to it. And with the trouble that Uncle Eric got involved in with Alice's da, he hasn't shown his face since Friday night. Mind, our Jackie prepared it all, I've only got to check it, which I'd better do as I'd hate to spoil it. Jackie has a way of making the most meagre ingredients into a tasty dish.'

94

'She's a bucket full of talent, that one. But you know, I'd like to bet that we haven't much more than you for dinner, Marg. Ma was getting it on when I came out.'

When Marg left Edith, she didn't like to think what Betty would cook up, but smiled to herself as she imagined her supping from a bottle as she did.

As she went through her front door she was met with, 'Oh, Marg, I'm glad you're back.'

'Why, what's up, Jackie, lass?'

'Gran's crying in the front room. She's sat on her bed, and Ma went to go in to her but she's had to sit down as she can't catch her breath. I was just coming to get you.'

Marg went over to her ma, while reassuring Jackie. 'Don't worry, lass. Gran's been crying a lot lately. You go in and cheer her up. She's probably visiting the past in her mind again, and that sometimes makes her laugh, but often makes her cry . . . Ma, what's up, love, is it serious?'

'Naw. I – I'm just having a bout. I . . . tried to get outside for . . . air.'

'Come on, then. Let me help you.'

Once outside, they leant against the wall. 'Ma, you're always bad after Uncle Eric's been. Is he . . . well, I mean, is he treating you all right? Eeh, Ma! Don't cry.'

'I – I've to tell you sommat, Marg. I – I tried not to. I . . .'

'Ma, what is it? Is it anything to do with Uncle Eric?'

'Aye. Oh, Marg. He forced me at first . . . but, well, we needed the money . . . but I can't do it anymore.'

'You mean . . . Ma, is he . . . does he, well . . . you know?'

'Aye. I've never liked it, no matter what your gran insinuates, but, I – I feel as though I am helping out with the extra

95

he gives us because of it. But ... well ... Friday, he hu – hurt me.'

'Catch your breath, Ma. You can tell me when you're ready, eh? But don't worry, he won't come near you again.'

'How – how're you going to stop him? You won't tell him I said as he forced me, will you?'

'Why? He should know as I know, it'll shame him then.'

'Naw, please don't ... He ... well, he might turn nasty.'

Marg couldn't understand this. She'd have thought her ma would want her to tell Eric she knew about his ways.

'Besides, how can you stop him? And ... oh, Marg, how'll we ... manage without what he tips up?'

'I know a few things about him, Ma. I'll threaten him with the police. And anyroad, don't worry, we'll manage somehow.' Though she said this last part, Marg didn't know how she was going to make ends meet and keep up with paying for Jackie's lessons as well.

Inside she was seething, and felt dirty at having it confirmed that her ma had been selling herself to her brother-in-law to help out.

She put her arm around her ma. 'Come on, Ma. Don't upset yourself, it makes your breathing worse. And from now on, no fags and no booze, not even on the odd occasion, right?'

'Aye, well, I'll not be able to afford them, will I ... but, aw, Marg ... I'm glad. Glad to the heart of me ... But, be careful ... lass, your uncle can be a nasty piece of work.'

'Dinner's ready, you two,' Jackie called out. 'I'm just helping Gran to the table. She's settled now. I'll ... Eeh, Ma, what's the matter?'

Marg answered. 'Nothing, lass. Well, nothing other than Ma's not feeling well. She'll be better once she gets a lie-down. I'll help her to bed. Would you put mine and Ma's dinner in the oven a mo? But get yours and Gran's, Jackie, there's a good lass.'

As they passed the dinner table, Gran was sat with her knife and fork at the ready and a big smile on her face. Whatever magic Jackie had woven had cheered her.

'Come on, you two, sit yourselves down, I'm hungry. I don't knaw, our Marg, you're late in from school again! Been in trouble, have you?' Gran nodded at Jackie. 'Always in trouble that one.'

Jackie giggled.

Marg smiled. 'Aye, Gran, I had to stay behind. I'll be down in a mo. Start without me.'

When she came back downstairs, it warmed a small part of Marg's heart to see her gran eating heartily. She loved her food did Gran.

Though how I'm going to provide it in the future, God knows.

An immediate pang of guilt stabbed Marg at this thought. She had to admit to herself that she'd suspected her Uncle Eric's game for a long time, but what he gave them made their situation a little easier so she had pushed those thoughts aside.

Now she knew and felt ashamed.

Oh, Ma, Ma, how could I have turned a blind eye?

But why had Ma never said anything before? And why now? It must have been going on for years.

'Marg, lass, you've got to try harder, you know. Follow our Jackie's example. She's a good 'un, our Jackie.'

With this, a tear traced a cold path down Marg's cheek. Just once it would be nice to have her gran say something nice to her, but it seemed her mind was stuck in the past when the growing-up blues had made Marg a bit of a rebel at school.

'Eat your dinner, Gran, you look like you're enjoying it.'

'There's naw meat. That daughter of mine spent the meat money on fags. Well, serve her right if she chokes on them.'

'Gran, don't talk like that. You don't know what Ma does to get money for meat. It ain't her fault she didn't get it with all the trouble going on.'

'Aw, I knaw all right, she—'

'Gran!'

'What are you talking about, Marg?'

'Nothing, Jackie, lass. Nothing ... Only, well, things might get a bit tough for a while. Uncle Eric's not going to be welcome here ... Now, don't ask me why, just accept it. But it means that he won't be helping us out, and he might even call in my debts to him.'

'Didn't you say he'd said you were all square?'

'Aye, but he might cut up a bit spiteful after I tell him he can't come here again.'

'What about my stout? How am I to get me stout?'

'We'll think of something, Gran.'

Exactly what, Marg didn't know. Gran loved her stout and Uncle Eric had bought her a couple of bottles a week – more than likely to keep her quiet, or to send her off to sleep while he ... A shudder went through Marg. Her mind couldn't cope with the truth of it all.

And yet, doubts crept in. Why hadn't Ma ever said anything before? How come she always looked happy to see Eric? And how could she have taken his money – strung him along, if . . .? But no, she mustn't think like that. Times had been difficult, Ma had only tried to help.

'Are you all right, Marg?'

'Aye, lass. I just had someone walk over me grave.' But she wasn't all right and wondered if she would be for a long time. Facing the truth of what she'd avoided acknowledging had shaken her and shamed her. Now she was to somehow sort out how they were going to manage, because one thing was for sure, she meant to stop her Uncle Eric's games, no matter what it took.

They'd finished dinner and Gran was snuggled in her armchair. 'Let's go outside a mo before we do the pots, eh, Jackie?'

Once outside, Jackie said, 'If you're worried about money, Marg, I'll stop me extra lessons. There's naw need for them now. I'm the cleverest in the class and me teacher said I'm sure to get me school certificate with honours.'

'No. That's not going to happen. I mean, not you getting your certificate, but you not having lessons. Being the cleverest in a church school in Blackpool ain't going to get you into a college, but a recommendation from Mr Grimshaw might. He could have some influential friends he could talk to. I met him down the town, you know, and he told me you were exceptional.' She didn't say that he also mentioned that he wasn't a charity and if she couldn't afford to pay him, then he would have to stop the lessons.

'Aw.' Jackie gave a lovely giggle. But then became serious again. 'But Mr Fairweather would give me more work if I had more time and that'd bring a bit in for us.'

'No, Jackie, I don't want you to ease up on your studies. That's how you're going to get us out of this poverty, lass. You're my one hope. But not only that. I don't care if you never do it for us, I want you to do it for yourself. I want you to have a better life, lass.'

After a moment an idea occurred. 'Do you think Mr Fairweather might need more help then?'

'Aye, he's asked me a couple of times but I couldn't because I had me lessons. Last time he said if I couldn't fulfil all the hours, he'd have to ask me to leave and get someone who could. He wanted me to work the shop in the evenings as he said his feet swell up by the end of the day and he can't do it for much longer. But finding someone he can trust is his problem.'

'I'll do it is the answer! If he pays me right, or if he lets me have some groceries in lieu, we could be sorted.'

'But, Marg, you're tired out when you get back from the factory.'

'That's me going to bed so late. I'll just have to change that, lass. I'll manage. Just as long as we have enough money for our needs and you get your education, that's all that matters.' She put her arms out to her young sister, who came into them willingly. 'And as long as we have each other, lass, we can't go wrong, can we?'

'Naw, Marg. Aw, you're the best sister ever. I do want to learn. It's like I'm addicted to it and can't get enough knowledge. Mr Grimshaw is a fountain of it and has some great books. He won't let me bring them home, though.'

'What books do you like, me little lass? Can't you get them from the library?'

They came out of the hug. 'Encyclopaedias mainly, and reference books. And you can't bring those out of the library either, you have to sit in and study them. But it ain't always sommat in particular that I want to know, I just like reading facts. Mostly about science.'

'Science! I never knew that, lass. I thought only professors studied that. Goodness knows where we got you from.'

'Gran once told me that I took after Granddad's brother, that he always had his head in a book.'

'Aye, that's right. I have heard of him. Great Uncle William. A bit of an inventor he was, always trying to make things. Gran once had us in stitches telling us about how he thought that there were men on the moon and that one day we would be able to go there and meet them.'

Though Marg laughed at this, Jackie didn't. 'It wasn't his idea. It's known as "panspermia" and it was in the writings of the fifth-century BC Greek philosopher Anaxagoras. And I think it's possible.'

'What? Eeh, Jackie, I reckon you're from another planet yourself, lass.' She hugged Jackie to her and laughed once more. 'Come on, let's go in and do the pots, as no man from the moon is going to do them for us.'

Jackie laughed with her, and to Marg it felt as though her cares had lifted. This sister of hers could always do that for her.

As she'd hugged Jackie, she'd felt her love for her surge through her. She'd protect Jackie no matter what and do anything for her. Anything.

ELEVEN

Edith

Edith linked arms with Marg and Alice as they walked to work the following Tuesday. The July morning was swirling with sea mist, creating an eerie atmosphere and making the other workers, clad in the same white overalls that she, Marg and Alice wore, appear ghostly as they walked along in their groups.

The changing weather that living by the sea brought was one of the things Edith loved most about Blackpool, and this morning she wouldn't have minded if it had been chucking it down, because nothing could dampen the feeling she had that all was right in her world.

Ma had been on the wagon for a week now and the atmosphere at home had been the best she'd known it, with even Albert being civil. Even Alice's da had hope, and Marg seemed happy too, though Edith worried she was taking too much on, especially after the latest happening with her uncle. Not that Marg had told them why he was banned from her home.

'By, I feel we've been given a new beginning; so much is changing and most for the better.'

'Aye, you're right there, Edith, it does feel like that. As if everything is going to come right. I start me new job tomorrow night.'

'That'll be so different for you, Marg. But why have you got to do it? I know something's gone wrong between you and your uncle, but surely that will right itself eventually and he'll carry on helping you?'

'I'm not taking anything else from my uncle ever again, and next time he does call I'll show him the door for good. I've found out something – don't ask me what, but, well, there'll be no more handouts from him.'

'Eh, Marg, though I'm sorry that whatever has happened has put such a load on your shoulders, I'm glad in a way that you're rid of your uncle. I don't like him, and I worried about you.'

'Well, you've no need to, Edith.'

Edith thought Marg snapped this out at her, but she let it go and changed the subject. 'You're quiet, Alice. I bet you can't wait for tonight when your handsome Gerald brings Harry home.'

'Well, yes and no. I felt safe with Harry out of harm's way in the hospital. I know Da's trying to be better than he was, but he's still quick-tempered so I'm worried about not being home during the day. It'll just be Harry and Da.'

They were all quiet as they absorbed this information.

'I know how you must feel, lass. I'll see if my ma'll have Harry during the day. Can he hobble up to mine, do you think?'

'He could, Marg, but your ma ain't well. She looked awful this morning.'

'I could ask mine. She's not been drunk for a few days; says she's done with all that. Taking care of Harry might help her – give her something to focus on.'

'So she's still not touched a drop, Edith? Good for Betty, let's hope she keeps to it.'

'I hope that more than anything in the world, Marg, but, well, I'm not sure about it.'

'You can't be, lass. Betty's tried a few times and failed, but each time there's a chance she will make it, ain't there? Think positive.'

'I'm trying to. Anyroad, I know you snapped at me just now, but I have to say it, Marg: you be careful when you see that uncle of yours, eh?'

'I'm sorry, Edith, it's all got to me. But, no, I'll not be able to take care, not with what he's done. If I had a gun, I'd shoot him. Has your Albert said anything about seeing him?'

'Not recently. He's been out every night, but he doesn't tell us who he sees or what he does. We've fallen into letting him get on with it – if we say anything, he gets wound up and into a temper. I just wish you could get your uncle out of all of our lives.'

'If Albert wants to be involved with my uncle, there's nothing that I can do, but I'm sorry my family's brought problems to your door, Edith, you don't deserve it. Anyroad, we're here now. Ooh, look at that car – as good as the one your doctor has, Alice. Wonder whose it is?'

Edith looked in the direction that Marg pointed. The car was a flash sports car.

'It is the same, an MG Midget, only I like Gerald's red one better than that bottle green.'

'By, you noticed a lot, didn't you, Alice? You know the name of his car, when to me it was just a red sports car.'

Edith laughed at Marg's rigging as Alice blushed, but before she could say anything a young man came out of the office entrance with a briefcase.

'He's a bit of all right ... Oh, it's him! Him from the ballroom!'

Edith couldn't say anything. She hadn't forgotten a single detail of how handsome Philip Bradshaw was, and how his black wavy hair, brushed back off his forehead, matched his handlebar moustache.

Rita Sharpe turned around from the group in front. 'That's the boss's son, girls. No point in having designs on him, he wouldn't be interested in any of you.'

'We ain't looking at him, just his car, Rita,' Marg snapped back.

'Well, I'm looking at him. As old as I am, I can see he's a bit of all right.'

This from Mavis carried to Philip. He looked up and smiled.

'Ha, Mavis, you'd kill him, he's only a young 'un.' Rita didn't say this quietly either, and Edith saw Philip blush. She felt embarrassed for him. He caught her looking and nodded his head. Though a friendly nod, Edith felt mortified at him possibly thinking she was as cheap as the others were behaving.

Things went from bad to worse as Rita called out, 'Ooh, watch out, Edith.'

And a banter started between Rita and Mavis.

'Oh, shut up, Rita, you're making the girl blush.'

'Eeh, Mavis, not many girls of her age can still blush, I'll tell you.'

'Ha! Them today ain't like you – opening your legs for all and sundry.'

Edith lowered her head, her sense of shame burning deeper into her.

'Hey, don't mind Rita and Mavis, you know what they're like.'

'Aye, I do, Alice, but what must he think?'

'Aw, don't worry, lass. He had a good chat with you on that dance floor, so he'll know what kind of girl you are.'

'Don't let the others know about that, will you? They'll make me into minced meat and stuff me into a pie.'

Marg laughed out loud, but Edith felt more like crying.

'Come on, don't take it to heart. You know how they carry on, it keeps them going. Let's beat them to the bench and get a head start.'

When they got inside and began the ritual of washing their hands and arms, Edith couldn't get Philip out of her mind. But as she donned her cap and pushed through with the throng, the familiar smell of the biscuits baking assailed her. Then came the sound of the conveyor belt jumping to life and she was left with no time to dwell on the incident – the biscuits were on their way to them and they had to hurry to get in line and be ready to start work.

By home time, Edith felt up to her eyes with the silliness that had been the day's gossip – speculation over Alice's visitor, rigging for Marg over her new job and rude jokes heard on the radio. She didn't know why, but what were normal everyday carry-ons had given her a headache and quashed the optimism she'd felt this morning.

Walking home with Alice and Marg, she tried to shake the feeling of dread that sat deep inside her, but even their chatter and the relief of having the day's work done with didn't lift her.

When they entered their road, her heart sank and the dread became a reality.

Her ma was in the middle of the street singing her head off and doing a jig that showed her bloomers. '*Pack up your troublesh in your old kitbag, and shmile, shmile, shmile.*'

The street was alive with women on their doorsteps clapping and egging her on.

'Go on, Betty, lass.'

'Eeh, you should have been on the stage!'

Kids were dancing around, goading Ma and calling her names. Ma was oblivious to it all.

But then, the mood changed as Albert appeared at the other end of the street. 'What the bloody hell, Ma!'

He scooted the hundred yards and waded in with his fists flailing, knocking the kids off their feet and shouting abuse at the women until Ida Higginbotham came out of her door brandishing a rolling pin and went for him.

Edith stood watching in horror, unable to move.

'Eeh, Edith, lass.'

'Stop it happening, Marg, please! Stop it!'

Marg had always been the toughest out of the three of them in these situations. Edith knew she had the strength of character herself, but in that moment fear held her in its grip as she watched Marg go for Ida.

'Now then, Ida, put that down. The kids should have been stopped. They deserved a clout from Albert. They were out of order.' Marg turned in a circle. 'As you all are ... Ma! By, I'm ashamed of you. Get back inside, all of you. And Albert, calm down now, lad. Let's get your ma inside, eh?'

As everyone listened to Marg, a calm settled on the street. Though looking at her ma, Edith guessed what she was about to do, but had no time to stop her.

Bending over, Ma showed her bum to them all.

It was then that a sickening pain grabbed Edith's insides as Albert lifted his boot and kicked Ma so hard on the backside that she toppled forward and fell flat on her face.

Ida had been walking towards her front door but turned back and swiped Albert before he knew what was happening. He fell to the ground. His screams filled the air and echoed around the now quiet street.

Edith rushed forward. 'Ma, Ma!'

When she got to her ma and helped her up, her ma was in tears. 'I only had a glash or two, me lash. I needed a dwink.'

'Oh, Ma, you promised.'

Albert's cry of, 'Help me. Edith ... Sis, help me. I can't move me arm,' left Edith unsure of what to do, but then she saw that Marg and Alice were going towards him, until a voice calling out, 'Don't move him!' stopped them.

No one had noticed Gerald or heard his car turn into the street. Edith saw Alice freeze. Her mortified expression tore at Edith's heart and deepened her despair. But Gerald didn't sound judgemental of the terrible scene as he took charge.

'Alice, help to get the lady into the house. Sit her down and I'll be there in a moment.'

With Ma seated, Edith straightened. 'I'm sorry, Alice, so sorry.'

'It's not your fault, nor your ma's. It's that lot out there enjoying a spectacle instead of persuading her to go indoors. Any one of them could have taken her in for a cup of tea and sobered her up. They disgust me. And I'll skelp our Joey and Billy when I get them in; they should know better than to join in the catcalling and making fun of Betty.'

'Aw, they're only lads. But you've been embarrassed in front of your doctor.'

'Don't be daft. He'd never look at me anyroad, so nothing the likes of your ma could do would make a difference.'

Edith felt torn. She could see Alice was hurting and knew she really did have hope where Gerald was concerned, and yet her worry over her ma made everything pale in significance. 'I thought Ma was getting better, Alice.'

'I know. Maybe this is just a slip. She's bound to have them, but it's like Marg said earlier: if she keeps trying, she might get there.'

Edith had forgotten all about her da until he spoke. 'Betty? Betty, lass?'

'It's all right, Da. Ma's took a fall.'

'Eeh, Betty . . . Are you sure she's all right, Edith, lass?'

'Aye, Da, you know Ma.'

'Was that our Albert I heard out there? Where is he? Is he hurt an' all?'

'He'll be fine. He was mad at Ma and Ida attacked him with a rolling pin. The doctor who was bringing Harry home is with him.'

'Albert hurt your ma?'

'He . . . he was trying to get her inside, that's all . . . Da, how did Ma get the drink?'

'She was suffering, lass. I had to help her.'

'No, Da. You should help her through them patches, not give in to her.'

'She begged me; the poor lass were crying and shaking. I couldn't let her suffer like that.'

'So, you told her where the money we'd put by was? Oh, Da, what are we going to do now? Has it all gone?'

'Naw. Not all. She just took enough for a drop of gin. I'm sorry, lass.'

A feeling of despair overwhelmed Edith. With Albert tipping up a bit more at the weekend they'd put ten shillings aside thinking they might build up a bit to help them in the winter months. Now half of that was probably gone and she didn't know if Albert would help out again, not after Ma had shown him up like that. And Edith didn't blame him in a way. What sixteen-year-old wanted to have his ma embarrass him? Especially Albert, who thought himself the cock of the street kids.

Alice's arm coming around her gave a little comfort. 'Don't worry, Edith. It'll blow over, lass. Look, your ma's all right now.'

'She's too quiet and look at the colour of her. She's not all right, Alice. I'm worried about her.'

Edith's heart sank as she looked at her ma. She had a strange pallor – a greyish tinge to her skin under the bruising and scrapes – that made her look such a sorry sight.

Ma's breathing seemed laboured too. 'Ma, Ma, open your eyes.' There was no response.

Beside her, Alice stood up. 'I'll go and see if Gerald can come and look at her. Don't worry, Edith, we have help at hand.'

Edith nodded, but her da, who must have remembered her telling him about Gerald, became anxious. 'Naw, Alice, ta ever so much, but we can't afford naw doctor. Will you fetch Ada for us, lass?'

'I don't think he'll charge you, Mr Foreman, he just happened to bring Harry home at the same time. It isn't as if we called him, he's just helping us.'

'All right, lass, but make sure you let him knaw we can't pay him.'

'I'll go. You stay with me ma, Alice. I can explain that we can't pay, and besides, I want to see how Albert is.'

When she got to the door, Edith saw Gerald was strapping Albert's arm in bandages. Ada, who was nowhere to be seen before, was now kneeling beside him and Marg, and was no doubt offering her tuppence worth of advice.

Marg saw her first. 'Don't look so worried, lass, Ida's not broken Albert's arm, but it's badly bruised and cut. How's Betty?'

'Bad. I'm so worried about her.' Looking over at Gerald, she told him, 'Me ma needs help, Doctor – but, well ... we can't pay. Though if we have to, I can give you something each week.'

'There's no need for that. I'm just helping out, so don't worry. It's Edith, isn't it?'

Edith nodded. Gerald seemed such a nice man, but what must he think? She felt she'd let Alice down.

'I'm sorry about what happened, Edith, but like Marg said, it's not as bad as it looks.' Turning to Ada, he asked if she could carry on seeing to Albert.

111

'Aye, I'll take over here, Doctor.'

Gerald stood. 'Thanks, Mrs Arkwright, and very capable hands he'll be in too.'

'Call me Ada, Doctor, everyone does.'

Gerald smiled down at her before turning to Edith. 'Right, Edith, let's go and have a look at your mother.'

As they walked towards the house, he asked, 'Are you all right, Edith? You're not hurt? And is Alice all right? Where is she?'

'She's with me ma. None of us were involved, we just came home from work and found it all happening. But I'm really worried about me ma, she's gone a funny colour.'

'I'll see to her. It's probably the shock, don't worry.'

When they got inside, Edith noticed the lovely smile the doctor gave to Alice, and how gentle his voice was when he asked her, 'Are you all right, Alice? Edith says you're not hurt, but it must have been distressing for you all.'

'Aye, I am, we're used to these happenings in our street. There's always a rumpus of some sort.'

'You do seem to see life. Do you want to go and help Harry out of the car and get him inside? I'll be down to see you when I've sorted Betty out.'

'Oh God, I'd forgotten all about poor Harry. Will you be all right, Edith? I'll be back as soon as I can.'

Edith nodded. She seemed held in a cocoon of fear for her ma and a feeling of being mortified that her family had embarrassed Alice and might even have spoilt everything for her.

'Now, let's look at our patient, shall we?'

'Is Albert all right?'

The doctor turned to look at Da as he said this.

'This is me da, Doctor.'

As Gerald went to shake hands with Da, Da had a fit of coughing. 'It – it's me lungs. Coal miners' disease. Don't worry about me, just see to me Betty.'

'Oh dear, I'm sorry about that. Are you receiving treatment?'

'There is none as I know of.'

'Well, it's true, there's no cure, but a lot can be done to make you more comfortable. Let me see to your wife and we'll have a chat. Your son's all right, by the way. Badly bruised – his ego as well as his arm – but he'll be fine.'

Da laughed at this and the sound was good to hear. If only Edith could shake the feeling that all the good in the world she'd felt this morning had now crashed down around her.

'Your mother's all right, Edith. She needs to drink some water as the shock to her system and the alcohol she's consumed has made her dehydrated. Fetch a glass of water, will you? And then a bowl of warm water so I can clean her up and see to her grazes.'

The thought came to Edith that they didn't have a glass, it would have to be a mug, but she went into the kitchen without voicing it. Once there, she set the tap running, not to get the water cold, but because of the lead pipes they were always told to allow some to run off before taking a drink.

The sound of the water hitting the sink grated on her fraught nerves. A tear seeped out of her eye, but she rubbed it away with her sleeve as she knew that crying wouldn't help anything.

When she went back into the living room the doctor was talking to her da. The thought that something could be done to help him cheered her. Her lovely da didn't deserve to suffer how he did, just because he'd worked hard all his life down a stinking pit.

There was no justice in the world.

Ma rallied after a couple of sips and looked a lot better now that Gerald had gently cleaned her face. 'It'll be sore, I'm afraid. Have you any soothing cream, Edith – antiseptic would be best?'

'Aye, we've some Germolene. Mind, we've had it since we were kids. But what's left of it seems to be all right.'

'That will do fine. It shouldn't deteriorate as long as the lid's been tightly screwed on. Wash your hands well, then apply some to your mother's open wounds and she'll be fine.'

'Ta, Doctor. Yoursh that one Alish is shweet on, aren't you?'

'Ma!'

Gerald laughed. 'There, I told you she was fine. But you do need to stop drinking alcohol, Betty. And your family need to help you to do that. I can see by the yellow tinge in your eyes that all is not well with your liver. Drink can really harm you and disease your liver.'

'I can't help it, Doc . . .'

'Yes, you can, Ma, you stopped for a whole week.'

'Keep doing that, Betty. Keep trying to stop. Your family need you to, and you need to for the sake of your health.'

'Does me liver being bad meansh I'm going to die, Doc?'

'No, not if you stop punishing it. Your liver can repair itself, but you can't live without it, so it's up to you. Look, I'm not saying you are a bad person. Drink is addictive to some people

114

and addiction isn't easy to fight, but try, Betty. For yourself and your family.'

'I will. I'm shorry, Edith . . . I . . .'

'Drink some more water, Ma, then I'll help you to bed, eh? You can sleep it off like you always do. Then we'll help you, we will.'

'I – I'm shorry, lass.'

The tear that trickled down her ma's face cut Edith in two. 'Don't worry, Ma. You did well and you can do it again. Marg said the same as the doctor – that each time you try, you succeed a little bit more until one day you'll kick the drink for good. That'll be a good day, won't it?'

'It will, lash. I don't knaw why I do it. Albert won't forgive me this time.'

'He will. He's just embarrassed, so don't expect anything from him for a while, but he'll come around, he always does.' Suddenly, Edith saw the funny side and giggled. 'By, you can do a good jig, Ma.'

Ma smiled a weary smile. Her lips flapped as she let out a sigh and Edith felt the pity of their lives. But she wouldn't give up. Everything could get better and she'd try hard to make it so.

'Well, I missed that, didn't I?'

Ma grinned at Gerald.

Turning back to Da, Gerald said to him, 'Try to get some help, won't you?' and then to her, 'I'll have a word with the physiotherapist who comes to the hospital, Edith. I'll ask him what movements will help your father, and maybe you and Albert could help him to do them?'

'I'm past exercise, Doctor, but thanks for your kindness.'

'But you need help of some sort, you must be in pain?'

Edith wanted to tell Gerald about the blood her da spat up, but something in her da's face held her back. As she saw Gerald to the door, she said, 'I'll talk to him, Doctor. He's upset at the moment and worried about Ma and Albert, and worry always makes him worse.' She could see that Gerald wanted to pursue it further, but he gave in.

'All right, but I am worried about both of your parents, Edith. It must be very hard on you. I'm sorry, I wish I could do more.'

Apologising and thanking Gerald in equal measures, Edith didn't look to see what was happening with Albert. She was angry with him and yet understood him, but it was all too much for her right now. Ma needed her the most at this moment.

Turning, she let out a sigh. *Why did it all have to happen? Why?*

TWELVE

Alice

In all that had happened, Alice had forgotten Harry.

As she came out of Edith's she looked over to see Billy and Joey trying to get him out of the car. Poor Harry looked in agony as she called out to the lads to be careful. 'Don't hurt him.'

'I'm all right, sis. I'm still a bit sore, that's all.'

Alice smiled into Harry's pale face. 'You're home now, lad. Everything's going to be all right.'

'Da's going to get help, ain't he, Alice?'

'He is, Billy.'

'There, I told you, Harry. It's all going to come right.'

'I knaw. Doctor Melford's been telling me all about it. But what's Da like? Will he . . .'

'You're not to worry, love. Da knows he did wrong. He's been very quiet since it happened. Let's just get you inside, but don't mention anything about the other night and then I think he'll be fine.'

Marg came over to them then. 'Hey, Harry, lad, how are you?'

'I'm all right, Marg, a bit sore, and it's difficult to breathe and move as I'm all strapped up.'

'Aye, and only one arm is of any use to you at the mo. Well, this pair'll take care of you, won't you, lads?'

'Aye. Anything you want, Harry, me and Joey'll do it.'

Joey didn't speak. His face was white and his eyes stared out.

'Come on, Joey, lad. Everything's all right. Though I have to say I'm ashamed of you, and you an' all, Billy. I thought better of you than to join in catcalling poor Betty.'

Joey hung his head.

'It was only a bit of fun, Alice, we didn't mean anything.'

'It was cruel, Billy. You should have stopped the others, not been part of it. Betty's sick, and she's a person, not an object to entertain you.'

'But she was dancing and singing. Aye, and she showed us her bum.'

Harry grinned. 'Oh, don't make me laugh, Billy, it hurts.'

'It's not funny, Harry. Betty's ended up hurt and Albert an' all, though he deserves it, kicking his ma like he did. You lads are to say you're sorry to Edith and to offer to run any errands for her da. He'll need some help now that Betty's hurt.'

'Huh, you'll have us like slaves to the neighbourhood at this rate, Alice. What with us having to offer help to the butcher and now Mr Foreman.'

'Serves you right.' They entered the house then and Alice wasn't surprised to see that her da wasn't in the living room. 'Da's taken to his bedroom a lot since it happened, Harry. Like I said, he's changed. He's ashamed about what he's done to us

118

over the years, but he's also realised that he needs help. Be kind to him when you do see him, Harry.'

'I will, sis. I don't blame him for this, not now that you've explained everything.'

'That's good. Right, Billy, make Harry a brew. Joey, you keep Harry company and I'll go back and see if Betty's all right.'

Marg was waiting for her outside her door. 'Are you all right, Alice, lass?'

'Aye. You?'

'I'm fine. A bit shook up, though.'

'Me too, but I'm disgusted at the women in the street. How could they behave like they did?'

'Eeh, lass, we have to think on. What entertainment do they ever get to brighten their day? Betty's a card.'

'I know that, but look what has been caused, and poor Edith, she's so upset. Her ma hurt and ridiculed, and her brother showing violence towards her ma. I felt like dying when we came into the street.'

'I did an' all. I'm just trying to put it into perspective. I'm mad as hell with me ma. Not just for being party to it, but she's meant to be resting in between looking after me gran . . . Oh no, Uncle Eric!'

As if they hadn't enough to contend with, Eric Porter had turned into the street in his huge black Austin. 'I'll see you in a bit, Alice.'

'No, I'm coming with you. You're not facing him on your own.'

'Don't do that, Alice. Ta, but I've things to say that I don't want you to hear. Besides, Gerald could be out any moment.'

'I can leave you when he does, I just want to show him you're not on your own.'

When they got to the car Eric Porter was just about to alight. 'You needn't get out, Uncle Eric. You're not stopping.'

The look on his face made Alice regret she'd chosen to back Marg up – not that she'd ever not do so. She glanced over to Edith's and saw Gerald and Edith talking to each other just inside the door. Ada was walking Albert back into the house and Gerald offered his arm and helped him inside. Eric's voice sounded menacing as he answered Marg. 'Oh? And who says? You'd better explain, Marg, lass.'

'I say. I know what you've been up to. Well, it stops now. We want nothing from you, nor do we want you visiting us.'

'Huh, you don't convince me that you've only just sussed out what's been going on! You knew a long time ago, Marg. Why are you on your high horse about it now? Me and your ma go back a long time and your ma's happy with how things are. Besides, there's stuff you don't knaw 'cause she's too afraid to tell you.'

'I don't want to know. But if she's ever wanted to go with you before, she doesn't now. She wants you to leave her alone.'

'And who's going to make me? You?'

'Yes. I know stuff about you, and if you come around here again, I'll go to the police with it.'

'Oh? And you've got proof of this stuff, have you? Don't answer that until you get rid of your shivering friend who looks like a fly-catching machine!'

'You go, Alice. Ta for coming with me, but I'll be all right . . . Look, Gerald's coming out, he'll want to see you.'

Alice could only nod. The confrontation had shocked and frightened her, but she felt confident that Marg could handle it. Turning, she ran to meet Gerald, relieved to be away from the menacing Eric Porter and wishing with all her heart that Gerald hadn't been subjected to the street in all its rawness, which was part of her life. *Will he still want to know me after this?*

'Alice! Is everything all right? Is that man bothering you?'

'No, he's Marg's uncle. I'm all right, Gerald. How's Betty?'

'She'll be fine. The alcohol has numbed any pain she might be in. But she'll be stiff and sore tomorrow and have a black and blue rear. Does this sort of thing happen regularly? What with your father beating your brother and now a son kicking his mother?'

'No.' She tried to smile. 'It's the hot weather got to them all.'

'So, you just accept it as normal behaviour?'

'No, I don't, I'm appalled by it, and I steer the lads – me brothers – on a better course. They slipped up today, but they will apologise and offer to do some jobs for Edith's da, as he has the burden of Betty during the day.'

'Doesn't the son help?'

'No. He's a nasty piece of work and is always violent towards Edith.'

Gerald shook his head.

'Afore you judge us all and put us all in the same basket, most have reasons for their behaviour. Albert is a rough diamond now, but he wasn't as a lad. His da becoming ill from years down the mine, the poverty they've endured and his ma taking to drink and forever humiliating him has led him to

121

seek a get-rich-quick life, which is tied up with gangs and extortion. Their way has become his. He's an impressionable lad.'

'I see. And the lady with the rolling pin?'

'A brutal husband – not the one she's with now, but her first – leads her to reach for a weapon when she feels under threat. Again, I'm not condoning her behaviour, but trying to give a possible reason for it.'

'And the braying crowd?'

'Boredom, and a bit of spice in their humdrum lives. Something they can gossip about for a long time. They've given up thinking about the right thing to do, and follow like sheep. That to them was the most fun they've had in a long time. And the young 'uns? Well, a bit of sport that their mas didn't see the wrong in – and that's where the pity lies as no one is ever going to break the cycle.'

'Alice, you're special. You have a wonderful talent for reading people. That's not easy. Most just judge, but you look for a reason why. I'd like to get to know you better.'

'What, me? You want to know me better? I – I . . .'

'Yes, you. Like you said to me – and rightly – don't judge. That should apply to yourself. Don't think of yourself as not worthy. You are, Alice. I find you very attractive and intelligent, and . . . well, as I said, I want to get to know you better.'

'Like friends, you mean?'

Gerald laughed. 'That's a good starting point, yes. Do you think you could look on me as a friend?'

'Well, you're not like me usual, but I'd like to see how you pan out.'

Gerald put his head back and laughed out loud. A sound that Alice loved and would never forget. 'You're lovely, Alice. I've never met anyone like you.'

'Nor me you.'

He stood and gazed at her for a moment. She couldn't take her eyes away. Mr Porter's car speeding away with an angry roar broke the spell.

'Oh dear. Another scene on Whittaker Avenue. You'll soon know the neighbourhood as well as me.'

Again, Gerald laughed. 'Well, I think I'll enjoy the learning process, there's certainly plenty going on. Where I live you're lucky to even *see* your neighbour. Anyway, I'd better tell you about Harry's care and then get on my way.'

'Is there any news about me da?'

'Yes, you can expect an appointment to come through in the post this week.'

'Oh, that's good news. Ta for all you've done for us, Gerald.' Alice looked up and down the street. Marg had gone in and all seemed quiet. 'Well, looks like the show's over for today. Shall we go inside?'

'Yes, thank you.'

As Gerald followed her, Alice was shocked to see her da sitting in his chair. 'This . . . this is me da, Gerald . . . The doctor, Da. He treated Harry and—'

'Aye, I knaw who it is, I'm not daft. What's going on? What did you have to talk about out there for so long, eh? Is it me you're going to treat or are you more interested in what you think you can get from me daughter? Well, you can forget any notions of that.'

Alice was mortified. She couldn't speak, but Gerald didn't seem put out.

'Both, in a way, sir. Though I don't mean it how you put it. I would like to get to know Alice better – as a friend. Nothing dishonourable . . . That is, with your permission.'

Alice's cheeks burnt. Her heart thudded.

'Ha! I like a straight-talker. Well, Alice ain't in your league and you can only make her unhappy, so forget it. She isn't worldly like you and your mates. You'll only show her up and make her uncomfortable.'

'I wouldn't dream of that, but I think you underestimate your daughter, sir. Alice is highly intelligent—'

'I knaw me own daughter! State your business and sling your hook.'

'Da, please. The doctor is the only one who has ever offered you any help. Please be civil to him. He doesn't deserve to be humiliated like this.'

'It's all right, Alice, I'm not humiliated. On the contrary, I admire your father, and how he is protective of his daughter. I wouldn't expect anything less of him. I hope that one day he changes his mind, but I will respect his decision . . . Now, Mr Brett, my father has instructed his secretary to offer you an appointment for a consultation as soon as is possible. I have been telling Alice that you will get a letter very shortly. If you can't get there – it's in his private clinic on Whitegate Drive – I'll be very happy to fetch you. Just get one of the lads to drop a note in at the hospital reception addressed to me.'

'Right. Ta.'

'As for Harry. I've a bag in my car with some clean dress-ings. If you come with me, Alice, I'll explain to you what is needed to keep his wounds bathed. You will also get an appointment, Harry, for the outpatients' clinic at the hospital to check up on how your injuries are healing.'

Da dropped his gaze and his head drooped. Shame oozed from him, and at this moment Alice thought he deserved it too.

As Gerald left he said, 'Well, nice to have met you again, Mr Brett. I really hope my father can help you.'

In response, all Da could manage was a feeble, 'Ta.'

Outside, Alice didn't know what to say.

Gerald smiled at her. 'Don't worry, Alice, that was a typical father's reaction. It must seem strange that I ... well, not strange in the way that I'm too good for you, I'm not. But, well, a father might see me as someone taking advantage of his daughter.'

'Aye, I suppose so. It don't happen every day that someone of your standing wants to know someone of mine.'

'Yes. That's just it. He's afraid for you. There are those who would, well, use that in a bad way, and you could get hurt. But I haven't changed my mind.'

'Nor me. But, well, it's hopeless, Gerald.'

'Don't say that. If everything goes to plan, once your father gets onto one of my post-op wards I will make sure I get to know him and gain his respect. I shall see you a lot then too, when you visit.'

'Well, good luck. Me da's a hard nut to crack.'

'And I'm a determined one, so we're a good match for one another. Besides, I'm an only child and used to having my own way.'

She smiled up at him.

His expression showed surprise and then something she couldn't determine. 'Alice, you're very beautiful.'

'Oh! I . . .'

'I'm sorry. I shouldn't have said that. I meant it but shouldn't have said it. Forgive me.'

'There's nothing to forgive. I didn't expect it, but ta . . . You are an' all.'

'Ha! A man can't be beautiful!'

Alice blushed. 'I – I have no other word.'

'Oh, Alice . . . I – I'd better go. Here, this is all you'll need. Use the blue pack to cleanse with hot water and a tiny drop of Dettol. It will sting any open wounds, but it is essential it is done. Then cover the wound with this gauze . . .'

He finished by saying, 'Take care of yourself, Alice. I have now seen a little insight into your fears. I will ask my father to speed up things otherwise I will worry about you.' His eyes bore into hers. Her heart was captured by the gaze. For Alice, a whole new world had lit up.

'Everything will work out. You'll see.'

With this he got into his car. She smiled and waved as he drove off.

'Don't you be getting ideas above your station, Alice,' Da watched as she stepped back inside and closed the door behind her. 'I ain't saying that he ain't an honourable man, but the fact is that men from his class generally don't go for girls like you with a view to marrying them. They have other things in mind. You watch your step.'

'Oh, Da. Gerald's not like that. Look what he's doing for you, and he needn't do. Not when you treat him as if he's some kind of lecher after only one thing from your daughter!

He's a doctor, a caring man, who's gone beyond the call of duty for Harry and now for you. That ain't all to get what he wants from me! It's the man he is. I like him. I like him very much.'

Expecting a backlash from standing up to him, her da surprised Alice by just grunting.

Sighing, Alice asked Harry if he was comfortable.

'Don't you go mollycoddling him, Alice. You've made a baby out of him as it is. He needs to be made a man of and that good hiding I gave him was deserved!'

Harry cringed, fear etched onto his face.

Alice's worry compounded. How could she leave Harry with Da? He wouldn't be safe. For all the talk, her da still had a grudge against Harry. Why? To Alice, it was all a mystery. Her only answer was that Harry showed weakness, whereas Billy didn't and Joey just did what Billy did. Why men thought all boys, and in particular their sons, should be tough and take everything like a man, she didn't know – and even more, why they thought that anything that showed weakness in their sons should be knocked out of them!

For herself, she felt a lot more confident since she'd opened up with her da and been more direct with him. Could she get Harry to do that? Looking at him, she didn't think so.

At a loss as to what else to say, she just turned and went towards the kitchen. 'I'll get the tea on the go.'

With there being a small bit of the cooked scrag end left over, Alice busied herself adding onions and carrots to a pan and getting them on the boil, then cutting the meat into small cubes to put in with it. Using gravy salts and cornflour, she made a tasty thick gravy with the juices and left it all to

127

simmer. She'd made bread dough before she'd gone out to work and left it proving. She soon had this in the hotter oven, happy that the stew and chunks of fresh-baked bread would fill the lads up.

As she worked, Alice let her mind dream of Gerald. Until she heard her da growl, 'You're a cissy, Harry, nothing but a bloody cissy.'

Every bone in her body stiffened as she waited, hoping Harry would answer back and stand up for himself, but he didn't. When she went into the living room, her da was just going through the door to the stairs. 'I'll have me tea later, I'm going to bed. I'm not hungry anyroad.'

A sob from Harry tore at Alice's heart. 'Harry, love, don't take on. You know what he's like.'

'I – I can't take it, Alice. I'm frightened. Don't leave me with him. Please don't leave me.'

Alice sighed. There was only one thing for it. She couldn't take Edith's offer now, but she could take Marg's.

Calling out to Billy, she told him to keep an eye on the stew. 'If the lid starts to lift, turn the gas ring down for me. The bread will take another forty minutes or so, so you needn't worry about that, and don't open the oven door to take a peek, you could ruin the loaf.'

'Where're you going, sis?'

'Just up the road to see Marg. Send Joey if you need me, but I won't be long.' Looking at Harry, she said, 'Don't worry, lad, I'll sort something out for you.'

When she knocked on Marg's door, Edith came out of hers and called over, 'Are you all right, lass? I saw you talking to Gerald for a while.'

'Aye. I'll tell you in the morning, or later tonight if we can gather outside. How's your ma and Albert?'

'Ma's fast asleep and Albert's gone out. Poor Ma. She's badly bruised. I'm so angry with me brother, but what can you do, eh?'

Marg opened the door as Alice answered Edith, saying, 'Nothing, lass. I know how you feel. See you in a bit, eh?'

Marg waved to Edith as she went inside. She turned to Alice, 'Eeh, lass, I can't wait to hear your news. You and Gerald were looking into each other's eyes when I looked out of my bedroom window.'

'Nosey parker! Ha, I'll tell you and Edith later as I haven't got much time, but how did everything pan out with you after I left you? I know he's your uncle, but he frightens the life out of me.'

'Aye, he threatened me and it's scared me a bit, but I told him I know things – quite a lot of things about what he gets up to – and that I'll go to the police with them if he don't leave us alone.'

Although all of this worried Alice, she was on a mission, and she felt better about everything when a few minutes later, after also calling into Ada's, she was able to tell Harry, 'Here, lad, I've arranged for you to go to Marg's while I'm at work. It won't be a lot of fun for you, but better than being here with Da, as he ain't going back to work for a while. Ada'll go into Marg's around noon every day to do your dressings, so you're to take all the stuff that the doctor left with you.'

'But what will Da say? He'll think me more of a wimp than he does now. And I don't knaw if I can stand being with Marg's gran and ma. What will I do?'

'As far as Da goes, he'll probably be relieved to be by himself and we'll tell him it's so that he can have some peace in the day and not have to be bothered with your dressings, which he couldn't do. We would have to rely on Ada to pop in – that'll be our best persuasion point, as he can't stand Ada. Marg said she'll leave one of the kitchen chairs outside so you can sit out there when you feel up to it, and that'll mean you can talk to anyone who is passing. And you like to read, don't you? Well, I'll ask around and get books and comics for you. Didn't Albert use to pass on comics to you years ago when you were kids?'

'Aye, he did. I've still got some. I couldn't always understand them then, but I'd be able to now. If you could get them down, they might help a bit with the boredom.'

'And we could send a note with Billy to your school. Ask for them to send you some work to do. I don't want you failing your school certificate. You've just got to make the best of it, Harry. And at least I'll know you'll be out of danger. I didn't like how Da was with you. He spoke to me of being sorry for what he did, but it seems to rile him when you're actually here and he don't seem sorry at all.'

Harry dropped his head.

Going on her haunches in front of him, Alice brushed his hair back. 'I know it's awful for you as Da seems worse with you than any of us. But it will come right, Harry. I just know it will.'

Harry gave her a little smile and nodded. Her heart went out to him. She gave him all the love she could, but she couldn't replace the ma they'd lost. She just hoped that Gerald's father could give them back their da.

THIRTEEN

Marg

The three girls sat on the pavement outside Marg's house.

'Well, that was quite an evening. Drama for all three of us, and they say nothing happens around here.' Marg looked from Alice to Edith. 'So, who's going first with an update?'

They all giggled, though Marg knew that none of them felt like doing so.

'I want to hear Alice's first. I can't wait.'

'No, save mine till last. Tell us if your ma's woken, Edith, and if she's all right.'

'Yes, she woke up a bit ago. Crying like a baby in me da's arms. I've never known a man to love his wife like he does. He finds all the excuses for her, mostly taking the blame on himself, saying his illness is the cause of it all . . . On that score, there was a little help offered by Gerald, but Da refused. Well, at first, but Gerald said he'd look into it anyway, something about breathing exercises and pain relief . . . Anyroad, as I was saying, his love for Ma is such that he embarrasses me when

131

he says he can't be a proper husband to her. It's not what you want to hear your da talk about.'

'Some good news then. You didn't think your da could be helped at all.'

'He won't do whatever it is, Alice, so I'm not getting me hopes up.'

'Men! Mind, when he says he can't be a proper husband, maybe he means with not being able to work and being sick all the time?'

'No, Marg. Because he says that in another sentence. He feels guilty because I'm the one who has to bring in enough to keep us – well, to top up what he gets from the miner's pension and welfare. And because he's lost control of our Albert, who earns a reasonable amount of money at the rock factory and goodness knows how much from his antics in the evening – whatever they are.'

'It's a rotten trick of Albert's to expect his meals and his washing done and not to pay anything towards the household.'

'I've a plan for that. I'm going to tackle him, and if he still refuses to tip up anything, I'm not going to cook his meals or do his washing, and I'm going to tell Ma that she's not to either, nor make his bed.'

'Good for you. He needs pulling up.'

'So, what about you, Marg?'

Marg told Edith all that had happened. 'But I ain't going to worry.'

Though she said this, she did feel afraid. Her uncle was a nasty man and the look of evil in his eyes when he said she would regret ever having said that she would tell the police about him made her shudder.

As they both turned to Alice, a voice called out, 'John! Where's John gone?' Gran appeared on the step. 'Have you seen me husband, eh? A big man with a moustache and lovely blue eyes? Did he come this way?'

There was no recognition of Marg in her face. 'Gran. Eeh, Gran, me granddad John's not here. He – he passed on. You remember, Gran?'

'Who's your granddad, lass? By, I'm sorry to hear he passed on. Do you live around here?'

'Gran! It's me, Marg!'

Gran began to tremble; her bottom lip shook. 'Marg?'

'Aye, Gran.'

Gran's vacant stare went from one to the other of them. 'Why are you here, me lasses?'

Marg pushed herself up to a standing position. 'Come on, Gran. Let's fetch you a nice mug of cocoa and get you to your bed, eh?'

'But I have to find me husband. Have you seen him, lass? He's a big handsome man. A builder. By, he can lay more bricks per hour than any of them. It's the amount he can carry on his hod, you see. The more bricks you take with you up the ladder, the more you can lay in the time. He brings in good money.'

Deciding on a different tactic, Marg took Gran gently by the arm. 'Aye, he's the best. But you remember, he's working away. Liverpool. He won't be back till the weekend.'

Gran, the woman who used to look down on Marg and ruffle her hair, who took her to the park and played with her, who made her special cakes on her birthday and little frocks with frills on, gazed up at her, 'So, you knaw me John, then?'

133

'Aye. I know him. A grand chap. Kindly and fun-loving.'

'You're crying, lass. Has sommat happened to me John?'

'No. When you wake in the morning, he'll be back with you.'

'Ooh, I can't wait. He's a grand chap. Me soulmate. I'm lost without him . . . Eeh, I'm tired, lass, so tired.'

'I know. Let me help you.'

'You're kind. Funny how you knaw me John.'

Gran leant heavily on Marg, but Marg took the burden of her weight willingly. Her heart was breaking, for more and more it seemed to Marg that she was losing her lovely gran to a world where she didn't even exist for her.

When she came out to Alice and Edith, having got Gran tucked up in bed, they were standing. 'We'll go, Marg.'

'No, Edith, lass. I need your company. I'm making cocoa for Gran. Jackie'll be back from her lessons soon. She gets back at around half eight to nine, and me ma likes a mug of cocoa taking up then.'

'All right, we'll stay, won't we, Alice? But, oh, Marg, you have so much to contend with. How is your ma?'

'Well, you saw her braying with the rest of them for more of your ma's antics and she was full of life then, but that's how she can be one minute and knocked back by the effort it took the next. She seems to drain, as if someone's put a syringe into her foot and drawn the life from her. She needs to see a doctor really, but now . . . well, with me uncle gone, I'll never find the money.'

'We'll pay you back what you spent on that Simon taking us to the hospital, and the flicks money, and the Tower an' all, won't we, Edith?'

'Aye, we will.'

'Ha, you daft apeths! How're you going to do that? Look, times like that – as rare as they are – keep me going. Well, things like going to the flicks, not you having to go to the hospital. We're in the same boat, and if you weren't in it with me, I think I'd go mad.'

'Aw, give us a hug.'

Marg went into Alice's arms and felt Edith's come around her too. Her head flopped onto Edith's shoulder. 'I love you two. My life would be nothing without you and our Jackie.'

'We're the Halfpenny Girls, remember? We stick together.'

'We do, Edith, and I love you both too, and without you, I'd be left drowning under the pressure of everything.'

'I know, me too, Alice.' Edith sighed.

'Well, we all have a boatload of troubles, but we'll not sink while we have each other. Now, I'll put the kettle on and you get ready to tell all about the look that went between you and Gerald, Alice, because there was more behind that than a passing glance, lass.'

Alice giggled and the sound lifted Marg.

'We'll all help you, Marg. By, you must be made of cocoa, you're always getting someone or other a mug. And you're the best at it, an' all. Ain't she, Alice?'

'Aye, mine tastes like ditch water! Ha, even our Joey won't drink it and he's the dustbin of the house – he'll eat and drink anything usually, he's got a belly made of iron, but not for me cocoa.'

They were laughing as they went inside.

'Mine ain't too bad, but no one really likes it but me. Me da and ma prefer a mug of tea, and Albert, well, he's a tea belly an' all.'

Jackie came through the door just as Marg put the kettle on. Her face was beaming, and the sight warmed Marg. 'What're you so happy about, lass?'

'I've got news. Mr Grimshaw has a friend who was a lecturer in the sciences. He's going to ask him to give me lessons when I get me school certificate. He said that if he'd have been my headmaster and had known how bright I was as a youngster, he would have got me a scholarship to a private school!'

'By, our lass. I've always known you were a bright spark.'

As Marg put the kettle back onto the stove, Jackie rushed at her. 'Eeh, Marg, I couldn't have done any of it without you. You've always believed in me.'

Marg held her sister to her. 'I have, lass, and you've never let me down. Bring your cocoa outside with us. Alice has got news too, only on her love life, and that'll be an education.'

They went outside giggling like a lot of kids. Marg was enthralled by the turn Alice's relationship had taken with Gerald. 'By, Alice, it sounds like he's falling in love with you.'

'Aye, it does an' all, Marg. I reckon you should take no notice of your da, Alice, and meet Gerald in secret.'

'I've thought of that, Edith, but no. It won't happen because Gerald wouldn't walk out with me behind me da's back. He's an upfront kind of fella.'

'Not to mention handsome, rich and, by the sounds of it, a true gent. Lucky you, Alice.' Marg looked wistfully at Edith. 'I wonder who you and me'll meet, lass, though you made a good start on Friday night with the boss's son, no less.'

'Ha! Fat chance I've got of him ever looking my way again after Rita's antics this morning. I had high hopes on Friday. I came out of the flicks dreaming that I was the girl Cary Grant couldn't get over, and thinking there was someone like him who would walk towards me along the prom and sweep me off my feet, so when Philip asked me to dance, I thought it was me moment. But no, not now I don't.'

'Never say never, lass. He couldn't take his eyes off you when he was by his car.'

Edith just smiled. It was a wistful smile that Marg understood well.

Alice got up. 'I'd better get back, then. Harry'll need help to get snuggled down on the sofa and he'll want his cocoa an' all. The others went up afore I came out here.'

'Aye, Alice, I'd better go and see if Ma and me da's all right.'

'Righto. And me and you had better go in, Jackie, you're up late as it is.'

As Alice put her hand out to Jackie to help her rise, Jackie asked, 'Why didn't you bring Harry over? I'd have liked to have seen him, but then, he wouldn't want to join in with women's talk, would he?'

'No. But it ain't easy for him to move much. It's going to be a job to get him over here in the morning. But if we'd have thought, you could have gone over and sat with him.'

'I will tomorrow night. So, he's coming here during the day?'

'Aye, I'll tell you about it all, lass. Let Alice and Edith go now. Night, both, see you in the morning.'

Curled up in her bed, Marg's worries over her gran gnawed at her. It broke her heart that her lovely gran hardly ever knew her these days, and if she did remember, it was only a version of her from the past. It was as if someone had wiped her recent memory clean.

She thought about her ma too, and how she'd struggled, even with Marg's help, to get up the stairs. She was still angry over the way Ma had enjoyed the spectacle that Betty had made of herself, but Marg had more pressing concerns on her mind. Why had she agreed to taking Harry in? How was her ma going to cope?

Turning over for the umpteenth time, she cried into her pillow. Even helping out her friends was a task too far these days. But not only that – where was she going to get the money for Jackie's education, and to pay Ada to pop in on her ma? Though at least Alice had offered to pay Ada tomorrow since she would be dropping in on Harry at the same time.

As her eyes began to close, Marg was startled fully awake by a cry echoing through the house. She threw back the covers, slipped her feet into her slippers and hurried onto the landing. 'What's happened?'

The landing flooded with light as Jackie came out of her bedroom and flicked the switch. 'Marg, what was that?'

'I don't knaw, lass.' Flinging open her ma's door, Marg saw her ma sitting up, gasping for breath. 'Ma, oh, Ma, did you call?'

Ma's head shook from side to side.

'Stay with Ma, Jackie. Help her. Pat and massage her back like Ada does.'

Marg couldn't have said how she got downstairs – her flight was sheer panic. 'Gran, Gran, are you all right?'

A quick glance told her that Gran wasn't in her bed. Marg

was through the living room like a shot and was horrified to see the front door open.

Gran was toddling up the street, her felt hat skew-whiff, her shawl wrapped around her, with only her long nightdress under that and slippers on her feet.

'Gran, Gran! Oh, you're all right, I've got you. Where were you going?'

'I knaw where me John is and I'm going to him.'

'Oh? Well, why not wait till morning, eh? It's dark now.'

'He's down the Layton Institute. He'll be playing snooker. He loves a game of snooker. Well, I'm going to fetch him home 'cause I want a cuddle.'

'Oh, Gran. I'll give you a cuddle.'

'Ha! You can't give me a cuddle like me John can ... Do I knaw you, lass?'

'Aye, you know me. I'm Marg, your granddaughter, your Vera's lass.'

'Eeh, our Vera's a rum 'un. Her and that brother of her husband's. Been having it off for years, they have. Even when her husband was alive. Had a kid they did. I had to keep it secret. Scandalous it was.'

Marg's stomach came into her throat.

'What was the kid, Gran, a boy or a girl?' She held her breath. Fought the urge to scream out against what her gran was saying.

'A girl. Her name was Margaret. I loved Margaret. Where did she go? We called her Marg. Is she at school?'

The gasp Marg took pained her lungs. Her uncle's words came to her: *Me and your ma go back a long time ... there's stuff you don't knaw 'cause she's too afraid to tell you.*

Her legs wobbled. *Oh God, don't let it be true!*

But as she thought this, a realization came to her of how her Uncle Eric was so generous with her and yet never did much for Jackie.

No, no, I can't take this, don't let it be true. Please, please don't let it be true! How could Ma be so deceitful? What else could she be lying to me about?

FOURTEEN

Edith

Edith turned over. Her sigh didn't release the tension that tightened every sinew of her body. She was alert to every sound. Waiting. Wanting to be ready if Albert came in and he was in a mood.

How does he get so out of control? she wondered.

But then she knew the answer to that: with her da ill and unable to discipline Albert, and with how her ma acted, making him angrier and angrier, it was an impossible situation.

The sound of the door banging caused her to bolt upright. A chair crashing to the ground sent her heart racing.

'Where's me bloody dinner, Edith?'

Throwing the covers back, Edith ran to the top of the stairs. 'Stop shouting, Albert, you'll wake Ma and Da.'

'I'm hungry and me dinner ain't being kept warm on the saucepan! Where is it?'

'You haven't got any.'

With this, Edith went to go back into her room, but stopped as Albert came tearing up the stairs. 'You what! Naw dinner?'

141

'That's right. And you're not getting any until you start to cough up your share to pay for the food, rent and coal.'

He stood open-mouthed gaping at her, but he didn't go for her as she'd expected. After a moment, he turned and went back downstairs.

Edith felt as though she'd won a battle. Sleep came easier to her when she snuggled back between the sheets.

When she opened the door the next morning she saw Alice struggling across the road with Harry. She went over to them to help. 'Eh, Harry lad, you look in pain.'

'Aye, I am.'

'Aw, will it help if you hold on to me arm?'

She took the weight of him leaning on her. 'I forgot you were going to Marg's, I'd have come out earlier and helped you, Alice.'

'No, it's all right, we've managed to here. I just hope Marg's ma'll cope. We've nothing else we can do, have we, Harry?'

Harry shook his head, but grimaced as he did so.

Edith felt the pity of all of their predicaments. It seemed they hadn't much that was good in their lives at the moment, when just a short time ago she'd thought them on the up. Well, Alice did have hope with her friendship with Gerald deepening, but even that was tainted by her da not accepting the situation.

When Marg opened the door, Edith was shocked to see her eyes puffed up and bloodshot.

'Eeh, Marg, lass, are you all right?'

'No. I'm tired. Had a bad night with Gran and Ma's not

well. I can't come into work. I've sent over for Ada, but she can't come till noon.'

'Marg, I've told you I'll stay off school. I can watch over everyone.'

'No, Jackie, you have to go to school and that's that.'

'Marg. I reckon one day off for Jackie won't hurt, but you could get the sack.'

Alice backed Edith up. 'She's right, Marg. Moaning Minnie seems to have it in for you lately. But look, Harry won't stay, will that ease the situation?'

Harry's head swivelled round to look at Alice. Edith saw the look of fear that crossed his face.

Marg must have seen it too. 'No, we won't change the arrangements for Harry. But I can't let Jackie stay off school, she must get her school certificate with honours.'

'By, she'd get that if she had a year off, she's the cleverest in the school.'

'Aw, Harry, ta, but you're not far behind me. You should get yours an' all.'

Edith saw Alice's mouth drop in surprise.

'He is, Alice. I know he don't say much about it at home, but if you were to talk to Mr Vale, he'd tell you. If I come first in any test, Harry comes second, and that's only because I have extra tuition and never have a day off.'

'Harry? Is this true, lad?'

'Aye, it is, Alice. But don't go turning into Marg and have me nose to the grindstone every minute of the day!'

They were all shocked into silence. Harry coloured. 'I – I'm sorry, I meant it as a joke, but I ain't much good at jokes.'

This lightened the atmosphere as Marg laughed. 'Don't worry, lad . . . But is that what I do, Jackie?'

'Aye, you do. It's relentless, but I don't mind. I love you for it and I love learning, but I need you to stop worrying so much about my education. Let me do my bit around here.'

Marg looked lost for a moment. She looked from Edith to Alice and back to Jackie. 'Righto. Let me get me overalls and I'll get off to work. You and Harry are in charge. But watch Gran. She went wandering last night. Don't let her out of your sight.'

'Yes! Oh, Marg, you've made my day. Me and Harry can study together. I've a heap of books you'd like, Harry.'

As Edith linked arms with Marg and Alice, leaving the two youngsters sitting at the kitchen table, she squeezed Marg's arm. 'I reckon you've been told, lass.'

'Aye, I think you're right.'

'Marg, did something else happen last night? You said your gran got out?'

'She did . . . But nothing else. I'm just worried about her, and it took me a while to get her back in. She don't seem to know me at all now. Well, not the me of today.'

'It's sad. It's like you're losing her bit by bit. I always laughed when someone said their gran or granddad had lost their marbles, but I won't now. Seeing the effect it's having on all of you, I think it's heartbreaking.'

'It is, Alice, it is.'

'Eeh, Marg. Don't cry, lass.' Edith put her arm around Marg. Alice did the same.

'Ta. I needed a hug.'

'Well, that's all you're getting. Moaning Minnie'll have our guts for garters. Come on, put a spurt on.' Edith tried to sound cheerful, but inside she couldn't shake the feeling that their lives were getting worse once more.

'You two go on, I'll have to go and tell Mr Fairweather I can't come tonight.'

'Don't do that. We can help out, can't we, Alice?'

'Aye, we can take it in turns to check on Jackie, and your ma and gran.'

'Would you? I really need this job. I – I might have to give up the factory, and then the money from Fairweather'd be all I have.'

'Oh, Marg, love. Is there no other way?'

'No, Edith, how can I find someone to watch Gran *and* take care of Ma? I can't. And I ... well, anyroad. I'll manage somehow.'

Hoping to take the pressure of Marg, Edith asked, 'Right, tell us, what have you got planned for your tea? We can get it all prepared for you and even get it on the go.'

'I've only got a few tatties and some eggs. I was going to make chips and fry the eggs. I've got a pan that I keep me dripping in, it's under the sink behind the curtain. If you could help Jackie ... Mind, she's a good little cook. Tell her to have hers then feed Ma and Gran as I won't be in till eight. I'll get me own.'

'Think of it as done, lass. What a night we had, eh?'

'Aye, I never want another like it. Oh, I don't mean your ma, Edith.'

'I know you don't. What's really wrong, Marg? It's not just your gran, is it? Something's happened?'

145

'N – no, nothing,'

Edith caught a look from Alice and nodded. She knew Alice was trying to tell her not to pursue it further.

Getting their mob caps on after clocking in, the girls could hear Moaning Minnie's voice over all others. 'Edith! I want you in my office.'

Edith grimaced. Then laughed as the women around her started ribbing her.

'You're in trouble, lass! What you been up to?'

'Ha! You'll get to stay behind as a punishment.'

'Naw, she's teacher's pet that one.'

Ida piped up. 'Eeh, you don't need any more trouble after last night. By, I sorted that brother of yours out for you, though, Edith.'

Edith took no notice of them, except to smile at Marg and Alice who both offered to come with her. 'No, lasses, I'll be all right.'

'Come in, Edith.'

'Ta, Mrs Roberts.'

'I've heard a lot of gossip about the goings-on last night, lass.'

'Oh?' Edith wanted the floor to open up and swallow her. 'It's all sorted, Mrs Robinson, and won't affect my work.'

'Good. Only, me son reported sommat he heard. I should go to the police really but I thought I'd give you a chance to sort it out. My William knaws your Albert; they were having a chat about his injuries and Albert said that he was going to get his revenge on Ida ...'

Edith gasped. 'It'll be just talk, you know what lads are like.'

'I do, but I also knaw as your brother is into a lot of things he shouldn't be and that some of that is of a very violent nature. Now, Ida is a valued member of our team, she's one of us, and I don't like to think of her under threat. What she did was more than she should have done to your brother, but as I heard it, she was protecting your ma. I want you to sort this out and let me knaw that you have done, or I will go to the police.'

'I will, I promise. Our Albert has a short temper and shouldn't have done what he did, but I ain't happy with what Ida did either, though I understand her action. Me brother's been in a lot of pain and, well, I know he's only young, but he's been drinking an' all. He's on the wrong path and needs . . . Look, I'll sort it, I will.'

'Good. Make sure you do, because if Ida gets hurt, I'll never forgive meself for giving you the chance to deal with this yourself.'

'I appreciate it. Ta, Mrs Roberts.'

The day dragged for Edith after that. She felt weary-boned when at last the factory hooter sounded.

With the cleaning down done, she joined Marg and Alice.

The walk home was something she usually took in her stride, but today she found it heavy going – made worse by a downpour.

When Marg said she wanted to run so she could call at home before going to her second job at the grocery shop, Edith knew she wouldn't be able to, so was glad to hear Alice say: 'No, you'll be exhausted, Marg, lass. You go now and if anything's amiss, I'll send our Billy to let you know how things are at home. If he don't come, you'll know all's fine.'

For a moment, Edith thought Marg wouldn't agree as she said, 'Eeh, Alice, I'll be on tenterhooks.'

'All right, I'll send him anyroad, then. The moment we get back, so you'll know then, won't you?'

'Ta, Alice . . . By, Edith, lass, you're quiet.'

Edith hadn't had a chance to tell them what Moaning Minnie had told her and they hadn't pressed her in the few minutes' break they'd had together earlier.

As her tale unfolded, she didn't miss the look that passed between them.

'I ain't sure what to do. If I bawl our Albert out, it'll start him off, and then he's hard to handle. But if I do nothing and Ida gets hurt, I'll never forgive myself.'

'Eeh, Edith, lass, there's always something with one of us.'

'You're right there, Marg.' But though she said this, Edith felt bad at having put them into the doldrums once more. As it was, she still felt there was something really wrong in Marg's life, besides what they already knew. She just hadn't been the same today. Her thoughts seemed confirmed with Marg's heavy sigh.

'How I'm going to get through the next couple of hours, I don't know. Mr Fairweather gets on my nerves if I just pop into his shop for something, let alone work with him for two hours! He's such a know-all and judges everyone. If you did one thing wrong when you were a young 'un, he has you down as a bad 'un, and says, "That trait will out one of these days!"'

Marg had imitated Mr Fairweather's voice – a sort of squeaky, high-pitched sound. They all doubled up, the mood noticeably lifting.

Alice suddenly started another rendition of the song 'Pack Up Your Troubles'.

Still laughing, she and Marg joined in and, as daft as she felt going through the streets singing her head off, Edith felt her spirits lift and nothing she'd been worrying about seemed as bad as it once had.

Just as they'd promised Marg, she and Alice popped in to check on Jackie and Harry as soon as they got home. They found a calm and peaceful atmosphere, with Marg's gran asleep in the armchair next to the fireplace and her ma sitting doing a bit of knitting. Harry and Jackie both had their heads in a book, but looked up and smiled a lovely greeting.

'Well, you all look cosy! It's a shame to disturb you. How's thing been? Are you all right to get the tea on, Jackie?'

'Aye, the tatties are chipped and ready for the pan – I'm all organised.'

Alice had gone over to Harry and was asking him about his day. 'I've been in pain, but me and Jackie have had a giggle. By, that gran is a one, she's had us in stitches – caused most of me pain she did.'

Listening to how Gran had been looking for her spectacles when she was wearing them the whole time made them all giggle.

Jackie added, 'And she was treating me ma like she was her little girl again, getting on at her sommat rotten she was – a real nagging session about all Ma's faults, didn't she, Ma?'

'Aye, and she weren't that kind of a ma. She must have bottled it all up as it was all true.'

As Vera Porter laughed at this, a fit of coughing took her that frightened Edith. There seemed no chance in between the coughing for Vera to take a breath. Jackie jumped up and started to rub her chest and back. Edith didn't know what to do and she could see the same dilemma on Alice's face.

'Ma, take a breath, Ma!'

Vera's face turned blue.

'Do something! Somebody do something!'

Edith stood frozen to the spot, but Alice dashed out of the door screaming for Ada Arkwright to come. This mobilised Edith. Coming out of her shock, she went to Vera and shook her while blowing hard into her face. Somehow – Edith didn't know how – this did the trick, and Vera took a huge gasp of air before collapsing back in her chair, exhausted.

Her colour gradually came back, and the fear and tension in the room lifted.

When Ada came through the door, the panic was all over.

'She was blue in the face, Ada.' Ada listened open-mouthed to the method Edith had used to revive Vera.

'Well, I've never heard the likes of that afore, but it worked and that's the main thing. I'll have to try it meself sometime. So, are you feeling all right, now, Vera?'

'Naw, I'll never feel all right again. Me lungs have had it, Ada, lass. I'm ready for the knacker's yard.'

Though Jackie laughed at this, Edith knew the worry would fill her upon realising just how poorly Vera was, and it brought to her mind the predicament of her own da.

As they left, supporting Harry, Alice caught hold of her hand. Edith could feel Alice's body trembling, but she understood. The experience had been terrifying.

'I'll send Billy along to Marg, but what do you reckon I should get him to tell her, Edith?'

'The truth. We always said we'd never lie to one another.'

'I know that, but ... well, I got the impression today that there was something troubling Marg. Did you?'

'Aye, I did. And it's something massive, I can tell. I know she must be feeling even more exhausted, having to go to a new job when she's already dog-tired from the first one, but, well, I felt something bad had happened. We'll tackle her later.'

They parted at Alice's door and Edith let out a huge sigh. She still had Albert to deal with, and now she was worried sick about Marg too.

FIFTEEN

Alice

When Alice got in and had helped Harry to a chair, the house felt strangely quiet. She hadn't seen the lads in the street either, which was unusual. Hurrying to the door that led to the stairs, she lifted the latch and called up, 'Hey, where are you all?'

Billy and Joey appeared at the top of the stairs. 'We came in out of the rain and have been playing in our room, Alice.'

'All right. Well, I've got an errand for you, Billy.'

'Eeh, I'll get soaked.'

'You won't, it's stopped now.' Giving him the message for Marg, she turned her attention to Joey. 'Is Da in his room, Joey?'

'Naw, he went out. Said he was going to the factory to see his mates and his boss.'

'Oh . . .? Righto, well, let's see about some tea, eh?'

'Da had a letter, Alice.'

'Oh? Did he take it with him?'

'Aye.'

Alice was busying herself, trying to find something she

152

could make for tea, when her da appeared. 'I've got chips here, lass.'

Shock left Alice unable to answer. Nothing like this had happened for a long, long time. Her da, all cleaned up and in his best Sunday suit, and bringing home chips!

'Aw, Da, that's grand, I was just wondering what we would have for our tea.'

'I've a loaf an' all, and some butter, so we can have doorstep chip butties!'

His smile filled her with joy. She didn't know what to say. Harry caught her eye, his smile holding a question, but she ignored it. 'Ooh, let's get the table laid. We'll put the chips in the oven for a mo. Billy won't be long, I sent him on an errand. Sit down, Da, and I'll make a brew.'

As he sat, he let out a deep sigh. Alice looked over at him, worried about how the sigh sounded so weary.

'Me boss at work gave me a payment, Alice. It's to pay me off really, so he can fill me position. It's a nice little sum and is meant for compensation. If I wasn't so tired, I would have got us some shopping in, but here you go, lass, here's ten bob to make a start getting in what we need.'

Alice couldn't believe it. She could stock up a few things with this, to add to what she was able to get at the weekend.

But then Da surprised them all by looking at Harry, and asking, 'How're you feeling, lad?'

Harry didn't seem to find his tongue at first, but then smiled at his da. 'I'm getting better, ta.'

'Good. I think I've made a man of you, son. You'll need to step up and I think you can. I – I, well ... maybe, I was a bit heavy on you.'

'Naw, it's all right, Da, it wasn't your doing.'

Da reached over and ruffled Harry's hair. The beam on Harry's face was a good sight.

When they sat having their chips, Billy and Joey looked a bit wary of this new da. But Alice couldn't blame them; they didn't know how to act around him when he was in his usual mood and this was new territory for them all. Harry, though, looked like a new lad, all confident and relaxed.

'So, Joey says you got a letter, Da? Was it from Mr Melford?'

'Aye.'

Nothing more, and yet she was dying to know what had been said, when his appointment was, and, most of all, to have the chance to go the hospital and see Gerald.

'Anyroad, I won't need knaw lift. I can get a taxi now.'

Disappointment filled Alice. 'When do you go, Da?'

'Tomorrow. I called in on Simon, he's picking me up at ten in the morning.'

'Oh, Da, I'll have to wait all day to know how you got on, but I hope you can have the operation and it takes your head-aches away.'

They ate in silence for a while. The chips were delicious – crisp on the outside and fluffy in the middle. When Alice took a bite of the big fat one on her fork, the steam from it took her breath away and traces of vinegar ran down her chin as the flavour burst on her tongue.

A giggle started and then another joined it. She opened her eyes and saw Joey and Billy watching her.

'You need a bib, sis!'

All three of the lads laughed at this from Joey, but a sudden thump on the table shut them up as a terrible, agonising moan came from their da.

'Shush, shush! Oh God, help me!'

Fear clutched at Alice's chest and she could see her three brothers had frozen. She looked from them to her da. He'd gone deathly pale and held on to his head. Beads of sweat trickled down his face.

'Da, Da! Oh naw! You were so well.'

The chair scraped on the floor as her da stood. Almost losing his balance, he staggered back towards the sofa still clutching his head. Before he landed, his scream sliced the air. As it died, her da closed his eyes and fell silent.

Panic gripped Alice, but as she looked at the shocked faces of her brothers, she took control of herself for their sake. 'Billy, run for Ada, but don't come back with her . . .' She rummaged in her da's pocket for some change. 'Here, run like the wind to the phone box and ring 999. I don't think you have to put money in the slot for that number, but just in case.'

Billy didn't argue, and in moments Ada was coming through the door. 'Eeh, what's to do? What with Vera and now this, a body can't rest five minutes.'

'It's my da!'

'I knaw, lass, I was halfway here when Billy rushed at me. Your da's terrible scream brought everyone out.'

Going to Da, Ada stood and stared down at him. Her head shook from side to side. 'I'm sorry, lass, there's not much I can do but make him comfortable till the ambulance gets here. It looks to me that a big part of your trouble is about to come to an end.'

'No, Ada!'

'If I were you, after what you've put up with from him, I'd be in the street cheering, but then, your da's your da.'

An anger she rarely experienced shot through Alice. 'Yes, he is, and we love him. He can't help what that illness does to him.'

'Well, naw, if you put it like that, lass, then I was out of order. But, by, he's a lucky man to have you all still think of him like that. Especially when you see the state that he put poor Harry in and what he's done to you all at times.'

Harry hadn't moved. Alice looked over at him to see his face awash with tears as he stared at his da. 'He couldn't help it . . . Da, Da, don't die, Da.'

Alice rushed over to Harry and held him to her. 'He'll be all right, lad. He will.'

'I'll put the kettle on. I can see you've had a cuppa with your chips, but another won't hurt.'

Ada had hardly got into the kitchen when the street filled with the sound of bells ringing just as Edith came through the door. 'Eeh, Alice! Alice, love.'

Alice went into Edith's outstretched arms. 'Me da, me da . . .'

'The ambulance is here, love, he'll be all right.'

'I want to go with him, Edith, will you watch the lads?'

'I will. Of course I will, lass. Oh, Alice, I'm sorry. Just as you had so much hope an' all.'

Alice nodded.

'Right, miss.' The ambulanceman spoke in a gentle voice. 'Can you gather all you can for your da: pyjamas, a towel and shaving gear and soap? We'll lift him into the ambulance.'

'I've got them all ready. Here you go, Alice.' Alice hadn't seen Ada moving around the house, but she must have skipped up the stairs when she heard the bells. She gave her one of the brown paper grocery bags that Alice always folded and put in the basket next to the fire, ready to use to set the tinder alight. The bag was stuffed with all the ambulanceman had asked for.

'Now, I take it you knaw all your da's particulars?'

'Aye.'

'Right, so are these two good ladies going to see to things here, then?'

'We are. You get Mr Brett on up to the hospital. Off you go, Alice, and don't worry, lass, they'll see to him up there.'

Alice smiled gratefully at Ada, forgiving her for what she'd said. It had been a natural assumption and a backhanded way of trying to comfort them – an easy misunderstanding of how they felt.

Running to Harry, she hugged him, then grabbed Billy and Joey at the same time. 'Be good, lads. I'll be back later with good news on Da, you'll see.'

Joey clung to her, but she eased him off and got into the back of the ambulance. As they closed the doors, she saw he was in the circle of Edith's arms. The tears were running down his face, but she knew he'd be all right with Edith.

At the hospital, it seemed a whirlwind hit her as white-coated doctors and nurses in their blue uniforms and flowing white veils seemed to appear from nowhere and whisk her da away.

It was a lifetime measured in minutes before she saw the vision of Gerald coming towards her, his steps hurried, his own white coat billowing behind him.

157

Jumping up, she ran towards him. 'Me da! Oh, Gerald, what's happening?'

'Sit down, my love.'

Despite her agony of emotions, Alice's heart soared at the endearment.

'He isn't well at all, my dear. Father is operating on him now, but he . . . well, I went in with him and saw . . . Oh, Alice.' Gerald's eyes filled with tears. 'It doesn't look good, I'm afraid, you must prepare yourself.'

A huge gasp caught in Alice's throat. Her mouth stretched, but the scream she wanted to release came out in a strangled sound that rasped her throat. Gerald pulled her to him and held her close, giving her comfort – just that, nothing more, but she had dreamt of this moment. Now she had to shut down her dreams as her hopes to ever again see her da well tumbled around her.

Gerald rocked her back and forth as his soothing voice told her how much her da would suffer if he were to live, and how much better it would be for him to go now.

'W – will me da ever wake up again?'

'No, I'm sorry, Alice.'

Her head shook from side to side as her tears spilt over and snot ran from her nose. Gerald fumbled in his pocket while still holding her and handed her a huge hanky.

'I can only hold you, my love, I cannot make this right for you. If I could, I would.'

Between sobs, she said, 'Ta. It means the world that it is you telling me. Eeh, Gerald, me and the lads . . . well, we thought . . .'

'I know. But it wasn't to be. Hold on to those memories you told me of and try to keep them alive for your brothers.

Poor Harry. I so wanted him to see his father well and have time to forgive him.'

'He has. Da was in such a lovely mood just before ... He even sort of apologised to Harry. Harry was distraught when this happened almost straight after.'

'That's good – not Harry being distraught, but that he will have that moment to take forward with him.'

Alice nodded. 'Gerald ... will they let me see my da?'

'I can find out for you. But, my dear, he may ... well, he may have passed on by the time I get back. My father was doing his best but ... well, there was a bleed on the brain that he couldn't stem. And as was always a possibility, there was a tumour ... I'm sorry, but it would have been inoperable. I want you to remember that if your father does die now, it will have been the kinder thing for him. He wouldn't have wanted to live his last days in agony.'

As Alice stood looking down at her da, she felt a sorrow too deep to express.

Touching his hand, she whispered, 'I love you, Da, and I always will. I'll come back soon.' Her 'goodbye', she said silently to herself, not wanting to voice it in case that made it the last time.

Gerald stepped forward. 'Do you want to stay with him?'

She shook her head, 'I need to be with the lads, to comfort them, then I'll come back.' He didn't protest.

They walked in silence to the hospital exit where they stood a moment.

'Alice, keep thinking about what I told you of how your father would suffer so much, it might help you.'

She nodded. Closing her eyes, she prayed. *Don't let that happen. Take him to me ma, please, Father in heaven.*

With this prayer, she felt a sense of acceptance and peace come over her and more so as Gerald took her in his arms. 'Ta, Gerald, I have prayed for his passing.'

'Yes, my dear, I thought as much when you closed your eyes. I joined my prayers to yours and asked that you and the boys find comfort.'

'We will. I have a lot of stories to tell them that will help them, things I know they don't remember. I was reminded recently of picnics on the beach, and the brief moment we had with him when he was so kind reminded me of the loving father who was stolen from us by that accident.'

'During an act of heroism, I understand? Well, we can see about that being recognised officially. He should have been given a bravery medal, something tangible for you all to see. If. . . well, if he passes before we can get it, it can be awarded posthumously. I will have it framed for you, and you can give it pride of place in your home.'

It seemed to Alice that Gerald was holding her for the love of her now, and not just for comfort, and this was confirmed when he said, 'I hope that I can be included in seeing it too, Alice, and many times as our . . . our friendship grows.'

'I hope so an' all, Gerald, and for a long time to come.'

She couldn't believe her forwardness, but Gerald seemed only to see joy in what she'd said.

'You mean that? You really would like to be friends . . . maybe more, even?'

'I would, Gerald. I'll need you by me side through all of this, and then after as well . . . and yes, as more than a friend.'

'Oh, Alice. My love.'

He held her closer. And this time her emotions were that of joy, not sorrow. Sorrow still had a place in her, but for the moment she just wanted to hold on to the wonderous love that Gerald was offering her. She lifted her head. His eyes held hers. They moved closer and closer, until their lips met, and though hers were still trembling with the shock she had received, the kiss took her soaring into a happiness she never knew this world held for her.

SIXTEEN

Marg

For Marg, unaware of what had happened to Alice since they'd parted earlier and she'd gone off to her second job, her relief at finally being home was tempered with all that weighed on her shoulders. Her body ached all over and her heart was heavy with the news she'd heard last night, and hadn't yet absorbed, about her true father. Anger seethed in her.

Ma, how could you? How? But though she was fuming with her ma, she was also worried about her and had fretted from the moment Billy had brought her the message earlier to say that Ma had had a bad turn.

Jackie met her with a mug of tea. 'Here you go, Marg.'

'Ta, lass. How's Ma now? I nearly came home, but I knew you'd have told Billy to tell me to if Ma needed me.' She didn't say that the anger that festered in her had impacted her decision not to come home.

'She's all right. Her breathing's still bad, but you knaw, it was Edith who helped her the most.'

Marg listened to what Edith had done. 'We'll have to remember that,' was all the enthusiasm she could muster at this moment where her ma was concerned.

'Aye. It worked like a miracle. Are you hungry? I've dropped your chips in the pan for you.'

'Ta, lass.'

'So, how did you go on?'

'It wasn't so bad. To be truthful, I enjoyed it. I had a good banter with the customers and Fairweather left me to it after about half an hour. Then, when the shop shut, I was left to fill the delivery boxes. I enjoyed that an' all. I mean, I fill boxes all day, but that's repetitive. For this, as you know, you have a list and have to get the order together. Gives you something to think about, instead of feeling like a machine.' Marg paused to take a sip of the tea Jackie had made for her. 'By, this brew's lovely, lass, and them chips smell good. But you shouldn't have saved some for me, we only had a few spuds.'

'Ma didn't want anything after she had that bout. Anyroad, now you've had a drop of tea and a minute to catch your breath, I've a bit of bad news for you.'

Marg was shocked to hear of Alice's da. 'Eh, that don't sound good. Poor Alice. Have you heard any more?'

'I went over to see if Harry and the lads were all right. They seemed really scared. Alice ain't back yet and they've not heard anything, but Edith's with them. She said she'd watch for you coming and if they were all right, she'd pop over to see you.'

'Well, I won't go over then, they don't want too many people asking them questions. How's the chips doing? I want to hear how your day was and how Gran is an all. You can tell me while I eat.'

'Don't you want to go up to Ma? It ain't like you, Marg. I thought you'd take them stairs two at a time when you got in. And you didn't react much to hearing about Alice's da. What's up? Are you all right?'

'Aye, I'm sorry, lass. Just tired. I'll go up when I've eaten and heard your tale. I'll have more energy then.'

This seemed to satisfy Jackie as she went into the kitchen without commenting further. She started straight up with her chatter when she put Marg's plate of chips in front of her, mostly talking about her time with Harry.

'You're sweet on him, ain't you?'

Jackie blushed. Marg laughed out loud. 'Eeh, me little sis . . .'

Sis. A sudden thought made Marg gasp, which in turn caused a small piece of chip to catch in her throat, sending her into a fit of choking.

When it passed, she brushed her tears off as a result of the coughing, but really it was because her heart was full of sorrow at the realisation that she wasn't Jackie's true sister.

At least, that would be the case if only she were Eric's daughter. But what if he'd fathered Jackie too?

Though Gran had only mentioned one child, and their Uncle Eric didn't treat Jackie the same. He wasn't unkind to her, but the more Marg thought about it, the more she realised how different he had always treated them. Her body shuddered with disgust.

'You looked sad there for a minute, and then angry. Is there sommat wrong, Marg?'

'No, honestly, I am just tired. These chips are lovely; I might give you the job to cook for us.'

'I'd love that, Marg. I like the science behind cooking.'

'Science? There's nothing scientific about boiling spuds and veg, lass.'

'There is, and in how different foods react with each other and what nutrients they give to our body. Please say it's my job to do it, and the shopping. I reckon I could cut the cost of that an' all. I could get cheap cuts of meat, and veg from the market that's just on the turn, and do all sorts with it – casseroles, sauces, pies, soups – and I can bake the bread myself, that'd save us sommat. I just need a few ingredients in, like a store cupboard of essentials.'

'Well! Good grief, Jackie, I didn't expect such a passionate plea, lass. But aye, of course you can, I'd be glad to have it off me hands. I've never been much good at it. Alice is the cook amongst us, you could get a few tips from her – though by the sound of it, you could give her a few an' all.'

'I could, but I'd like to hear her ideas. We could swap recipes or even write a cookbook – one for poorer folk.'

'Ha! You're away now, you always have a head full of ideas. Come here, I need a hug.' Taking Jackie into her arms, the thought came to Marg that it didn't matter what their true relationship was. Jackie was her sister, nothing could change that.

When they parted, Marg resigned herself to carrying on as normal, even though her world felt like a lie. It hurt badly to lose the man she'd thought of as her father all her life. The pain sealed the wretchedness of him having gone for ever, as now he wasn't hers to claim as her da.

'Marg, why are you so sad?'

'No, I'm not. I'm all right. We've a lot on our plate, but me and you'll get through. We will . . . Well, I'd better go and see

Ma, but I'll pop in on Gran first. Is she all washed and in bed proper?'

'Naw, I ain't had time. She toddled off after tea saying she was going for a lie-down and I haven't seen her since, and it was a bit of a relief to have her from under me feet.'

'Ha! I know what you mean.'

Marg found her gran fast asleep, fully clothed in her grey frock that she seemed to have had forever and which wouldn't have been out of place thirty years ago. Her legs were clad in thick lisle stockings and her brown court shoes were still laced to her feet.

Marg gazed lovingly at the picture – this was the gran she'd adored for as long as she could remember, and she thanked God that Gran was her maternal grandmother and truly hers no matter what.

Tears filled her eyes. She meant nothing to her gran now. What an awful thing losing your marbles was.

Shame clothed her as she thought of old Mrs Pike. Poor soul used to walk out in her nightie, her hair tangled as she'd tried to put it up with what looked like a million hair grips, and ask if they had seen her cat, which had long died, or her husband who'd never returned from the Great War.

To the kids that they were then, it had seemed funny. They'd teased her and giggled behind her back. Now she knew the pain behind the humour as she herself was one of the marbles her gran had misplaced, and she wished with everything she had that she wasn't. She wanted her gran to remember her and love her as she used to; she wanted to be able to go to her with her problems. Gran had always known the answer to everything that hurt you, and always gave a way forward.

Gently nudging her awake, Marg smiled down at Gran as she opened her aged eyes. 'Shall we get your nightie on, Gran?'

'Aye. And you can come into me bed, Marg, like you used to when you stayed at mine, eh? I've been dreaming that you were me little secret and I was cuddling you to me. You used to always come down in the morning, really early, and get into me bed, lass . . . but by, your feet were always cold and I'd have to rub them for you.'

Smiling through her tears, Marg helped Gran to stand, then felt even better as Gran put her arms around her and snuggled her head into her bosom.

Holding this lady who had been there all her life, and stroking her hair, Marg felt filled with love. 'Eh, Gran. My lovely Gran.'

Gran let go of her and plonked on the side of the bed. Her head hung, giving her the look of someone deeply sad.

'Gran, what is it? Are you all right? Shall we get you undressed, eh?'

Gran looked up. The lost look was back. 'Would you help me, lass?'

'I will, Gran. Stand up so I can lift your frock over your head, that's right.'

Gran didn't speak again until she was washed, in her nightie and snuggled up in bed.

Then she said, 'Ta, lass . . . What's your name, by the way? You're a kind girl, helping an old biddy like me.'

'Marg, Gran. Your little Marg.'

Gran looked confused. Marg wanted to take that away for her. Bending over, she kissed her forehead. 'You're the nicest stranger I've ever helped to bed. Now, have a good night's sleep.'

167

'Ta, lass. Will you come and help me another time?'

'I will. I'll always be here for you.'

Gran smiled. Her face looked at peace as she closed her eyes.

In her ma's room, Marg found her sitting up in bed. She'd taken to propping herself up using cushions as well as all the pillows from both sides of the big double bed. Though her breathing wasn't normal, Ma didn't seem to be struggling too much.

'Hello, lass. Eeh, it seems a long day since you left this morning. I heard you go.'

'Aye, it has been. I'm shattered.'

'How did you get on, love?'

Marg didn't want to talk about her day, she wanted to bawl her ma out, call her names, make her pay for what she'd done, but as she looked at her, failing rapidly in her health, other emotions took over and she knew that whatever her ma had done, she would always love her – she was her ma.

These realisations didn't stop her from tackling her – she had to know if it was true or simply a creation from Gran's confused mind.

'Ma, I need to talk to you.' She sat on the side of the bed where her da used to lie, and lifting her legs onto the bed, faced her ma. 'Ma, who was me da?'

'What? What sort of daft question is that?' Though Ma sounded incredulous, Marg could see her fear.

'It's not a daft question, Ma, I just want to know. Only Gran said something . . .'

Ma's face went through a whole host of emotions in a short space of time, before she scoffed. 'You don't take notice of Gran, do you?'

'Ma, tell me.'

Ma's head dropped. 'I – I, oh, me lass, your da was your da, really, he loved you like you were his own, he did.'

Marg hadn't wanted it to be confirmed. She just stared at her ma. 'Did he know?'

'Aye. Look, lass, it's not that simple. Your da, well, he was a good man, but weak. His brother, your Uncle Eric, ruled him. Your da ... well, I loved him, I did, but ... Oh, me lass, this is hard. I don't want you to feel bad about your da, or any of us ... well, except your Uncle Eric, your real da. He's evil, Marg. Evil.'

'What happened? Did he ... well, did he force you?' Marg hung on to this. She didn't know how she was managing to keep so calm, or why, but now it was confirmed, she wanted the reason to be that neither her ma nor her da could do anything about it. What she heard ground a hate into her for the man who fathered her.

'Marg, lass, I can only tell it to you as it was. It ain't nice and I don't want you to knaw. I never wanted you to knaw, nor did your gran. She couldn't help having told you, her mind has gone altogether now.'

Marg didn't like to think of this as the truth. Hadn't her gran come back for a few seconds just now?

She looked at her ma and waited.

'Your da – well, me husband – he was a gambler. I couldn't stop him. Sometimes he won, he even won big a couple of times, but mostly he lost and Eric had to bail him out. You see, the folk he owed money to were nasty – brutal. Anyroad, Eric always fancied me, he took a shine to me from the moment he came back from the war.'

Ma went on to tell her how Eric began to want favours in return for bailing Horace out, and how Horace begged her to comply because his life was in danger. She embarrassed Marg by saying she preferred to go to bed with Eric in the end, that he made her have feelings. Horace never did in his hurried, satisfying-himself way.

'I lost me head to Eric. Not me heart, that was Horace's, but, well, the rest of me was Eric's. He wanted me to leave Horace and live with him. He's never stopped obsessing over me, even now, and look at me – a physical wreck.'

A tear ran out of the corner of Ma's eye. Marg felt sick to the stomach at what she'd heard so she stayed quiet and just listened.

'Me ma – your gran – knew about you. She took me to task over the rumours and I confirmed them with her, but she never spoke of it again and I never thought she would.'

'So, did it come to an end after I was born? I mean, I know about lately, but . . . well, Jackie?'

'Jackie's Eric's an' all, only he don't knaw it and neither does Gran.'

'What? Oh, Ma! How? Why? I mean . . .'

'I knaw. It all sounds disgusting, don't it? But your da – Horace – couldn't after that, not after you were born. And, eh, lass, don't think bad of me, but . . . I had me needs. And Horace made the most of that by using me to get money from Eric to feed his habit . . .'

'That's wicked! You sold yourself to feed Da – *Horace's* – gambling! How could you? How could he allow it, let alone encourage you? And what of Eric? God! You lied to him, extorted money from him . . . Ma . . . I don't know what to say or think!'

'Naw, don't take it like that. Horace was weak, but he loved me and wanted me to have . . . well, it's hard to put into words, but what he couldn't give me.'

'So, it was a good arrangement for you both.' Marg couldn't keep the disgust out of her voice. 'Did you never think how you were both using Eric?'

'Naw. It weren't like that.'

'But it was, Ma. Eric loved you and offered you a life with him, but you loved Horace and stuck to taking Eric for all you could get, not even telling him he had a second child. How did you keep that from him, then?'

'You're making this sound all my fault. It wasn't, lass, I was between the pair of them. The Porter brothers used me like a pawn.'

'You used yourself, Ma. You were in it up to your neck. Tell me, how did you keep Jackie a secret?'

'The minute I knew, I told Eric that I didn't need him anymore, that Horace had started making love to me and it was better than anything he could give me, and that Horace had even made me pregnant.'

'By, Ma, you're going down in my estimation by the minute.' Marg felt her emotions shut down. Nothing her ma said embarrassed or shocked her now, she just felt nothing.

'Naw, lass, you don't understand. You see, Horace promised me he was over the gambling, that we could make a life together if I broke it off with Eric. Telling Eric that I was pregnant with Jackie and that the baby was Horace's did the

171

trick – he left me alone and Horace did manage to stay on the straight and narrow for a while ...But before long he started his gambling again and we were back where we started. I had to go back to Eric. Eric begged me to leave Horace and get a divorce, but I couldn't, it would have killed your da ...*Horace*.'

Ma's tears flowed freely now, but Marg could feel no sympathy for her. 'It seems to me, Ma, that Eric and Horace didn't use you, but that you and Horace used Eric. All he was guilty of was loving you, but you both took advantage of that – especially Horace. He sold you to his brother to feed his gambling habit. It's disgusting!'

Her ma didn't protest.

Marg sighed. 'So me and Jackie are proper sisters – the only good thing about all of this – and we do have a da who's alive, one who has helped me out while keeping your secret, but hasn't bothered too much with Jackie because to him, she's a sign of your betrayal. Ma, you've a lot to answer for.'

'And I've paid, believe me, I've paid. Eric treats me rough, as if he can't stand me and yet can't let me go. Oh, he'll lie low for a bit, but by, he'll be back with a vengeance.'

Marg didn't feel that this was the truth, not from what she'd seen – Ma looking pleased to see Eric, and Eric giving her looks that told of his feelings.

Or am I just questioning everything Ma says now? Ma's not who I thought she was – all these years spent planting bad things into my head about Eric ...Well, that'll stop now.

'I'll talk to him, tell him about Jackie. For all his faults, though he is a rogue and a notorious gang leader, he's not the wrongdoer here. I mean, he's done wrong, but he was manipulated by you and the man I'd always had a good memory of.

By, you two were cunning, I knew nothing of my . . . *Horace's* gambling, or of your affair with his brother. Where did all of this happen?'

'Mostly at Eric's place. I used to go there when you thought I was out with me mates, or visiting Gran, but your da's gambling—'

'Don't call him my da! I don't ever want to think of such a deceitful man that way.'

'Don't raise your voice, lass. I'm still your ma! Aye, it may look to you like I did wrong, but they were hard times, and Horace—'

'I know, got all his excitement with the bookie's runner. But you didn't have to act in the way that you did. I'm ashamed of you.' Marg's anger was such that she turned away, afraid that she might slap her ma. She only made it to the door before Ma called her back.

'Marg . . . Marg! Where are you going, lass? Don't go to Eric, don't. You don't knaw what he's capable of.'

Coughing hacked her ma's chest, frightening Marg. She ran back to her. 'Ma, I'm sorry, I won't do anything, I promise. Catch your breath, Ma.'

As if by magic, her ma calmed. 'Oh, Marg, I had naw choice, we'd have starved if it was left to Horace. Forgive me, Marg, and promise me you won't go to Eric. If he finds another way in, and a way of getting at me, he will. I can't stand his ways anymore, Marg . . . Look.'

Ma pulled the sleeve of her nightie up to reveal horrible bruises – some the shape of fingertips, others as if she'd been punched.

'And they're on me body an' all. He's angry with me all the time and when he gets me on me own he punishes me and then forces me to do things I don't want to do. He's cruel, Marg, cruel.'

Shocked and sick to her stomach, Marg held her ma and rocked her back and forth. She didn't know what to think anymore.

'Calm down, Ma, it's all right, I'll not let him near you again, I promise.'

'And you won't tell Jackie?'

'Naw.'

Though she promised this, she knew one day she would. But now that Marg knew the truth, she didn't want Jackie to go through what she was coping with.

SEVENTEEN

Alice

Alice was nearly home when Gerald pulled up beside her in his car. He jumped out. 'Alice, I'm sorry, but I think you should come back. Will the boys be all right?'

'Aye, Harry's capable and I know that Edith and Marg will keep an eye on them – why, what's happened?'

'Your da. He's agitated. It happens sometimes, but if a relative is with them they become peaceful again. I know you would want that so I got permission to come and fetch you.'

When she was sat beside him, Gerald took her hand. 'I'm by your side, Alice, where I hope to always be.'

Alice swallowed hard, the enormity of what might happen soon vying with her certain knowledge that Gerald loved her.

As they went along the corridor, following the sister who was waiting for them, Alice's thoughts continued to be a confusion of happiness at the implication in what Gerald had said, fear and worry for her da and anxiety for the lads. How must they be feeling, with all that had happened today and her not back yet to let them know how their da was?

This last shocked her. Was it really just a day? *It seems like a lifetime since I set off to work with Edith and Marg this morning. As it did since I left Marg on the way home and she went to her second job. And was it only a few hours ago that I was so happy as for one brief moment I had a glimpse of my da as he used to be, and life held so much hope for me?*

Before she could dwell further on this, Gerald whispered, 'Are you sure you are up to this, Alice?'

With the turmoil in her mind having stopped, the reality of it all hit her. She looked up into Gerald's beloved, concerned face. 'No, I wish that I was anywhere but here, but I can't leave him and not help him to be peaceful.'

The side ward where her da had been taken after coming out of theatre led off from another ward of sleeping men, whose snores sounded too much like normal life and an intrusion to Alice in the unusual world she found herself in.

She clung to Gerald as she saw the sweat standing out on her da's forehead and the writhing of his body, and yet, his eyes remained closed.

'I'll leave you here a moment, but I'll be back. Oh, by the way, we have the priest coming. Would he like that?'

'Aye, I think so.' Alice moved closer to her da. 'Da, it's Alice, you're all right, Da, I won't leave you.'

Da became still.

The sister spoke then in the whispered tone that befitted the situation, 'We'll leave you a moment, Alice, but won't be far away.'

Alice nodded.

When she was on her own with her da, Alice took hold of his hand. 'Da, I want you to know that we all understand that none of it was your fault. It was the accident. You were a very brave man and Gerald's going to see to it that you get a medal for what you did. He said you should have been honoured.'

Her da didn't move. Alice sat quietly now, watching his breathing, seeing it become more erratic – one minute he would take a breath and then not another for what seemed like ages, but suddenly, he'd breathe again. She could hear a rattling sound and knew this was what she'd heard spoken of – the death rattle.

'Da, oh, Da, you didn't get the chances you wanted. This was meant to be a turning point for you, for us all. I'm so sorry. I'll make sure the lads know you as you were. And, Da, that was a good thing you did for Harry when you said he'd make a good man. That'll set him up to know you didn't hate him as he thinks, and that you only wanted the best for him. The other two'll be all right, you never came down hard on them – not that you could help anything you did.'

Alice noticed that Da's face was becoming paler and more sunken in by the minute. Then another long pause in his breathing, before an intake and a long rattling breath out, and Alice knew her da had gone.

Letting go of her da's hand, Alice leant over and kissed his still face. 'Go to Ma, and be happy, Da, you've been through so much.'

The door opened and Sister stood there with Father Malley.

'He – he's gone, it's too late.'

'No, Alice, it is said that the soul is not for leaving the body for a few hours after the last breath. I will anoint him and send him on his way to heaven, so I will.'

177

As Alice stood with her head bowed listening to the prayers, she couldn't cry, as to her it was good to think of her da out of pain and at peace, so she just gazed at him until the priest had finished and Sister gently took her by the shoulders.

'Doctor Melford was called to another patient, dear, but he will be back soon. He will write the certificate for your father. If you wait in the waiting room, I'll bring it to you and I'll instruct you about what you need to do next. I'll send a cup of tea in for you too. Now, is all that all right? Are you all right? You did so well. You helped your father to go in peace. Well done.'

Alice hadn't been aware that the Sister had been watching, but it didn't matter. She had felt as though she was alone with her da, as she'd wanted to be. Now she had the strange sensation of everything being unreal, as if she were being directed what to do and had no part in it.

The waiting room – a small room painted in shiny cream with green doors and window frames – gave no welcome. Alice chose a seat near to the window; not that she could see out of it, but it just made her feel less alone. Someone brought in a mug of tea and shared their sympathies, but she didn't register who it was, nor could she drink the tea.

When the Sister came in, Gerald was with her. Alice listened to all Sister had to say about going to the council office the next day to register her da's death, without properly taking it in. Her eyes held Gerald's. This stopped her feeling the sensation of drowning under the pressure of all she had to contend with.

A cough brought her attention to Sister. 'Did you get all of that, Miss Brett?'

'Yes, thank you.'

'Good. Well, I'll leave you with Doctor Melford, who has kindly offered to take you home. I am sure he will take care of you.' She gave Gerald a disapproving look. 'Goodbye, Miss Brett. I hope all the formalities go well and that you find comfort in all you told your father tonight. I am sure he heard it and you helped him to go.'

'Ta.'

With the door closing, Gerald took her in his arms. This felt like the place she belonged now and she was filled with a feeling of being safe once more.

'Did he hear me, Gerald?'

'If Sister said he did, then he did. Sister kept watch the whole time. It is something we have to do, and she said you were wonderful. She would have known if your da heard or not.'

Alice wasn't convinced and took all of this as a kindness to her.

She let Gerald direct her out of the building and into his car. When there, surrounded by darkness and swishing trees, he held her once more. 'Oh, Alice, I never want to let you go.'

Alice couldn't speak. She was overwhelmed with emotion – she'd just lost the man who'd meant most to her till now and was taking on a love that far surpassed any her da gave her as a little girl. It all felt so strange . . . so surreal.

'Don't say anything now, my love. Let's get you home.'

Throughout the few minutes the journey took, Gerald held her hand, only letting go to change gear. When they arrived, he leant over and kissed her cheek. 'I'll always be here for you, Alice. May I come in and help you to tell the boys?'

She nodded, but then hesitated. 'I don't know how I'm going to do it yet, Gerald.'

'You'll find a way. It isn't anything you can rehearse.'

He kissed her hand.

Edith greeted them when they opened the door, her question unspoken, but Alice knew what her look was asking and confirmed it with a nod. Edith stepped aside to let them pass.

Gerald smiled at her. 'Hello, Edith.'

Edith seemed tongue-tied and just nodded her head.

'How's your mother?'

'She's doing all right, ta.'

Alice had never seen Edith so shy and this told as she whispered, 'Shall I get going, Alice, love?'

'No. I – I . . .'

'Aw, come here.'

Edith took her in her arms and whispered, 'Be strong for the lads, lass. We're all here for you.'

Before she could answer, Marg appeared at the door. 'Eeh, Alice, lass, how are things?' The three of them hugged. Alice felt the lump in her throat break, but swallowed hard.

Gerald took charge. 'Hello, again, Marg. It's good that you've come over, but shall we give Alice a moment with the lads? And I think she could do with a hot cup of tea with plenty of sugar, and maybe the boys too?'

'We'll see to that, won't we, Edith? Only I think the lads would like some cocoa. They like me cocoa. I make it different, you see. I . . .'

Alice knew it was Marg's nerves that were making her waffle on and she found she could smile to herself at this. Not everything had changed – Edith and Marg were just the same.

They'd be there for her whenever she needed them, like always.

Though she wanted to run through the door and never stop running, Alice turned towards the lads.

Three pairs of eyes stared at her. She held out her arms. Billy and Joey ran to her and the three of them hugged. 'How's Da, Alice?'

She took their hands and led them back to Harry, whose face paled with fear. 'Let's all sit on the sofa with Harry, eh?'

She sat with Harry one side of her and Billy the other. Joey, seeming not to want to be far from her, squatted at her feet. She wanted to hold them all, but with the pain etched on Harry's face she knew she couldn't, so she kept her hands on her lap. 'Da's gone to our ma, lads.'

'Naw.' Harry's protest was a deep gasp. She took hold of his hand. Billy didn't speak or move. Nor did Joey, who looked up at her, his face unreadable, his mouth open.

'He didn't suffer,' she told them. 'He went into a coma after his operation and it kept him safe. The doctors tried, but lads, we have to be grateful that Da went now, without knowing anything about it, because, well, Da had sommat that couldn't be taken out of his brain – a tumour. It would have grown and grown and, had he lived, he would have only lasted a short while but would have been in terrible pain. This way, he went to sleep and just drifted away up into Ma's waiting arms.'

Still none of them spoke.

'We've got good memories, haven't we? We have to forget the part when Da was ill and remember the man that used to play footie and take us on picnics. How we would run to

181

him and he'd give us each a special cuddle. See him in your mind, smiling and lifting you in the air. Forgive what the horrible tumour that changed him, made him do. And think of tonight an' all. His last, when, before the terrible thing happened, we saw our real da. How he apologised to you, Harry, and bought us chips, and he was almost back to our old da again, the one who loved us and would have done anything for us.'

A tear plopped onto Joey's cheek and his lips quivered. 'I want me da, Alice.'

Alice put her arms out to him and he climbed up on her knee. As big as he was, at this moment he was just a little boy and he snuggled into her. Billy's head came down onto her shoulder and Harry, though it made him wince, put his arm around her as he asked, 'What's going to happen, Alice?'

'We're going to look out for each other. We're all going to muck in, and you lads are going to do well and make our ma and da proud.'

'How will we manage?'

'We will. I haven't looked yet, but at the hospital they gave me an envelope with Da's things in it. It'll be his pocket watch and his money. When he gave me that ten bob earlier tonight, Da said that the factory had given him a good payment, so I'm hoping that will sort everything out initially. Then we'll have me money from the biscuit factory coming in.'

'And I'm next in line for the paper round, Alice. I put me name down a while back, and when Jimmy Black leaves school at the end of this next term the job's mine.'

Billy said this with pride and Alice smiled at him.

'That'll be grand, lad.'

'And I can do errands for them in the street. I do a few now, but they just give me a biscuit or a toffee. I'll tell them I'm doing it for money only now.'

'Good lad.' Alice didn't dampen Joey's little enterprise by telling him they gave him a biscuit because they had no spare pennies to give him; she'd tackle that another time. For now, she could see he needed to be able to contribute.

'And I can get a job and leave school. You're allowed to once you reach fourteen, really. You don't have to wait for the end of the term when you should officially leave, just as long as you have a job.'

Alice agreed, though she suspected the term would end before Harry was well enough to get a job. In any case, now that she knew how clever he was, she wanted to try to keep him studying for as long as he could – maybe even, like Jackie, try to get him into college after leaving school, though she knew this was perhaps just a dream as the cost wouldn't be within her pocket. Jackie had recommendations from respected tutors that might help her to get a scholarship. But again, like with Joey, she didn't share these thoughts. This wasn't the time to say anything that might dash Harry's enthusiasm for helping out the family. 'Aye, you can, Harry. So, you see, there's loads we can do, and the main thing is, we'll have each other and always will have.'

Joey's quivering lip turned into a sob. This set all the lads off. As Billy snivelled and took Alice's hand, it was as if he'd shrunk in age and was a young 'un again. Harry held her tighter, not seeming to feel the pain of his broken ribs, and she heard a sniffle from him too.

It was all too much. Alice's strong armour cracked and she sobbed along with them.

After a few moments, Gerald, Marg and Edith came through the door and, as if they'd planned it, Edith took Joey and stood him by her side, in the circle of one of her arms, while beckoning Billy to her other side. Gerald pulled Alice up and Marg sat down beside Harry and took his hand. As Gerald took her into his arms, she saw Harry lower his head onto Marg's shoulder. None of them were urged not to cry – their sobs were allowed, as loving, comforting arms held them all.

'You did so well, my darling.' Alice's heart soared at Gerald whispering this, her love for him conquering all other emotions. She clung to him for strength. He kissed her hair. 'I'm here for you, my darling. Now you've come into my life, I'm never going to let you leave it. I'll always be by your side. You will get through this and with our help the lads will too.'

She nodded, then took his hanky and blew her nose.

'Help the lads some more now, darling. They needed this crying time, and will over the next days and weeks, but bring them some comfort now as only you can.'

She nodded, wiped her face, then turned towards where Edith was holding the sobbing Billy and Joey, and Marg was comforting a weeping Harry. 'Didn't someone promise us some nice cocoa, then?'

'Aye, me. And I bet these lads are looking forward to it 'an all. They don't often get a drop of good cocoa, do you, lads?'

Billy answered. 'Naw, our Alice can only make ditchwater!'

'Ha, the truth is out, but I knaw, I've tried it! Scandalous. A Blackpool lass – and a Sandgronian at that – who can't make cocoa? Never been heard of. And I tell you, lads, I've tried to teach her, but no. Useless.'

184

They all giggled, and Alice felt her giggle bubble over and turn into a laugh.

They all looked at her but she couldn't stop.

Gerald held her firmly. 'I think this one needs some fresh air.' With that, he walked her to the door. Once the air hit her, she was able to control herself.

'Eeh, I'm sorry, I just felt like I was running away with myself and couldn't stop it.'

'Well, that's the best description I've ever heard from someone bordering on hysteria. Are you feeling all right now?'

'Aye. Ta, I'm fine.'

'Oh, Alice. I mean it, I am going to be here for you and I'll help you all I can.'

'I know, Gerald. In all of this, that's like a shining light for me.'

'I'll always be that to you, Alice, if you'll have me.'

'Me! Have you? By, I thought it'd be the other way around. Aye, I'll have you in bucketloads.'

They both laughed then. Not the hysterical giggles that Alice had just experienced, but the laughter shared between two people in love.

'But you know, Gerald, I don't know much about you. You know all my family and all about me. All I know is that you're a doctor, you're daft enough to look at a lass from Whittaker Avenue who's so below your station in life, and you have a da who's a top surgeon and live on posh Newton Drive! We don't sound as though we match, do we?'

'No, we don't, but we do have the most important thing – hearts that we've given to each other. All other obstacles we can overcome.'

At this moment, as she looked into his eyes, Alice felt that they could.

'Cocoa's up!'

Marg's voice broke the spell. They giggled and turned to go back inside. There they found the banter about the cocoa still in full swing. 'I'll teach you lads how to make it. I'm sure you've got more up top than Alice has.'

'Hey, cheeky!'

They all giggled. And Alice thought, *We're going to be all right, me and the lads. We've got the best friends ever in Marg and Edith, and now we have Gerald too. My darling, adorable Gerald.*

EIGHTEEN

Edith

Edith arrived home after what seemed like a mammoth day full of hurts to the surprise of her life. Albert sat at the table, eating the dinner she'd left keeping hot on a saucepan of boiling water for him. 'You're early?'

'Aye, I don't knaw what's up with Eric Porter. He only had a bit of bookies' running for me and that was it. He usually has other errands, but he gave me a bob and told me to hop it off home. The bob's here for you, sis. Ta for making me dinner. I was starving.'

'Aye, well, you're welcome. I saw that you'd made your bed and brought your washing down, and aye, polished me shoes an' all, so you deserved a bit of something back.' She smiled at him.

Despite everything, she loved this brother of hers and was always wishing she had the same relationship with him that Alice had with her brothers.

A little hope settled in her as he said, 'Well, I knaw you do your best for us all, and I could help out more. It's just that I've

187

always felt that me ma and da – well, not me da as much – owed me for all I'd missed out on.'

'Eeh, Albert. I know what you mean, but punishing a wrong with a wrong don't work. If Ma had some of her troubles lifted, she wouldn't drink, I'm sure of it. We can do that a little for her. We can't give her Da back how she wants him, or make all her troubles go away, but if we're kind to her and do all we can for her, then it might help, and Da deserves that from us, don't he?'

'Aye, I shouldn't have kicked Ma. I feel bad about that. I just don't seem able to hold me temper. Where are they?'

'Sitting in the backyard together.'

'They still love each other, don't they, Edith?'

'Aye, I've never seen a love like Da has for Ma. It's such a pity he's taken with the miners' disease. You remember how things were before, don't you? Ma always giggling, and all of us eager for Da's return at the end of whatever week's shift he'd done.'

'Aw, they were good times, weren't they? Though I used to play me ma up because I missed me da.'

'You did, and she spoilt you instead of disciplining you. So a lot of how you are ain't your fault. But now you've grown up, Albert, and can make your own decisions, you should think on, like you're doing now, and act in a different way.'

For a moment, she thought she'd lost him as he scowled. 'All right, don't make a meal of it, you've got faults an' all.'

'I know. I nag you, for one. I don't know how you put up with me, Alley boy.'

'Ha! That took me back. You called me that until you were

188

about ten and I was seven, then I told you off. "Me name's Albert, after me grandda! Not Alley boy, you stupid thing!" You went crying to Ma, but she stuck up for me and said it was a silly name.'

Relieved to see he still had his good humour, Edith laughed with him. 'We didn't do bad as kids, did we?'

'Naw, and it's good to remember them times. I don't let meself, because I feel a sort of grief as if I've lost sommat really good and can't get it back.'

'Aw, Albert. I need a hug.'

She braced herself for him refusing, but he got up, scraping his chair and grating her fragile nerves. When he came over to her and held his arms open, she went into them gladly. The lump in her throat hurt.

'I'll try to deal with it better, sis. You don't deserve how it's all affected me.'

He pulled away, and for all him thinking himself the man and the big I am, she could see he was near to tears.

'That'd be good, Albert. We're in this together, you know. Me and you. And we can help the situation by being close. Alice and her brothers get by that way.'

'I knaw. How's things there? They took the old man to hospital, didn't they?'

Edith told him what had happened.

'Well, that's a relief for them, innit?'

'No, it ain't, they're devastated. They all understood what made their dad how he was.' She told him about Gerald. 'And he's going to see about getting Mr Brett a medal – he said it could be awarded, post ... aw, I don't know, some big word that means "even though he's dead".'

'By, that'd be sommat. With how he was, it made you forget what he'd done, and it was brave of him. They still talk about it at the factory. They say he could have just run out of the building like the rest of them, but he went back when he saw the roof collapsing and Clive, the boss's son, right underneath it. It was heroic what he did ... And all his moods were because of that, then?'

Albert was surprised to learn what the injury had done to Mr Brett.

'And to lose his wife while he was still unconscious and know nothing about what she was suffering ... well, it all just turned him,' Edith explained.

'I'll nip over and see Harry. He's a year and a bit younger than me, but he's a good lad. We used to hang out in the same gang in the street.'

'I know. I think he'd like that, especially as he's suffering the double hurt of his da having beaten him up so badly just a few days ago.'

This conversation was so wonderful to Edith that the one thing she wanted to bring up she daren't, for fear of sending Albert right back into his usual mood. But despite him seeming to have had a sudden change of heart, she still worried that he might harbour a grudge against Ida.

Albert went towards the door, then hesitated. 'Would you come across with me, Edith? I don't want them to think I've come bothering them.'

She nodded; she knew his fear. Bothering people was all he'd done for a long time. The kind gesture he proposed was so out of character that Alice might be wary of him and upset him. 'I'll just nip out back and say hello to Ma and Da and make sure they're all right.'

190

'Aye, I'm not ready to tell Ma that I'm sorry yet, but I will when the time's right.'

'All right, I understand.'

Edith found Ma and Da relaxing in the late warmth of the dusk. She greeted them both and told them the sad news. 'Is there anything you need afore I go over with Albert? He wants to give his condolences to Harry.'

'Albert does?'

'Aye, Da. Just treat it as normal, don't make a thing of it. Albert's been a different lad tonight, saying he's going to apologise to Ma, give me a couple of bob towards the household, and we've been talking about old times. I don't want to damage that. Let him come out of his shell in his own time with as few recriminations as possible.'

'You've a wise head on your shoulders, Edith. And naw, we don't need anything, do we, Betty?'

'I'd like a cuppa in a bit, Edith, but do what you've got to with our Albert. I'm glad he's thinking different. I knaw I ain't helped matters.'

Ma wiped away a tear.

'Naw, Betty, love, don't take on. We can all change, you knaw.'

Edith closed the door and left her da to it. Coming back through the kitchen, she saw Albert stood at the door having a fag. 'Right, shall we go?'

'Aye. You knaw, I can feel the eyes of all the neighbours on me, judging me every time I leave the house. It sickens me; there ain't none of them that's got anything to shout about, and they've all got secrets and ways that they do wrong. I could tell of a few of them, and their antics – the men gambling, some of the women going after other men, and her across the road, laughing at me ma when she's been Eric Porter's floozy for years.'

This shocked Edith. She knew there'd been gossip recently, but for it to have gone on for years set her wondering if that had anything to do with whatever was bothering Marg.

Knocking on Alice's door, she told Albert, 'We won't go straight in like we usually would in case it's not the best time.'

'Righto. I see that doctor who tended to me the other night's still here.'

'Aye, that's what I meant about him and Alice ... well, they're walking out.'

'What? Flipping heck!'

There was no time to say more as the door opened. Alice looked from her to Albert, then back to her without speaking. 'Albert wanted to come over to see Harry and the lads. Are they still up?'

Not showing the surprise she must feel, Alice opened the door wider. 'Aye, they are, we're letting them go when they feel like it ... Ta, Albert, that'll mean a lot to Harry.'

As Albert walked in, Alice gave Edith a look that said, *That's a turn-up*.

Edith nodded.

'Hello, Harry, mate. I came to say I'm sorry for your loss, and you, Billy and Joey. It's a bad job. And just to say that if you want owt, I'll do me best to get it for you. We used to be big pals back in the day.'

'Aye, till you got that you thought yourself above mucking around with the likes of schoolkids!'

Edith held her breath, but then she saw Harry was laughing.

'Ha! You'll feel the same when you leave, it's called growing up. But when the going gets rough for a mate ... well, none of that matters.'

Alice offered Albert a chair. 'Naw, thanks, Alice, we're not stopping. I hope you're all right?'

'Well, you know, Albert. It's not easy, but having friends like you call makes it a bit easier to bear.'

Albert grinned. Edith felt so proud of him.

'Albert, this is Gerald.'

'The doctor, aye, I knaw.'

'How's that arm, Albert? Is it giving you much trouble?'

Albert hung his head. 'A little.'

'And your mother? Edith tells me that she's all right too?'

Edith wanted the floor to swallow her as she waited anxiously for Albert's answer, thinking that any little thing could topple him over the edge and trigger his temper.

'I'm only asking as a doctor, Albert, nothing more.'

'Aye, she's all right.'

Inside, Edith felt a bit cross with Gerald. She'd already told him how her ma was. 'I've told you, Doctor, she's doing all right; she's not complaining at all and she's trying to stay off the drink.'

'Gerald. Please call me Gerald, Edith. I know I had my doctor head on just now, but I want you to feel that I'm a friend, not someone in authority.'

'Well, if you keep changing heads, you'll confuse all me mates, Gerald!'

They all laughed at this from Alice and the tension broke. Gerald smiled shamefacedly. 'You're right. I apologise to you, Albert and Edith. I don't want to be your doctor, though I'll always help you out if I can. In future, I'll just ask Alice how everyone is.'

'Good idea, as it sounded as though you were opening a surgery.'

Gerald grinned at Alice. Edith had a pang of jealousy for a moment. How she wished she could find the kind of love that Alice had. Philip came to her mind and she knew a longing that wasn't strange to her, as it hadn't left her from the moment she'd met Philip – just to be near to him and to chat to him in this easy way.

'Well, shall we go, Edith?'

'We'd better. The lads look tired and you'll be wanting to get settled, Alice. I hope you sleep all right, lass. Don't worry about work tomorrow, I'll tell Moaning Minnie what's happened. No doubt she'll say you've got to come in the day after, but that's how she is.'

Harry and Albert shook hands. Harry winced, but his smile said the contact had been worth it.

'I'll nip in after work tomorrow, Harry. I'll bring you all some sticks of rock – we can buy those that are a bit misshapen for a halfpenny.'

'Ta, Albert. And will you do me a favour? Will you ask if me name can go down for a trainee job? Tell them who me da was and that might give me more of a chance.'

This surprised Edith. She'd thought that Harry would want to work anywhere but the factory, given that it was the scene of his father's accident.

'That'll give you every chance in the world, and I'll tell you this much, you'll see just how much your da was thought of despite the change. He's a hero in the men's and women's eyes who remember what he did. As soon as anyone new comes they hear all about him. The foreman was saying yesterday after your da left how they might put a plaque up to honour him as he didn't think he'd be back . . . Aw, I – I didn't think what I was saying. I'm sorry, lad. Me and me mouth!'

'Naw, you've helped me, Albert, ta. It's good to knaw how me da is well thought of.'

Edith saw Alice wipe a tear. 'It is, Albert. Ta for that. Will you tell those at work who remember me da that I'll let them know when the arrangements are, and that they are all welcome?'

'They'll like that, Alice, ta. I reckon a couple of the bosses will come an' all.'

Edith could see pride in Alice's face and she herself felt bursting with it for Albert.

When they were back out in the street, Albert was quiet and Edith could feel that he was uncomfortable, so decided to reassure him. 'By, that was a bit of an ordeal for you, Albert, but you did grand. Just grand.'

'I was embarrassed in front of that doctor, that's all. And it made me think how everyone must see me.'

'You can change that, Albert. You can. You can stop being so angry and talk to folk in a civil way.'

'Aw, don't start, our Edith, you're jumping on the band-wagon now.'

'I'm not. I'm your big sis, and if anyone can spout advice, then it's me, because I think the world of you and want others to see what I see.'

'Ha! You're some different kind of girl, Edith. Most would have given up on me by now. But not you. It shocked me when you got cross and cut me dinners off, and you and Ma didn't make me bed. You've always done everything for me.'

'I know, but it was getting hard, Albert. More on the money side of things.'

Albert kicked a stone. The kick was more a vicious swipe than moving the stone out of the way.

Edith's heart came into her mouth as Albert quickened his pace to pass by Ida's house. She knew this was the reason for his sudden mood change – he was still badly affected by the humiliation he'd suffered at Ida's hands. Her fear increased. She wouldn't be able to bear it if Albert did have a plan to hurt Ida.

Thinking it would be best to leave the subject alone for now, she caught up with Albert just as he reached their door. 'I'm going to make some cocoa, love, do you want a mug?'

'Naw, I'm going out.'

He grabbed his jacket from where he'd left it on the back of the chair. Edith felt saddened that she'd only had such a short glimpse of the brother she so wanted him to be. Now, that Albert had gone, and the usual short-tempered, rude and moody Albert was back.

Leaving him to it, she went through the kitchen to her parents. 'It's getting cold out here now, are you coming in for your cocoa?'

The light from the kitchen lit up her da's lovely smile. 'We are, lass, we are, but make mine a tea.'

As he rose his coughing started, filling Edith with the knowledge that she too faced losing her da in the not too distant future.

Please, please God, don't take him yet. I couldn't bear it, I couldn't.

NINETEEN

Marg

Going from house to house with Edith, collecting for Alice and the boys, was a distraction for Marg. This was a tradition amongst the Whittaker Avenue neighbourhood and nearby streets when a family had suffered a death. The money raised bought a small wreath from everyone, and they all signed the card they took around with them. What was left over went to the family to help out with the funeral expenses.

More than one household had been a bit hesitant as no one liked Mr Brett. Marg knew she'd have been the same before all this happened, but now she understood how much he meant to Alice, she felt differently.

Rhoda Clarke from Rathlyn Avenue opened the door and stood arms folded. 'I didn't put anything in the collection box at work and I ain't giving anything now. Good riddance, I say. George Brett was nothing but a sourpuss who gave lovely Alice more black eyes than anyone should have to bear, poor lass. She's naw doubt relieved he's gone.'

'Naw. She ain't as it happens, Rhoda.' For the third time on this round, Marg told the truth of how it was for Alice. 'But in any case, she needs our help now. This ain't about Mr Brett, but about the young 'uns and Alice, and the help they need from us all.'

'Aye, well, I'll give a few coppers for them, but I ain't signing naw card.'

'What difference can it make, eh? You can't spite a dead man, Rhoda, but you can make a difference to those left behind. A few words, like "Sorry for your loss", cost nothing.'

'Bloody hell! Quite the preacher. Give it here, then. Mind, this is for Alice and them lads, not for that sod who's turned his toes up, because we're all glad to see the back of him.'

Edith, who hadn't spoken till now, said, 'I take it you like Clive Barnes, the son of the rock factory owner, who does such a lot for this town?'

'Aye, I do, Edith. What's that got to do with anything?'

'Mr Brett saved his life and lost himself – well, the lovely version of himself we all used to know – in the process. And he's likely to be honoured for it. Can't you have a thought for that?'

'Aye, well, that's true, and he lost his wife an' all. Eh, go on then, I'll put towards his flowers.'

Coughing up another copper, Rhoda hmphed.

Marg wanted to tell her that if she were giving grudgingly, she shouldn't give at all, but she wanted to collect all she could for Alice.

'Eeh, Edith, this is hard work.'

'It is, lass. Folk just didn't like Mr Brett and you can't blame them. Anyroad, let's finish this street and call it a day, you look exhausted. We can do some more tomorrow.'

'Having two jobs and worrying about me gran and me ma is taking it out of me, that's all.'

'I don't think that is all, Marg. There's been something up with you for a few days now. Can't you talk about it?'

'No ... Well, I suppose, but I wanted to tell you both together, like we do when any of us have any troubles. But seeing as though I can't now after what poor Alice has gone through, it would be good to get it off me chest and see what you think about it all.'

'All right, but I tell you what, why don't we cut through to the Layton Institute. I've got enough for a lemonade and me da's a member so we can go in.'

'That'd be a treat. Aye, let's.'

They gained a skip in their step as they linked arms and giggled at each other.

'Right, what is it, lass? What's weighing you down, then?'

Unburdening herself gave Marg a feeling of relief, but compounded the enormity of what her ma had done. 'I can't forgive her, Edith, and that's the worst part. Me and Ma have always been close and I've lost that now, along with losing respect and love for the man I thought was me da. It's like I'm grieving all over again, and yet, I have to be strong for Alice as she needs us, and for Jackie and Gran, who depend so much on me.'

'Oh, Marg. I don't know what to say. None of us ever liked Eric Porter, and now ... well, he's your da! I can't take it in. I mean, how come me ma and da didn't know, or the neighbours? Nothing happens that they don't know of, but I've never heard tell of anything.'

'That's what gets me, because ... Eeh, Edith, for the neighbours not to suspect, then me da – I mean, *Horace* – must have

199

been in the house sometimes when it went on. It's disgusting and I feel ashamed.'

'And your gran. Didn't she move in before your da . . . well, who you thought of as your da, died?'

'No but, by, even me gran was a party to it.'

They fell silent. After a moment, Edith reached over the table and took Marg's hand.

'She may not have been. You said she didn't know about Jackie being fathered by Eric Porter.'

'No, but she knew about me, so knew sommat was going on, and since Horace died, what about then? Ma says she went to Eric's house a lot in the early days, but I've not known her do that for years, so . . . under the same roof as me and Jackie an' all. It all makes me feel sick.'

'Maybe your ma couldn't do anything to stop it and so shielded you and Jackie as much as she could. I mean, you had no idea and you lived in the same house, and there wasn't a lot your gran could do about anything either. She must have hated it, but by putting up with it she saved her daughter from being scandalised, and shielded you and Jackie from it all. It must have been a terrible time for her.'

'Aye, that would explain her knowing and not saying anything, or trying to stop it. And means that me ma's a scheming, get-what-she-can prostitute.'

'Aw, don't say that, Marg.'

'Why not? She is, Edith. She doesn't even like Uncle Eric. If she did, why didn't she marry him after Horace died? It could all have been above board then. And if she didn't want to be with him, then why didn't she finish it? It can't have just been something she did to get money for Horace's gambling.

200

No, whichever way you look at it, me ma ain't a nice person and she's been taking Eric for a ride all his life.'

'Ironic really. I mean, Eric Porter being taken advantage of when he spends his life as a money lender who uses violence if his creditors can't pay. Not to mention his other criminal activities that cause hardship and pain to others. You couldn't make it up.'

Marg didn't know why, but this tickled her and she giggled uncontrollably.

'What? What have I said?'

Marg couldn't say as she didn't know. She couldn't even see anything funny in any of it, and yet she rocked with laughter and tears flowed down her face.

Before long, Edith was laughing with her.

Marg snorted when she caught her breath, making things worse. A gang of men who were playing cards shouted over to them to shut up or get out, and this increased their hysteria.

'Right, girls, that's enough.' The manager, a large man with a bright red nose that told of him enjoying a pint or two stood over them. 'This is an hour mostly for the menfolk to unwind when they leave work and you're disrupting that. You either quieten down or you leave, which is it to be?'

Marg couldn't speak. She got up and made as much noise as she could by scraping her chair along the floor. Edith did the same.

Outside they sat on the small wall and leant on each other as they dried their eyes. 'Eeh, thrown out of the Layton Institute! Me da'll be mortified, Marg.'

'Don't tell him and he'll never know. Oh, but it was funny. It was a tonic. And we aren't barred.'

'No, we can always go in again and be on our best behaviour and be forgiven.'

'We can, and I'd like that to be one Saturday night when they have a turn on. It'd be good fun and needn't cost us much – as long as we have the price of a lemonade each we can sip them all night.'

'By, that'd be grand. I've heard a lot about the club's social nights at the factory. They play housey-housey in the interval and Ida won the jackpot of three quid once. She and her Jack went to Morecambe for a week's holiday.'

'I remember that. It seemed daft to me to travel all that way for the same as you've got at home.'

'Aye, but she said it was a nice change of scenery.'

'I'd not want to change being in Blackpool for anything.'

As they walked home, chatting away, Marg began to feel normal again, something she hadn't felt in a long time.

When they got back to Marg's house, Jackie greeted them with the good news that though Gran had been upset earlier, she was in her bed now.

'Is Ma still away to her bed an' all, Jackie, love?'

'She is. I'm worried about her, though, Marg, she's not the same. Are you and her still at odds?'

'A bit, but don't worry, lass. I'll go up later and have a chat with her.'

This seemed to cheer Jackie as she joined in with helping her and Edith to count the money they'd collected. She took the pennies as her responsibility because there were a lot more of them and she was quicker than the others. Edith counted the threepenny bits, and Marg the smaller number of silver coins.

The total was fifteen shillings and two buttons.

'Well, I never noticed who put them in, Edith.'

'Well, they are metal and would sound the same. Flipping cheek!'

'Aye, but do you know what? I'm going to keep them and use them myself when the Sally Army rattle their tins.'

'Marg! You can't do that.'

'I can, Jackie. Besides, they'll never know.'

'Eeh, Marg, no! I'm with Jackie on this one. They don't deserve that. They do some good work, you know.'

'I do know, but I feel embarrassed when I ain't even got a halfpenny to give them, so I can pretend the next couple of times when that happens that I am contributing.'

Edith giggled at this. 'Ha, Marg, you're never down for long, lass, I'll say that for you. Come on, let's add this to the seventeen and six we collected yesterday and take it to Alice.'

'Aye, good idea, and it'll be a relief to do so, as now we know that she's going to be all right for money. The box at work is almost full too, and I saw one in the Layton Institute as well. I reckon she'll have enough to cover everything.'

'And more, as her da had that payout from the rock factory. Alice never said how much it was, but she said she'd be all right for a few weeks.'

For Marg, this was an easing of one of her worries. 'Right, Jackie. Are you all right if we go over to Alice's, lass?'

Jackie's head drooped. 'Can't Edith take it? I thought you'd sort things out with Ma. I don't like how everything is at the moment.'

Noticing for the first time how upset Jackie was tore at Marg. 'Eeh, lass, what's up? 'Cause that face says it's more than me and Ma being at odds with each other. Why didn't you say something?'

'I didn't want to spoil things. You seemed so pleased with how much you'd collected ... and well, you ain't been yourself lately so it was good to see you back to normal.'

'Aw, come here, lass.' Taking Jackie in her arms, Marg could feel that she was trembling. 'Jackie, lass, what's to do?'

'Gran's been saying things ...'

'Aw, no ... Look, I know what she's been saying. Me and you'll have a talk about it all. You're not to worry.'

'But she said me and you aren't sisters. You are me sister, ain't you, Marg?'

'I am. I'm your true sister, lass. We have the same ma and da, but Gran doesn't know that.'

'I don't understand, how can Gran not knaw it?'

Edith interrupted. 'Look, I'll pop over home, I have to check on me da. We'll go to Alice's later or see her tomorrow, eh?'

'Righto, Edith. Ta, lass.'

Turning back to Jackie, Marg held her close. 'It's quite a tale, lass, but I know you're strong and can take hearing it. But I warn you, it's not nice. I've only had a couple of days to get used to it and it knocked me for six, but you won't be alone with the knowledge. I'm right here with you, and nothing need change in our lives unless we want it to.'

'Naw, Marg ... naw!'

Both she and Jackie turned to see their ma standing at the bottom of the stairs in her nightie. Her skin had a blueish hue to it and her breath came in shallow gasps.

'Ma, I have to. Gran has told Jackie things.'

Ma swayed. 'Not – not all . . . please, Marg.'

Leaving Jackie's side, Marg went to her ma, catching her as she collapsed forwards. 'Help me, Jackie, lass, help me! I can't hold her.'

Together, they got Ma to the sofa. 'Run for Ada, lass.'

When Jackie reached the door, she stepped back. Marg's heart dropped as she saw who stood on the doorstep. She couldn't speak and had no time to react before Eric took great strides and reached the sofa.

'Vera! Eeh, Vera, me lass!'

'Leave her alone, Uncle Eric, she told me she don't want you near her.'

'Naw. Not this time, Marg. There's things you don't knaw about me and your ma. I'm not leaving her, not now, not ever!'

Not giving her time to argue, he lifted Ma up as if she was a baby. 'I'm taking her to the hospital. I've asked her many a time to let me take her to be treated. I can pay and would pay all I had to save her, but she never let me. Naw one's going to stop me now, Marg, so get out of me way.'

Marg was shocked and confused as she did as he said.

When he passed by Jackie, he told her, 'Don't worry, lass. They'll get your ma right.'

When he'd gone, Marg plonked down on the chair next to the fire and stared at Jackie – all she saw was fear and a sister who looked lost.

'Eeh, Jackie . . . Jackie, lass.'

'Marg?'

'Come and sit down, lass.'

Without telling her all the sordid details, Marg told Jackie the truth of who their da was.

'But ... Ma? I mean, she couldn't help it, could she? She's afraid of him, and I am an' all. He's a beast, I hate him. I don't want him to be me da and I'll never accept him. He must have hurt Ma ... made her do that thing with him. And where was da? Where was he? Was he out at work?'

Marg shook her head. 'I don't know all the answers, Jackie. I heard it from Gran in the first instance. I was shocked and I tackled Ma, but ... Look, it's all mixed up, all of it. And I'm beginning to think that even how we see our real da is all mixed up an' all. We've been brought up to hate him and never give him the time of day. I – I just don't know now. Not after seeing how he was with Ma just now.'

'Will ... will Ma die?'

'Aw, Jackie, no. Don't say that, I couldn't bear it, lass.'

A huge sob came from Jackie. Marg got up and went to sit next to her on the sofa.

Taking her sister in her arms, she wept with her as they rocked backwards and forwards. She had no words of comfort, only her love to give to her sister, for inside she was churned up with worry over her ma. This, and the new knowledge she'd gained, gave her a feeling of being lost.

TWENTY

Alice

Alice felt her heart lift as she, her brothers and Gerald alighted from the car which had slowly followed the horse-drawn hearse from their home to St Kentigern's Church. She'd thought no one would turn up to give her da a send-off, other than those close to her, but there were many standing outside the church waiting for them.

Glancing this way and that, she saw both familiar and unfamiliar faces and wondered where they had all come from. Catching sight of her da's old boss standing with his son, Clive, in amongst one group, she guessed these were all from the rock factory.

Others stood with Mr Flanagan, the pub landlord, and she recognised a few of these.

It all seemed unreal to Alice and she questioned why she was so interested in the mourners at such a time, but it was as if all her weeping during the night hours had drained her, and now she couldn't feel anything.

Gerald tightened his grip on her arm and gave her a little smile that asked if she was all right. She nodded.

Alighting from the car, Father Malley came over to her. 'Alice, how are you feeling, my dear?'

'I feel as though I am in a strange world, Father. I'm just getting through, but can't seem to feel anything most of the time.'

'Aye, it is the protection the Good Lord gives you. He puts you in a world of your own but allows you to function, though that doesn't last for ever, you will need your friends and those who love you ... And what about you, boys?'

The lads just nodded their heads. Alice's heart went out to them. In the week that had passed, they had gradually come to terms with how their lives were now. She hated to think it, but they were all much happier and a feeling of calm had settled on their home.

'Now, I need to ask you before I start the service. Clive Barnes would like to say a few words during the mass. What do you think – is it that you are all right with that?'

Clive left the group from the rock factory and came over to her. Alice had met him many times. Often, he'd offered help to them, but her da would have none of it. He'd tried other means: whenever he'd seen her or her brothers, he would offer to buy them a bag of chips or a hot tattie, but they'd not dare accept in case Da found out.

'Hello, Alice, lass. I'm sorry for your loss. I hope you'll let me say a few words for your father.'

Alice nodded.

'Thank you. I hope you like what I intend to say. I'll see you afterwards?'

The priest went into his role then, blessing her da's coffin with holy water and leading it into the church, saying prayers as he went. None of it registered with Alice, not even the readings, but when Clive Barnes, dressed in a black suit and startling white shirt, stepped up onto the altar, she knew she would listen to every word and prayed that many would gain an understanding of the man her da truly was.

'I stand here today because of George Brett. My youngest son, George, is alive because George Brett saved me. Born just a year after that terrible accident at our factory, he is now a healthy and happy four-year-old. I thank George Brett for that ... My ... my wife did too.' Clive took a deep breath. 'And so do his grandparents. For our little George is a joy to us and he represents the life George Brett gave me.'

Alice bowed her head. She felt the ripple of feeling that went around the congregation for Clive, as his wife had died not long after their child had been born.

Alice hadn't known that Clive had honoured her father by naming his child after him.

Oh, Da, Da, did you know? How I wish I had, as this has made me so proud and helps with my grief.

'I cannot describe the fear I felt when I heard the massive crack that sounded like an explosion, and looked up to see that beam hurtling towards me. In that instant I saw men scrambling away, heard screams of terror, and my own body froze. In this split second I saw one man coming towards me, not running away – though I am not decrying those that did. Two hands pulled me, then pushed me forward. Behind me there was an almighty crash. That man running towards me was George Brett. Those hands that pushed me to safety belonged to George Brett.

'George suffered injuries that would have killed a lesser man. Injuries that have impacted on his life and his family ever since, and contributed to his untimely death. I have never been able to thank him in the way I would have liked to, because George was a proud man. And because of this, his bravery was never formally acknowledged with an award. Today, I am going to put that right. I have here a framed citation signed by Lord Winterton, the Chancellor of the Duchy of Lancaster. It says, "Awarded to George Brett. For outstanding bravery in saving the life of a fellow citizen, without being mindful of his own safety." I am proud to be able to give this to his children: Alice, Harry, William and Joseph. Who richly deserve to have their father's action recognised.'

Stepping down, Clive came forward and went to hand the frame to Alice, but she turned and indicated that it should be given to Harry. Harry blushed, but then his face beamed with pride as he said, 'Thank you, sir.'

Going back to the altar, Clive bowed to her father's coffin and then turned and began to applaud. Gradually, all the congregation stood and applauded.

Alice looked around her and saw that not one man or woman had remained seated. Pride filled her and she found herself smiling. *At last my da is known for who he truly was – a brave man.*

After the service, the burial that took place in the Layton Cemetery seemed to happen without Alice being fully present. Once more her emotions were distanced as she threw the earth onto her da's grave, cringing inside against the hollow sound it made.

Stepping away so that others could do the same, she stared across at her ma's grave.

How she had wanted to put her da in with her ma, but as they hadn't paid for a double grave – and not even a proper grave, just a pauper's one for Ma – the permission wasn't granted. At least with the money that the rock factory had paid Da off with, they had been able to lay him to rest in consecrated ground in a proper grave.

As the mourners filed away, many of them shared kind words with her.

'You must be proud, lass.'

'I remember your da before the accident, lass: a kind man who always helped me ma if she needed it. God rest both their souls.'

'I was at your ma and da's wedding. It was a lovely day, with dancing and laughter. A lovely couple.'

Alice greeted and thanked them all, filled with comfort by their kind words.

All through the day, Gerald stayed by her side, supporting her, while Marg and Edith looked after the lads. Jackie did her bit too, as she stood close to Harry, looking pale and faraway, as if she had the world's troubles on her mind. Alice knew that her and Marg's ma had been taken into hospital and that this was likely the cause for it. She hadn't had a chance to ask how Vera was or who was looking after their gran, but she assumed it would be Ada.

The eight of them turned to walk towards the gate and go back home with Alice, where she'd prepared a small buffet of cold meat pies, cheese flan and pickles.

As they were leaving, Clive Barnes came up to her. Gerald shook his hand and thanked him.

'No. Thank you for coming to see me and making the suggestion, and for asking for the signature of the earl. Once that was done it was a simple matter of me talking to him on the phone to tell him what had happened, and then the citation arrived. I soon got it framed.' He looked at Alice. 'You know, Alice, lass, I feel as though I have repaid my debt a little. I know your father doesn't know of it, but you four do and that's important to me.'

'Ta, Clive, it was a lovely thing to do. My da wasn't able to take your appreciation, but we are and we're grateful for it.'

'I want you to know that my door is always open, and if there is anything that I can do, I will.'

Before she could answer, a voice behind her said, 'I have sommat to ask.'

They all looked at Harry. 'I leave school soon and I want to follow in me da's footsteps and train to be a rock-roller.'

'Well, we'd be honoured to have you on an apprenticeship, Harry. I'll be in touch when I've been able to arrange it. I'll leave you now, but if I can ever be of help in any other way, please let me know.'

'Clive, would you like to come back to my house to have a cup of tea? We'd really like you to.'

'Yes, I would like that, thank you, Alice . . . That's if I won't be intruding.'

'No. We'd like you to come.'

Once they were seated in the funeral car to be taken home, Alice snuggled into Gerald.

'Ta for arranging that with Clive, Gerald, it meant the world to me and the lads. It's as if my da's name's been cleared and folk no longer look on him as a bad man, but with understanding.'

'I wanted that for you, dear. And so did Clive – well, for himself, too, as he'd long wanted to thank your da and would have made sure you were all taken care of. As it was, they did continue to let him work there, allowing any time off, as you know, but to Clive, that wasn't enough … And Alice, if he offers compensation now, you must take it. Your father died through an accident at the factory, which may have been prevented if Clive's father had spent money on long overdue repairs.'

'Oh? I didn't know that.' Alice felt anger fill her as she thought about how much she and the lads had lost of their once loving da, and how Ma had too, as she died without her beloved husband by her side, and all because of someone's negligence.

'Alice, darling, don't dwell on that side of it all. Clive and his father tried very hard to compensate your father, and offered far more than your father would take as a final payout from working at the factory.'

'I can't help it. I'm not angry at Clive, but I am at his father.'

'With good cause. But there is nothing more to be done now, and I don't want you getting bitter about it. That emotion can only destroy you.'

Alice looked out of the window and watched Talbot Road disappear as the car turned into their street. Gerald was right, she knew that, but a part of her would never forget what he'd told her, and yes, if more compensation than her da had accepted was offered, she would take it for the boys and their future. Harry was a clever young man, something she'd always been aware of and yet had ignored until Jackie had made her see it, and it was too late to do anything about it. Lately, though, through his deepening friendship with Jackie, she saw it more and more, and regretted that it was never possible for her to have paid for private tutoring like Marg was doing.

Her da would have stopped any such ideas.

Now, she would dearly love for him to continue his education and get a better job than working in the rock factory.

The atmosphere back at Alice's house wasn't sombre. Edith and Marg took charge of making the tea for everyone, and Jackie served the snacks. Alice so wanted to ask her if she was all right and tell her how sorry she was to hear about her ma, but a little warning from Marg stopped her.

'You'll notice our Jackie ain't the same, Alice. There is a reason, other than Ma being in hospital, and I'm trying to help her. Me and Edith are thinking of having a chinwag outside mine tonight. Can you come over for a bit? Only I'll have to be near for Gran and I've a lot to tell you that will explain what's been on mine and Jackie's mind.'

'Aye, I will. Gerald has to leave before tea, as he's on a late shift. Perhaps Jackie'll come and sit with Harry? The lads will be happy enough kicking a ball around outside and I can keep me eye on them. I can't get them to bed these light nights.'

Alice lost Marg after they'd made these arrangements, as when Marg took Clive his cup of tea the pair got into deep conversation.

'That was good to hear, Alice, and will make me feel more settled in my mind about you, knowing that you're going to be with the girls tonight. I've been worrying about you and wishing I didn't have to leave. Oh, I know you have the boys, but it's you that has to be strong for them when you need someone to give you comfort.'

'Eeh, you never need worry. There's always someone in the street to turn to. And after having suffered a loss, your door-step's never empty, with the neighbours checking that you're all right.'

'I still can't get used to that. We've never had visitors that haven't been invited first. I like it. It feels like you belong to a family much bigger than your immediate one. It's made me think that, when I do get around to having my own practice, I want it to be around here, or in a community like this one.'

Alice still struggled to accept that someone like Gerald could love her. She lay awake at night thinking of what it will mean for her, and asking herself what a doctor's wife would have to do or need to know, and the burning question – would his family and friends accept her? Always, she consoled herself with knowing that Gerald would steer her through it, and she swore to herself that, should it happen, she would do whatever it took to be the best wife that she could be.

These thoughts made her giggle – here she was thinking of marriage and Gerald hadn't even asked her, and might never do so.

'Oh, and what's so amusing about me being a doctor in this area, then?'

His half-smile and the way he cocked one eyebrow made her want to take him in her arms and hug him. She so loved every new expression and all the little ways of his that she was discovering.

'I was giggling at me thoughts, not at you being a doctor around here. I can think of nothing better for us than to have someone like you – we usually end up with a grumpy old doctor who is about to retire and can't wait to do so, but wants every penny he can get his hands on. They always make us pay the going rate when most around here can't afford to. The best doctor we had left us about six years back. He'd come and see us the minute we sent for him, and we could pay him in jars of homemade jam if we couldn't afford to pay the penny insurance.'

'Penny insurance? I've never heard of that one.'

'No, it was something he started himself. If we all paid a penny a week, no matter if we never needed him, then he would treat us for whatever ailed us, no question of what the cost was to him.'

'That's ingenious. What a good fellow he must have been.'

'He was. When he retired, if there was a family that had paid in but never used his services, then he paid them every penny back. A few got a nice little sum – as if they'd been saving for all those years.'

'Hmm, that was generous of him. So, this penny insurance – did it cover the whole family, or did each member have to pay?

'It was a penny for each adult member of the family over sixteen and a ha'penny for each child. I know my da paid it as I used to take the fourpence to the surgery every Saturday morning. As it happens, it was nowhere near what it would have cost for the attention me and my brothers needed – we caught everything going. But then, it evened out with those who paid and didn't need much care from him – a sort of just-in-case payment. Now, most folk around here rely on Ada Arkwright as she charges a lot less.'

'Oh, yes, I met Ada. She seemed well versed in first aid. Has she any qualifications? Where is she, by the way?'

'She nursed in the Great War, and she's taking care of Marg's gran at the moment.'

'Oh? Is her gran sick?'

'No . . . well, not as such. She's lost her marbles, so we never know what she'll do next. She wanders off a lot and has lost her memory – at least, her recent memory; she knows all about the past and thinks that is now. She's a lovely woman, though, and Marg won't hear of her going to an asylum.'

'She probably has Alzheimer's disease. Not a lot is known about it, but it was identified by a doctor of that name thirty-three years ago. There's nothing that can be done, it just requires patience and taking care of the sufferer. There's no one better than a member of the family to do that, but in some sad cases the asylum is the only option we have.'

'Aw, poor things.'

'Yes. Well, my dear, I have to go. Will you walk to my car with me?'

On the way, Gerald said his goodbyes to everyone.

They made their way to his car in silence. He'd left it just around the corner so that it was out of the way of the funeral cars. When they reached it, Gerald held her close for a moment. 'I hate leaving you, Alice. And not just because of the circumstances. I feel that I want – no, *need* – to be with you all of the time.'

'I feel the same about you.' A shyness came over Alice and she kept her head down.

'You've so much to contend with at the moment, but do you think we could go out to dinner soon?'

'I work in the daytime, so I can't.'

'Oh, I meant in the evening.'

'You mean tea? Aye, I could do that. Harry could watch over Billy and Joey – they always do as he says anyway – and Edith would be on hand as Marg works in the evenings. We could go to the chippy.'

Gerald was quiet for a moment. He looked taken aback, but his expression changed in an instant as he put his head back and laughed out loud.

'Shush! Gerald, I don't want folk thinking I'm being disrespectful to my da!'

'Sorry, darling, but that was so funny. I didn't mean . . . I mean, I wasn't . . . Oh dear, forgive me.'

'I do, but I don't see anything funny in what I said.' Alice was mystified – what could be funny in them going out at teatime instead of dinnertime?

'No, you're right. Tea it is. I would love to go to the chippy with you sometime. Is there one we can sit in?'

'You're a Blackpool lad and you don't know that! Aye, there's dozens of them. The best is The Cottage on Newhouse Road.'

'Well then, how about Monday? I have a mixture of shifts till then as I've been put on call all weekend.'

'No, they close on a Monday after the busy weekend.'

'Tuesday?'

'Aye, that'd be grand.'

'It would be grand to see you on Monday too.' Again, Gerald chuckled, before kissing her lightly on the lips. Alice saw a longing in Gerald's eyes as he held her gaze, before jumping in his car and starting the engine as if his life depended on it.

'Bye, darling. I'll see you on Monday evening.'

He blew a kiss and was gone, leaving Alice feeling lost for a moment. When she was with Gerald, she felt whole and strong, as if she could cope with everything.

Banishing the feeling, she took a deep breath. *This won't do. I have to be strong with or without Gerald by my side. The lads need me to be.*

TWENTY-ONE

Marg

The evening was warm, though there was a breeze that whipped down the avenue as the three of them sat on the pavement in their usual positions – Alice and Edith each side of Marg.

Marg put her arms around them both and pulled them close. 'It all went well today for you, Alice, love. I'm glad. You must be feeling a bit . . . well, as if you've got to somehow fit back into normal life, when yours has been anything but normal for a week . . . or rather, for a long time.'

'Aye, I do feel strange. As if none of today happened, and yet it did.'

'It was a lovely service with what Clive did,' Marg changed her tone. 'Eeh, he's a nice man.'

Edith winked at Alice. 'We knew somehow you thought that.'

'By, give over, we were only talking.'

'Aye, as if there was no one else in the room!'

'Don't you start, Alice! Ha, you'll have me married off next.'

Edith laughed. 'Aye, and into money an' all. That'll be you and Alice moving up into the posh world. Don't leave me behind, will you?'

'No, you daft apeth, we'd never do that ... Flipping heck, you've got me talking as if it's going to happen. It wasn't like that. Clive talked about his sons, and about how he'd been lost since his wife died. Oh, and a bit about the rock factory and how they're going to open their own shop on the front.'

'That's a good idea, though there's a few of them already. Not that there's not room for another – no one who visits Blackpool can resist buying rock. You see them walking around with bags full, as if they're going to give one each to everyone in their street when they get back ... Anyroad, enough about today. This is meant to be us listening to you, Marg.' Alice squeezed her arm as she said this. 'Come on, out with it. I'm sure it isn't as bad as you think.'

At this, Marg explained all that had come to light. She was crying by the time she'd finished and it was Alice and Edith who were cuddling her. Neither spoke for a while, then Alice, always the one to say the right thing, said, 'None of this is your fault, Marg, and it doesn't sound as though it was your uncle's – your real da's – either. But you know, it's easy to judge others. I know that better than most, so though it sounds bad on your ma, maybe she didn't have a lot of choice. Love can make you do things you wouldn't normally do.'

'Alice is right. I told you that the other day – Marg told me about this when we were collecting for your da, Alice. Anyway, Marg, it seems to me that the worst one in all of this was the man you thought was your da. He didn't seem to care enough

221

about your ma or his brother. He only seemed to care about himself.'

'I know, Edith, and yet, well, I remember him being such a good da, kind and loving. I can't separate that from what I know now – he was evil. None of it fits.'

'I don't want to upset you more than you are already, Marg . . .' Alice hesitated, made Marg wonder what she was going to say. She didn't interrupt, but waited for her to continue.

'Well . . . supposing the man you thought of as your da used you and Jackie an' all? I mean, you were another weapon to use against his brother to get what he wanted – more money to feed his habit – and maybe his demands were such that his brother had to do more and more bad stuff to get money to keep what he most desired, your ma . . . and, well, you an' all. He's always been different with you.'

'He has, though there were times I was scared of him.'

'I can understand that. But when I think about it, I'd say I'm more afraid of his reputation than him. And that's probably the same for you – worse, as you've been fed hatred for him from your ma and your gran. But he's never done anything to you, has he? Even when you couldn't pay him back what you borrowed, he made a really reasonable payment schedule for you.'

Marg had to admit that Alice was right.

'So, what about your ma, Marg? This isn't like you. It's seemed strange all day. I mean, I know there was the funeral and we all wanted to support Alice, but for you not to want to go early to see your ma. Nor Jackie – she never once tried to get away. Your ma must be breaking her heart alone in that hospital.'

'That's if she is alone, Edith. Eric most likely stayed with her, which makes me feel better that she's got someone, but I just don't feel ready yet.'

'But from what you said, she wouldn't want him, she would want you both. Besides, Jackie needs to know how her ma is. Why don't you go up to the hospital to see her, eh? Me and Alice'll look out for your gran and Jackie.'

'I don't know . . .'

'I agree with Edith: I think that you should go, love.'

Marg knew they were right. She stood up. 'It'll take me a while to walk it, but aye, I reckon both me and Jackie should go. Will you run over to yours, Alice, and tell Jackie to come home?'

'Aye, I will, lass. I'm so glad you're going. Your ma has always meant the world to you, don't change that because you've found out some bad things about her. Like I say, it's so easy to judge, but not easy to live through what she had to. And you don't have to walk, I'll get Billy to run to Mr Riley's on Talbot Road. I'll pay whatever he charges, I have a bit of money left of what me da had.'

As they sat in the back of the small car, hardly able to see out of the windows, Marg held Jackie's hand. 'They might not let us see Ma, lass, but at least we can leave a message to say we've been.'

'I'm not sure I want to see her, Marg.'

'I know, I've felt like that too, but let's do this, eh? Do it for the ma we've always known, and forget for the time being the one we've discovered.'

'I'll try, but I feel so angry with her.'

Marg couldn't say anything to this. She knew the feeling and didn't blame Jackie.

'Oh no!'

'What? What's wrong, Marg?'

'Look who's standing at the hospital doors having a fag!'

Jackie visibly cringed when she caught sight of Eric. She grabbed Marg's arm.

'It's all right, lass.' Marg squeezed Jackie's hand.

Eric came over to them as they alighted. 'Jackie, lass, I had naw idea! I'm sorry, lass. God, that brother of mine's got a lot to answer for.'

Jackie stiffened and her grip on Marg's arm tightened. Marg tried to reassure her. 'It's all right, lass.'

'Aye, it is. I don't blame you for being afraid of me, I ain't exactly given you the time of day. But you knaw, well, I didn't know the truth until now.' He put his head in his hand and turned way. 'God! I've treated me own daughter like she was a carbuncle on me happiness. But I didn't knaw, I swear.' He turned to face them. 'I don't blame you if you're afraid of me, or can't stand the sight of me, lass. Nor you, Marg. I always had to act in a different way to how I felt. One day I'll explain, but for now I think you need to visit your ma. She's pining for you both.'

'Will they let us in?'

'Aye, they will, Marg, lass. Your ma's in a private ward and that means that I call the shots, not them. I'll lead the way. But no upsetting her, or you'll have me to contend with.'

This wasn't said in a truly threatening way – more how a father would warn a child.

Marg's anger began to waver. She looked at Jackie, but couldn't read what was going on in her mind.

When the door to the side ward was opened by a nurse who'd seen them coming, Marg wanted to dash forward, but Eric's hand stayed her. 'I'll go and make sure she can take your visit.'

He closed the door behind him.

'Eh, Marg, Ma must have told him about me … I feel strange in me belly, like I've got a whole army marching around inside me.'

Marg had to smile. Jackie had always had a way with how she expressed things – the usual butterflies in her stomach would not do, it had to be a whole army marching!

'I've a feeling that it's going to be all right, lass. Uncle Eric seems different somehow.'

'Will we still call him Uncle Eric, even though he's our da?'

'I don't know. I think we'll wait and see on that one.'

The door opened. 'Right, in you both come.' Eric's smile was kindly. Marg didn't know how to deal with this new version of him, but on seeing her ma sitting up against a mound of pillows with an oxygen mask on her face, she forgot everything but her concern.

'Eeh, Ma. I'm sorry I haven't been. It was the funeral.'

'I knaw … I … didn't expect you, me lasses.'

'She's been very poorly, and out of it for most of the time. The doctor said that some of the breathing problems are caused by panic – you can't get your breath so you panic and the whole situation gets worse. But they gave her sommat that knocked her out, you see, and then they took over the work of her breathing. She's a lot better now.'

Again, Eric sounded kindly. He looked at Jackie and smiled. Jackie looked away, as if about to take flight.

'Jackie, I knaw I ain't given the best impression of meself, but once you get to knaw the real me, it'll all be all right, I promise. I'm going to see to your education. Your ma's always on about how clever you are and she says you want to study with a scientist bloke. Well, you will, me little lass, you will. And how do you both feel about us mo—'

'Naw ... naw, Eric ... not ... yet. Leave it!'

Ma started to cough, after struggling to get her protest out.

'I thought you wanted them to knaw, Vera?'

Ma shook her head and gasped, 'Not yet ... leave ... us, Eric.'

Eric sighed heavily. The look he gave Ma as he left showed that he was none too pleased.

'Ma, what's all this about? Eeh, Ma, look at you.' Marg's tears rained down her face as she bent over her ma and tried to hold her. Hearing Jackie sob helped her to control herself. Straightening, she put her arm out to her sister and held her close.

'By, what're we like, eh, lass? Poor Ma lying there and we come and mope over her. Sorry, Ma, but it's such a shock to see you like this.'

'I knaw, me lasses ... but you coming, has helped me. G – give Eric a chance ... he knew nothing of you b – being his, Jackie. It's your ma to blame ... I – I'm sorry.'

'No, Ma, don't upset yourself. I'm all right, ain't I, Marg? I'm only upset to see you like this.'

Ma gave a little smile.

'She is, Ma. She was shocked, but she's all right, she just needs time. We both do. It's a lot for us to take on board.'

'I knaw. I – I wanted Eric to take it steady ... he never does. He's like ...'

'Don't talk so much, Ma, all can be said later. I've a lot of questions – well, we both have – but when you're better we'll sort it all out.'

'Aye, lass ... I can ... con – concentrate on getting better now.'

'Jackie will come to see you tomorrow, Ma. I can't leave Gran with someone again and Jackie needs a rest from taking care of her, but I'll come on Monday. It'll be late, like this, as I've to go to Fairweather's after work or I'll lose me job and we'll be in a right state then.'

'Naw, we – we're going to be all right ... Eric, he—'

'We'll see, Ma. Like I say, let's have time to think about everything first. Me and Jackie need to do that. Just carry on how we are for now, eh?'

Ma nodded. Marg kissed her and squeezed her hand. She waited while Jackie said her goodbyes then took her hand as they walked out.

Eric stood outside. He seemed to have calmed and his eager expression asked questions of them.

Marg shook her head. 'We need time, Uncle Eric.'

'Aye, I could have done with that meself, but your ma wanted things settled.'

Marg understood this. Ma would be afraid she was dying and needed something in place for them, but this was too big for them to handle in five minutes.

'Look, me lasses, I'll go and say me goodbyes to your ma then run you home.'

For all the world, Marg wanted to refuse as she would have enjoyed the walk home, and wanted to be away from Eric for a while, but that would mean being out for another half an

227

hour and that wasn't fair on Edith and Alice – especially Alice, with the day she'd had.

On the journey home, Eric didn't speak. Marg was glad of this. She couldn't have taken it if he'd started telling of his plans he had for them. She wasn't ready to accept him as her da yet and didn't know if she ever would be.

When they arrived home, Edith was at the door to meet them. 'So, how's your ma, Marg?'

'I'm worried for her, lass. It was upsetting to see her like that.'

Before she could say more, Eric leant out of his car window. 'Well, I'll leave you to it.' He looked at Jackie then. 'I'll pick you up tomorrow afternoon, if you like, lass. Your ma said you're going to go up to see her.'

'Naw, I'll be all right, ta. I can walk.'

'All right. So, can I give you a lift on Monday night, Marg, lass?'

'Ta, that'd be grand, Uncle Eric. I finish at Fairweather's around eight.'

'You can pack that in now, lass. Didn't your ma tell you?'

'No, we stopped her. Please, Uncle Eric, just leave it for now.'

'Righto. But you can't expect me not to look out for you.'

'I know. Ta. I'll see you tomorrow. Goodnight.'

Marg ushered Edith and Jackie inside and closed the door. Leaning on it, she sighed heavily. Her life seemed broken at this moment.

'Not good news, then?'

'No, Edith. Worrying really. Anyroad, how's things been here?'

'Well, not long after you left, your gran started wandering. She's been upset. She was trying to find you all, but not as you are now, bless her. She got so frustrated she started to cry. I took her over to me ma and she helped her. It was lovely to see as your gran remembered me ma and da, and she's sat chatting with them at ours as if nothing's wrong in any of their worlds.'

'Eeh, Edith, ta, lass.'

'Come on over, the pair of you, and I'll make you a drink.

Marg felt tired to her bones, but just smiled and agreed.

'The thing is, Marg, me ma didn't challenge your gran. Me and Alice tried to remind your gran of where she was and how you were no longer a child, but she got in a state. Oh, Alice had to go home to bed, by the way; she said to give you her love. Anyroad, Ma took a different approach; she handled your gran really well. She just said, "Hello, Sandra, lass, have them young 'uns gone off again? Eeh, they give you the runaround. I bet your Vera has taken them off to the park, she's always doing that." And your gran just giggled, and agreed to having a cup of tea. Ma then asked her about her brother and her hubby, and before long she was back in the present and remembering they were both gone and telling of their antics. She was having a real laugh with Ma. Me da joined in an' all. Eeh, they've got some tales of the goings-on when they were all young.'

'I knaw. I remember when we were young 'uns, we used to love to listen to them, when they didn't know we were there.'

'Ha! We did. But they never meant a lot to me then. Now I know just what devils they all were.'

'You'll have to tell me about it sometime ... So, you're saying that it's best to agree with Gran and give her reasons why she can't find who she's looking for?'

'Aye. Ma didn't say that your gran's husband had passed on, she just said he'd popped out for some fags. Your gran was happy then and soon forgot she was even asking for him. I know it's lying to her, but surely it's best to keep her happy than have her all upset?'

'I reckon it is. I've done this sometimes and it has settled her, but to know that someone else thinks it best has cheered me and made me see it is the right way. Ta, lass, you've put new life into me. By, when you said I was to make cocoa for you all, I didn't know how I was to put one foot in front of the other, but now, well, I could jump through hoops.' They laughed as Marg hooked arms with Edith and Jackie and said, 'Come on, we can get through all of this, as long as we can always have a giggle – and by, I ain't drinking yours or Alice's cocoa ever again. I'll make it, even if I'm dropping on me feet.'

When Gran's lovely giggles met her as they went into Edith's house, Marg felt her spirits lift even more.

Nothing's as bad as it's painted, I should remember that.

TWENTY-TWO

Edith

As Edith got ready for bed, she felt the weight of her friends' troubles, but was glad that her own problems had eased a little. Albert had promised to contribute a weekly sum, which would help, though his better mood would help even more, and her ma had been sober for more than one day, which made her da happier and had a good effect on his health.

Sighing, she knew that though all was good, it was fragile, and could come crashing down at any minute. Albert was unpredictable, and Ma even more so. Edith knew that she could come home from work any evening and find that all had changed.

Her thoughts turned, as they always did, to the night that she and Alice were treated by Marg to the flicks and a trip into town.

Was it such a short while ago that I was in heaven, dancing with Philip Bradshaw?

Such a lot had happened since.

Feeling the same restlessness she felt whenever she thought of Philip, she turned over, trying to displace the silly longing to have him hold her again. It could never happen. But though she tried, he didn't leave her, and she was in his arms as she drifted off to sleep.

The restless feeling stayed with Edith when she awoke the next morning. Trying to shake it off, she tackled the cleaning downstairs, but no matter how much heart she put into sweeping, dusting, mopping and beating the rugs over the washing line, she couldn't get Marg's and Alice's problems out of her head, and neither could she get Philip Bradshaw out of her heart.

'You're up early, lass.'

Ma came through the door to the kitchen, her hair still tied in the rags she put it in every night to make it curl.

'Morning, Ma. Aye, I couldn't sleep. There's so much sadness in the street at the moment.'

'You mean with Alice and Marg, love? Don't worry. I know you say Alice loved her da, and I don't doubt it, but I've a feeling her and the lads are going to be better off without him. And she's got that doctor sweet on her an' all; that's a turn-up for a lass from this street. Alice'll be fine. And Marg will be an' all when her ma comes out of hospital.'

'I know they will up to a point, but they've a lot to contend with.'

'I knaw, lass. Eeh, poor Marg, I feel for her. Her gran's hard work, but she'll cope, we can all help her with that. I enjoyed me time with Sandra. We used to always get on well afore she lost her marbles and didn't knaw who I was . . . Look, I'll just go and have this fag while your da gets up, then I'll cook them bacon strips you got from the butcher yesterday. They'll make a nice bacon butty for us all. You go up and get our Albert up, eh?'

'No, Ma, he don't like to be got up on a Sunday morning. He came in late last night. Let him sleep. If the smell of the bacon frying wakes him, well then, that's all right, but I ain't going to disturb him. It'll be like waking an angry lion.'

Her ma laughed at this. 'Aye, all right then, lass.'

'Ma, I thought I might go to church.'

'Church? You ain't been for years! What's brought this on?'

'Well, you know that it's tradition to go to mass as soon as you can after someone's been buried? Alice said something about it last night. She wants to be there when prayers are offered for her da, and I said I'd go with her. We talked about going to the eleven o'clock.'

'Well, it'll be nice for Alice to have you support her. I'll get your butty done while you get ready, but I'll have me fag first. It's only half past nine.'

Edith considered offering to cook the bacon, but she got the feeling her ma really wanted to do it for her, so instead she went through to the front door and unlocked it. Stepping outside, she found the street alive with nattering women and kids kicking a football – Billy and Joey among them as if they hadn't a care in the world, and Edith supposed that, like her ma had said, they hadn't now.

At the sound of her neighbours calling to one another, and the delicious smell of food frying wafting through open doors, Edith was overcome by the feeling of being part of a family of folk she'd known all her life.

Just then, Marg appeared and called over to her. 'Morning, Edith, want a cuppa? I've just made a full pot.'

'Aye, I will. Ta.'

A few moments later, they were leaning against Edith's wall sipping the steaming mugs of tea that Marg had brought over. To Edith, Marg seemed like a different person to how she was the evening before. 'You sound cheerful, Marg, did you sleep well?'

'Aye, I did. Did you?'

'Apart from my dreams. They woke me a couple of times.'

'Ha! I can guess who they were about. Did he get you into bed?'

'Marg!' Edith grinned. 'As it happens, he was just going to when I woke up.'

'I know, always happens at the best bit. Then you try to direct the dream and it's not the same. Anyroad, I reckon you've got a chance with Philip Bradshaw. You just need to get a meeting with him again – an accidental-on-purpose one that you make happen.'

'How can I do that, you daft apeth?'

'Well, we know he lives on Newton Drive, near to Alice's Gerald. You should walk down there, you might bump into him.'

'No, I couldn't do that. Anyroad, me and Alice and the lads are going to church. We decided last night while you were at the hospital, but I don't suppose you can come?'

'No. I ain't one for church as you know, but I've made me mind up not to leave Gran today. I don't have much time with her as it is. I want to give Jackie a good break – she has to go to the hospital this afternoon 'cause she promised Ma.'

'Is she up yet? She might like to come as Harry's coming.'

'Ha! More than likely. They seem inseparable now. Funny that, when you think how they never showed much interest in each other when they were kids – not that they're much more than that now.'

'That's because Jackie was always at lessons or with her head in a book. She always struck me as a lonely kid.'

'No, not Jackie. I've never worried about her. She's happy enough. She just loves learning. I doubt she'd have been interested in other kids even if there were some girls of her age. While I can't imagine life without you and Alice.'

'Me neither. Has it felt strange to you, with Alice courting now?'

'It has a bit. As if we're losing her, little by little. She's seeing Gerald tomorrow night, and then on Tuesday they're going to the chippy together.'

'Aye, I suppose it had to happen. I wonder which one of us'll be next?'

'You with your dashing boss's son, most likely, Edith. Whereas me? I've no chance.'

'What about the rock factory owner's son, then? Clive?'

Marg hit her playfully. 'Ha! Don't start matchmaking. He's at least twelve years older than me.'

'You didn't say you didn't like him, though, did you?'

'No, he's a lovely man, and attractive an' all, if a little sad. But we chatted as if we were brother and sister, there wasn't anything else in it. We just clicked, that's all. He was easy to chat to and needed someone to hook on to as he didn't know any of us – well, only in passing. It was nice of Alice to ask him back, though; he strikes me as being a lonely soul.'

'Ha, you've analysed him already. I told you, you've a spark for him.'

'I ain't! Anyroad, I'm leaving you now, you're a daft apeth. See you later, and say a prayer for me, won't you?'

'Aye, I will. I'll pray that Clive comes down the street riding a white charger and sweeps you off your feet!'

They both laughed out loud at this.

The smell of the bacon lured Edith back inside. Her whole mood had lifted and she skipped through to the kitchen.

Finding her ma standing at the stove deftly tossing the bacon pieces in the sizzling fat, she was filled with an over-whelming love and went to put her arms around her waist from behind.

'Eeh, lass, that's a good cuddle, and very welcome.' Her ma turned and took her in her arms. 'By, I've not been a good ma, have I, Edith?'

'You've always loved us, Ma, you couldn't help your sickness.'

'Aye, it is that, me darling. Sommat as has got hold of me. I shouldn't have let it, but I'm trying hard to fight it now.'

'I know, and I'll help you all I can.'

'Maybe say a prayer for me while you're on your knees in the church, lass?'

'Ha! God's going to be very busy on my behalf, I've such a lot to ask Him – not least for a white charger to bring Marg the man who's sweet on her.'

Her ma let go of her and turned back to the bacon. 'What you on about? What white charger? Eeh, you're a dafty some-times, our lass.'

As her ma slapped some lovely crispy bacon onto the door-steps of bread that she had laid out, Edith had her laughing with her tale of Clive.

'He's a nice bloke from what I saw of him yesterday in the church. So, he made a beeline for Marg, did he? She could do worse, though I agree he's a little old for her, and he spoke of having a child, didn't he? Naw, I wouldn't wish him on her, for all he's handsome and well set up.'

'Children – well, he did say his youngest son.'

This made her ma chunter more about unsuitability. Edith didn't agree, but then, she was party to more than her ma was, and would like nothing more than to see Marg taken care of by someone as nice as Clive, who could make sure that horrid uncle-come-da of hers didn't cause her harm.

As they walked to church, the boys and Harry, along with Jackie, who'd jumped at the chance to tag along, lagged behind a little, giving Edith and Alice a chance to chat. Alice wanted to know how Marg was when she came back from the hospital.

Edith told her how cheered she was to see her gran lucid and having a laugh.

'I feel for her, Edith. I wonder how all of this business with Eric Porter will pan out?'

'I don't know, lass. All we can do is be there for her as we always are, though it seems funny as she always seemed to be the strong one.'

'No, I think you are. You're level-headed and take stuff in your stride more than we do. You cope better an' all, as you've as much to put up with as we do.'

237

'I didn't know you thought that. Ta, love, I do try to keep me chin up through it all. My biggest worry is my da. I can see him failing every day.'

'I know, lass, and I'm sorry. There should be more help for the miners. They work in awful conditions for long hours and end up diseased like your da. It ain't right.'

'Well, if I'm the strong one, you're the one who always wants to put things right, Alice. Not a do-gooder, but a kindly soul who takes on the troubles of the world.'

'I'm always wishing that I could be of some help to folk. I feel wasted packing biscuits. Since meeting Gerald, I feel that I would have loved to do something medical – a nurse maybe – but there's no chance that lasses like us can be anything like that, we'd never afford the training.'

'Well, there's other work in hospitals, ain't there? I saw some volunteers who were packing away books they'd taken around to the patients on a trolley.'

'Aye, I know, but they're a posh lot an' all. I'd never fit in with them.'

They were quiet for a moment. Alice broke the silence with a change of subject. 'I've been thinking lately about it being our twentieth birthdays soon. We should organise a party for the three of us. It could still be nice in September and we could arrange a picnic in the street. It was lovely in May when we had the street party for the King's coronation. We all said then that we should do that more often.'

'That's a good idea, lass. The coronation party was great fun. Eeh, that sketch your lads did had us all in stitches. Billy was hilarious as Charlie Chaplin.' They both laughed out loud at the memory.

The younger ones caught up with them and asked what they were laughing at, and then joined in the banter as they all reminisced.

'I'd have loved to have joined in with you all, I could have been Gracie Fields.' With this, Jackie went into a cackling take-off of Gracie Field's best-known song, 'Sally', which set a dog barking and had them all doubled over with tears running down their face, until an old lady put her head out of the upstairs window of her house and shouted, 'Bugger off, making that racket on a Sunday morning! Get down your own end and wake that lot of lazy arses up.'

With this they ran as they giggled, and didn't stop to wait for Harry, until they were a good distance from the woman's house. 'Eeh, you grown-ups should knaw better than leading us astray. I thought she'd empty her piddle pot on us.'

'Ha, the cheek of it, Jackie-Gracie-Fields! It was your doing! Mind, you sounded a brilliant mimic of the real Gracie. I think we'll book you for our show. What do you think, Alice?'

'Aye, I agree. The four of you can start practising. We want a proper show, mind.'

Harry, Billy, Joey and Jackie began a conversation after this that kept them happy for the rest of the way, and judging by their giggles, they were cooking up some good acts.

As they came to the end of Collingwood Avenue and turned into Newton Drive, Edith shushed them all. 'We're nearly there now so we'd better behave.'

When they arrived at St Kentigern's they chose to slip into a pew at the back, and then took a minute on their knees before sitting and waiting for the priest to come to the altar. Edith prayed hard for everything in her family to stay normal

– well, what she would like normal to be for them – and for Marg's and Alice's situations to get better too.

When they sat back, Alice nudged her and pointed towards a family just getting seated. A warmth crept through Edith as she saw who it was. Philip Bradshaw looked beautiful with the sun shining down on him through the stained-glass window as he helped an elderly lady into her seat. Once she was settled, he turned to seat himself in the pew behind.

It was then that he caught sight of her.

He looked startled for a moment, then smiled and nodded. The warmth in Edith spread to her face. She smiled back at him, trying not to make her joy overspill into a grin, which would have made her look silly.

The service went over her head after that as her imagination had her with Philip, sitting next to him, holding his hand, and even seeing two little children in her mind's eye – one sitting each side of them.

'Edith . . . Edith.' Alice nudged her.

Reluctantly turning her eyes from the back of Philip's head, she whispered, 'What?'

'The collection, I forgot all about the collection. Have you got some coppers on you?'

Edith's heart stopped. She hadn't brought her purse. She hadn't thought about the collection either, but in any case, her purse only had enough for the rest of the week's groceries in it. 'No, I forgot too. Shall we go before it comes to us?'

Too late. Two men were walking towards the back of the church to collect the brass plates and make their rounds. Edith died at that moment as she saw that they were Philip and his father.

Please let his father do our row!

But it was Philip who came to them, a lovely smile on his face.

Alice shook her head. Edith, her face burning, looked up at Philip and mouthed, *Sorry, we don't have any money.*

Philip winked, then to her surprise, he put his hand in his pocket and dropped coins noisily onto the plate. His dark eyes held amusement as he smiled at her, as well as something else that she couldn't understand, but it took away her embarrassment and had her smiling back at him.

Once he'd moved a few pews away, Alice whispered, 'Is that all you two are ever going to do, smile at each other?'

Edith giggled, earning herself a look that could kill from the woman in front, who hmphed loudly as she turned back to face the altar. This set the lads off. All three were stuffing their fists into their mouths in an attempt not to giggle out loud, but it was infectious as they spluttered anyway.

Edith wanted to die as the woman turned again and in a loud whisper told them, 'Be quiet! You are being disrespectful! Go outside if you can't control yourselves!'

After this it seemed that everyone looked in their direction. Joey's giggles turned to tears, having the effect of sobering the other two as they helped Joey to clamber towards Alice.

The lovely priest surprised everyone by saying, 'Suffer little children to come unto me. Is it that you are all forgetting why Jesus said this? These young people are the children of the gentleman I had the sad duty of burying yesterday. If it filled them with joy to come to God's house, who are we to condemn? Little Joey, don't you be shedding any tears. It is that we prefer to hear you giggling, and I'm sure it is that the same is true of the Lord too. He doesn't want to see you weep, but to be happy in his house.'

The lady spoke up. 'Sorry, Father, I didn't know, and I didn't mean to upset the child.'

'No, I would never be thinking that of you, Mrs Crowath. Perk up, Joey, the best bit of our mass is coming, where I perform my magic and a miracle happens as the bread turns into the body of Christ. Watch carefully or you will miss it.'

There was a ripple of laughter and the atmosphere became relaxed again. Philip hadn't turned around before, but he did now. He looked straight at Edith, his amusement clear to see.

Edith glanced at Alice, but with her being preoccupied with trying to calm Joey she hadn't noticed, leaving Edith to savour the moment and feel hopeful that she and Philip could be friends.

It's a start. I want to be more, but I never thought I'd achieve even this.

But then, she told herself off for being so fanciful, and concentrated on what the priest was doing. As she did, she began to enjoy the sensation the mass was giving her – the peace and the sense of being lifted out of the humdrum world she lived in. The prayers she said meant more to her than those she'd uttered when they'd first come into the church, and it felt to her that she was being listened to.

Outside in the sunshine, with mass now over, the priest was greeting folk as they came out of church, causing a delay to the crush of people eager to leave.

'Hello again.'

Edith turned. Just behind her, Philip was patiently shuffling forward with the rest of them. 'Hello, I didn't think you'd remember me.'

'Oh, I do. How can I forget? I came out of the Tower looking for you. But you were like Cinderella, only you didn't wait for midnight before you disappeared.'

'Oh? I – I'm sorry I missed you, but we had a bit of a crisis.'

'Anything to do with the death you suffered? I was sorry to learn of that. Nice to hear the prayers for the gentleman's soul at the end. The priest called him a very brave man.'

'Aye, he was, and yes, a little to do with that, but he was Alice's da, not mine. You remember, Gerald was dancing with her? I'm just supporting her.'

'Oh, I see. Gerald's told me about her, of course. And the boys – are they the brothers Gerald mentioned?'

'Aye, they are. They've been through a lot.'

'I'm sure. Is that why you're attending mass, to hear the prayers for the deceased? I know it is a tradition to do that.'

'Aye, but, well, I enjoyed it and might come again.'

'I, too, enjoy mass. The peace after a busy week, and the feeling that someone is listening just to you. I know you'll be very welcome so don't worry about what happened. Some are a little stuffy about it all, but as you see, the priest isn't.'

'Aye, I felt that, and understood. Anyroad, I'll not forget the collection next time. Ta for covering for us. I felt such a fool.'

'Not at all. I just didn't want you getting looks, though you got those anyway with the giggling. What amused you?'

Edith blushed.

'Oh, I see, you can't tell me, sorry. I hope it wasn't something I did?'

'Oh no!' Suddenly, Edith didn't want to leave it there. Though she knew it would be forward of her, she wanted to grab the moment. 'Well, it was, actually.' She told him what Alice had said about them smiling at each other.

'Oh? Well, we could do more than that. I would love to go for a walk with you and get to know you better. I know you work in my father's factory, have a beautiful face, a lovely smile, and can dance like Ginger Rogers, but that's it.'

Edith's heart leapt with joy. 'I'd love that.'

'Are you free this afternoon?'

Edith could hardly speak, she just nodded.

'Can I pick you up at home or do you want to meet somewhere?'

For the first time ever, Edith felt ashamed of her home. On top of that, she feared how her ma would be, and if Albert would be about – she didn't trust either of them not to let her down. 'I can meet you in Stanley Park around three-ish, if that's all right?'

'That would be splendid! I look forward to it.'

There was no time to say more as the queue in front of them lessened, and they were greeted by the priest.

Alice linked arms with her as they moved away. 'So, what were you and Philip talking about, then?'

She told Alice what had been arranged with him.

'By, Edith, I'm that pleased for you, I think he's really sweet on you, I do.'

'Shush, he's coming.'

'Well, Edith, I will see you later. Bye for now.'

Before Edith could answer Philip, a young lady came up to him and grabbed his attention. As they walked away laughing together, Edith's hopes felt dashed as she took in the beauty of the lovely young woman and how she looked up at Philip, completely capturing his attention.

I'm an idiot! How could I think Philip could ever be interested in me? I'm just a plain girl, and from the poor end at that. I work for his father in the factory, for goodness' sake!

Making up her mind that he could only want her for one thing and probably thought of her as forward, she determined she wouldn't meet him that afternoon, or ever.

'Edith? What's up? You've gone from being happy to look-ing like thunder in moments.'

'I reckon he's only playing with me. Probably thinks of me as a pushover. Well, I ain't going this afternoon and that's it!'

'Edith, don't be so daft. He's bound to have friends like her, he moves in those circles; she might be his sister even. You'll soon tell if he's up to no good, then you can kick him and run, like our ma's always told us to.'

'Eeh, I don't know. Anyroad, I was going to spend the day with you, I don't want you on your own.'

'Well, I'm only going to walk to the cemetery with the lads. We want to make sure the flowers have been placed nicely and to read the cards an' all. I'd rather do that with just the lads, so that they can express themselves if they feel sad. They'd feel awkward in front of you, like they've got to keep a stiff upper lip. I don't want that for them.'

'Aye, they would. Best that you go alone to do that. But I don't know what to do.'

'Just go to the park, you daft apeth. You might never get another chance and if nothing else, you'll know one way or the other what his intentions are.'

Edith felt a smile coming on. 'Ha, you make it sound as though he might want to marry me!'

They both laughed out loud. Edith glanced towards Philip's car. He was on his own now. He looked back and lifted his hand to wave to her, and she knew in that moment that she would go along to Stanley Park. She only prayed that she wouldn't find that her fears were right.

When Edith set out, she realised they hadn't said what entrance they would meet at. She decided to go to the main entrance in West Park Drive and hoped she'd guessed right.

She'd changed the beige two-piece outfit she'd worn for a pretty white cotton frock patterned with blue cornflowers. It was calf-length, slightly flared and had a fitted bodice and a large, shawl-like, white lace collar, which fluttered in the breeze, keeping her cool. She'd bought the frock at a jumble sale about three years ago. It had been a church jumble, one that the posh ladies donated to, and so she knew it was of good quality, which gave her confidence. She'd slipped on some white sandals with a kitten heel. Though not the best for a long walk, she couldn't think of wearing her pumps as she had done that morning. She wanted to look her best.

By the time she arrived at the gates, Philip was already there. He waved to her as soon as she came into view, then came to meet her. 'I was beginning to think you weren't coming. You look beautiful. Very hot, but so lovely.'

With her face already flushed from the effort of walking in the heat, Edith thought he wouldn't notice her blush at this.

'Let's get ice cream. I saw a cart pull into the park a few

minutes ago. I'll tell you what, you sit on the first bench just inside and I'll run after him and bring each of us back a cone.'

Glad of the chance to sit down, Edith agreed. Once he'd gone, she eased her pinched feet out of the sandals and regretted ever putting how she looked above her comfort. She didn't know if she could manage walking around the park with Philip.

'Ha, they're melting! Come and meet me and get yours, Edith!'

Edith looked towards Philip, saw the beauty of him in his beige-coloured casual cotton suit, and caught her breath.

'Come on! We'll have none left!'

Getting up, forgetting to put her shoes back on, she ran to him, laughing at his antics of trying to lick one of the ice creams as it dripped down the side of the cone and onto the floor.

When she reached him, she went to take one from him, but he stepped closer to her. His gaze held hers and his eyes clouded over. 'Edith, I – I . . .' He looked away, and down at the ice creams. 'Here, take this one.'

The ice cream dripped onto her frock.

'Hold on.' Producing a handkerchief, he started to wipe her skirt when his own ice cream fell out of the cone and plonked onto his foot.

A giggle rose up in Edith, and try as she might to suppress it, it burst from her in a loud laugh. Philip looked astonished for a moment, but his face soon relaxed into a smile and he joined her laughing just as loud but then, before she knew what was happening, he mischievously grabbed her cone and ran away with it.

Though her feet were bare, she chased him over the grass, but he was too quick for her. At last he stopped way ahead of her, turned, grinned, and stood licking her ice cream for all he was worth.

Edith's giggles left her breathless as she tried to protest, calling to him to leave some for her. When she came alongside him, he held on to the cone, but offered her the ice. She bent forward and licked it, loving the sound of his playful mocking as his giggles joined hers.

'That'll teach you to laugh at me losing mine!' His arm came around her. Edith quivered.

'Are you cold?'

'No.'

His eyes stared into hers, making her feel as though there was no one else in the world but them. But suddenly, the spell that had held her splintered as he dropped his arm and handed her the cone and abruptly turned away from her. His tone was quiet as he said, 'Come on, let's get your shoes.'

They walked back in silence. Philip kept his hands in his pockets and stared ahead, leaving Edith confused.

When they reached the bench, he picked up her shoes. 'I'm guessing that you don't want to put these on again?'

'No, they're pinching me. I should have worn me pumps, it's quite a walk from home to the park.'

'I've never asked you where you live?'

'Whittaker Avenue, just off the top of Talbot Road.'

'Of course, the same street as Alice. You should have let me pick you up, I would have gladly.'

'I know, but—'

'Come on, let's walk, we'll keep to the grass as much as possible.'

When they reached the Italian gardens, Edith was struck by the beauty surrounding her. She'd visited the park many times as a child and had run through this area hardly noticing it, eager to get to the play area with Alice and Marg, but now, having not been to the park in a long time, she was in awe of the stunning layout of the gardens surrounding the water fountain.

Her gaze took in the smooth lawns and the flower beds bursting with vibrant colours, and her senses were soothed by the gentle tinkling of the water.

'Shall we sit?'

She took Philip's outstretched hand and allowed him to guide her to a bench. 'It's lovely, I should come here more often.'

'I come all the time. I always discover something new.' When they sat down he said, 'Tell me about you, Edith. As I told you this morning, I know a little, but, well, have you brothers and sisters?'

'I've one brother.' She told him about her family, trying to make her home life sound better than it was. 'And you?'

'I have a sister. You probably saw her this morning; she came up to me outside the church and we walked to my car together. She's married and I have two little nieces.'

This pleased Edith and settled the questions in her mind.

'She came to church on her own as one of the children is poorly with a summer cold. She ... well, Father and Mother don't approve of her husband and they have fallen out, so she sits on the other side of the church. If her husband comes, they'll leave with the children before the service ends and wait in the car for me to come and have a chat with them . . . Look, this is all boring for you – families, eh?'

'No, it isn't, I – I'm interested. I imagine you lead a very different life to me, and I'd like to hear about it.'

'Well, more privileged, but probably not as happy.'

'I'm not happy . . . I exaggerated, trying not to put you off coming to pick me up. I mean, well, things at home aren't good.'

'Oh? I'm sorry, Edith, you always come across as being happy and carefree.'

'I am when away from home. Well, I try to be, but my situation . . . well, I don't think you'll want to know me if I tell you the truth.'

'You're not your family, Edith, you're you, and so far, I see a nice, kind person who supports her family and friends, nothing less.'

'Ta. I do try. But you know, where we live, everyone has problems. Never enough money for basic needs, angry parents who take it out on their kids . . . and, well, in my case, a ma who's got a drink problem, a brother who's going down the wrong road and has a temper, and a da who has the coughing sickness from working for years down the mines.'

'Oh dear, I'm sorry. And I thought I was hard done by with an overbearing father, and a mother who thinks she's a duchess or something and looks down on anyone who hasn't got wealth, even though she and my father started with nothing. Oh, she came from a good family and was left a small bakery, but having grown from that to owning the biscuit factory, she now thinks of herself as somebody and is a proverbial snob.'

Edith didn't know what to say. She could see that Philip had problems, but they paled against the enormity of her own.

'They won't accept Patricia's – my sister's – husband because he comes from a working-class family who were mill workers in Blackburn, but who did all they could for their son and got him an apprenticeship in carpentry. Oh, but that means nothing to my parents, even though Dennis is a superb carpenter and sculptor, and has done some beautiful work on Blackburn Cathedral. He is also a thoroughly nice man. But Mother and Father won't give him a chance. They wanted her to marry Gerald, you see, but they're just good friends.'

'So, your parents won't approve of my friend who Gerald is courting then, but do you reckon his own parents will?'

'Oh, they will. Gerald's parents are what I call bohemian. Brilliant surgeons, both of them, but never happier than when they're living life in a carefree way. They spend their holidays camping in some of the remotest parts of the world – sometimes in a gypsy-type caravan. They love music – Gerald's dad plays a guitar most of the time – and flowers. Well, all nature. His mother paints beautiful pictures and floats around in what looks like a negligée most of the time, with flowers pinned in her hair. Once they retire, they are going on their travels to help distant tribes of God knows where. They're pretty adorable, actually, and would work for free if not bound by rules and a need to see their son launched in the career he loves.'

'They sound wonderful.'

'They are. I mean, my own parents can be, but they are so . . . well, suffocated, by what they think acceptable or not!'

'So, you'll no doubt be looking for a girl of the right class to be your bride, then?'

251

'No, I'm looking for a girl that I fall in love with . . . I may have found her.'

He fell silent then, and Edith felt pain in her heart as she wondered who this girl was.

When Philip did speak again, he shocked her by asking her if she would like to meet again sometime.

'Won't I hinder you in your getting to know this girl you think you're falling in love with?'

Again, that look of astonishment followed by a small, but lovely laugh. 'Not at all, you'll help me.'

She didn't want to meet him on these terms. 'Well, I've more things to do than help you find your bride, so we'd better make this the last time. But ta, anyroad. I've had a lovely time.'

'What? No, you've got it all wrong! I'm talking about you.'

'Me?'

'Yes, you're the girl I think I am falling in love with, Edith. And I definitely need your help in that! I haven't been able to stop thinking about you since we danced that night . . . I wanted to find you . . . well, I didn't tell the truth when I said I didn't know where you lived, I did. I – I looked you up on the factory records. Only, well, I didn't know how to meet you. I thought of asking Gerald to arrange it, but he's only known Alice a short time and it's early days for them so I didn't want to put pressure on him . . . Oh, Edith, I'm waffling, but . . . well, do you like me a little?'

'Aye, I like you a lot . . . This ain't true, is it? How will your ma take to you seeing a girl like me?'

'A girl like you? A beautiful, funny, easy to talk to, kind and very sensitive girl. Is that who you mean?'

Edith blushed. She had no answer to the way he saw her. She didn't see herself like that – well, not the beautiful bit – but she was glad that he did.

'Edith, you're exactly that girl. I really want to get to know you better, so will you meet me again?'

Edith felt she would burst with the joy that filled her. 'Aye, I will. But nowhere posh, mind. I've no posh clothes, and I'd let you down.'

'You could never do that. I'm not the sort that all of that matters to.'

'But your ma and da? They are, and if they can't accept your Dennis, then they'll never accept me.'

Again, he fell quiet, and Edith prayed this wouldn't make a difference to him.

'You're right, and I apologise for them. They'll probably cut me off without a penny, and leave the factory to my cousin, Alfred, who they greatly admire – he's a snob too. So, you see, if I do fall in love with you, and you with me, I'll probably end up penniless.'

'Oh, well then, that's it, as it's your money that I'm after.'

That look of astonishment appeared on his face once more. Edith burst out laughing. 'I was only joking, you daft apeth!'

'Daft apeth, what does that mean?' He was smiling again.

'It's what you are when you don't get my jokes. You gawp at me as if I'm from another planet or something.'

'You are. A planet of fun and laughter, despite all you must go through. So, yes, you do astonish me, and long may you continue to do so.'

Edith looked at him – his handsome face, his expressive smile, his easy manner – all things she was falling in love with.

253

However, his posh voice, expensive clothes that spoke of money and the upbringing he'd had, so different to her own, told her that in loving him, she had a lot to learn and possibly a lot to put up with. But none of this put her off. 'Aye, I will meet you again, and be honoured to. Just tell me when and where.'

His smile widened. 'You're willing to face the wrath of my parents, then?'

'No, you can face that, but I'm willing to get to know you more, and I want to, as I like what I've seen so far.'

Philip took her hand, sending waves of shivers through her. He leant over her and looked into her eyes. 'May I kiss you?'

She could only nod her head, then his lips touched hers and she felt herself transported to another world – a world she never wanted to leave. And she had the feeling that she never would, despite any nastiness his ma and da could throw at her.

When they parted, he held on to her hand and in a low voice he told her, 'You're doing a good job of helping me with the girl I think I'm falling in love with, I must say.'

Edith laughed. 'It's easy work as I feel the same way.'

'You do? Oh, Edith. We can make this work. We can. Let's meet again next Saturday. I don't want to wait that long, but I've a few things happening this week. Where shall we go? You choose.'

'It'll have to be after seven in the evening as I look out for me friend's gran while she goes to her second job on Saturdays.'

'How about the Tower Ballroom where we met? I love it there and love dancing. I'll pick you up.'

She shook her head to him picking her up as she still worried over what might meet him if she consented to this, and how it would affect him. 'I'll walk to Talbot Road and stand opposite Layton Cemetery. I'll be there at seven thirty.'

'But what about your poor feet?'

'I'll be sensible and wear me pumps and carry me heels.'

He didn't question her further and she was glad of this. She didn't want anything to spoil the feeling of looking forward to Saturday night. Now she needn't worry what her ma got up to, or what mood Albert was in as Philip wouldn't be subjected to them.

As he kissed her again, all of these worries left her. A new world was opening up for her, one she never dreamt would, and she'd let nothing spoil it, not ever.

TWENTY-THREE

Alice

As she linked arms with the others, Alice had the sensation that she was walking on air, and yet she felt guilty for feeling such a way.

Shouldn't I be in the doldrums? After all, I only buried my da three days ago!

But the sadness of that was overshadowed by Gerald's visit last night. He'd arrived late and she'd thought he wasn't coming at all. The lads were in bed and she'd prepared everything for the morning and was about to go up herself when she heard his car.

They'd hardly spoken, but had huddled up on the settee in each other's arms having what they used to call as kids a snogging session. It transported her to a place where she didn't feel like Alice, but some beautiful film star, and Gerald was her dashing hero. It gave her feelings, longings – times when she wanted Gerald to do more to her – and she got to a pitch where she had to stop herself from moving his caressing hands to her breast. But she had held back, knowing such moves should come from the man, and it was her job to stop him.

But would she? Could she?

'That was a big sigh, Alice. You're not listening to us, are you? You're in a world of your own, and aye, I bet I know who's there with you.'

'Sorry, what were you saying, Marg?'

'Nothing as interesting as your thoughts, I wouldn't think . . . Eeh, I feel that we're coming to the end of an era.'

'No, never. Things might change a little, they've always done that, but nothing will ever come between us. We won't let it, will we?'

'No. Take no notice of me, Alice, I just feel that way at the minute.'

'But I do want to take notice. I'm sorry, Marg, I was daydreaming then. Tell me what it was you were saying, lass.'

'Well, I've got this worry that Ma wants us to move in with Eric . . . By, I don't know what else to call him. He ain't my uncle anymore and I can't call him Da.'

'Don't worry about that, it'll resolve itself in time. But moving! Eh, I hope not.'

'I know. It'll unsettle Gran and our Jackie. Besides, I don't want to live with him. I have seen a nice side to him since it all came out in the open, but that doesn't mean I want to live with him.'

'Has he said as much then? I mean, asked you to move?'

'No, he just keeps dropping hints and then Jackie said Ma asked her how she would feel moving to a nice home in a better area.'

Edith spoke then. 'I must say, Eric must love your ma as it's a lot for him to accept her being his brother's wife, and still be interested when she wouldn't even take him on after she was widowed.'

'I'm not sure that me ma feels the same for him, or ever has. She's used him, that's for sure, and now I reckon she's just thinking of me and Jackie. Now that it's in the open about Eric being our da, she thinks she can get us well and truly established as his daughters so we'll be taken care of by him if ... well, I don't like to say it, but Ma ain't got long.'

'Eeh, Marg, have you been told that?'

'No, Alice, they tell us nothing, but I think that Ma knows it ... I do. I can see it, and it's breaking me world up into little bits to think of it.'

Alice could only put her arm around Marg. She had no words as Marg's despair opened up raw wounds for her.

Edith's voice held emotion as she tried to comfort her friend. 'Marg, lass, none of us know when our time is, but aye, I feel your pain. I have the same feelings about me da and dread it happening.'

They walked on, none of them speaking for a while. Alice felt as though she'd dropped out of the happiness cloud she'd been floating on and had landed in a pit of misery. She didn't want to feel like this, so changed the subject. 'Did your Jackie tell you that she's a regular Gracie Fields, Marg?'

Marg looked bemused. 'A what? Singing, you mean? Our Jackie! She's got a voice like a foghorn.'

They all laughed and Alice felt better for having thought of something to lift the mood as she told Marg about the fun they'd had on the way to church and the idea for their birthdays.

'Oh, that'd be grand. Let's do it … Mind, no falling out over which birthday we have it on. I think we should either pick a day that's not any of our birthdays, or pick one of our names out of a hat and all stick by it.'

'I've thought of that. Edith's and mine are weekdays, and yours, Marg, falls on a Saturday! So, I think we should have it on the Sunday. It's the best day anyway as no one goes shopping, or to work, and everyone is usually just hanging around the street. Eeh, I just so want to experience that day again.'

'That's a great idea, Alice. We could do an egg and spoon race for the young 'uns as them with grandchildren will have them around, they do most Sundays, and that one where the kids have to try to get an apple out of the bucket of water with their mouths … By, I can see it now. We could make it an annual event!'

'We could, Marg.'

Edith just giggled, which showed her excitement, though her mind seemed far away and she hadn't put her tuppence worth in. 'You haven't said how your afternoon went, Edith. Did he show up?'

Marg answered. 'He did, and by, we're on the way to losing Halfpenny Girls member number two!'

'Don't be daft. Ha, I've only spent one afternoon with him!'

'Well, that's enough for you, by the sounds of it. She's to help him find the girl he loves, Alice, only it's her, so she hasn't got much of a job on.'

Edith laughed out loud. A laugh that was full of happiness, and Alice felt so pleased for her. 'I want to know every single detail, lass.'

259

This took most of their walk, but Alice loved hearing how far Edith and Philip's relationship had travelled.

When she came to the end of her tale Edith shifted the focus. 'Now, I want to hear all about your date an' all, Alice.'

Alice felt herself blush. She knew she could never share with them what she and Gerald had done – the intimacy of the kissing, the sighs of wanting more, the love Gerald had whispered, and the feelings she'd experienced.

'Uh-uh, I don't think you're going to learn much, Edith,' Marg teased, 'and nor do I think you should. As close friends as we are, there's some things that we can't be expected to share.'

Edith laughed again. 'I know, I just wanted to see her blush. You do so, so easily, Alice. Sorry, I don't want to know more. From now on, we can talk about the lead-up to the men of our dreams becoming ours, but once they are – well, that's our own secret to cherish.'

They all agreed on this as they arrived at the factory gates.

Alice saw Edith look around hopefully, but she was disappointed as there was no sign of Philip in the grounds of the factory. Nor of his car, which meant he probably wasn't coming in today.

She wondered about his role, as he didn't seem to have one. Sometimes he was in the office all day, but that was only a couple of times a week. No one had ever questioned this, or even let it bother them, but now, with him becoming a focus of their gang, Alice was curious.

'What does Philip do exactly, Edith? I mean, is his main job here or elsewhere?'

'He's learning the business. He's been on something called a sabbatical, which, when he described it, sounded like no more than a long holiday after leaving university.

'Anyroad, he's got to knuckle down now, as his father wants him to know every aspect of how the business is run, from the accounts down to the making of the biscuits. So he spends time here, in the office, and with their accountant. And some time at a bakery that his mother owns. He told me that he did the wages last week and couldn't believe how little we get.'

'By, he'll be giving us a pay rise, then?'

'No, he's got no powers here, and doesn't even like it. He wanted to teach. But he's ruled by his da.'

They'd entered the building and were donning their white overalls and tucking their hair into the white mob caps, leaving them no time for further chat.

For Alice, it was a long day. She hurried them along on the way home, eager to get ready for her second date tonight with Gerald, but worried about how much she was putting on Edith's shoulders. Once they'd said their goodbyes to Marg as she went into Fairweather's grocery store, Alice asked, 'You'll be all right looking out for Marg's gran for her, and keeping an eye on the lads, won't you, Edith?'

'Of course, you go and enjoy yourself. It'll be your turn on Saturday as I have a date.'

'Eeh, you didn't say.'

'No, I suddenly felt very sorry for Marg. Here we were going on about our love lives and she's got no one. On top of that, her life's crumbling.'

'Aye, I know. It's difficult. But it's hard not to show happiness when you're feeling so much of it. Love is a wonderful emotion, ain't it, Edith? It makes everything else pale.'

'Aye, it does, and I reckon we should do all we can to find Marg someone.'

'Aye, we should. I mean, if we're all in couples, then we can go out as six ... Trouble is, we've only got Clive in the pipeline, and she ain't having none of it.'

They laughed as they parted, but Alice couldn't shake the feeling that Edith was right. Marg did seem to be sliding into more unhappiness. She made up her mind to help her all she could.

This thought stayed with her as she dressed in a light grey, slightly flared cotton skirt that hung to her calves. She teamed this with a pale blue blouse with a large collar that draped over her shoulders and short, puffed sleeves. Pleased with the look, she gently unwrapped the rags she'd curled her hair into, brushed it through gently, then parted it on one side before clipping it back behind her ears. She smiled as she teased the curls around the brush, getting a lovely neat roll on each side. Adding a little rouge to her cheeks – just a blush, which was hardly discernible – some mascara and a lovely red lipstick, she felt happy with her appearance. When she came to choose shoes, she did heed what happened to Edith and chose pumps in case they went for a walk along the prom after their fish supper.

The serene calmness she felt left her the moment she heard Gerald's car. Her heart thumped with joy and her stomach felt as though a million butterflies had taken residence there and had all decided to flutter at the same time. She was down the stairs and opening the front door in the time it would take to bat an eyelid, only to find Gerald surrounded by her brothers.

'I'm taking them to the chippy, as you all call it, and treating them to some chips to bring home with them, Alice. I won't be long.'

With this the lads jumped into the car – Billy and Joey in the bench seat with Gerald and Harry sitting on the rolled-down roof with his legs dangling between the lads, and left Alice standing.

Those monkeys! I'll tan their hides. I bet this was their plan all along.

She smiled and guessed they'd told Gerald that they would have to have waited over an hour for supper. Her fault as she'd thought she'd put a stew on the side of the stove before she went out to work that morning, but found that she'd forgotten to move it from the side onto the warming plate where it would have simmered all day.

Harry had made some remark about her being in love and they'd all giggled, going outside to mess around while they waited for the stew to cook – or so she'd thought.

The stew had hardly warmed through, so she could stop its cooking process and they could have it tomorrow. It would be fine on the cold slab in the pantry.

Alice readily forgave them when they came back, drawn into their excitement as they were full of giggles and tales of what it was like to have a ride in Gerald's car with the roof down.

'Now, behave for the rest of the evening, lads. Edith has a lot on her plate looking out for you all and Marg's gran.'

'I just saw Edith's ma go into Marg's, Alice, so Jackie should be over in a mo. We're all going to share our chips with her.'

Alice smiled a greeting to Gerald over Joey's head as she told him, 'That's good, Joey. Now, promise me, as you haven't started well.'

They all looked a bit shamefaced as they nodded their heads.

'Right, are we ready, darling?'

Alice loved it when Gerald called her this. 'Ready. Will I do?'

'You look lovely. And I'm starving. I can't wait to try these fish and chips.'

'I can't believe I've met a Blackpool lad who's never had fish and chips!'

'I know, I've always wanted to try them. Some of the nurses send for them if they're on a late shift – husbands and boyfriends deliver them to open windows on the ward, driving us all mad with the smell – but my mother has always packed me up a magnificent concoction that tastes delicious, and is meant to be very healthy for me, so I've forgone the pleasure until now!'

'Come on then, you're in for a treat.'

The Cottage was busy as usual, but they were given a table near the window that looked out onto the road. Andrea, the owner, who'd recently had an operation, recognised Gerald and couldn't be more attentive. They were served what she called 'the best fish in the house', with a mound of chips, bread and butter and a pot of tea – a meal so huge that Alice struggled to eat it all, but she managed it somehow.

They chatted about this and that, but what Alice really wanted to know was more about Gerald's family. The snippets that Edith had told her had made her curious. She asked Gerald if they were really like Philip had described.

'Yes, and more! And I'm so glad that Philip has met up with Edith again. We knew there was something on his mind, but he said he hadn't wanted to bother me with it as you and I were only just getting to know one another. Anyway, I saw him yesterday evening and he was the happiest I've seen him for a long time.'

'Eeh, I'm glad, Edith deserves some happiness. Though she's worried about Philip's parents.'

'Oh, Philip will work that one out. Tell her not to worry. She may not meet them for a long time – Philip said he has no intention of subjecting her to such an ordeal anytime soon. Anyway, yes, my parents are all of what he told you. What you saw of my father was not the real him; he takes on a different persona when with patients and their families. He is bohemian – gypsy-like – and so is Mother. They are adorable and will love you. Mother's already jealous that Father has met you, though he keeps telling her that it was in difficult circumstances, and he is yet to get to know you. They're quite admiring of you, as I told them about your life and how you cope.'

This embarrassed Alice. She couldn't imagine what they thought of her – they probably wanted to tell her to leave their son alone – but then, Gerald dispelled this fear.

'Father told Mother how beautiful you are, and that, like me, he can see your goodness shining from your face.'

This made Alice laugh. 'You really are different to our lot, but I like what I'm hearing and won't be shy to meet them now.'

'Shyness is something I love about you, Alice; the way you blush, it makes you appear so innocent.'

He'd said he loved her! That was twice now. He'd whispered it so low last night that she'd not reacted in case she'd heard wrongly. Now, the shyness he'd spoken of left her unable to look him in his eyes and she was glad when Gerald changed the subject: 'Shall we go for that walk you talked of? I'm full to bursting.'

Alice was relieved at this suggestion as she felt as though the space between them shouldn't be there, and yet at the same time, she had been dreading Gerald showing her too much affection in front of the many folk who were ogling them – most of whom knew her.

Despite them being looked on as common folk, Alice knew they had a moral code that didn't take kindly to young people canoodling in public, and some would feel she'd overstepped the mark by being with a young man from a higher standing than them.

She didn't object to Gerald taking her hand once they were seated in the car, though. 'I really enjoyed that, Alice.'

His smile and the look in his eyes thrilled her.

They drove to the promenade and parked near to the South Pier. Still buzzing with people, Gerald remarked on the number of soldiers and air force personnel there were as they stood leaning on the railings next to the pier. Alice had been lost in the feelings that were assailing her from the nearness of Gerald, as they'd watched the sea gently brush the sand. She looked around her.

'Aye, I've never seen so many. Maybe a new lot of recruits at Weeton and Warton?'

'Hmm, perhaps. I've noticed the numbers growing for a while. It makes you think that the powers that be are training more men for fear of a repeat of the Great War. There's so much unrest in the world, and I don't like this Hitler fellow, or his bloody Nazi party.'

Alice felt out of her depth. She'd heard Hitler mentioned on the radio, but had never taken any notice of who he was, or what he was doing.

'What do you think, darling?'

'I – I don't know much about it.'

'Oh . . . Of course not, sorry.'

Alice cringed. 'Why "of course not?" What are you implying?'

'Oh dear, are we having our first cross words? Well, I deserve your rebuke, it was a terrible thing to say, and you can slap me if you want to.'

His smile undid her. She giggled. But then became serious. 'Gerald, you will have to make some allowances for me; you've had such a different life. I haven't had your education – mind, that don't mean that I'm thick. If you take the time to teach me, I'll soon catch up.'

'I know. I'm sorry. And I've got all the time in the world to teach you as I'm not going anywhere. But I won't force things on you that don't interest you, so if I start preaching, just tell me I'm boring you.'

'I will. But you know, I can't ever see you boring me. I am interested in all the things you talk about and I love it when you talk about your work.'

'That's good to hear, darling, as my work is my life.' Gerald squeezed her hand.

To her the gesture was as if he was glad of the change in subject, but she didn't want that. She wanted to know more about what he'd said about Hitler as a fear had been planted in her with him mentioning war. Some of the older women talked about this possibility, and now, with Gerald mentioning it, all the rumblings seemed a reality.

'You can make a start with your teaching, Gerald, by telling me why you don't like Hitler and his politics, and why you think the government might be getting ready for war.'

'Well, Hitler's party are Nazis. Now the Nazis . . .'

Alice listened, fascinated by his knowledge, and yet feeling her fear deepen by all she heard. She couldn't believe, or understand, the awful things she heard about the treatment of the Jews in Germany. She knew a few people of Jewish faith and liked them very much.

'So, do you think the Nazis are a threat to us, Gerald? I mean, we have fascists here an' all, don't we?'

'Yes, Mosley's lot, but, well, I don't want you to worry too much as we don't know how far this unrest will go. But there is a concern, as we have alliances and treaties with some of the countries that Hitler has an interest in. What we would do if he set his greedy sights on those I don't know.'

'But you reckon it could mean a war?'

'No . . . well, I'm not sure, is the truthful answer. There's only rumblings of that so far, but with what is going on in Europe, and seeing all the extra troops here, it had me thinking. Though Chamberlain is a pacifist, so there is no way he would prepare for war; he's more likely to try to keep the peace. That's why he kept Churchill out of his cabinet.'

This was something Alice had heard of and was able to make the comment that people thought Churchill a warmonger. But then found that Gerald admired him.

Alice was so enjoying this conversation, despite it churning her insides. She'd never had one like it in all her life and was disappointed when Gerald said, 'Anyway, that's enough talk of war and politics. Let's walk along the pier. I might be able to win you a teddy bear.'

As they strolled along holding hands, they passed a couple snuggled together in front of a lifebelt which proclaimed *South Pier – Blackpool* in large writing around its circumference. A photographer was snapping them.

'I'd like a photo of you and me, Alice. Shall we?'

'I'd love that.'

They took their place as the other couple left it, and settled themselves down while the photographer adjusted his camera.

Gerald pulled her to him. 'Snuggle up, Alice.'

Alice laughed up at Gerald as he took both of her hands in his.

'Hold it right there, lady, and you, sir, perfect! Lovely.' There was a flash just before the photographer came out from under the black cloth. 'I'll take another couple of poses and then you'll have some to choose from. Put your arm around your girlfriend, sir.'

To Alice, her world completed as Gerald did this, whispering, 'Oh, Alice, I love you.'

She went to look up at him to utter the words herself for the first time, but the photographer stopped her. 'Now, look straight ahead this time, lass.'

Once he'd taken this, and another shot of them with her head on Gerald's shoulder, he said, 'That's it, and may I say what a lovely couple you are.'

They giggled at this as they'd heard him say the same to the previous couple.

After giving him their details and receiving instructions about how to collect their photographs, they walked away laughing, but they didn't go far as Alice pulled Gerald back towards a bench asking if they could sit a while. She had an urge to tell Gerald how she felt, but he was having none of it. 'No, darling, let's keep going. I want to win you a prize! I want us to remember tonight forever.'

'Well, I want to tell you something that I hope you'll remember forever, and I don't want to tell you while we're walking along.'

'Oh, that sounds ominous.' With this, he did as she asked.

Before she could lose her confidence, she turned her body to face him. 'I love you, Gerald.'

His eyes filled with tears; his lips stretched into a smile like none she'd seen just as the lowering sun lit him in a beautiful light. Alice wanted to keep this picture in her heart and never lose it.

'Oh, Alice. That's the most wonderful thing to ever happen to me. I love you, darling. I've been in love with you from the moment I heard you talking to Harry. Something happened to me as you said those loving and understanding words to your brother. Then when I pulled the curtain back and saw you, it was as if I'd been enveloped in such happiness, and had found the other half of me. My soulmate.'

The tears were welling in her own eyes now. She couldn't believe this was happening to her and it humbled her.

Gerald's face came close to hers. 'I can think of no better place than this to ask you: Will you marry me, my darling, and very soon?'

'I will, Gerald, darling, I will.'

His kiss was light, and yet held a promise that burnt into her heart.

Happiness soared through her — mixed with disbelief that this was happening. Was she dreaming? If so, she never wanted to wake up. She just wanted to fling her arms around Gerald and hold him to her for ever.

TWENTY-FOUR

Marg

As she came along the street towards home, Marg was surprised to hear Jackie laughing as she jumped out of Eric's car. For some reason, this unnerved her. She'd fought against accepting Eric in the new role she had to place him in, but now wondered if she should as it seemed that Jackie was all right with everything. At least, she certainly sounded as though she was at this minute as she called out to Eric, 'I will. Ta. See you tomorrow.'

'Eeh, you sound happy, lass?'

'Oh, I am, Marg.' Jackie ran into her arms.

'I hope that means good news. Have you visited Ma? How is she?'

'I did, and she's a lot better. She sat up and hardly coughed. She's been having a new medicine. I can't remember its name. I knaw it costs a lot of money as I heard Uncle Eric say that he didn't care how much it was, he'd find the money somehow. But it's made no end of difference to Ma.'

'That's good. So, what made you laugh? And I heard you call Eric "Uncle Eric", lass?'

'Aye, well, I told him that I didn't knaw what to call him, that I couldn't take it in that he was me da, and he said nothing need change, I can carry on calling him Uncle if I wanted to . . . He's so different now. I don't understand it, but it's nice. I used to dread him coming to the house. I always felt in the way and as if I'd done sommat really bad.'

'You hadn't, me little lass. Anyroad, I'm glad you're more comfortable with him. So, how did you come to go to the hospital, then?'

Marg listened to how Eric had turned up to see if she wanted to go. 'I was having chips with Harry and the lads. I felt bad leaving them, but they understood. And then Edith said it would be fine.'

She went on to say how nice Uncle Eric had been to her, not pressuring her, but telling her once more that he was sorry for always being gruff and not taking much notice of her.

'Eeh, lass, we're all mixed up, ain't we? I don't know what to make of it all. Did he mention anything about moving into his?'

'Naw. Why? Is that sommat we'll have to do?'

'I don't know. I just get a feeling, that's all. But I don't want to, do you?'

'I hadn't thought about it. I saw his house on Preston Road once, it looked really nice.'

'Aye, I saw it when I was a lot younger, but he's always come here and never asked us there. I remember Da . . . I mean . . . Eeh, it's all a mess, ain't it?'

'It is. But you're all right with it, ain't you, Marg?'

'I am, up to a point. Come on, let's go in and see Gran.'

Inside, Marg found that Betty was sat playing cards with Gran. 'Now, that's a grand sight. Hello, Gran, are you winning?'

'Naw, lass. She's took all me fortune, I ain't got a button left.'

Marg laughed at the sight of the pile of buttons in front of Betty. 'Are you cheating, Betty?'

'Naw.' Betty giggled. 'I might be winning now, but I'll tell you, this one's got a gift; she's been running rings around me all night.'

They all giggled as Gran screwed her face up into an expression that Marg knew so well. 'Me? Eeh, it's not a gift, it's skill, lass.' Gran turned to face Marg. Her face clouded into a blank stare as she looked from Marg to Jackie and back to Betty. 'I've seen these lasses afore, do I knaw them?'

The joy Marg had just felt melted away and her heart filled with pain.

'You're tired now, Sandra. I'll get off. Marg and Jackie'll take care of you.'

Gran didn't object – something that Marg dreaded happening, and wondered how she would handle. Strangely, Gran still accepted her, so something about her must still feel familiar and safe.

This thought cheered Marg. 'Aye, I'll help you to bed and get your cocoa, Gran.'

Gran smiled up at her. 'Ta, lass, that's kind of you.'

The pain eased a little as she looked into her Gran's light blue eyes and saw love there. It was a strange world her gran had entered, and she knew it must be a confusing one too. Though much of the confusion had gone since they'd all followed Betty's lead in not trying to make her see the real world, or challenge her about not knowing them.

'Well, ta for a lovely evening, Sandra.'

Gran looked at Betty. 'Eeh, when did you pop in, lass? I didn't see you come.'

'Naw, I surprised you. But you're just going to have your cocoa now, and I'm ready for me bed, so see you tomorrow, eh?'

'Aye. Try to come earlier, eh? This time's naw good to me.'

'I will. Night, lass.'

Marg smiled at this exchange. Though none of what was happening to Gran was easy to take, it helped to see that it wasn't just her and Jackie who Gran could forget.

Her heart lifted further as Gran looked at Jackie. 'You can help me to bed, Jackie, lass, then Marg can get on and make me cocoa, as I'm that tired I want everything to happen at once so I can get off to the land of nod.'

Jackie's expression showed Marg the joy this had given her. It matched her own.

Winking at Jackie, Marg made her mind up to stop getting upset when Gran didn't know her, but to enjoy the times when she did.

Betty nodded her head and smiled as she reached the door. 'Well, she sounds quite happy now, bless her. But I tell you, Marg, she's hard to beat at crib. Mind, she always was. Not many of us would play her, but then, she taught us all in the first place. She learnt it when she was in service, you knaw. She used to play it with the young mistress she looked after.'

'Aye, I know, Betty. She was always telling us tales of that time in her life. She'd say it was a sad time but a happy time. Sad because her ma had to send her away to work and she missed her, but happy because she loved the young mistress whose maid she was. She was called Matilda, and Gran had Christmas cards from her every year. I remember them coming when I was a little girl. Gran's got them all in a box under her bed. But then she had a notification that Matilda had died and that ended her contact with the family.'

'Aye, she can tell some tales of them days and I love to hear them. Anyroad, Edith'll pop over in a mo, she wouldn't miss having her cocoa with you. She put her head around the door a bit ago and said the lads were all listening to the wireless . . . Though ain't that Harry sitting outside?'

'Aye, no doubt watching for our Jackie to come home. They're right sweet on each other.'

'Ha, I knaw! Edith said Harry was like a wet week when Jackie went off to see your ma; he'd thought they would spend the whole evening together.'

'I'll send her over with cocoa for them all and she can sit and have hers with Harry. Ta for sitting with Gran, Betty, I'll repay you one of these days.'

'You can do that now by making me one of your cocoas an all – you're known for the best ever, lass. Edith thinks I don't like it, but I just don't like how she makes it. I had a sip of one you'd made for her once as she was always going on about it, and I enjoyed it. Be a nice treat for me.'

'I can't, I haven't enough mugs, Betty.'

'I'll get Edith to bring a couple over, then she can bring them back for us to wash them up, lass. It'll save you having to do it. I'll send over some cocoa an' all; we've got half a tin and a full one, as it's rarely drunk in our house. I'll send the full one.'

'That'll be a good help, ta. Well, I'd better get Gran's on the go.'

As she went into the kitchen, Marg was bemused as to why her cocoa was said to be better than anyone else's. Mind, she always skimmed the cream off the top of the milk and kept it just for her cocoa. But tonight, they wouldn't all find it so good as she had only enough cream for three.

Betty would get her share. She deserved it.

An hour later, as Marg and Edith sat speculating about Alice and Gerald – whether they would marry, if they were having a good time tonight, and where they could have ended up – Gerald's car pulled into the street.

Not just Alice but Gerald, too, got out. They waved as they stopped to chat to Harry and Jackie, then went inside Alice's house. Harry went in after them.

'Well, we'll soon know the answer to some of our questions, Marg.'

'Aye, and I hope they're all good. Alice deserves all the happiness she can get. But it's awkward for her marrying anyone. I mean, as she has the responsibility of the lads, and that's a lot for any man to take on.'

'Your Jackie's coming back over. You don't think they've asked her to leave, do you?'

'If they have, it would be because they need to tell the lads something . . . Eeh, lass, it's exciting, ain't it?'

Jackie told them nothing they didn't already surmise – that Alice had asked if she wouldn't mind them having a quiet word with the lads in private. Jackie had hooked on to their excitement, telling them that she'd never seen Alice looking so happy.

They didn't have long to wait as soon Alice and Gerald came out of the house and headed across the road towards them.

Alice beamed all over her face. 'That birthday party we're planning, are you two still up for it?'

Marg looked at Edith, then back up at Alice. 'Well, lass, that's a funny greeting! Of course we are. Why do you ask?'

'Well, I was wondering if we could make it into an engagement party an' all.'

'What!' This came from both girls as they spontaneously jumped up and hugged Alice, the three of them doing a jig, laughing and talking while they did.

'Oh, Alice, lass, congratulations!' from Edith.

Marg told her, 'By, Alice, you're a quick mover when you get your man!'

They laughed more at this. Edith sobered them as she broke away and went up to Gerald. 'Congratulations, Gerald. As you can see, we're really happy about it.'

Gerald shocked Marg as she saw him put his arms out to Edith – she hadn't thought that posh blokes did anything like that. She ran over for her turn.

'I'm so glad, Gerald, I know you'll make our Alice really happy.' She didn't wait for him to extend his arms to her, but joined in the hug.

'Hey, you two, put him down! He's my man, you find your own!'

They all three laughed at this and Marg had the warmest feeling that they weren't losing a member of the Halfpenny Girls, but gaining a fourth.

'I haven't had a hug yet, Alice, and these two haven't given me a chance to say me congratulations.'

'Ta, Jackie. Well, go on then, but be quick because I want me Gerald back.'

Marg's heart warmed as she saw Jackie get a hug from Gerald. Jackie glowed. And Marg felt the pity of her young sister probably not able to remember hugs from a man, as their da wasn't a big one for hugging them – then again, he wouldn't have been, knowing the deceit he'd been party to.

She was glad that Alice didn't give her time to dwell on this, as soon she was in the circle of her Gerald's arms. She continued the conversation around the celebrations: 'Well, it's settled then! The street party has been partly hijacked for me and Gerald to celebrate. Though instead of everyone mucking in, Gerald would like to see to the cost of the refreshments.'

'Aye, that has my vote, lass, as long as it's plain food like everyone's used to and none of your posh stuff.'

As Gerald laughed at this, Alice beamed. 'Ta, Marg.'

Edith chipped in with, 'You've no need to ask when suggesting a free feast! It's a grand idea. And I'd go further and say that I think we should hold it just as an engagement party. What do you think, Marg?'

'I agree, Edith. It'd be grand. The grandest engagement party to ever be held in this street.'

'Well, you'll have to put up with my father playing the guitar and my mother dancing with the tambourines; I'm afraid my parents are a bit crazy.'

'Ha! I heard, Gerald; Philip told me ... I mean, well, he didn't say ...'

Gerald laughed at Edith's embarrassment. 'He did, no doubt. Philip loves them, but does think them crazy, which they are!'

They all giggled.

Marg felt a little left out, as if they all were in on something that she wasn't, but Gerald soon changed this.

'So, I've only been able to surprise you, then, Marg. Well, I'm telling you, when you meet them soon, you'll see what I mean.'

She hadn't thought to be included in meeting them – well, not until the engagement party. She smiled as Gerald said, 'I'm going to arrange for Alice and me to have dinner – I mean, tea – with them on Thursday, then you're all invited to a garden party they have planned for Sunday. They'll love you all, I know they will. And so will their friends, who are just the same as they are. In the twenties they were called the Crazy Gang and were known for their Rag Week antics at Cambridge University.'

Marg was glad when Alice asked Gerald what Rag Week was – he explained that it was held every year by students to raise money. 'I think it started in Victorian times, when the students didn't collect money but clothes for the poor. But it soon took on the connotation of Rag standing for ragging people – playing tricks for a forfeit of money for charity, and selling a joke magazine to raise funds. I can't tell you some of the things my parents got up to, they would make you blush, but one prank was that all the girls rode horses through Cambridge wearing only their birthday suits! They were emulating Lady Godiva, but saved themselves from being arrested because they did it under the cover of darkness at three o'clock in the morning. Ha! The policeman who stopped them didn't arrest them, thank goodness, as that would have been the end of their aspirations of a medical career. But when giving them a verbal warning he told them they'd had more complaints about not being able to see the ladies than about the noise the horses made on the cobbles!'

Marg laughed at the thought of this sight, and at the daring of these ladies – they sounded like real cards to her. But she had to admit she was a bit lost by some of the words Gerald used, and didn't have a clue who Lady Godiva was.

Ethel Jones, opening her window, quietened them all. 'You lot ain't got naw consideration for other folk. Shut your racket, will you? I've told you afore that you'll get me piddle pot! Well, I'll give you one minute to pack your noise in, or else!'

Marg grabbed Jackie and Edith, and Alice grabbed a bemused Gerald. Once inside they fell about laughing as Alice explained what Ethel was threatening to do.

'Oh dear! Wouldn't you be wise to hold your chats indoors then?'

'There's plenty of time for that in the winter. She's just an old spoilsport. She knows I can't go far from me house because of Gran. She could cut us a bit of slack.'

Gerald just nodded as he asked, 'How is your gran?'

Marg told him about her lapses of memory getting much worse and then took the opportunity to ask him, 'If we could afford it, Gerald, is there something that could be done for Gran?'

His reply and explanation of what little was known about Alzheimer's and how there was no known cure made her feel saddened, and yet this was tempered with relief at knowing they weren't letting Gran down by not seeking treatment.

Gerald had added how much he admired her for taking care of her gran and not putting her in a home.

'Ta, Gerald, you've helped us a lot saying that, hasn't he, Jackie?'

'Aye. I've never said anything, Marg, but I worried that there was something that could be done if only we could get the money together.'

'Me too, lass.'

Gerald asked then if Gran was ever violent. This shocked Marg. 'No, never. Gran's not got a bad bone in her body.'

'That's good, because the condition can take that route – not always, and we think it is borne more out of frustration than anything. But your gran sounds very content.'

'She is now, since Betty – Edith's ma – took on caring for her when we can't and is spending time with her. She told us all to stop challenging Gran with things she can't remember and that's made a lot of difference. She even recognises us sometimes.'

'Yes, that's a good way to be. You can always ask me anything, Marg. I know it isn't easy coping with a relative in this condition. And if I can help, I will – that goes for any of you. I can't administer to you as I'm not your doctor, but I'll always be happy to give you advice.'

'Gerald's hoping to set up a practice around here one day. And he'd restart the penny insurance.'

'Eeh, that'd be grand. And ta, Gerald, you've already made me and Jackie feel better about everything.'

'Well, after Alice saying, "yes" to marrying me, that's the next best thing to be said to me today. I became a doctor to help people, so it's good to be able to achieve that.'

Marg thought him one of the nicest fellas she'd ever met and couldn't be happier for Alice. It felt good that something had at last given Alice the happiness she was due. But marrying a doctor! That was something she'd never imagined for any of them. And Edith, too, in love with someone of the same class as Gerald. It all beggared belief.

She just couldn't shake the feeling, though, that all she'd known was coming to an end. But when she saw the happiness on Alice's face, and on Edith's too, she knew some of the changes were for the better.

Though she couldn't help wondering what her own future held.

TWENTY-FIVE

Alice

Nerves made Alice's body tremble as she alighted from Gerald's car outside his home two days later. She looked up at the large, white-painted house with its window frames and door picked out in a shiny black paint, and each of the windows draped with lace curtains. She thought it was beautiful.

There was no front garden, only a pebbled area to fit two cars, but this was brightened by large, ornate stone vases either side of the door brimming with flowers, and marble statues depicting ladies swathed in cloth at each corner of the house.

Gerald took her hand and winked at her. 'Don't be afraid, darling. I know they will love you and they are so excited to meet you.'

'They won't think you've rushed into things, will they? I mean, we've only known each other a few weeks.'

'No, they met at Cambridge and secretly married within three weeks of meeting. They didn't tell my grandparents until their graduation and then had a huge celebration to pacify family, and two years later I arrived. Mother gave up practising medicine for five years until I went to school, then she returned to it. She retired three years ago – early, I might add – and Father intends to do so once I am settled. As that can't come soon enough for them both, they're more than delighted to welcome you.'

'But wouldn't they want you to marry someone of your own class?'

'Darling, I've told you before – they don't hold with dividing people into classes. They know they're privileged to have been born into money and have the means to follow the life they want to, but they don't think of that as their right and they don't look down on those who aren't so privileged. Look, my darling, take a deep breath and come and see for yourself.'

With this, Gerald walked with her towards the front door, and as if his mother knew their every step, she flung open the door the minute they reached it.

Alice was struck by a vision of long flowing chiffon in what looked like all the colours of the rainbow, floating around a slim, tall figure of a beautiful lady, with long fair hair and the same lovely deep blue eyes Gerald had.

'Darling, you're here! Oh, and this is Alice! You're so pretty, Alice, and dainty, just like I imagined.'

'Ha! Mother had a picture of Alice in Wonderland in her head.'

Alice grinned. For once she didn't feel out of her depth as she knew the stories of her namesake. As Gerald had said would happen, she immediately liked and felt comfortable with his mother. 'Pleased to meet you, and I promise not to disappear down a rabbit hole, Mrs Melford.'

Gerald's mother laughed a lovely tinkly laugh. 'Oh, that's good. And you look lovely, my dear, come on through. And it's Averil, call me Averil as all my friends do . . . Now, it's this way as we're having drinks in the garden before we sit down to dinner.'

This threw Alice a bit, but she remembered Gerald referring to his tea as being his dinner, which was odd to her, but she didn't mention this. 'Ta, me frock is me Sunday best. I only wear it for special occasions.'

'And this is very special, my dear: the day that Roderick and I get to know our future daughter! Oh, I have so longed to have a daughter, but it just didn't happen. Not that I minded as I had my darling Gerald.'

'Yes, and you treated me like a daughter sometimes.'

Alice found this very strange, but then Gerald laughed. 'Oh, I mean in how she is always so open, talking to me about anything and everything. But then, you will find doctors are a little like that – they lose all of their inhibitions.'

'Not all, darling. Some are very prudish and won't even discuss "private matters" with patients! Ridiculous . . . Ah, here we are. Rod, come and meet the delightful Alice, who promises that she won't disappear down a rabbit hole.'

'Ah, but we have met, my dear, remember? Albeit in my official capacity and at a very sad occasion. How are you, Alice?'

'I've been in something of a whirl since I saw you last time.'

'That's my son for you. Like his mother, he sees who he wants and sweeps them off their feet before they can take a breath. Averil did that to me – I went to university and before I knew it, I was a married man! Well, I must say, my dear, I like Gerald's choice. I always loved that frock and—'

'Come and take a seat, dear. Never mind Rod, he always prattles on.' Averil gave Rod a look that would wither a lesser man. 'Now, what can I get you to drink, Alice, my dear?'

Alice asked for a lemonade as she sat down on the wicker chair – one of four set around an oval-shaped wicker table. Her cheeks burnt as she remembered how Gerald had looked taken aback when she'd stepped out of the house; he'd hesitated before he'd told her she looked pretty.

She'd chosen to wear one of the frocks she'd bought when at a jumble sale with Edith and Marg. She'd loved both her choices but had particularly fallen for this white flared frock with clusters of yellow flowers decorating it, but had never even considered wearing it until today.

Thinking about this as she looked at Averil, busy at a small bar-like construction in the corner of the garden, she realised why it had been recognised and was now the cause of her extreme embarrassment. Averil was the same size as herself, and yes, this flowing frock, with little bell-like sleeves, would be just the kind of thing she would wear.

Oh, why didn't Gerald tell me when he picked me up?

All of a sudden the lovely feeling she'd had deserted Alice, and she felt cross with Gerald for letting this happen.

The banter went on around her, as they all tried a little too hard to cover up the embarrassing moment, until Alice could stand it no longer. 'I'm sorry, but yes, I bought my frock at a jumble sale at the church, and I never thought to own such a lovely one as this, or even to have somewhere to wear it to. I just couldn't resist it. I now know it must have belonged to you, Averil. I'm sorry if I've embarrassed you all. I – I didn't mean—'

'No, no, my dear, you haven't. We thought we'd embarrassed you and were mortified. Rod is hopeless; the most undiplomatic man you could meet.'

'I am, my dear. I only meant to say what lovely taste you have as that was one of my favourites of Averil's frocks, but do you know? I'm going to be even more undiplomatic now and tell you truthfully that it suits you much better than it ever did Averil.'

Averil hit him playfully. 'Talk about digging yourself a hole!'

'Well, at least it isn't a rabbit hole, or I am sure I would have made Alice scramble into it!'

Alice saw the funny side of this and giggled. The atmosphere lightened and even more so as Averil said, 'I didn't say when I met you, Alice, but I have seen you before. I was at that same jumble – I was on the china stall. You didn't notice me, but I saw you buy my frock and felt so pleased as you were exactly the person that I had in mind for it. I could have jumped for joy when I opened the door to you wearing it. I bought a lovely shawl there. Hand-crocheted with a thread that has tiny speckles of silver running through it, I love it.'

'I saw that hanging behind the stall and thought it grand. I wanted to purchase it, but I'd already bought two things that I thought I'd never go anywhere to wear.'

'Oh, I wear that sort of thing every day. I never stand on ceremony. I dress according to my mood and I hope that you did tonight? As to choose that frock, you must have felt bright – maybe a little nervous about meeting us, but excited too, and above all, wanting to look your best.'

'Eeh, I did. I chose it for just them reasons.'

'Well then, buy something frivolous next time. We'll go together and I can help you – we'll look for a similar shawl. Then if you feel like dancing barefoot in the grass, wrap it around you and dance! Fling it in the air, make circles, whatever you feel like doing!'

Alice laughed at the image of her dancing barefoot on grass, and yet a spark lit in her as she realised that's exactly how she had felt on many occasions – restless and yet full of joy.

'By, that'd be grand. And there's nothing I'd like better than to have you along with me and my friends when we go to the jumble. You'll love Edith and Marg.'

Gerald spoke for the first time since her embarrassment, the crossness she felt towards him having left her. She would take him to task over not warning her, but for now she forgave him.

'You will love them very much, Mother. They, like Alice, have so much weighing them down, but they're always ready to giggle. You will meet them on Sunday.'

Averil clapped her hands. 'Wonderful! I can't wait. Oh, and wear that other frock I saw you buy, Alice, darling – the lemon one with the square neck. It will so suit your olive skin, an unusual feature with you being so blonde.'

'Oh? Was that one of yours an' all?'

'No, I did have my eye on it, though. I'd looked at it while we were sorting the jumble, but when we organise the stalls, we're only allowed to buy one item each before we open the doors, and it was either that or the shawl. When you saw it, I had already purchased it and hung it there.'

'So, no one'll recognise it when I come on Sunday?'

'No, and nothing else any of us wear as my friends are not from close by. They are friends from our university days who are all just like us, despite having attained high positions in life. They love music, fun, and just being themselves.'

'Some of the chaps and I will be providing the music, dear.'

'Gerald told me you would. You play the guitar, don't you? I love music. I listen on the wireless.'

'Oh, and what do you like – what music in particular?'

'I love it all, especially the dance music programme. But eh, when they play Benny Goodman's records, I just want to jig and fling myself around. Though I like the jolly music and the waltzes that Reginald Dixon plays an' all.'

'Well! You cover a lot of genres there, but I think you'll love our little band then, as we play all of those – swing in particular. We have a sax player who can make his saxophone talk.'

They all laughed.

'Gerald plays the piano, you know? But he loves guitar too, he just doesn't play it as well as his father, do you, son?'

'I'm not as good at anything you are, Father, but keep looking over your shoulder as I'm catching you up!'

Again, they laughed and Alice couldn't believe how relaxed she felt. She seemed to belong here with these folk and she never would have thought that in a million years.

'My brothers love music an' all. You should see Billy dance; he loves swing music.'

'Well, I hope you will bring them on Sunday, my dear. It will be lovely to have some youngsters about, and really nice to meet your brothers, as they are to become our surrogate grandchildren.'

'Ta. Averil, I didn't know whether Gerald had told you that he's willing to take them on when we marry.'

'Oh, yes, he's told us everything! We cannot shut him up when he starts talking about you, your family and your friends, and the street you live in. He seems to have found his home with you all.'

This sent a warm feeling through Alice. She turned her head and looked at Gerald. His smile was so beautiful. This garden setting, with its lush green lawn bordered by hedges, a huge tree in the corner and beds of flowers, seemed to relax him and she wondered how he could like her street with its hustle and bustle of people calling out to one another and the rumpuses that broke out at the drop of a hat. But he'd once said something similar to them being like a huge family, and he was beginning to feel part of it – maybe being an only child meant he longed to have a bigger family. Well, she loved that feeling too, and hoped they had a whole rook of children of their own when they were married.

She blushed at this thought and at how her body longed so much to experience Gerald's lovemaking.

'Well, we'll leave you two love birds together while we go and get dinner on the table. We'll shout you when it's ready.'

As soon as they'd gone, Gerald reached for her. In a low voice, he said, 'I'm guessing that you had the same feelings as me just now, darling? I saw it in your expression when you looked at me.'

She nodded, knowing what he meant.

'Let's marry soon. Let's set a date and announce it to Mother and Father over dinner.'

'Yes, Gerald, let's make it soon.'

'Christmas?'

'That'd be grand.'

Gerald rose and pulled her to her feet. 'You haven't seen the summer house yet. I'm going to take you there and seal our promise with a kiss.' With this, he took her hand and ran with her across the lawn. 'It's in a secret place, through the gate behind the tree.'

'But your mother might call us in to eat.'

'Not for at least half an hour. They had everything prepared but have to cook it all. They'll leave us alone during that time.'

'Oh, have you brought many girlfriends here, then? You sound as though there's a routine.'

He giggled. 'Hundreds! Ha, no, you're the only one, darling. Mother always said, "Go with as many young ladies as you like, but only ever bring the one you are going to marry home here."'

'And did you have loads?'

'A few, some very nice ones, but after a couple of dates, they just became friends. What about you? Any boyfriends?'

'I fancied a few, but didn't dare to go with any if they asked me. But then, it never mattered to me. When I met you, that was it, and I was ready to stand up to me da.'

They'd reached the gate, out of sight of the house as it was, like Gerald said, tucked behind the huge tree. 'Oh, Alice, it was like that for me, darling, an instant falling in love.' He pulled her to him. 'I can't wait till we get to the summer house, I want to kiss you now.'

She drowned in love as his lips met hers, gasping his name when they parted and going into a deeper kiss as he drew her to him. She could feel his hunger, and matched it with her own as their bodies moulded so closely it was as if they were one.

Gerald broke away first. Sighing heavily, he lifted his eyebrow. 'Maybe before Christmas?'

'Yes, yes, Gerald, darling! Make it soon.'

'Oh, Alice, I don't know if I can wait another minute, let alone a month or two.'

'Nor me. I love you, Gerald, and want to be yours. All of me wants that.'

His groan thrilled her as he took her hand and pulled her through the gate.

Alice tingled with nerves and anticipation, but felt an acute disappointment as he whispered, 'Not here, not now, I want us to be completely alone. I'll sort something out. That's if you're sure, darling?'

'I'm sure. I love you, Gerald, with all of my heart.'

'Oh, Alice. Alice.'

He kissed her more gently and led her into the summer house. 'Let's sit and plan our wedding, darling . . . But, well, I need to say to you that at any time you can change your mind on anything – and I do mean anything that we decide to do.'

'I know. I – I would only have one worry, well, about, you know . . . It's just that I don't want to be pregnant before we wed.'

'Oh, darling, don't worry, I will protect you.'

'I know, and I know you'll still marry me, but I don't want anyone saying you were forced to marry me. That'd taint our love and put doubts in my mind.'

'Don't ever doubt me, my darling. Look, I'm going to make you a promise now – it goes against all that I want to do, but I have changed my mind. We won't come together . . . I mean, I won't make love to you until after we are married.'

'But—'

'I know you want to as much as me, and that bodes well for our future as man and wife, but now that I can think without being in the throes of extreme desire' – he smiled, a kind of apologetic smile – 'this, for both of us, is the best path to take. You will know beyond doubt that I wanted to marry you because I love you and cannot live without you, and I won't feel that shame which I am bound to if I take advantage of your feelings for me.'

Alice could see that he was right in what he was saying and agreed. 'Aye, let's save ourselves for our wedding night.' As she said this it occurred to her that she had to pick the date carefully. She'd heard those about to be wed say how they'd worked their special day around making sure they weren't on their monthly, and she wanted nothing to spoil her own special wedding and first night of being married. She now knew with the feelings that had awoken in her that she wanted to be able to give herself fully to Gerald that night.

Quickly doing mental arithmetic, she told Gerald. 'I think five weeks from now.'

'What date will that be, darling? I haven't got my diary on me?'

'I think the first week in September . . . But, eh, I'm not sure we can be ready. We haven't said where we would live . . . Well, I don't think you'd want to live at my house, would you?'

'I don't see why not. It's a lovely house, very cosy, and it's where I imagine you are when I think of you. But it wouldn't really be suitable . . . well, for a short time maybe. Look, I think for now it's best if we plan for as soon as possible, and we iron out all the arrangements and see how soon we can settle all the details.' He took her hand. 'I will do all I can to make it around that date, darling. Did you pick it for a reason?'

Alice felt her colour rise.

'Oh . . . right, very good thinking. I too want to avoid any delays after we say I do.' He dispelled her embarrassment with a smile. 'So we'll get everything in place then fix a date, and I promise to be on my best behaviour until it arrives and you are my wife.'

Alice giggled. Before she could answer there was a shout from over the fence: 'Ten minutes, if you want to freshen up.'

Gerald called back before saying, 'Well, darling, saved by the bell, as I was just about to kiss you again. Come on, I'll show you where the bathroom is.'

'Bathroom? You've got a bathroom?'

'Yes. No going up the yard or dragging in a tin bath here. We're very lucky, and this is what I want for you and the boys, Alice. I want to give you a proper life and I want the boys to have every chance in life too.'

She couldn't speak. None of it was anything that she knew or had dreamt of, but it all sounded wonderful.

As they settled down to what Gerald said was the first course – a dish that looked lovely, but Alice had no idea what it was – Gerald made the announcement. 'We have something to tell you both.'

'You're going to get married very quickly! Good. The quicker the better – one, because you are so very much in love and that's always a danger, two, because we are in love with Alice too and want her for our daughter, and three, I will then retire and your mother and I will go travelling. Your wedding gift will be this house, and we will use our house in the Lake District as our main residence when we're back in England – which won't be often as we want to travel to far off places and help those who need our skills.'

Alice couldn't believe what she was hearing. She looked at Gerald. His mouth was open, his eyes staring.

His mother's words reflected this. 'Gerald, my dear, you look like a fish. You only have to close and open your mouth a few times to complete the picture.'

Gerald burst out laughing. 'Oh, Mother . . . Father . . . I – I don't know what to say.'

'Don't say anything. Give your lovely Alice a hug and then us.'

At that, Alice was in Gerald's arms, but she still couldn't register what she'd heard. As Gerald hugged his mother, Alice looked around this beautiful room, furnished in soft greys and gold. It was magnificent, and with its ornate furniture she imagined it would be fit for a film star. Though she had to admit that it was more in line with Averil and Rod's person-alities than hers and Gerald's own. Gerald expressed the same thoughts after she came out of a hug from Averil and then Rod. A hug that spoke of love and acceptance and filled her with joy.

'We can't thank you enough, can we, Alice?'

Alice, still held in the amazement of it all, could only shake her head and smile at Gerald, but then he hesitated as he said, 'Only . . . well, I don't know how you feel, Alice, but . . .' He turned to Averil and Roderick. 'I – I might sound ungrateful by asking, but would you mind terribly if we furnished the house to our own taste?'

Averil's lovely tinkling laugh gave Alice a sense of relief. How Gerald knew she would agree with him, Alice didn't know, but she was glad he'd approached the subject and that he knew her feelings without having to ask her.

'Of course not, darling! This will be your home. As you know, it has never been our favourite of the two, has it, Rod, dear?'

'No, never. It was just a place near to work and to bring you up in, son. Our dream house is in the woods in the Lake District, Alice. Averil furnished this in our style to help us to feel at home, and she has accomplished that, but we can walk away from here with happy memories and no regrets. We plan on extending our Lake District house and will want most of this furniture for it. In the meantime, it can all go into storage, while we commission the work and go on our travels.'

'Thank you, Father. How will I ever repay you both?'

Averil answered, 'You have done already, darling, by giving us such a lovely new daughter, as we look on you as that already, Alice. We are so proud of you, Gerald, and this was always our intention for when you married. Now, shall we open the champagne and have a toast before we eat the next course?'

By the time Gerald took her home, Alice felt as though she had been transported into a dream.

Gerald had taken her on a tour of the house and she'd loved every room. The wonderful kitchen in bottle green and cream, with cream cupboards, green and cream tiled floor and a stove like she'd never seen before, which Gerald told her was a Rayburn. It was heated by a fire behind one of its doors. Its

297

other two doors were ovens and the hotplate on the top had its hottest spot over the fire and a simmering place over the ovens. She could imagine cooking so many lovely dishes on it for Gerald and her brothers.

And, oh, her brothers! How they were going to love having space. Even though Billy and Joey would have to share a room, Harry could have his very own, as there were five bedrooms in all. The other two would be a nursery and a guest room.

Gerald had suggested their first guests be Edith, Marg and Jackie and Alice had readily agreed. They would hold a party after they married and everyone could stay the night.

Not that she knew how they would make that work with the ties her lovely friends had, but that was a problem for later. For now, she'd been plucked from Hell and transported to Heaven, and nothing was going to spoil that for her.

TWENTY-SIX

Edith

Edith woke to the sound of Alice calling her through the letter box, in a voice that exuded happiness. 'Get up, Edith, come on! I know it's early, but I just have to tell you something!'

'What's all the noise, Edith, love?'

Edith jumped out of bed and went and stood outside her ma and da's room. 'Sorry, Da, it's Alice. I'll just go and let her in.'

Running down the stairs, dying for a pee, she opened the door and stood crossed-legged in her nightie. 'Alice, have you gone mad, lass?'

'No . . . Yes! Eeh, Edith, come over to mine as soon as you can! I'll get some doorsteps toasted. Hurry, while I just go and get Marg up.'

As she turned, Marg stood on her step. 'I'm up, and so is half the blooming street. Eeh, Alice, lass, I can see you're happy, but is there need for all of this?'

Marg was laughing, as Edith was as she called over to Marg, 'I think she must have wet the bed, it's only just on six!'

'Stop being daft, the pair of you, and hurry, I want us to have breakfast together before we go to work. I've so much to tell you!'

'All right. Can I bring Jackie?'

'Oh, aye, I've got the lads up an' all. Will your gran be all right?'

'Aye, she's still in the land of nod . . . Well, she was. I'll just check, but I'll bring her with me if not. I'm not missing out on this! What a treat.'

'I'll be over in a mo, love, I need the loo.' Edith closed the door and made a run for the backyard, ignoring Albert shouting for everyone to shut up.

Back in the kitchen Edith took the almost full kettle from the side of the hotplate and filled the tin bowl they used to have a wash. Swilling herself and leaving a fresh kettle full of water on the hotplate, she hurried upstairs to dress. Never had she felt this excited as she'd got ready for work, but now she was filled with anticipation.

'I'll bring tea up for you all, won't be a mo, then I'm going over to Alice's to have breakfast before work.'

Three grunts answered her.

When she got to Alice's it felt as though a whirlwind had hit her. Marg and Jackie were already there and the lads looked bright as buttons, as if it were nine o'clock and not six thirty.

'Morning, Edith. It's all ready for you on the table, help yourself. I'll just pour you a mug of tea.'

'Eeh, Alice, what's to do?'

They all stood and stared in amazement as Alice told them. It sounded like something out of a film.

'I can't wait for you to see the house on Sunday. You'll love Averil and Rod and it is as Gerald said, all of their friends are like them.'

'By, Alice, you've fallen on your feet, lass, and I can't say how happy I am for you.'

'Ta, Marg. And I know something good'll happen for you an' all, lass. But I'll always be there for you. My door'll be open to you all.'

'Eeh, I can't take it in, Alice. It seems like no time since you were . . . well, since things weren't good. I can't say how happy I am.'

'Ta, Edith. I know, my life's changed beyond anything I could have imagined or dreamt of. And it's all helped me cope with my da's passing and forget all that went before that. What about you, lads? How do you feel about it?'

'You say the lawn's big enough for us to play footie, and that Gerald'll put goalposts up for us? And we'll still be at the same school and can have our mates around sometimes?'

'Aye, I said all of that and it's true. Your lives will only change for the better, Billy. What about you, Harry?'

'By, our lass, I like Gerald, I like him a lot, so I think I could live with him. But it's going to be strange. I don't knaw if I'll be happy or not.'

Jackie encouraged him. 'You will, Harry. You'll have your own room and I can come and study with you. It'll be grand.'

Harry smiled at her. To Edith, the smile held love, and she could see by the wink Marg gave her and Alice's raised eyebrows and smile that they had seen that too.

'Well, in that case, it might be all right. As long as life don't change too much and I'm not expected to be posh.'

'No, no one'll expect anything of you, Harry, they just want you to be yourself and to be happy. You'll see what I mean when you meet Averil and Rod. They're so nice – so ordinary, and . . . well, accepting.'

This, Edith could see, meant a lot to the lads.

'You haven't asked me yet, Alice.'

'I was getting around to you, Joey. So, lad, what've you got to say?'

'I feel all strange in me tummy. Like I did when you told me Da had gone. Like everything I know ain't going to be like it is no more.'

Edith watched Alice go to Joey and hug him. 'You're right there, lad, it's going to be a hundred times better.'

Joey grinned.

It was Marg who asked, 'What about our street party that was to be your engagement party? You'll be married by then. Aye, and for almost two weeks!'

'We can have it for our birthdays, just as we first planned.'

'By, lass, you've a lot to do. Your wedding's in five weeks' time!'

'Well, that's another bit of me news. I'll be handing in me notice today.'

'Oh?'

Marg sounded as though she'd been hit by something, and when Edith looked over at her she saw tears brimming in her eyes.

Edith decided to take a different view; she wanted nothing to spoil Alice's excitement. 'Good for you. You'll give hope to every lass who stands on their swollen feet for hour upon hour with nothing in the future to look forward to. Come here, Alice, let me give you a hug.'

This did the trick as Marg came forward too. 'I'm not missing out on a Halfpenny Girls hug.'

They clung together and Edith could feel that the atmosphere was charged with mixed emotions. For Marg, she knew it felt like the end of an era. For herself, a beginning and a hope that she too could find happiness with Philip, and for Alice, excitement and joy came from her in bucketloads.

'Right, lasses, I've to go. I've not packed mine and Albert's snap yet and he'll want some fried tatties afore he goes out to work. See you at eight as usual.'

Edith ran across the road, knowing she was going to be hard pushed to do everything in time, but feeling as if she'd just had a Christmas Day.

The morning had dragged for Edith. Her thoughts had been on Saturday night, which seemed so far away and as if it would never get here, so she was glad of the break when she was distracted by the chat about the wedding.

As soon as they were sitting in the canteen eating their sandwiches and drinking tea, Alice told them that she, Marg and Jackie would all be bridesmaids, that Harry would give her away, and Billy and Joey would have the job of taking care of everyone. For this task they'd be practised in where everyone was to sit in the church and would give out the hymn books. 'And a bit of news for you, Edith. Philip's going to be our best man – at least, Gerald told me he was going to ask him.'

303

At the mention of Philip's name, Edith's heart did a little flip. But there wasn't a lull in the conversation for her to dwell on the feeling as Marg said, 'By, Alice, your mind must be working overtime to have sorted all that out.'

'I never slept all night, I can tell you, me mind was that active. I even know what the frocks you're all going to wear will look like – cream, with satin sashes of different colours. Ruby red, royal blue and a rich dark green that I can't describe, but which I have seen on the cushions in Averil's front room.' She went on to tell them all about the house, finishing by telling them, 'Every room gives you the feeling that you are in a film star's house, but then, that's Averil's personality, she is just like you imagine a film star to be. Anyroad, you'll see everything on Sunday. Averil can't wait to meet you, and don't be nervous because there's nothing to be nervous about; it'll be like being around our own folk. I promise.'

Edith caught Marg's expression and could see she wasn't sure, which is how she felt herself, but she decided she'd wait and see.

'By, it all sounds like a fairy tale, and I for one can't wait to wear me frock and support you on your wedding day, lass.'

'Ta, Edith. But I've taken over the conversation – what about you and Philip? Aren't you seeing him again this week?'

'Aye, I told you, Saturday night. We're going to the Tower Ballroom.'

'Oh aye, you did. Ha, my head's in the clouds! It'll be grand, you love dancing. What're you going to wear?'

This had been worrying Edith all week. 'I've to have a rummage through all three of me going-out outfits yet, so I don't know.'

They all laughed at this.

It was Marg who became practical about it and helped her out. 'Look, we're all about the same size, so why don't we pool what good bits of clothing we've got and you can pick something from the lot?'

'That's a good idea, Marg. I'll take that lovely chocolate-coloured, pencil-slim skirt of yours, as you're nearer my height, and that red satin blouse of yours, Alice; I love the frills down one side of the buttons and the little puffed-up sleeves.'

'You'll look lovely. We want a parade afore you go.'

Edith grinned at Alice as she pictured herself dressed in these items of theirs.

'I'd forgotten about that skirt, Edith. It'll look grand on you, and I'll tell you what, Ma's got some lovely brown shoes with a little heel. She's never worn them and they'd go lovely with it. What size are you, Edith? These are a five.'

'Perfect, but would she mind?'

'Well, if she ain't out of hospital, she won't know, but of course not. I'm seeing her tonight, I'll ask her.'

'Oh, Marg, I hope she comes home soon. It's a worry for you, and something else you've got to sort out – going up to the hospital. But don't worry about your gran, me ma'll keep her happy. Though if she's lapsed and had a drink, then I will.'

'Do you think she might?'

'I don't know, Marg. This is the longest she's gone without, and she seems happy. But, well, that could all change.'

The bell went then and they all scampered to the lav. 'Eeh, we should have gone at the beginning of our break!'

'Don't worry, Edith, me and you'll go first as they can't sack Alice for being late back now she's given her notice in.'

As they hurried along the corridor, nerves made them giggle. It was when Edith came out with Marg that they were met by Moaning Minnie, her arms folded across her chest. 'You two looking to join your mate and become ladies of leisure, then? You're five minutes over your time so expect a quarter of an hour docked from your wages next week!'

'Eeh, we're sorry, Mrs Roberts. The time ran away with us.'

'Aye, well, that's as may be, but this ain't the first time. You get back to the line, Marg. Edith, a word.'

Marg scurried away.

'I know what you're going to ask, Mrs Roberts. And yes, it's all sorted. Albert's forgotten about his threat now. He's a different lad to then. He's changed a lot of his ways, so you needn't worry about Ida.'

'Glad to hear it. But another little bird has whispered in me ear. You were seen with Philip Bradshaw, getting up close and comfortable. Pack that in. It don't go nowhere, believe me. He's way out of your league and'll be out for what he can get. I wouldn't want you to become a fallen woman.'

'I won't, and aye, it's true, I am seeing Philip. We're going out on Saturday night as it happens.'

'By, you're getting above yourselves, ain't yer? You lasses are from the backstreets – Whittaker Avenue, not Newton Drive or any other posh area of Blackpool – so you mind yourselves. Setting your sights high will end in broken hearts.'

'It hasn't for Alice.'

'Yet! Though I have to admit that in life there can be fairy tales, but they don't happen often so don't go thinking you can nab yourself a prize as big as Alice has. You'll end up hurt. Settle for one of your own type, like the rest of us.'

In a strange way, Edith knew that Mrs Roberts was looking out for her as they all did one of their own, but she couldn't heed the warning. Neither did she feel that she should.

'Are you listening to me?'

'I am, and I'll be careful. If there's any suggestion of . . . well, doing anything I shouldn't, I'll take to me heels, I promise.'

'Good lass. Aye, have your fun, but just be careful is all I'm saying.'

'I will, ta, Mrs Roberts.'

'Go on, get back to the line.'

Edith hurried back to the line, glad to escape, though she had to admit, Mrs Roberts wasn't as bad as she was painted. She did care about them all, but she had to do her job.

Walking back home with Alice after Marg had left them to go to the hospital, they chatted on about Alice's wedding, and whether the same might happen for Edith. 'I don't think it will be quite the same if it does. Philip has declared his love for me in a roundabout way, but he does have problems at home. If it came to it, he may choose his family over me.'

'Oh, Edith, I don't think so. You know, it seems to me that people with money don't care as much about having it as people who are poor. I mean, we'd be hard pushed not to take what money came our way, sometimes sacrificing things for it just so we don't starve, but they have never had to look at it that way.'

'I suppose, but to give all that up to live in relative poverty with me would be a big ask. But you know, his parents have proved you right. They had nothing, and now they'd sacrifice their own son's happiness to hang on to what they've got – and I don't mean their money, but the standing they have. They'd see me as a threat to that.'

'It's sad really. Then you get Averil and Rod, who have always been privileged, and yet would give it all up to go and help some tribe in the back of beyond.'

'Really?'

'Aye, that's part of their plan after they've travelled a bit.'

'Eeh, there's no accounting for folk. We're all different, whether we're the haves or the have-nots. Anyroad, will you be coming over to Marg's for cocoa tonight?'

'Aye, I will. Hope that cloud doesn't decide to empty its load on us, though, I like it when we can sit out.'

'Me too. I'll see you later, I've to get tea sorted. But I'll call in on Jackie first and see if she's all right.'

Edith found that all was quiet in Marg's house. Jackie had the tea on – a stew that was simmering on the stove and smelt delicious, and was sitting at the table with her books. Her gran was snoring in the chair.

'Glad all's all right, lass. Give me a call if you want a break. Eeh, I bet you're missing school, aren't you? The holidays can drag at times.'

'No, I ain't had time, Edith. Me gran gives me the runaround most of the day. But ta, and aye, I would like a break in a bit, but Marg said she wouldn't be late and then I can go over to Harry's.'

'All right, lass. See you later.'

The cloud broke as Edith stepped outside so she had to run across the road. When she got in her da sat in his chair, looking pale and dejected. She went up to him and kissed his cheek. 'By, it's decided to bucket it down all of a sudden, Da. Where's Ma?'

'She were bored, lass. She said sommat about nipping to the church hall as the ladies meet up on a Wednesday afternoon. I don't knaw how she knaws that, though.'

Alarm bells rang for Edith. 'Da, when was that?'

'Aw, about two-ish.'

'Did she have any money?'

'Aye, I gave her a couple of bob as I managed to get to the post office to get me pension cheque cashed.'

'Eeh, no, Da . . . It's nigh on six now. She'll have gone drinking. Did she have a coat?'

'Naw, it were a nice afternoon till this lot started.'

'I'll get hers and mine and go look for her. I'll shout Alice to send Harry over to make you a brew. I won't be long.'

Dashing over to Alice's, Edith was almost in tears as she asked the favour of Harry and was glad when he willingly agreed.

'Ta, Harry. You know where everything is, don't you? Da's told me that you've popped in afore and made him a cuppa – I've meant to say ta for that.'

'Aw, there's naw need, I like spending time with your da.'

Alice gave her a pitying look. 'Oh, Edith, lass. I hope your fears are unfounded. Will you be all right, it's chucking it down?'

'Aye, I will if I find me ma, Alice. I'll get off, lass.'

Running as fast as she could, Edith made for the Layton Institute which, being a club, could stay open longer. The sight that met her when she arrived made her heart do a somersault.

'Ma, eh, Ma! You're getting soaked ... What happened? You're bleeding!'

'Is that you, Edish?'

'Oh, Ma. Get up, them steps are cold. What're you doing here, and how did you cut your head?'

'I jush wanted a little drink, but landlord threw me out.'

'What? Bodily? Did he make you fall?'

'Naw, but he made me leavsh, and I tum ... tumb ... fell on the shteps.'

'Eeh, Ma, you said you'd not drink again. Come on, let's get you home.'

'Whersh Albert? He wash here.'

'Albert? How?'

'He came to buy shome fagsh, only he wouldn't give me one.'

'Come on, Ma, get up, there's a good 'un. Let me help you home.'

'Me legsh won't work.'

'How many have you had? Da said he only gave you a couple of bob.'

As she lifted her ma, an empty bottle of gin rattled down the steps. 'Ma, where did you get that from? Ma?' It was no use; her ma gave a snore. Despairing, Edith looked around. No one was about to help her. Feeling foolish at having to do so, she knew her only way was to go into the club and ask for help.

As she climbed over her ma, the sound of screeching tyres had her turning. Then the bottom seemed to fall out of her world as she saw Philip's car coming to a skidding halt.

'Edith! Edith, are you all right, my love?'

Though the endearment penetrated the horror of the moment, Edith just wanted to die. She turned to face Philip fully, saw that he'd got out of his car and only had a shirt on that was now soaked through. Saw too how his parted hair fell in wet strands on each side of his face and that a raindrop was ready to fall off the end of his nose, and she had the over-whelming urge to just jump into his arms and have him take her away from this hell of embarrassment and the disgust she felt in her own ma.

'I – it's me ma, she's in a bit of a state and I can't lift her. Eeh, Philip, I'm sorry, I – I told you, you shouldn't bother with the likes of me.'

'You're not going to stop me, nor is your unfortunate mother, or mine and my father. I can't help myself, Edith, you know how I feel. Let me help you, my dear.'

With this, Philip lifted Ma, and between them they half walked and half dragged her to Philip's car. Ma didn't help by swearing her head off at Philip and passers-by.

'Ma, please, behave! Come on. Please, Ma.'

Tears flooded Edith's eyes. Tears of humiliation and despair. When they spilt over, Philip looked at her with such pity in his eyes. 'Edith, darling, don't. We're winning now. Ignore everyone. We'll get your mother into the front seat with you, you'll be cramped as it's not the biggest bench seat. But it can be done.'

Though Edith did as Philip directed, she couldn't stop her tears.

Why? Why does Ma need to do this?

Once they were all in the car squashed on the bench seat, Edith put her arm around her Ma to soothe her. She daren't think what would happen when she arrived, as it seemed Albert would be there by then.

True to her fears, Albert stood outside their house, his arms folded, smoke from his fag curling up and making him squint – his expression and stance telling of his anger.

'Ma, don't do anything to upset Albert, love. Just get out of the car quietly, please. Let's get you inside and get you a nice cup of tea and something to eat, eh?'

'I'll help you in with her, Edith.'

'No, I'll be all right, ta.'

'Edith, you'll never manage, my dear, and by the looks of who I am assuming is your brother, he isn't up for helping you. Don't worry. I'm not here to judge you. I know your circumstances.'

His hand reached out and covered hers. She wanted so much to have all this go away, but sighing, she knew she couldn't.

'At least the rain has stopped so I can put the roof back down and get you both out more easily. Hold on, it won't take me a mo to wind it down.'

Edith listened as Philip spoke to Albert. Every sinew of her body tensed. 'Good evening. I'm a friend of Edith's. I've brought her and your mother home.'

'Who are you, then? How come you know our Edith?'

'I'm Philip Bradshaw.'

'Her boss!'

'No, but the boss of Bradshaw's is my father. Edith and I are very good friends.'

'Well, I've never heard tell of you.'

'No?'

Philip sounded a little hurt. Edith willed him to understand how difficult it was to tell her brother anything that he might not like.

'Anyway, I'd appreciate your help with your mother.'

'I ain't helping that old bag. She's a disgrace, showing her family up how she does. She can fall in the gutter if she likes, and I'll spit on her as I pass.'

'Very well, Edith and I will manage.'

'You can just sod off, Edith can manage. We don't like snobs like you around here.'

'I'm not a snob, I'm a friend – well, more than a friend – and I'm going to help her.'

There was something in Philip's tone that Albert responded to. He shrugged his shoulders, threw down the fag he'd held in his mouth and went inside.

The roof was down now and Philip half lifted Edith out as she tried to climb over the low side. 'Please don't be upset, Edith.'

Edith looked around. Every door had opened and her neighbours stood watching, making her feel as though they were a sideshow. Alice came running across the road, followed by Harry, and calling out if everything was all right. Jackie was soon following them as she'd opened her door too.

'By, Edith, is it your ma?'

'Aye, it is, Alice. Philip came across us when I was trying to lift her and couldn't.'

'Hello, Philip. Nice to see you again. Come on, Edith, I'll help you, lass.'

As Philip stood Ma up and Alice took one side and Edith the other, Philip said, 'Nice to see you, too, Alice. I can congratulate you now. I was going to on Sunday as I'm invited too. I was thrilled by the news and very happy for you both. And very happy to hear that you will be at the garden party too, Edith, dear.'

Edith just nodded. Inside she was dying and this was made worse by her ma calling out, 'What you lot staring at? I'll piss on the lot of yer!'

'Ma! Ma, please don't.' Edith's tears found the dried traces of her last ones, making her nose run, and completing her humiliation.

'Edith, darling, please, don't let this affect us. It isn't in anyway upsetting me. Will you still be on Talbot Road on Saturday night?'

Alice passed her a handkerchief. 'Use that, love. She will, Philip. I'll see to that, but better if you go now.'

'Yes, piss off. Me son wash right, you snobsh are not welcome here.'

'Eeh, Ma. Ma . . .'

'I'll see you on Saturday, Edith.'

Edith couldn't even look at him. She just wanted him to disappear, and for her to get out from under the eyes of the laughing neighbours.

Once inside, Alice took charge. 'Sit down and be quiet, Betty. Harry, you make a cup of tea. Jackie, lass, go back to your gran, she can get into a lot of mischief in a few minutes. Harry will come over to yours when he's made the brew.' Turning to Albert, she gave him what for. 'You don't help matters talking like that to Edith and her friends, and bullying your ma, lad. Why can't you have a civil tongue in your head?'

'Well, it gets me down. She shows us up. And she steals. She had a bottle of gin away while the landlord turned his back. He told me he ain't putting up with it anymore, even if I do pay him. Next time he's getting the police to her.'

Edith wiped her face. This was a chance for her to help Albert out of the hole he'd dug for himself and probably help to get him out of his mood. 'You paid for the gin?'

'Aye, I did.'

'You're a good lad, Albert. I understand how you feel, but to do that to save Ma from going to court, that's good.'

'Aye, well, I'm sorry how I spoke to your man ... He is your man, ain't he? He ain't got you for a ... well, he'll do right by you, won't he?'

'We like each other, yes. And aye, I know how it looks, but when you get to know Philip, you'll like him.'

'I'll apologise.'

'Ta, lad.' Edith looked over at her da. He looked afraid, upset and concerned in equal measures. 'It's all right, Da. We'll have a cuppa and then help Ma to bed.'

'I'm shorry, Reggie. I wash only going to the meeting, but the shtuck-up cowsh wouldn't let me in, shaid I hadn't paid me duesh. Then—'

'Eeh, lass, stop worrying, I understand.'

Edith thought that if only he weren't so understanding, then Ma may not lapse so often. But then she couldn't blame her da, she could only hope that she was lucky enough to be loved how he loved Ma.

Would Philip love her like that? He did seem to, as nothing about what had happened had put him off. How blessed she would be to have him love her how she knew her da loved Ma.

Oh, Philip, it seems my love for you and yours for me will be fraught with hurdles.

But then, somehow, she knew they would overcome them.

TWENTY-SEVEN

Marg

'Ma, I want to ask you something.'

'I knaw you must have a lot of questions for me, but Marg, I can't tell you any more than I have. And I can't apologise more than I have either. I've tried to make me peace with you, and have made it with the Lord. Now, me darling, l just want to rest until He sees fit to take me.'

'It's not about any of those things, it's about you saying as Eric hurt you. Did he?'

'Not intentionally, but I'd had enough, I wanted it over with and he ain't one for taking naw for an answer.'

'So, he would have hurt you if you refused him?'

'Naw, I don't mean that. He's just ... well, persistent and then, well, he makes me want to ... Look, this ain't anything you should hear, lass.'

'You didn't mind me hearing that he hurt you. Ma, you're playing games with me, I can just sense that you are. You want us to move in with Eric and let him take care of us, and that makes me think you'd say anything.'

'Oh, Marg, Marg. I knaw I'm naw age, but lass, I'm in a bad way. I can't get better. Please be forgiving of me for mine and your sake, me little lass.'

Feeling peeved at her ma and not able to let it go, even this sounded like another of her tricks. 'How can you know that you'll not get better? You're in a good hospital, Eric's paying for every care for you, and for the new medicine. Of course you will get better, Ma.'

This last she said in desperation. She didn't want her ma to die, even though she was angry with her. She couldn't live without her ma.

'Marg, I've got lung cancer.'

'What? No! Ma, no!' Gasping between sobs, Marg's heart felt clenched by a great force.

'Marg, eh, me lass, I – I don't want to die.'

Feeling as though she was falling at a great speed, Marg caught hold of the bedstead. 'No, Ma, no.'

Her head flopped onto the bed, her body heaving huge sobs that scorched her throat as her world splintered.

Ma's hand came onto her hair. Marg was transported back to when she would do this when she was a child. Her sobs calmed. 'Ma, I love you so much.'

'I knaw you do, and I knaw you've found me out and I'm not the person you thought I was, but do you think you can remember the times before that? When you look back, I mean, lass?'

'Aye, I can. They came flooding back to me just then, but I wish I understood.'

'I can't help you to understand without spoiling your memory of your da.'

Marg decided not to pursue this. She'd never know for sure if her ma was telling the truth or just blaming someone else again. 'Well, we'll talk no more about it, eh? I've had enough revelations as it is. Anyroad, I've probably pieced it all together, and already deduced that a lot could be put down to Horace. But what does it matter? It is what it is and I'll forget it now . . . And, Ma, I want you to come home. I'll give up work and look after you. I'll ask Eric to support us; after all, he's paying a fortune for you to be here. You'll be happier at home with me and Jackie and Gran.'

'Eeh, I would, lass. Lying here, I've got nothing to do for hours till I get a visitor, and me mind is like a horror story playing over and over.' Ma's voice cracked. 'Take me home, Marg.'

The door opening had them both turning. Eric walked in. 'What's all this, me little lass all upset? And, Marg, me darling, you've been crying! What's been happening?'

'Ma told me . . . I – I knaw what's wrong with her.'

'Eeh, Vera, we weren't going to tell them.'

'I knaw, but—'

'I made her tell me. I have to understand, then I can deal with it.'

'You take after me for that, lass. A problem faced is a problem halved, that's my motto. Would you let me hug you, Marg?'

The appeal in her ma's face made her relent. The hug was strange, she couldn't relax her body, but that didn't seem to bother Eric. 'You don't knaw how I've longed to do this over the years, lass.'

This beggared the question of why he hadn't. She'd thought of him as her uncle, after all – didn't uncles do that? – but then, as if he knew her thoughts, he said, 'I never dared approach you for fear of not being able to live the lie. I had to distance meself. Now, I'll probably pay for that way of dealing with things for the rest of me life.'

His voice was so sad that she pulled back and looked at him. 'I've asked you afore to give me time. I can't just adjust like that, I need time to accept the truth.'

'Aye, we've done wrong by you, that's for sure. But if there's anything that I can do to make it up to you, I will, lass, you only have to ask.'

'There is one thing I want, Eric. I want to take me ma home and care for her meself. To give up work and be with her every hour. But I'd need your support.'

'You've got it. Will you do that at my house?'

'No. Ma should be among her own. Her friends are our neighbours, and her surroundings are those she lived in all her married life. And I'll have my friends to call on to help me an' all. We need to be there together.'

'But Jackie? She's just a young 'un, she shouldn't—'

'What? Care for her own ma? Course she should and she'll want to do it.'

'All right. I'll take over your bills while you're looking after me Vera. If that's what you want, Vera, me darling?'

'I do, Eric. I'm lonely here, I need to be with me family, and you can visit me when you want to an' all.'

'That's settled then. So, how do you think the best way is? A bed downstairs and put your gran upstairs?'

'Aye, but Gran can stay down. Ma can have a bed in the living room. But I hope she'll get up most days and sit outside, or at least be comfy in the chair.'

'That sounds good, Marg.' Ma looked appealingly at Eric. 'They won't let me do anything here, and none of their cosseting is going to give me me life back.'

Eric plonked down on the end of the bed. To Marg, he looked like a broken man, shaking his head as he uttered, 'Eeh, me Vera, me Vera. Don't talk like that, lass, I can't bear it.'

Marg reached out for her ma's hand and held it. She could feel it trembling and knew that for all her facing up to reality, she was afraid.

Taking a deep breath, Marg made up her mind that she was going to be strong for her ma. 'I'll get everything sorted and we'll have you home by this time next week. I promise, Ma. I'll have to give a week's notice, but I'll pack the grocery store job in tomorrow. Then I can spend the weekend and every evening rearranging the house to make it suitable for you.'

'As long as that?'

'I can't do it quicker, Ma, but I'll make sure I come every evening for half an hour, and that Jackie does an' all.'

'Aye, and I'll be in and out all day so the time'll soon pass, me Vera.'

'I've to go now, Ma. I can't leave Jackie with Gran any longer. But I've a lot to tell you tomorrow night – we've a wedding coming up in the street. Alice! You'll be home and'll watch it all. I'm to be bridesmaid.'

'Really, lass, Alice marrying? Is it that doctor?'

'Aye'.

'Well, that's a turn-up. Who'd have thought, eh? I can't wait to hear all about it, lass.'

After kissing her ma and feeling the fear of holding her thin body, Marg straightened, only to see Eric with his arms open.

'I knaw you need time to accept me in me rightful place, but I reckon you need practice an' all.'

Marg giggled at his little boy expression and went more willingly into his arms this time. She needed a hug and didn't mind that it came from him.

Back home listening to Jackie tell about the goings-on, Marg was distracted. But though her heart wanted her to run to Edith to console her, she knew she had to do what she dreaded first – tell Jackie the truth.

A slurping sound took her attention away from this thought. Gran looked as though she was really enjoying her tea and she looked up at Marg. 'Nice drop of stew, lass.'

'Aye, I'm glad you enjoyed it, Gran.' Reaching for the tea towel, Marg passed it to her gran. 'Here, wipe your chin, you've dripped gravy down it.'

'I was saving that for later, lass.'

Marg laughed. Her gran could be so funny, but quickly the laughter turned to tears. Trying to wipe them away with her sleeve, she told herself off. She'd wanted to stay strong for Jackie, not blub like this. Now Jackie's voice held fear as she gasped, 'Marg? Marg, what's wrong?'

'I'm sorry, Jackie. I'm just tired.'

'Have you got a man, lass?'

'No, Gran, and you'll be the first to know when I have.'

'Right. Only they can keep you up half the night with their antics – mind, I never complained.'

Her cackling laugh had Marg and Jackie joining in.

'I can't remember me granddad. What was he like, Gran?'

Marg knew Jackie was using the distracting technique that Betty had told them always worked.

'He'll be in in a minute, lass, if you can wait to meet him. He'll enjoy some of that stew an' all. By, you'll fall for him. All the lasses do. He's a big strapping bloke. He can make me body tingle even at the thought of him walking through the door.'

'Ha, Jackie, I don't think your ploy's working this time! I think we're about to hear a full rundown.'

Jackie grinned. 'It don't even embarrass me now – it teaches me sommat, though.'

They grinned at each other and Marg felt all the sadness of having such terrible news to tell Jackie.

'Anyroad, if he's in a certain mood, you two lasses will have to make yourself scarce as there's naw putting him off, he'll want to march me into that bedroom as quick as you like. Not that I'll mind . . . Do you both live nearby? Eeh, it's good of you to come in and help me, but, well, do as I say and leave if he comes in, saying anything like, "Where's me lass? Sandra girl, get yourself on that bed, and get ready for me."'

Despite her sadness, Marg burst out laughing. 'Eeh, Gran, you're a card . . . Talking of cards, I bet you can't beat Jackie at rummy while I wash up?'

She and Jackie winked at each other. Marg was glad to see that Jackie wasn't upset by Gran not knowing her.

'There's not a chance you'll beat me, Gran.'

'Get the cards out, I'll soon show you. And me name's Sandra, not Gran. I don't knaw who this Gran is you keep talking about.'

This time the distraction did work as the two of them settled down to play. Marg sighed. She'd get on with the washing-up and by that time Gran would be nodding off. She rarely stayed awake for more than about five minutes after she'd had her tea.

Fifteen minutes later, Marg and Jackie were sitting on the low wall of one side of the backyard drinking tea. Gran, as predicted, was snoring away in the fireside chair.

'That drop of rain has made everything smell fresh, Marg.'

'Aye, and we're in for more according to the wireless. Thunderstorms.'

'Eeh, I still feel scared in a thunderstorm.'

'They ain't nice ... but, Jackie, lass, neither is what I've got to tell you.'

'I thought there was sommat up, Marg.' She put her mug down on the wall. 'Is – is it Ma?'

Marg took a deep breath. 'Aye, it is, lass.' Putting her own cup down, Marg turned to face Jackie and took her hand. 'Ma's very ill, lass.'

'Is she going to die?'

Marg nodded.

'Naw ... Eeh, Marg, naw. When? Why?' Jackie trembled. Tears filled her eyes and her body crumbled into Marg's. 'Don't let it happen, Marg, don't.'

'Aw, me little lass, I can't stop it. If I could, I would.'

Putting her hand gently onto Jackie's cheek, she lowered her sister's head onto her bosom and cradled her, joining her own sobs with Jackie's. Together they rocked backwards and forwards.

'Can nothing save her, Marg?'

'No, she has lung cancer. She—'

'Naw . . .'

The word was a long-drawn-out, strangled sound. Marg clung on tightly to Jackie, trying to stop her own world from falling apart further than it had.

'We can't leave her in that hospital. We've got to look after her, Marg. Please, Marg.'

'That's exactly what we are going to do. I'm going to give up work. Me and you'll see to ma, with a little help from Ada if we need it. But we won't do it in a sad way, mind. We'll keep everything happy around her and welcome the neighbours in to chat with her, and give Ma the best end of her life that we can. We'll bring my bed down for her and have it in the living room. I'll sleep in Ma's.'

'I'll sleep with you, Marg. You'll be cold in that big bed as you're not used to it.'

'Aye, that'll be good. I'd like that. And we'll get a bell, so if Ma needs us, she can ring it to wake us up.'

'Maybe we should take it in turns to sleep on the sofa, Marg?'

'Well, I was thinking that, but let's see how we go, eh? I like to think of cuddling up to you at night. You always slept with me, till Da . . . well, till we got another bed for you.'

'Are you going to be able to accept our real da, Marg?'

'I'm going to try. He's going to be supporting us through this. What about you?'

'I feel all right about it. He gives good cuddles, but I wish he wasn't, well, you knaw, someone like he is – a gangster.'

'Aye, but they say you can't choose your parents, don't they?'

They were quiet for a moment, clinging on to each other once more.

'Marg, me heart's hurting.'

Marg rocked her once more. Her own heart hurt too, but holding her sobbing sister eased the pain a little, as she knew she had to be strong for Jackie. But for all these brave thoughts, a tear plopped onto Jackie's hair, followed by more that she couldn't control.

Gran appeared at the back door. 'Ain't naw one going to come when I shout?'

This shocked their tears away. Jackie's eyebrows rose. 'Eeh, we've a lot on our plate, Marg, but we'll be all right, won't we?'

'We will, lass, we'll help each other through it. And if ever it gets too much, we'll come out here and sit on the wall and have a little weep and a cuddle, eh?'

'It'll be our Hawaii wall.'

'Our what?'

'They've got a wall that weeps in Hawaii. It's got lots of waterfalls flowing through it and so they call it the "Weeping Wall" and in Jerusalem they have a Wailing Wall.'

'By, Jackie, you're one on your own! Goodness knows where you get it all from . . . Coming, Gran!'

'I got that from Harry. He loves geography and he's got all of these facts stored in his head.'

'You're sweet on Harry, aren't you, lass?'

'Shurrup, you daft apeth!'

'Ha! I thought so! Well, you could do a lot worse. He's a lovely lad and handsome with it.'

'He's a lot cleverer than you knaw an' all. He'll be wasted in that rock factory, but well, he feels as though his da expected it of him.'

'Poor lad. Parents can put a lot on their kids' shoulders.'

'Our ma will, won't she, Marg? Will we cope with it all?'

'Aye, we will, lass. The love we have for Ma and for each other will shore us up and get us through. We can do this together, lass, we'll support each other.'

Despite Jackie showing her sorrow, Marg knew she'd done the right thing in telling her. Jackie would find the strength to do what lay ahead of them, and together they'd get through it somehow.

TWENTY-EIGHT

Edith

Marg's news devastated them all, and for Edith it far outweighed the incident with her ma earlier, which she had hoped to talk through on their usual meet-up at Marg's.

The three girls were in Marg's house as they huddled together, and Edith knew that, like herself, Alice didn't know how to console an exhausted Marg.

'We'll help you all we can, Marg.'

'We will, Marg. Like Alice says, we're here for you. You won't go through this alone.'

'I feel lost. And it's opened my eyes to the pain you've been through, Alice, with losing your da, and you, Edith, living with a sick parent.'

'Hush, it's all right. You and Alice are a rock for me to lean on, and we'll be the same for you.'

'Aye, and that's true for me an' all, Marg. We want to help. God knaws, you've been in the thick of it with your gran as it is.'

'This news has taken the stuffing out of me.'

'Well, it's bound to, but I know something. Your ma couldn't have better than you and Jackie to take care of her. And like I said, you won't be in this alone. Not only us, but the whole street will rally around you; that's what we do round here.'

Edith felt Marg getting stronger as she came out of their hug and dried her eyes.

'Eh, here's me hogging the limelight and yet you've been having trouble with your ma again, Edith. Was it Philip who brought her home?'

Edith felt the pain of earlier clutch her again. 'Aye, it was.' She told Marg what had happened. 'But you know what? In a small way, I'm glad now as it shows what Philip thinks of me despite me circumstances. He even dealt with Albert as his surly self.'

'That's good. I mean, it ain't, but at least you no longer need to be afraid of Philip leaving you.'

'Aye, it settled me some, but I'm worried about Albert again now. Ma getting drunk was bad enough, but she embarrassed him by stealing a bottle of gin that he was taken to task for, and had to pay for an' all. He's gone off in a huff about it.'

'Eeh, I'm sorry, lass. For that to happen when Betty had been so good . . . I thought she would make it this time. But if she keeps trying . . .'

'I'm not holding out much hope, Marg. You see, me da don't help, Ma can do nothing wrong in his eyes, but then, I suppose I've to accept everything as it is and enjoy the better times. I think I can do that now I have Philip's support. I just wish Albert was able to take Ma's antics in his stride instead of getting so worked up.'

★   ★   ★

329

By Friday, Edith knew that this wasn't going to be so. Albert had slipped back into his bad-tempered ways since Ma's setback and had moped for days. And now he was refusing to put his usual five shillings into the family pot.

Edith sat across from him at the table in the corner of the living room, trying to persuade him that he should give her something to help out. But she was getting nowhere.

'I'm telling you, Edith, I ain't paying towards that drunken cow's antics.' He pointed his finger towards the kitchen where they could hear Ma pottering about.

Edith knew she'd rather pretend to be doing something than face Albert.

'Besides, he'll give in to her if she wants to go out.' He nodded towards where Da sat in the armchair behind them. 'And that gin she stole set me back, so why should I give more?'

'Eeh, Albert, I thought you paid for that gin out of the goodness of your heart, not that you'd want to take the money back and leave us short.'

'Shurrup, will you? Don't try putting the blame on me or making me feel guilty. She's the one who drank me money away.'

Edith sighed.

'And don't come the martyr either!'

His chair fell to the ground as he suddenly jumped up and leant towards her. Edith's nerves jangled as Albert's bullying stance frightened her.

'I'm telling yer, and you'd better listen – I've had enough, right?' His face came menacingly near to hers. 'In fact, more than enough!'

330

A pain spliced Edith's cheek. Her senses left her as she fell sideways.

Stunned, she lay on the floor, her side hurting from where it had glanced the table edge and her face smarting from the blow.

Albert looked down on her. 'You deserved that. You're always going on and on; you're nothing but a nag!' He lifted his foot, but she rolled out of the way.

'Stop it!' Her own voice screamed in her ears. 'Don't you touch me again, you pig! I hate you.'

This stopped him in his tracks. He stared down at her, his foot slowly lowering, his hands clenched into fists.

Edith watched in horror as she saw Da appear behind Albert, his stick held above Albert's head. It crashed down. Albert bent over. His holler held anger as much as pain. Blood dripped through his fingers as he clutched his hair. His face grimaced into an ugly, evil mask. He turned.

Edith gasped, 'No!' but no sound came as she saw Albert's fist smash into Da's face. Da buckled at the knees and went down like a rag doll.

For a moment there was a silence, so heavy and yet so complete that Edith felt the world had stopped. Albert stepped over the prostrate, still figure of Da and slammed into the kitchen. Edith held her breath, but the sound of the back door slamming gave her the relief of knowing he hadn't touched Ma.

'Da?'

Da didn't move. As Edith pushed herself to a sitting position, the room spun around her. Vile-tasting liquid stung her throat. Her body retched, but she fought against being sick. Her voice croaked as she tried to say her da's name. Dragging her legs behind her, she got to her knees and crawled to him. 'Da, Da!'

Mumbling incoherent sounds, she took hold of her Da's hand. There was no reaction.

A trickle of blood from the back of her da's head spread into a pool as his vacant eyes died into a blank stare. His mouth fell slack, releasing a rasping breath, and Edith's terrifying fear came true. 'Da! Da! Naw, naw, naw!'

She lifted her head at the sound of the back door opening. There was a moment's silence before a fresh fear gripped Edith as Albert's voice filled the space around her.

'Get out of me way, you old hag! Think you can frighten me with that bloody rolling pin, eh? It might have worked when I were a lad, but not now, you drunken swine! This is all your fault, all of it!'

Ma's scream stopped abruptly and a crashing sound filled the space it had occupied. Edith stood, but couldn't move forward. It was as if she'd turned to stone. Albert appeared at the door, a bloodied rolling pin in his hand, his face ashen, eyes staring.

'What have you done?' The words rasped Edith's throat.

'I'm sorry, I – I, Edith, help me, help me!'

It seemed to her that her eyes were out of their sockets, such was the pressure she felt behind them as her horror-filled whisper asked, 'Ma?'

'I – I didn't mean it . . . Edith . . . Edith!' A river of tears fell from his eyes and snot ran from his nose in a spiral.

'Albert . . .' His name strangled from her throat.

He turned and disappeared through the door leading to their bedrooms. His footsteps banged on every carpetless stair before his bedroom door slammed shut.

Edith felt suspended in time. Her mind wouldn't tell her what to do. She looked down at her da hoping to hear him give her a gentle instruction, but his unseeing eyes held no hope for her.

Her body swayed. The room spun once more. The table saved her as she leant heavily over it. Then as if wading through water, she made it to kitchen.

Ma lay looking up at her with the same blank stare Da had, her head in a halo of blood, her mouth open and her body still, just like Da's.

The scream Edith released seemed to split the air as her home took on the appearance of a nightmare.

Its walls closed in on her. Her knees buckled and she sank into the blackness that welcomed her.

TWENTY-NINE

Alice

Alice finished ironing the blouse for Edith's date with Philip. She stood back and admired her efforts, as not remembering how lovely the blouse was, she'd discarded it as a creased-up mess a long time ago. 'I'll just pop this over to Edith's, then we are going over to Marg's to give her a hand with shifting some stuff. We could do with your help, Harry.'

'All right . . . I don't knaw how to act around Jackie, though, Alice. It's like she's broken, and I feel at a loss.'

'Why don't you give her a hug, eh?'

Harry blushed.

'It's all a body needs when they're hurting, lad. Not a hug that says, "I fancy you," but one that says, "I'm thinking of you, and I'm here for you."' Seeing him hesitate, she said, 'Well, I suppose there ain't much difference in them at your age, is there? But you'll learn the difference, lad. Now, watch the other two while—'

Billy and Joey came bursting through the open door. 'Alice, eeh, Alice!'

334

'What's up with you pair? You ain't broke someone's window, have you? I'll skelp the pair of you if you have!'

'Naw. There's a fight going on at Edith's but then we heard a scream and it's all gone quiet.'

Two ashen faces told her this wasn't the usual family row that could be heard from any of the houses in the street. She dropped the blouse and ran out of the house. 'Stay with Harry. Go on, don't follow me, there's good lads.'

Folk were outside, looking from one to the other. Ada was making her way to Edith's. Marg and Jackie were crossing the road, but Marg stopped Jackie in her tracks with a commanding, 'Stay with Gran!'

'Eeh, Marg, what's to do?'

'I don't know, Ada, but my God, that was some scream.'

Alice caught up with them and saw that Marg was trembling as she opened Edith's front door.

'Oh God . . . Edith, Edith, lass, what . . .'

Alice's heart came into her mouth as Ada gasped, 'Oh my God!'

'Ada, Marg, what . . .' They parted and the awful scene of Edith's da revealed itself to Alice.

Pushing past what felt like statues, Alice got inside. 'Edith? Edith, lass?' She couldn't understand how she felt so calm, but knew that the most important thing was to help Edith.

Rushing through the open kitchen door, she almost tripped over Betty. Her face imprinted on her mind in that moment. Her stomach retched, but she controlled it as she turned back to where Edith lay in a crumpled position. Her legs were bent to one side, her face flopped onto her shoulder and her eyes closed. Her skin looked deathly pale.

'Ada, quick!' She couldn't believe the strength of her own voice. 'See to Edith. I – I don't think Mr Foreman can be helped ... nor poor Betty ... She's in the kitchen. I think she's dead too.'

'No!'

Alice wasn't sure who gasped this out, but didn't take heed of it. Still in charge, she commanded Marg to send Billy to Fairweather's shop. 'Tell him to ask Fairweather to phone the police and an ambulance.'

Marg obeyed without question.

A sound behind Alice had her turning. 'Eeh, Edith, Edith, lass, are you all right?' Ada was holding Edith up and bending her over. 'We've to get the blood back to her head. She's fainted, and not surprisingly, poor lass. Come on, Edith. Take deep breaths, get some oxygen into your lungs.'

'Edith, eh, Edith.'

'Up – upstairs.'

'What do you mean, Edith?'

Ada looked up. 'Leave it till the cops get here, Alice, if she means that Albert's up there and he's done this lot. It won't be safe to approach him. Get Edith's other side and help me up with her. There's nothing we can do for her poor da, and you say Betty's a goner an' all?'

Alice nodded.

Together she and Ada took Edith outside. Someone brought a chair and they sat her on it. 'I'll go and get me kit; she's got a nasty cut over her eye and another across her nose. That swine's done it this time; he'll swing for this lot.'

'No ...'

'Don't try to talk, Edith, lass.' Alice took one of Edith's cold hands in her own. Not knowing what to say, she just gently stroked Edith's back with her other hand. When Marg came back over, she looked in a daze. Alice tried to give her a reassuring smile, but her face felt wooden.

Forcing herself to move, she looked from one to the other of her precious friends. Always they were there every step of the way for her, all her life, and now they needed her, she would help them. 'Edith, Marg, we'll get through this, we will. We Halfpenny Girls will pull together.'

The clanging of bells stopped any further talk as an ambulance and then a police car pulled up alongside the kerb.

'Now then, what's gone on here, eh?'

'There's two dead in the house and this young woman injured, and the culprit without doubt is her brother, Albert Foreman, who's upstairs in his bedroom.'

'Right, Ada. Well, let's not speculate.' Everyone stay out here while I go in to investigate.' Turning to the ambulance men, PC Bob Butcher said, 'See to the young lady – this is a crime scene and I want no one entering it.'

Within seconds, Bob Butcher came out of the house, his face drained of colour.

'Edith, lass, I'm so very sorry. Can you tell me . . . was this your brother's doing as Ada says?'

'Up . . . upstairs . . .'

'That's all she's said since I brought her round, Bob, only I wouldn't go and have a look, nor would I let Alice go. I've deduced she means that Albert's up there and he could be dangerous.'

'She's in shock, no doubt. But, yes, Ada, he could be, but he may also need help. We don't knaw that he did this, do we? Did you see anything? Did any of you see anything?'

Ada shook her head. Alice could only shake hers. But then she remembered. 'My brothers were playing in the street and heard screaming. They might know if Albert was involved.'

'Right, but I'd better take a look upstairs first.' Sighing heavily in Ada's direction, he re-entered the house. Alice felt Edith's body shiver with a violent tremor.

'Try to drink this, Edith.'

The kindly ambulance man handed her a drink that looked like water, but Alice wasn't sure whether he'd put anything in it or not. 'That's right. By, whoever saw to your injuries has done a good job, lass, we can leave them as they are until we get to the hospital. Do you think you could walk to the ambulance or shall we get the stretcher?'

'Upstairs.'

'Eeh, poor lass, she's in deep shock. Get her to finish drinking this, young lady. Now, everyone, can we have some space. We need to get the young lass into the ambulance.'

As they carried Edith to the ambulance, PC Butcher appeared at the doorway of the house once more. If Alice thought him white before, she couldn't believe how ashen he looked now as he stared at them all, before turning away from them and throwing up.

Ada went into nurse mode. 'Fetch a tumbler of water, Marg. And tell your Jackie to fill a bucket for swilling this lot away. Eeh, Bob Butcher, call yourself a policeman? You'd have been naw good tending to them that were injured in the trenches, lad. Whatever you've seen can't be near as bad as that. Drink the water Marg's fetching and tell us what's to do.'

Alice stood near to the open ambulance doors. Her whole self seemed to have shut down as she couldn't ask questions or

338

take any part in the horror that was unfolding. But then she remembered Edith and turned towards her. The ambulance men were settling her onto the bed that stretched along one side of the van. One was preparing a syringe. The sight compelled her to move.

Hurrying back to PC Butcher, she said, 'Don't tell Edith. Whatever it is, don't tell her yet.'

He shook his head. The action brought him back to his usual efficient self. 'I need back-up. Don't anyone cross over that doorstep. This is a major incident and a crime scene.'

'We've already been in.'

'Ada, stop with your backchat. I can do nothing about what happened before I arrived, but now I am here I am ordering you to obey me!'

Ada hmphed.

As PC Butcher went to his car and radioed through to his station, Alice heard the words, 'Triple deaths. Naw, I don't knaw much. The neighbours have theories, and from what I can see, they're borne out – the third death looks like suicide.'

'Right.' The ambulance man addressed PC Butcher. 'If there's naw more casualties for us, we'll get off and take Edith to the hospital.' He looked around. 'Can anyone come with her? She may need help from a friend.'

'I can . . . Harry, look out for the lads. Billy and Joey, do as Harry tells you.'

'I'll keep an eye on them, Alice.'

'Eeh, Marg.'

She opened her arms and Marg came into them. 'We'll get through all of this, I promise you, Marg. Stay strong, your own plate is full. Jackie, your gran and your ma need you.'

Marg straightened. 'Ta, Alice, I will ... See you later, Edith, lass. My love goes with you.'

Alice jumped aboard. Bells clanged and the folk caught up in the worst happening in the street gradually left her sight as she looked out of the ambulance window. She turned to look at Edith and found that her eyes were fixed on her. 'I'm here, Edith, I'll not leave your side, lass.'

'Albert ... upstairs.'

'Aye. He is. Don't worry, lass. Bob Butcher's seeing to him.'

'He – he didn't mean to.'

'I know, it ain't all his fault. We know how it is with him, poor lad.'

'They won't ... not ... oh, Alice, he won't hang, will he?'

'No, he won't, me lass.'

Torn now between telling her friend what she knew and waiting, Alice bit her lip. The ambulance man who sat in with them tending to Edith looked up at her. He shook his head, then in a gentle voice said, 'Go off to sleep, Edith, let the medication do its work.'

'I want—'

'Edith, do as the ambulance man says, there's a good lass. I won't leave you. We can sort everything out when you're well. You can tell Bob all that happened and he'll make sure everything is all right.'

Edith closed her eyes. By the time they reached the hospital, Alice saw that Edith was unaware of anything around her. She looked so peaceful.

★　　★　　★

Once Edith was settled in the ward, Alice was allowed to sit with her. She lifted the covers on her side and found Edith's hand. 'I've got you, lass. I've got you.'

A nurse came up to the bed with a glass of water. 'Get her to drink that when she wakes.'

'Ta, Nurse. Do you know Doctor Melford?'

'Oh, aye, we all know him. He's one of our most handsome doctors and we're all in mourning as he recently became engaged to marry some lucky so-and-so.'

Alice smiled a small smile. 'If you see him, will you tell him his fiancée is here with her friend.'

'Oh? Are you his fiancée or is . . .?'

'Aye, I am.'

'Congratulations, miss, you're a lucky girl.'

'I know, ta.'

The nurse scurried off and it seemed like no time at all before Gerald came through the door of the side ward Edith had been taken to.

'Gerald! Eeh, Gerald.'

In his arms, Alice nearly broke, but she held it together.

He kissed her hair. 'What happened? Is Edith all right?' He picked up the clipboard from the bottom of the bed. 'Shock? Why?'

She led him outside and told him what she'd seen and what the policeman had said. 'She will live, won't she, Gerald?'

'The danger they are guarding against is pneumonia. A severe shock of the nature you just described is a tremendous blow to the whole system. You say she doesn't know about Albert being dead and that you think he committed suicide?'

'Aye, I heard the policeman tell the station that on his radio.'

'Well, we must keep this news from Edith for now. She needs to stabilise first. Her body is erratic at the moment, judging by her charts. They will monitor her regularly. I'll ask to be kept informed. And I'll get a message to Philip. He'll want to know. He was so looking forward to meeting up with Edith tomorrow night.'

'Yes. If he comes to her, it will help Edith a lot.'

'Well, I must dash, darling. I'll pop back often. You are staying with Edith?'

'I am, my love.'

'Oh, Alice, my poor darling girl. How does so much unhappiness touch you girls, when you least deserve it?'

'This isn't all we're facing. Marg is facing more.' She told him about Marg's mother. He frowned. 'Oh? I haven't heard, and I have a lot to do with all cancer patients. What's her name?'

'Vera Porter.'

'Vera Porter? I need to look into this. Leave it with me. I have heard of the lady but not as a referral. Anyway, I'm bordering on patient confidentiality now, so I'll not say more till I find out.'

Alice didn't know what to say or to think as she sat back down next to Edith. Gerald said he would know if Marg's mum had a positive test for lung cancer, but surely . . . No, this couldn't be another of Vera's tricks, could it? She wouldn't be so cruel . . . would she?

Her mind went to all that Marg had told them, and somehow, she no longer doubted that Vera Porter could make up anything she liked to get what she wanted.

If she's made this up, it's the cruellest thing I've ever heard.

But then she looked at Edith and knew there was nothing crueller than she had to face. Poor, poor Edith.

THIRTY

Marg

Marg paced the floor, unable to settle to anything. She'd made cocoa and a piece of toast for the lads and Jackie, but she hadn't touched her own drink and her toast had dried up. She felt so restless and upset that she couldn't think straight, and thanked God that she still had a good few days to get everything ready for her ma.

'Oh, Ma, what with the awful thought of losing you hanging over me, and now this, I feel nothing but despair!'

'Who's that?'

'It's only me, Gran. Sorry, just talking to myself.' If nothing else, Gran had acute hearing.

'What's that about losing your ma?'

Marg sighed and went through. 'Nothing, Gran, I was just talking to myself, that's all.'

'Is me Vera going to die? Where is she? What have you done with me Vera? Has that Albert hit her?'

'No, Gran. How much of what went on over the road did you hear?'

343

'I knaw as that Albert's done sommat to me friend Betty.'

'Oh, Gran, I'm sorry. I forgot all the windows were open. It's such a stuffy night.'

'Well, thunder's about, lass. What's happened to me Betty?'

Seeming to have forgotten her own daughter, Gran looked very worried over Betty. Marg sighed at this thought as she tucked a blanket around Gran's legs.

'I don't want that on, you daft apeth. Eeh, I don't knaw where you came from, but you can go back there for me.'

'Eeh, Gran ... Gran.' Marg's tears, so close to the surface, trickled down her cheeks. Swallowing hard, she looked down at her beloved gran. Was this the time for truths or lies? She didn't know. But then decided that Gran was a tough old boot and that it was better to hear it from herself than anyone else. 'Gran, Ma – your Vera – is coming home from hospital. She ...'

Gran listened without making a remark while Marg explained about Ma's lung cancer, but then, emotionless, asked, 'And Betty?'

'Something terrible has happened at Betty's, Gran. Betty and Reg and Albert all died tonight.' The enormity of this hit her afresh.

'Ha!'

That was it. But thinking about it, her gran hadn't really shown any emotion over anything for a long time, except for things she remembered from the past, especially anything to do with Granddad. Perhaps this was all part of her condition. She'd ask Gerald one of these days, but part of her hoped it was, because she'd hate Gran to go through what she was experiencing right now.

Through the window and with the curtains almost closed, Marg had watched the comings and goings of the police, a black van arriving and taking away the bodies, and a cordon being put across the door. Soon after, a man and a woman had gone into the house, but had since left, and now Bob Porter stood guard, occasionally going to sit in his car. She wondered if he wanted a mug of tea, but she still felt too distraught to cross the road.

As she looked out now and saw him still sitting in his car, she decided to call out to him and went to the door. 'Bob!' He looked over. 'Can I make you a brew?'

'Eeh, Marg, I thought no one would ever ask. I've been here an hour; so much for the hospitality of Whittaker Avenue, eh?'

When she steeled herself to take it to him, she apologised. 'I'm so shocked at it all, Bob, I'm sorry. And the whole street must be – you never see it this deserted. Even Alice's brothers don't want to play out.'

'Aye, I knaw. Ta, lass. I've been the local bobby for over twenty years and I've never seen the like. By, this is going to be welcome. I emptied me stomach at the sights I saw in there.'

'I can make you some doorstep toast if you like.'

'That'd be welcome, lass. Ta.'

'How long have you got to stay here?'

'Till we can get a locksmith to secure the house.'

'I've got a set of keys, if that'll help.'

'Naw, we'll have to secure it so that no one can interfere with anything, and it don't get looted. Others might have keys an' all.'

'But what about Edith?'

'I doubt the poor lass will ever want to come here again after what she must have witnessed, though we won't knaw what that was for a couple of days. She's in complete shock. I am meself, so God knaws what she is feeling.'

'I know. Well, me and Alice'll look after her. She'll not be on her own.'

'No doubt. You three have been inseparable since you were born. The Halfpenny Girls, you once told me you called yourselves.'

'We still do, but you know, it's all changing. Our lives are going in different directions.'

'They'll never do that, lass. Aye, little things may change, but the root of your friendship won't, I can promise you that.'

When the toast was ready, she stood spreading it with dripping and thought about what Bob had said.

He's right. The stuff in our lives may change, but we won't. Me, Alice and Edith will always be pals.

This thought stayed with her as she waited for Alice to come home. The air, although still heavy and humid, hadn't brought the threatened storm. Gran was in bed and Jackie was getting ready to go, but before she did, she came out to Marg and sat on the doorstep with her.

'I feel too scared to go to bed, Marg. But Gran's fast asleep.'

'Good, she was a bit restless earlier.'

'The policemen have all gone, then?'

'Aye, Bob went about fifteen minutes ago.'

Jackie put her head on Marg's shoulder. Marg took her hand. 'There's nothing to be afraid of, lass. It's all over. Now we have to start grieving for Betty and Reg and Albert, and being strong for Edith.'

'Should we grieve for Albert? Everyone was saying that he did it.'

'It looks that way, but though the Albert we knew was a bit short-tempered and free with his hitting out, he'd been a lot better lately. We don't know what happened, but I'll never believe that he meant to kill his ma and da. I think that when he realised what his temper had caused him to do, he couldn't live with it.'

'I reckon I'll think like that an' all. And I think Betty were a bit to blame. When she drank, it did sommat to Albert. But he was always all right when she didn't. He'd been friendly with Harry recently.'

'Aye, but then, Betty couldn't help her ways either, it was like a sickness. She tried, bless her, but it always beat her. Have the lads gone to bed?'

'Billy and Joey have, but Harry said he'd read a bit as he couldn't settle till Alice came back.'

'Me neither.'

'Naw, nor me, Marg . . . Well, it ain't just what happened, it's what you told me about Ma an' all. I've not been able to cry over it for the last couple of days, and yet it feels as though me throat's burning with tears.'

'Aye, I know, I feel that. I remember I did after Da . . . well, after who I thought was our da, died an' all, and Gran said to me then, "Some things are too sad for tears. We cry when we hurt ourselves and when we fall out with someone, but some-how tears are not enough when you're so hurt and lost as you are when you lose someone." I feel like that over Ma.'

They sat quietly for a moment and Marg could feel tired-ness flooding her. Her eyes felt heavy. 'Eeh, I'd nod off here if the step weren't so flipping hard. Let's get us a chair out, shall we?'

'I think I'll go and lie on the sofa. I'll feel safe there with you just being out here.'

'All right, lass. I'll wake you to go up with me later.'

When Jackie stood, she flung her arms around Marg. 'You'll never leave me, will you, Marg?'

'No, lass, never. We'll always be together, I promise.'

When Jackie had gone to bed, Marg allowed herself a wry smile at what she'd said.

Eeh, lass, you'll be the one to leave, no doubt. You'll get a good position somewhere and marry someone posh like Alice is about to, and you'll all leave me behind, here in this little terrace, with no Ma and no Gran. All on me own – an old maid.

This thought had hardly died when a car pulled into the street. Through the dusk, Marg saw it was Gerald's car. She stood up.

She was by the edge of the kerb when the car pulled level. Alice alighted and came straight into her arms. 'Eeh, love, what's to do? How's Edith?'

'She's sedated and doesn't know that I've left her side. I'm going back. Gerald's on nights and is on his break, so he nipped me home to let you know and make sure Harry's all right.'

'By, I'm glad to see you, I've been worried sick.'

'Marg ... well, look, sit down, love. I've something – well, Gerald's got something to tell you.'

'Edith's all right, ain't she ... or is – is me ma ...?'

She couldn't say any more, but sat down and waited as Gerald spoke. 'Edith is as well as can be expected. Philip is sitting with her, though she doesn't know he's there. And yes, it is your ma, Marg.'

'What? Alice? No! What happened, Alice? Is my ma all right?'

'Yes, Marg, she's more all right than you think. She's lied to you. Eeh, Marg, I'm so sorry. I can't think what she's put you through, or why, but when I told Gerald your awful news he checked it out because, if it was true, your ma should have been under his team and she wasn't.'

'You mean, she ain't got cancer?'

'No, Marg.'

'But ... but why ...?'

'She won't say. She admitted that she lied, you see. Gerald had to ask her permission to tell you, because of patient confidentiality. She said yes, as she wouldn't be able to face you, but she said you would know why she did it. And, well, she asked us to ask you to forgive her.'

'But ... I don't know why she did it. Oh God, why would she put us through this? Why? I'll never forgive her.' But then it dawned on Marg that her ma would add this to her list of low tricks for one reason and one reason only – she wanted to avoid moving in with Eric. But then, wouldn't a simple 'no' do? Why did she go to these lengths to get what she wanted?

Gerald interrupted her thoughts. 'I'm sorry that you've been put through this, Marg. I can only say that there are such things as personality disorders. The whole field of how the mind works and the abnormalities that can occur is vast. The world of medicine has hardly touched the tip of the iceberg, but I have heard of a condition where a person cannot face reality or deal with situations that they find themselves in.

349

They resort to making up cover stories – lies are more real to them and give them a way out of a situation. It's all too complicated for me even, and medicine is my forte, so I cannot expect you to understand. But it's an easy solution to just condemn someone out of hand and brand them as a bad person, when they may be suffering from a real condition that just hasn't been identified.'

Marg tried to follow this. She wanted to hook on to it as it gave her a reason for her ma's behaviour. She wanted to find forgiveness for her, yet again, but it was difficult.

'How come all of this about me ma is only showing now? She's been just a normal ma till these last weeks.'

'We naturally trust our mothers and see nothing wrong in them – it's not programmed into our nature to. You have probably been noticing your mother's faults, her odd behaviour, but not seeing everything. But now, as you realised the role your uncle really had in your life, your real mother was exposed to you, making you a party to so much you would have been better off not knowing.'

All of this made sense to Marg. It was just like that: from the minute she realised what was happening between her ma and Eric, everything unravelled. 'Ta, Gerald, you've made me understand a lot. I know I've got to go on. And things are as they are. But I'd ask you both not to say anything to Jackie. I'll tell her as if it is wonderful news – that the doctors made a mistake, and Ma isn't going to die.'

'Marg, I have to be truthful – not having cancer doesn't mean your mother is well and has a long life. She does have damaged lungs and narrow breathing pipes – a condition we call chronic lung disease, which was a progression of her asthma and is incurable. Therefore, she is in danger as it is progressive. She will have attacks when she has difficulty breathing and her quality of her life will be affected. Look, I don't want to embarrass you, but Alice has told me what came out about your uncle and your mother.'

Marg felt mortified that Gerald knew what her mother had done, but she decided to put that to one side and listen to his explanation of her condition.

'Well, she may have felt discomfort and not wanted to continue with the intimate side of their relationship because she was breathless, and that can cause extreme distress and pain. She does need help. Her doctor at the hospital feels she would greatly benefit from having a nebuliser – in simple terms, it is a breathing aid, but it is very expensive. Not as much as keeping her in a private ward and her having private consultations and medication, so as your uncle – well, your father – is paying for that, maybe he could afford this treatment for her too. It isn't a guarantee of prolonged life, but it does help enormously with the symptoms and the quality of life a patient can have.'

'I'll speak to him. And again, I've a mind to tell him that mistakes were made in Ma's diagnosis.'

'Well, yes, that is a simple solution, but if he doesn't accept that ... look, please don't take this the wrong way, I will support you all I can, but if this comes to a complaint against my colleague, I will have to testify that you were fully aware of the truth and that I had your mother's permission to tell it to you.'

'Aye, I understand. I will tell Eric the truth if he starts to talk of making an official complaint, but for everyone's sake, I'll tell them for now that it was all a mistake.'

With saying this, and knowing that her ma was still in grave danger, Marg knew she would cope.

'It'll be all right. I can see how no one is perfect – not even me own ma. I'll get over this and try to make everything right. I'm the least of your worries. Go back and take care of Edith, she's the one that's going to need all our help. But keep me informed. I'm going to be suffering agonies of wanting to know how she is.'

Alice held out her arms. 'Eeh, love, let me hug you. I'm sorry about all of this, and for my part in telling Gerald everything. I felt in a position where, if he knew the truth, he could help you.'

Marg clung on to Alice. 'He has – you have. No regrets, you've both helped me more than you know. And look, lass, if you want the lads to come here rather than me keeping an eye on them over at yours, I can sort them places to sleep. Me and Jackie can share me ma's bed, Harry can have the sofa, Billy can have my bed and Joey Jackie's.'

'Eeh, lass, that would put me mind at rest. They're all right in the day, Harry's such a responsible lad and takes care of the others, but at night, well, as big as he is, Harry does suffer from a nervous disposition – Billy's much braver in the dark.'

Alice giggled as she said this. The sound made everything feel better – as if they could all be normal again.

'Leave it with me. I'll sort it, you get off back to the hospital – eeh, you could get docked fifteen minutes for being late like we are, Gerald.'

Gerald grinned. 'Yes, I must get back now, if you're sure you'll be all right, Marg?'

'I will. You've helped me no end by being honest and by taking the time to tell me so much. Ta.'

Marg waved them off, then stood for a moment leaning on the door. Her mind raced around the awfulness of everything – Edith's tragedy, her ma's illness, her lying, and the future that loomed without her mates being just across or down the street. Sighing, she decided the future could wait, she'd to deal with the now first.

Despite everything, Marg had to smile at Harry trying to conceal his relief at seeing her when he opened the door to her. She loved Harry – well, all of the lads – but Billy was at that annoying-boy stage, where he thought he knew it all and could be a bit of a handful. The natural way of things for a lad growing up. Joey, though, was a little darling, and a lot younger in his ways than he should be for his ten years, but that was down to all the lads and Alice babying him.

So as not to embarrass Harry, she used a tactic to make him feel needed. 'I've come to ask you all to stay the night with us, lad. Only with all that's gone on, me and Jackie don't want to spend tonight on our own.'

'Aye, of course we will. Me brothers are already in bed, but I don't think they're asleep. I heard them talking a moment ago.'

'Ta, Harry, you're a good 'un.'

As she made them all breakfast the next day, Marg felt exhausted, and yet better in her mind about all of her own problems. She'd been restless in the night and had prayed that Edith wouldn't lose her sanity over this and would find some kind of peace. And she hoped that Philip would be the key to that.

She'd been glad when morning arrived, even though, having finally dropped off to sleep in the early hours, she was left with a feeling of a cloud clogging her brain.

Being a Saturday, she'd crept out of bed, leaving Jackie to sleep in for a while. Somehow, she'd seen to Gran without waking Harry – changed her bed, washed her and donned her in a clean nightie, before making her a cup of tea. And had been heartened by this being one of the rare moments that her gran had known who she was and had given her a kiss and a cuddle. That gesture had gone a long way to lightening her load.

Now, she was busy getting an enormous pan of porridge on the go, and as Harry trotted through she said to him, 'By, it's like feeding the five thousand!'

'Ha! Well, I hope you've got five loaves of bread, I'm starving.'

He looked crumpled and his thick hair lay in disarray, but the picture was one of a lovely young man. She laughed at his joke and then told him, 'If it's something to eat you're after, cut a crust off that loaf to tide you over.'

'Ta, Marg.'

As he sawed the crust off with the bread knife, she asked him, 'Did you sleep all right?'

'Aye, I did. Though I couldn't keep me feet under the blanket. It was either over me shoulders and have me feet out, or the other way around, and I felt warmer with me feet out.'

'I know, I were tempted to tickle them when I came through to see to Gran.'

Harry giggled. It was a good sound. Marg felt the pity of Harry's life up till now, and was glad that, at last, everything looked rosy for him. She couldn't help wondering, however, how he really felt about the changes ahead.

'So, lad, you'll soon be living the life of the upper crust.'

'Aye. It feels as though everything's topsy-turvy. And as if I'm going to lose everyone. I was just getting on better with Albert. How could he have done such a thing? It's horrible.'

'It is, but . . .' Marg told him how she thought things may have happened.

'You mean . . . you really think he never meant to kill them?'

'I do. Not that that lets him off. Hitting his own sister, da and ma is despicable, and I hate him for it, but for all that, I'd say this was a fit of temper – him being out of control that ended in disaster – and that he's paid the ultimate price for it.'

'I knaw you're right about the hitting. I made me mind up a long time ago that I would never hit a girl. It used to make me feel sick when me da hit our Alice.'

'Eh, lad, you've seen some things in your life, and more than most should ever see, but hang on to your good memories, eh?'

'Aye, that's what Alice tells us to do, but it don't always work.'

'No, I know, lad . . . Look, tell me to sod off if you like, but I'd love to give you a hug.'

Harry hesitated, then said, 'Ha! Sod off, you've got porridge on your chin from tasting it, you only want to wipe it on me!'

They both went into a fit of giggles as Marg wiped her chin. 'Go on with you. I'll catch you one of these days, lad, and you'll have to put up with me hug.'

The small incident had cheered Marg. She always wondered at the resilience of young 'uns, but was glad for it and felt good that Harry was now feeling better enough to have a bit of fun.

And she knew that, in the end, everything came out in the wash and they would all find a way back, even from these horrific events. She herself must find a way back from what her ma had done this time. She'd start by telling Gran and Jackie that it was all a mistake and though Ma's life was in danger, it wasn't imminent that she would die, so they must all take care of her as they'd planned. She hoped this would make them feel a little happier about the future.

THIRTY-ONE

Alice

Alice looked over at Philip. The morning sunlight was splashed over Edith's bed as they sat either side in silence. 'Are you all right, Philip?'

These were the first words spoken between them all night, except when Gerald popped in and told them that Edith was now stable, out of danger, and that they were letting her wake up naturally.

'Yes, thank you. I have felt better since Gerald's visit, but I fear for Edith.'

'I know. She's going to need a lot of help. Shall I go and see if the nurse will make us a mug of tea?'

'Thanks, Alice. You're a good friend to Edith. She's going to need her friends; she has a lot to face.'

Alice couldn't imagine how Edith would ever get over what happened, but she just smiled and went in search of the nurse.

The young girl who'd first come to her and had been popping in and out said she couldn't make the tea as she had to start bedpan rounds, but she showed Alice where everything was. 'I feel so sorry for your friend, miss.'

'Aye, it's a lot for her, but we'll help her. Can I ask you something? Do you like being a nurse?'

'I do, lass. Love it. But it ain't easy, and weren't easy for someone like me to get accepted to train either. Usually, you need to have money to pay your way, but I'm an orphan and there was a good lady who helped us at the orphanage to achieve what we wanted to do. But the going's tougher for me as I get all the rough jobs. Mind, I hold me own with them and work at proving meself in me job.'

'Oh, I didn't know as it were like that. I thought if you had a vocation, then that was it.'

'Naw. And there's a lot of learning to it, but I've always been clever, so I'm not fazed by it. I doubt I'll ever be taken seriously, though . . . Well, I have thought of one way. If I could afford to have lessons to speak right, and move away where naw one knaws me, then I think I could climb up to be a staff nurse, and maybe a sister even.'

To Alice, this seemed so unfair. Why was everything open to those who have money, but not to the poor? And why should folk be judged by their accent? But that was the way of things.

'Well, I admire you and wish you all the luck in the world. I'd love to do what you do.'

Getting back to Philip, she handed him his tea and felt an overwhelming urge to tackle him about attitudes. But now wasn't the time. Besides, he would only agree with her and this would give her no satisfaction. She really felt the need to challenge someone who held the views that only money-folk could achieve, or be worthy of becoming a nurse.

This changed when Edith stirred. She wanted to rush at her, but held back as Philip stood, put his mug down on the side cupboard and leant over Edith.

'Edith, darling. It's all right, I'm here. Edith?'

Edith opened her eyes. Alice held her breath and gritted her teeth. For all the world she so wanted to reassure Edith, but knew that if she had a choice between a friend and the man she loved to be there for her, she would choose Gerald every time.

'Philip?'

'Yes, my darling. I'm here.'

'Where ... Eeh, Philip!'

'I know, darling. Hold on. I'm here for you.'

'Albert?'

Philip took Edith's hand. Alice drew back in the breath she'd released. A pain shot through her as she listened.

'Darling, you have to be very strong. Please don't become ill again, you nearly died, my darling. I can't bear to lose you.'

'No, I wasn't badly hurt.'

'I know, but you suffered a tremendous shock and you have more to face.'

'Albert didn't mean ... Don't let them hurt him, Philip, please ...'

'Oh, my poor darling. I know how much you loved your brother, I—'

'Loved? Albert's all right, isn't he?'

'Edith, please don't distress yourself, darling, you'll have a relapse.'

'Tell me, please tell me, where's Albert?'

'He – he's with your ma and pa, darling. He's at peace. Poor lad, he … he …'

'He's dead? Albert's dead! Oh, Philip, how am I to bear it all?'

To Alice, it was a relief to hear Edith crying, even though her sobs cut through her, as this was a natural reaction. She wouldn't mind if Edith screamed and screamed, but the important thing was that she wasn't shutting down again.

Philip held her in his arms for a moment and then gently released himself, saying, 'Alice is here, darling.'

As he turned to face her, Alice saw tears streaming down his face. It was all so unbearable.

'Edith, lass.'

Edith opened her arms to her. 'Eeh, Alice, Alice, how did it all happen? What happened to Albert?'

'I don't know the details, lass, I only know that … Oh, Edith, I'm sorry, lass, but Albert took his own life.'

'No! Oh, Albert! He shouldn't have done that, Alice. I would have stood up for him. He didn't mean any of it. He … By, what am I saying? The lad shouldn't have hit Ma and Da. They … they weren't strong enough, they couldn't … Is it true, are they all gone?'

'I'm so sorry, lass. If I could undo the last twenty-four hours, I would. You've got such a lot to face, but you won't be alone. Me and Marg will be by your side and so will Philip, and Gerald, and my brothers and Jackie. And all the folk in the street. We'll all support you, lass. We will. We can't undo what's happened, but we can hold you up.'

'I know. In some ways I feel strong and know I'll come through this, but my heart is breaking … I – I, well, I knew my da hadn't got long, and Ma wasn't helping her health, but I wouldn't have chosen for them to go this way, and Albert … he had his whole life in front of him … Eeh, why did he do it? Why?'

'You said yourself, he didn't mean to, lass. He acted on the spur of the moment, never expecting such a tragedy, and now … well, he would have faced …'

'Hanging? That's it, ain't it, Alice? He would have been hanged!'

Seeing this thought was somehow helping Edith, Alice confirmed it. 'Aye, and not only that, but an agonising time of living with what he'd done and the long wait, knowing the outcome. I reckon his uppermost thought when he took the course that he did would have been you, Edith, love. He were a good lad at heart, it was his temper that let him down. But then, that weren't all his fault, he was riled by … well, you coped better than him with the goings-on.'

'Aye, you're right, Alice. He'd have done it to save me all that agony. And he weren't all bad. Ma let him down.'

'Not intentionally, love, but yes, her problem was too much for him to cope with. They're all at peace now and together. We have to help you to carry on, Edith.'

'How can I? Where will I live? I can't go back there, I can't.'

'No, not to the house, but you could come and live with me, lass.'

Edith was quiet for a moment. Her body shook with silent rebound sobs. Her beautiful face, drained of colour, had a lost expression, and her fingers plucked at the bedsheet.

'Edith?'

'Oh, Philip. I'm glad you're here.'

Philip moved forward and sat on his side of the bed. 'I wouldn't be anywhere else, darling. I – I . . . Look Edith, I can take care of you.'

Alice stood. 'I'll leave you two alone a minute. I'll take the mugs out to the kitchen.'

As Alice went through the door, she saw Gerald approaching. 'Alice, is everything all right?'

Alice motioned for him to follow her. Once in the ward kitchen, she went into his arms.

'A bit better, my love. Philip has told Edith what happened – well, he started to, and I finished telling her about Albert. She took it quite well . . . as well as can be expected. I've left them alone. I think Philip is going to propose.'

'Oh? Not a good idea. I know he thinks a lot of her, but she is still in shock. She could either reject him and be very cross that he even suggested such a thing, or accept him as a lifeline, which isn't the best of reasons. He should wait.'

'I can't be certain he is doing that, but when I said she could live with me he said he could take care of her. He might have meant he'd find her a place or something. Anyroad, I made myself scarce, just in case.'

'I hope it's the latter. He'll need to take things slowly, for his own sake as much as Edith's.'

'So says the man who waited all of three weeks!'

'Ha! I know. But you were of sound mind, my darling. You could have said no. You weren't in a desperate place. Well, not when I got as far as asking you. I know you're still grieving for your father, but well . . .'

'You'll dig a deeper hole if you carry on, lad! But you're right. I wasn't clutching at anything to save me. I still had a life to get on with with me brothers. Edith has lost hers, and I see your point – she could make a decision that she later regrets. But I know how smitten she is with Philip. We've neither of us had time to really get to know our men, but we fell hook, line and sinker and are trusting our hearts.'

'And I won't let your heart down, and I know Philip won't let Edith's down either. Well, I must go and check on her as it is the end of my shift now. I was thinking of discharging her to your care and keeping an eye on her at your home, but I'm not sure now.'

When they got back to Edith's bed, she was sitting up, leaning on her pillows. To Alice, she looked much more relaxed and even managed a little tearful smile.

'I'm back, love, and Gerald's here to see you.'

'How are you, Edith?'

'I – I want to go to Alice's, I don't want to stay here, Gerald. Philip's made me see it is the best for now.'

'Eeh, lass, I'm so glad. Me and Marg'll care for you.'

Gerald was looking inquisitively at Philip.

'Philip made me see that I don't solve anything without facing it. It will be so hard, but I have to go back to the street. Whittaker Avenue is my home, and Alice and Marg and Jackie and the lads and all my neighbours are the best ones to make me feel better.'

'Philip's right, Edith.'

'And he's promised to visit me and help all he can. I want that, Alice. Will you mind?'

'No. Course not, lass. I can't always say you'll have privacy, but Philip's welcome any time.'

363

Alice did wonder what would happen when she married, and had the fleeting thought that she would cancel the wedding if she had to, but then, that wasn't an option as she'd given up her job and so much was in place already. The questions were answered with what Edith said next. 'And Philip has said that when you marry, I can choose what to do. Look at all my options then.'

'You can, Edith.' Philip's face held such love as he said this. 'And all of us will still support you. I have a lot of ideas, my dear, but now isn't the time to discuss them. We'll see to everything that has to be done first.'

At this a shadow crossed over Edith's face.

Gerald surprised Alice then by talking about what was on all of their minds. 'When I get home, Edith, I will ring the police and find out for you when arrangements can be made. Then as Philip and Alice have said, we will all put everything in place for you ... My dear, you will go through periods of deep grief and periods of feeling that none of it is real, as you probably are now. Times when you will feel angry at one or the other of those you have lost, and times when you feel lost yourself, but for each of those times, you will have someone to turn to.'

'Yes, and when you feel you need to run away, I'll be there to take you as far as you want to go – the Bowland Hills, the Lake District, anywhere – so you can run and run, but still I will be close by to pick you up.'

This from Philip was beautiful to Alice. He didn't know Edith well, but he loved her, and Alice could see that being Edith's salvation.

★   ★   ★

Once they got home, Edith sat in Gerald's car and stared at her own house. 'I – I can't. Don't make me, I can't.'

Gerald looked back at Alice squashed in the back. Alice leant forward and clutched Edith. 'I've got you, lass, I've got you.'

Edith clung on to Alice's arm. One or two doors opened as folk had heard the car, but they respectfully closed again. Except for Marg's. She came running down the road to them, her body hiding Edith's house from view. 'Edith, lass. Let me help you.'

'Eeh, Marg, Marg.'

'Come on, lass. I'll hold you the minute you step onto the pavement. By, I love you, lass. I do. You are the strongest person I know.'

'Marg, hold me, Marg. I'm falling.'

'No, we'll never let you fall, Edith. Hold on to me, that's right. Alice is getting out and'll go to your other side.'

Together, they helped Edith into Alice's house. 'There, I'll get the kettle on, shall I, Alice?'

'Aye. We could all do with a cuppa.'

'Marg, will you make Edith's very sweet? She is having a reoccurrence of the shock. Alice, let's get Edith sat down.'

Alice helped Gerald to seat Edith. When they'd done this, Gerald held Edith's wrist for a moment while looking at his watch. 'There now, Edith, that's right, try to slow your breathing. This is what we call a panic attack. It will pass. When you get your tea, I want you to drink it down as quickly as you can ... Alice, ask Marg to make it cool-ish. Edith needs the sugar as soon as possible.'

Alice rushed to the kitchen to find that the kettle still hadn't boiled but was sizzling. 'Pour some into a mug now, Marg. I'll get the sugar.'

Adding four heaped spoonsful to the warm water, Alice went back to Edith and put her arm around her shoulder. 'Here, lass, it won't be the best drink you've had, but'll help you quicker than waiting for the kettle to boil.'

'Good idea, Alice, I should have thought of that.'

'Aye, well, me ma used to say that women are better at thinking than men are.'

Gerald smiled and winked at her. Which, even in the terrible circumstances they were in, sent a tremble of love and anticipation through her body.

Tightening her grip on Edith, she could feel a calmness was coming over her dear friend. 'There, is that better, lass? I'll tell you, me marrying a doctor's going to be very useful to us all.'

'Ha! So that's why you took me on so quickly, is it?'

'Aye, I thought I'd find you beneficial to have around.'

A small smile appeared on Edith's face and some of her colour came back.

'See, even Edith agrees.'

At this, Edith made Alice's heart want to burst with the hope she felt as she said, 'You two aren't going to use me as a go-between, are you?'

'I might, lass, as I know you'll be on my side.'

Edith grinned. 'Don't you be so sure, you ain't as useful as Gerald.'

They all laughed at this, Marg louder than any of them as she brought the tea through. Her laugh seemed on the verge of tears, prompting Alice to go to her. 'This is welcome, lass. Shall you and me get some toast on while Gerald does his checks on Edith, eh?'

Once in the kitchen, Alice sipped her tea. 'You look like you slept in that skirt, and your blouse is all crumpled an' all, lass. Have you come to terms with what we told you?'

'Aye. I just couldn't relax. I lay on top of the bed for a while, then crept downstairs. Harry was snoring away – by, he's going to annoy some lass in the future if he don't get out of that habit.'

Alice grinned as she sliced a second doorstep of the large loaf.

'I know, it rattles the house sometimes. I might ask Gerald about it.'

'Anyroad, I had a few naps in the chair, but I ain't had long. Good job it's not a work day. I ain't told Jackie nor Gran yet about Ma. Neither of them are awake; Gran had a cuppa and a clean-up and promptly nodded off again. Harry and the lads are awake, they've had a good bowl of porridge. Anyroad, I'll bide me time before I give Gran and Jackie the news – get myself in the right frame of mind so that I know I can tell it as a joyful thing and not show bitterness about it.'

'Is that how you feel? Mind, I can't blame you, but, lass, remember what Gerald said.'

'I will. Eeh, what did we do to deserve such parents?'

'Aye, it's been a bit of a road for all three of us to travel, and you and Edith have still got a long way to go. For me, I feel at peace now. I'm glad me da is out of pain. I'm glad me and the lads know why he was like he was. And I'm glad that we don't live with the fear we felt every hour, and the beatings we had to endure. So, though it may sound cold-hearted, I think any grieving I'm doing ain't for me da as he was of late, but for what we lost a long time ago, when the accident at

367

the rock factory happened, for that's when we lost both of our parents.'

'I'm glad you're at peace with it all, Alice, as now you can build a good future for you and the lads. For me, I think my ma's deceit and this new side to her that I've discovered recently has soured what me and her had, because we were always close. And Gran ... well, I'm losing her bit by bit every day. And I've grieved for my so-called da for such a long time that I was used to the ache in my heart. But now, it's as if all that time's been wasted on a man I've found out so many bad things about that I've lost every respect and feeling for him. And, do you know what else I've found out, Alice? That there's more than someone's passing that you can grieve over – there's being so disillusioned that the bottom falls out of the world you thought you knew.'

'Aw, Marg. Give us a hug.' As they held each other, Alice told her, 'You will come to terms with it all and find happiness, lass. You will.'

'Aye, we all have to carry on. But Alice, where've our lives gone – the fun we should have had as young girls? That's all been taken away from us.'

'We did have some good times, and you'll remember them when your head clears and your heart mends a little. Let's take these in to the others, eh?'

When they went back into the living room, Edith was sitting back in the chair looking a lot more relaxed. 'We've just started talking about the times we had together, Edith. Do you remember that time we were on the beach and the donkey-ride man asked us to watch the donkeys while he went to get a cuppa?'

Marg nudged her. 'Eeh, Alice. Don't.'

'Ha! I knew you'd remember that, Marg. I can see us chasing them now. They were all tied together, and a blooming car backfired scaring the life out of us and the donkeys and they took off in fright. By, they say they're slow old things, but we couldn't catch them. They went under the pier and you'd have thought they were going on their holidays how they ran. Their bells were making a right racket!'

Marg laughed. 'And you caught hold of one and he dragged you along the sand. Me and Edith were screaming at you to let go. Eeh, Alice.'

Edith joined in the laughter. 'And when you did, they just stopped. As if someone had struck them dumb! Me and Marg ran like the wind towards you thinking you were a goner, but you sat up, your face covered in sand and said, "Blooming daft donkeys!"'

'Oh, but the best was when you went and mounted the front one, Edith, and rode them back to the railing and all the others followed. You were like a cowboy rounding up the cattle.'

At this from Alice, the three of them were hopeless with laughter. Between gasps of giggles, Alice said, 'We were exhausted when the handler came back. He never knew a thing about it.'

'Ooh, I know. We stood there all innocent, and he were that pleased with us he offered us a free ride . . . We all said, "No, ta."'

'And the look on his face, Marg, it was a picture as he must have guessed we'd been hanging around hoping he would offer that, but by the time it was offered, none of us wanted to see a donkey again!'

'Aye, but Edith, he didn't let us go unrewarded, did he? He gave us a penny and we went and bought an icy each and sat on the sand as happy as if it were Christmas.'

Edith dried the tears brought on by her laughter and smiled at Marg. 'Aye, happy times. And we will have such again, won't we?'

Alice and Marg both nodded. Alice moved over to Edith's side. 'We will, lass, we will.'

Edith's smile gave her hope that this would be so, and she somehow knew that, though they did have more to go through, they would all move forward from this horror and rebuild their lives.

THIRTY-TWO

Marg

Marg sighed. The last three weeks had flown by. They'd been filled with Ma coming home and taking residence in the living room, and her new so-called da Eric deserting them and leaving them in dire straits, the latest deceit he'd suffered from Ma being the last straw.

When Marg had told him that there was no cancer, the penny had dropped that this was yet another ploy of Ma's to get away from him. He'd been disgusted with her and told her that she'd finally got the message through to him.

'You don't want me; you've never wanted me. You've lied and cheated and kept me children from me, making them hate me. I'm nothing to you and nothing to them! Well, I'm off. You can have this, but it's your last. When that's gone you can fucking fend for yourself!' He'd thrown them one last lifeline of a crisp ten-pound note.

It surprised Marg later, and nudged her into admitting she had similar feelings, when Jackie had said, 'I didn't want our real da to leave, Marg. I've found I have feelings for him. I will miss him and hope every day that he changes his mind.'

'He'll calm down and come back, lass. He loves Ma, he'll make sure she's all right. And if not, we can go to him. Ask him if we can visit him now and again. These things need building slowly. That was Eric's trouble, he wanted everything to happen instantly.'

'I knaw, Marg, he wanted us to turn into his daughters just like that, but I couldn't.'

'Nor me, lass. But like you, I was warming to the idea.'

Eric hadn't contacted them, and as of yet she and Jackie hadn't called on him either. But Marg knew the day would come when she would drop in on him. For now, she had such a lot to contend with.

The money had tied them over the last three weeks. Marg had made them live on two pounds a week, but even then, she'd been able to get some good cuts of meat and had made inroads into paying off the back rent they owed by giving a shilling extra each week.

And she'd managed to keep her job at the factory on a part-time basis, while Jackie took over the job at the corner shop once more.

Reluctantly, Marg had to concede that Jackie should leave school, but no matter what, she was to continue her studies and start lessons with the science teacher recommended by her tutor.

Then two days ago, they'd had the horror of a triple funeral, and now today she and Alice were to help Edith to clear out her family home. A task they dreaded, for Edith's sake, but for

Marg it was like sealing the truth that Edith and Alice were moving out of Whittaker Avenue.

Aye, they won't be far, but Newton Drive might as well be a hundred miles away as far as I'm concerned.

With this thought, her heart felt heavy. No longer would she be able to pop down to Alice's or call across to Edith. There'd be no more sitting on the steps together late at night drinking cocoa and having a laugh, and even at work there'd only be Edith – that is, once she'd recovered enough to return.

Now Marg sat with Alice in her living room waiting for Edith to come downstairs.

When she did, she looked a shadow of her former self. The weight had dropped off her in the time since the death of her family.

'It'll be all right, love.'

To this from Alice, Edith gave a small tight smile, then nodded in Marg's direction to greet her.

'Aye, it's right what Alice says, Edith. And me and Alice'll be by your side, to make sure you're all right, lass. You just collect what you need to keep then we'll see to second-hand Parker.'

Second-hand Parker had made an offer of fifteen bob to clear the house, saying he'd take everything away for her whether he thought he could sell it on or not. 'And that's a generous offer on account of your circumstances, lass.'

Marg had wanted to spit in his face. He was the worst kind of scavenger, praying on people's need.

Linking arms, the three of them walked outside, but Edith took one look at the horse and dray parked outside her home and folded. 'I – I can't, please don't make me.' She pulled away from them, her body bent as if in agony. 'No! don't follow me ... I want to be on my own.'

Alice looked at Marg; the colour had drained from her face. 'Oh dear, I thought she were coping, bless her.'

'I did an' all, Alice. But I did worry about her, she was very quiet at the funeral and dealt with everything as if she was locked away inside. But she has seemed all right since.'

'Not really. After we left you that night she broke down upstairs, and not for the first time, as I've lain many a night with her in my arms.'

'Poor lass.'

'I know, I wouldn't have arranged the clear-out, but time is getting on. The new tenants take over the house on Saturday.'

'That's going to be a hard day for her.'

'I planned on us getting this out of the way so she'd have time to adjust before the wedding. Oh, I wish I'd put it off, she's not ready.'

There were just ten days to go before Alice's wedding, which Edith had insisted must go ahead, and she had thrown herself into helping with the arrangements. She'd seemed to be coping as she'd spent hours delicately stitching up the hems of the bridesmaids' frocks, which the dressmaker had left undone as she'd not been able to get in enough fittings with Marg, Edith and Jackie.

Edith had even been into her home before the funeral to get some items she'd wanted to put into each of the coffins – a cross and chain that her da had bought her ma, and the chain of a pocket watch that her ma had given to her da – he'd kept the chain, cherishing it after Edith's ma had told him she needed to pawn the watch. She never got the watch out again, but still, Edith had said her da wore the chain with the end tucked into his top pocket. And for Albert, a St Christopher medal his da had bought him for his tenth birthday, telling him it would ensure he was looked after on any journey if he took it with him.

The undertaker told her he'd placed each item in their hands and this had comforted Edith.

It hadn't been a pauper's funeral, which Edith had dreaded, as Bob Butcher had started a collection at the police station and that had escalated to the ambulance station and then further afield to all businesses. On top of that, the girls at Bradshaw's had made a magnificent contribution.

Nothing they did could get a burial in consecrated ground for Albert, though. He was considered to have died in sin, and suicides were not allowed a proper burial. This increased Edith's distress, but as it turned out his interment was under the same tree as his parents, just around the other side of it – something arranged by Philip.

Marg understood Edith's forgiving attitude towards her brother, and was glad for it, as she knew Edith would suffer bitterness if she hated him and blamed him, and that would destroy her completely.

'Eeh, Alice, lass, what should we do?'

'What do you think to asking Parker to make a start on just taking the furniture to begin with? We know she only wants to keep her da's footstool.'

'But what if she's changed her mind and wants something else?'

'I'll make an arrangement with Second-hand Parker. Come on, I've got the key, I picked it up from the police station for Edith before the funeral. There was two and I put one into the dresser drawer in case I needed it. That's how I managed to get her clothes and arrange for the cleaners that Philip had hired to be able get in before Edith had a chance to. You go and tell Porter while I fetch it.'

Marg put her head down against the driving rain and walked across the road on shaky legs. The women of the street were out on their steps. Most called out to her:

'It's a sad day, Marg.'

'Eeh, never thought I'd see the day.'

And suchlike comments. She acknowledged them all, but hurried on. Ida came out from next door to Edith's.

'By, Marg, what a to-do, but I see this is the end of it, then?'

'Aye, this is it, Ida.'

'I'm not sorry the lad's gone, but by, Betty and Reg, you couldn't get better neighbours.'

Marg wanted to ask if that was why she'd laughed and clapped at Betty's antics instead of calming the situation and getting Betty inside for a cup of tea, but she was past all that.

'Marg, lass . . . well, Betty knew I admired her dresser . . . If it's going, I could make room for it.'

Marg had to stop herself from saying, *I thought the vultures would come out.* But she walked on by, just telling her, 'Parker's bought the lot, you could buy it from him.'

Ida hmphed then went inside and banged the door shut.

'What's to do, Marg? I've been here five minutes and me time's money, lass.'

'Don't you dare tell me you're thinking of docking the amount you've offered, Sec . . . Mr Parker.'

Second-hand Parker was the name he was known as, but

no one ever called him that to his face. Though Marg nearly had done.

'If so, you can sod off. We're dealing with a girl who's lost all her family in a terrible tragedy, and you've already insulted that by offering a meagre amount for all she has in the world. Alice will be here in a mo with a key. Edith couldn't face this ordeal yet, so I'm to see that you just take large items of furniture on your first run, and hopefully by then we'll know what's to be on your second.'

'I was only saying. A man's got a right to voice his opinion, lass.'

'Aye, well, when your opinion hints at less money for Edith, then I ain't standing for it.' Marg marvelled at herself, but then, Ida had riled her and put her in the right mood to deal with him.

'Let's get on with it, then.'

'Right, here's Alice coming with the key.'

When Alice came up to them, she spoke to Parker. 'I want to ask a favour of you, Mr Parker. Edith isn't up to being here just yet, so we have a dilemma. If it happens that we accidently send something with you that she wanted to keep, will you hold on to everything for a couple of days until we can make sure she doesn't want something back?'

'Naw, I can't do that. I'm paying over the odds as it is. I need to shift it all as fast as I can. I have a dealer over in Blackburn coming to me warehouse on Saturday, and if he wants owt I take from here, I ain't holding back. You lot want sommat for nothing all the time.'

Marg lost her temper with hearing this. 'Something for nothing! Well, we ain't got nothing in the first place, so we can't get anything for it, can we? You're nothing but a leech, sucking the last blood out of us. Well, you can't get blood from a stone, so don't try!'

'Aye, you're right, lass, and you've not got any choices. It's me what takes away this rubbish, or you're stuck with it.'

A car pulled up just as Marg lost her control and sprung at him, bringing all the hurt and anger of the last few weeks raining down on him.

'Hey, Marg, lass, what's to do?' Clive Barnes, the rock factory owner's son who had said the kind words about Alice's father at the funeral, appeared from his car.

Marg stopped flailing her fists. She felt the shame of what she'd done and dropped her head, her body wracked with sobs as previously unshed burning tears were finally released.

'Never mind asking her what's up, Mr Barnes! Go and fetch the cops, she's assaulted me!'

Marg turned and was mortified to see it was Clive who had pulled up at the kerbside. He strode towards them.

'Oh? I didn't see anything. I don't know what you're talking about.' Clive turned to Marg. 'Are you all right, Marg, can I do anything for you?'

Alice answered. 'Aye, I hope you can. Clive, can I have a word?' Marg followed them over to Clive's car, though her legs felt like jelly and she felt such a fool.

Alice told Clive, 'Me and Marg are upset as Parker's trying to rip Edith off, and she's been through so much.'

'Aye, I know. I'm sorry, I wanted to come to see her, but didn't know if I should. I did attend the funeral, though I didn't know the family – just to pay my respects, like.'

'Ta, I'll tell Edith. Only she can't face seeing everything her family ever owned being taken away. Mr Parker's only offered a pittance for it, and he's trying every trick in the book not to pay that even, and besides that, he won't agree to hold on to it for a couple of days in case we let anything go that Edith wanted to keep.'

Clive looked at Marg then; she saw the concern in his eyes as he told Alice, 'Look after Marg, lass. Leave Parker to me.'

'Oh, Alice, I don't know what came over me, it seemed as if everything crowded me at that moment and Mr Parker were to blame for it all.'

'I know, love. Clive'll sort it, are you all right now?'

Marg nodded.

A crowd had gathered. 'About time someone gave that blighter a pasting, lass,' Ida called over. 'I was just coming to help you.'

Before they could answer Ida, who Marg knew was just trying to redeem herself, Clive came back to them. 'All right, ladies, the show's over.'

No one argued, but then Clive's father did own the factory where many of the men in the street worked, so they had to think of their livelihood.

'Now then, Marg, why don't you go and make us all a brew? And make Parker one too, though it might stick in your craw to do so. I've sorted him out and he'll do just as you ask. It took a bribe, but that's the nature of the man, and the least I can do for Edith.'

Marg was glad to escape and it gave her a chance to check on her ma and Gran as Jackie was out at the shop this morning.

Her ma greeted her with, 'Eeh, what's going on, lass? I was

just coming out when I saw you beating Parker up. I was cheering you on, but didn't make it from the window to the door. If I had, he would have got a mouthful from me, I can tell you. I knaw things about him that would make your hair curl and him do anything I ask.'

Marg didn't want to know what Ma knew. She had no capacity for further secrets and she was sure this would be just as sordid as the rest of Ma's past seemed to be.

And this was confirmed by Gran. 'Eeh, there ain't many men of your age in this town that you don't knaw from the inside out, Vera. A disgrace you were.'

'Aye, well, you didn't mind taking a penny from me to get food on the table, did you, Ma?'

Gran shut up, which pleased Marg. She couldn't take any more of this banter.

Making them tea helped her to calm herself. 'Now, I'll just pour Alice and the men one and help out all I can. Just call over to me, Ma, if you need me.'

'Aye, we'll be fine, lass. You're a good girl, Marg.'

Marg didn't answer her ma. She had a knot of anger in her that even her hysterics just now hadn't shifted, and it was towards her ma that she held it. Taking the tea out to them all, she left it to Alice to give Parker his. Coming back to her, Alice told her, 'Eeh, Marg, Clive really came here to see me and Harry. He wants to know if Harry's keen to start his apprenticeship soon. I don't know what to say, as I think Gerald wants to fund Harry continuing his education.'

Clive answered her. 'Find out what the score is and let me know, Alice. But as soon as you can, as we're in need of some-one . . . Ahh, this tea's welcome, Marg. I've a free morning so

I can hang around and help out here. I'll be a bit of a strong arm for you with Parker. He won't get up to any dirty tricks with me here.'

'You're welcome, Clive. And I'm sorry you witnessed that just now. It ain't like me, but everything boiled over.'

Clive laughed. 'Glad to hear it, I wouldn't fancy messing with you, and I hope I'm never the one to make you boil over.'

This made Marg blush, but she couldn't have said why. She turned quickly to Alice. 'I've made a brew for Edith, lass. Shall I take it over?'

'No, I'll do that, you carry on here.'

This was the last thing Marg wanted, but she couldn't make a scene by protesting. As soon as Alice had gone, Clive turned to her. 'What I mean, Marg, is that whilst I'd like to get to know you better, and part of me used coming here rather than sending Harry a letter as an excuse in the hope of seeing you, I hope that I never make you angry like that. You were packing some good punches there.'

Marg smiled, but found herself colouring as if she was a shy young girl, instead of going on twenty-one.

'Well, let's make a start. You direct and I'll help to lift and keep my eye on Parker.'

As she was helping Clive to lift a bureau that wasn't heavy but needed two people, Clive asked. 'I meant what I said about getting to know you better, Marg. Would you do me the honour of coming out with me one evening – maybe to the pictures, or for a drink?'

Again, she flushed, but found she wasn't averse to the idea, even though it was impractical and impossible at the moment.

She told him this, to which he said, 'That's not a "no" then, just "another time"?'

'I don't know. My life ain't my own at the mo, and it could be a long time before it is.' She told him about her ma and gran needing someone to be around. 'Our Jackie does all she can, but she's only a youngster, and she's such a clever bod. I want her to study so she has a better chance than I ever had.'

'That's such a nice attitude, Marg, and makes me want to know you even more. Could we meet and do something that only takes you away for half an hour, such as go for a walk?'

Marg felt trapped. She liked Clive, but she had no room in her life for another person. Not yet. She didn't want to offend him, though, nor make him feel that she didn't like him. 'All right, we could do that, but it'll have to be for just a short time.'

'Right. I'll come around Thursday night, then, about seven?'

Marg was glad he hadn't said tonight or anytime soon. She would need to adjust to the idea, but Thursday was three days away. 'Aye, but if anything ain't right with either Gran or Ma, I might have to turn you away.'

'Fair enough, we can make another date if it does.'

Him saying 'date' made her blush even more. She hadn't looked on it as that, just a friendly walk.

Alice came back then. 'Edith still isn't up to coming over, but I'm glad I caught you as that bureau is one of the things, along with her da's footstool, that she wants to keep.'

Marg and Clive lowered it to the ground. 'By, Alice, you're just in time.'

'Yes, we were just going to load it, but you know, it would do up really well. Can I take it with me and have a go at

382

restoring it for Edith? I like to do that kind of work and would have gone in for carpentry if my father hadn't a rock factory to leave me.'

'Eeh, that would be grand, ta, Clive. Will you get it in your car?'

'Well, no, that's a point, but I'll ask Parker to make it the last item he puts on his final load and to drop it off at mine.'

Parker moaned at this, saying it was the piece that would have fetched the most for him. It was then that Marg over-heard Clive say, 'I know your tricks, Parker. Well, it won't wash with me. I've offered you all I'm going to offer you to get this job done without any trouble. Now, do as I tell you and no more of it.'

At that moment, the sun came out and shone on Clive's dark hair, picking out the reddish shine it had in its depths. Marg involuntarily caught her breath as his features were outlined and she saw not a man ten to twelve years her senior, but a young man, handsome and, well, yes, she had to admit to being attracted to him.

He turned and smiled at her. A shiver went through her. She looked away.

'Well, that's settled, so don't look so worried.'

'You shouldn't have bribed him, Clive, he's a—'

'A leech, I know, but you have to manage men like him and on their own terms. And as it turns out, what I've promised him is no more than it would cost to have a removal man fetch the bureau to my home.'

She shrugged. She had no fight in her to object, and it was an act of kindness. 'Well, you're your own man. Not saying I agree with you, but I'm letting it go.'

'Well, I see I have a feisty lady to take for a walk, and no doubt you'll give me what for when we do.'

Alice turned from where she was folding antimacassars from the sofa and chairs to look at Marg. Marg stuck her tongue out.

Alice laughed, but grabbed her the minute Clive carried out a small table.

'You're going on a date with Clive? Woohoo …'

'For goodness' sake, Alice, don't be marrying me off. It's a walk, that's all. He's a nice bloke and I could do with a change. I told you before, we just get on well.'

'I know you told me before, but that bit of banter spoke of a lot more.'

Snatching one of the antimacassars off Alice, she hit out at her playfully, but Alice ducked and the cloth caught a few chipped cups and saucers that were on the sideboard, ready to be binned. They crashed to the floor, causing them both to go into a fit of giggles.

At that moment, Edith walked through the door.

Marg and Alice stood as if turned to statues. Marg blurted out, 'Eeh, Edith, it wasn't like it looked, we weren't behaving as if none of this mattered; it was a spur of the moment thing, I – I'm sorry, love.'

Alice's voice held a plea as she, too, tried to convince Edith that they hadn't meant it how it looked, 'Oh, Edith, I'm mortified you should walk in at this moment. It was an accident, but well, it set us off. You know what we're like, but we've given this task every respect, I promise you.'

Edith surprised them both by smiling. 'Ha, you look like two scared rabbits caught in a sudden torchlight! I know you both well enough to know I walked in at the wrong moment. But by, the sound of the china smashing was good.'

With this, she scooped the rest of the china off with her arm and sent it crashing to the ground, then turned and looked around her. Her eyes rested on two jam jars that Marg remembered Betty used as vases. Edith strode over to them and smashed them too.

Marg couldn't move, she didn't know how to handle this. Alice stayed still as if turned to stone. It was Clive rushing back inside who dealt with it.

'Edith, lass, smash all you want to if it makes you feel better. I'd do the same.'

They stood watching as Edith seemed demented, going from one thing to the other, kicking it and breaking anything breakable until, exhausted, she flopped down onto the sofa and hollered out a pain-filled scream.

Clive got to her first and took her in his arms. Edith didn't resist him. Never had Marg witnessed anything like what followed. Edith screamed out her hurt, ranting and raging against God and the vile effects of alcohol, of how a boy driven to his last limits could not be buried in a decent grave. Of how she'd never be the same as her life was over.

From nowhere, Philip appeared in the doorway. He hurried over to Edith and took her from Clive.

Philip held her and rocked her till she became still. Then he gently lifted her to a standing position, telling them, 'Just carry on, I'll take care of Edith. I'll take her away from it all. I'll bring her home later when it's all finished.'

Clive helped him to walk Edith to the car. When he came back, he told them that Philip hadn't been able to settle knowing what was happening here and so had come to see if he could help.

'He said he was taking her to the church of all places, to pray with him! I've never heard the like. I'd have taken her out into the country.'

Marg heard Alice say that Edith had reconnected with her faith lately, despite how she just ranted on, and that Philip was a religious man so she thought it was the best thing.

'Anywhere that she can find peace is a good thing, and I've seen her find that in the church.'

Clive looked surprised, but Marg wasn't. She'd always known that Edith was a deep thinker and had noticed a change in her since she and Alice had gone to mass.

Still shaking from the incident, she did as Clive suggested and carried on with packing things up into a box. It was only bric-a-brac, but it represented Edith's life. Tears fell onto Marg's cheeks at the pity of it all. And she sent up her own berating of God.

Why, eh? What did we ever do to you? By, I'll have something to say to you when we meet! I'll shame you that much, you'll let me in them pearly gates with a free pass.

But then she giggled quietly to herself as she imagined an astonished look on God's face.

Eeh, to have Him listen, and put everything right, would be grand . . .

THIRTY-THREE

Edith

Edith sat in St Kentigern's church, her head on Philip's shoulder, his resting gently on hers while he held both her hands. She felt so cold, so lost. She had no home of her own – no family, not even an aunt or uncle. Her ma and da had once had a brother each, but sadly they both lost their lives in the Great War.

She looked up at the statue of Our Lady. The beautiful porcelain face, so gentle, kind and loving, gave her comfort. And yet, she couldn't pray. Her anger was such that it prevented her from doing anything other than rant and rave at God. He could have stopped this.

'Are you feeling a little more able to cope, darling?'

She nodded at Philip. Her gesture spoke the truth as just sitting here in this calm with an atmosphere of something greater than all humans did help, if only to give reign to the turmoil inside her. And though angry, she did feel that someone was listening to her and allowing her to be angry – understanding it even.

'That's good, my dear. Would you like to go for a drive now? I'd like to take you up into the Bowland Hills. It's beautiful and not far out of Blackpool. We go through some pretty villages in the countryside and then we travel through a stunning area of woodland, with hills so rugged and high they think themselves to be mountains. Eventually, we'll come to a charming village called Chipping. It boasted seven mills during the Industrial Revolution and still has a couple of working ones now, so is a lively industrial place, and yet has a peaceful beauty and a very nice tea room – we can eat scones and jam whilst we sit on the bench outside.'

It all sounded so lovely, so far from what she'd ever known and the perfect escape from her life now.

The drive amazed Edith, not least because, halfway, Philip had to stop and refill his petrol tank from a large can he had in the boot. Getting back in, he said, 'I must think of a more practical car. I love this one, but it really is just a showy, sporty number for a young single gent.' He'd told her previously that it was a Morris TA Midget, but that hadn't meant anything to her as to her it was just a posh sports car and she loved it. Especially today, as with the top open and a warm breeze blowing her hair, she could feel a peaceful healing as they drove.

When they arrived and parked at the roadside, Edith could see why Philip loved it here. Stone cottages with little gardens filled with wallflowers and cornflowers gave a stunning picture, which neither the odd remains of non-working mills nor the churning working ones did anything to spoil. And set as the village was, against a backdrop of hills, to Edith it was a beautiful haven, not so far from and yet a world apart from Blackpool.

The scones were delicious. They crumbled when she bit into them, leaving her lips sticky with jam.

'Ha! You have a blob of jam on your chin, Edith!'

'Well, you have one of cream on your nose!'

They giggled at this, and Edith began to feel better than she had for weeks. She was now filled with hope for the future, something that had eluded her since the awful events had taken place.

'We should run away together, Edith, and never come back.'

How wonderful that sounded.

'Then we could eat scones and jam and cream every day.'

'Oh, yes, and end up like roly-polies who can only wobble around?'

Philip laughed. 'I wouldn't mind that, as long as we were free – free of all that traps us.'

'Do you feel trapped, then, Philip?'

'I do. I feel shackled to a life I don't want to lead. I know I haven't spoken well of my parents, but after what has happened to you, I realise how much I love them, and so have decided to knuckle down and try to be what they want me to be – take more than a passing interest in the biscuit factory, and prepare to take the reins one day. And to be grateful for the life they have worked so hard to give me.'

'Parents are meant to love their children as well. And in an unconditional way. My da did that. Ma didn't so much, as she had a selfish way about her that demanded anything that was done was done to suit her. Da pandered to that.'

'Oh? That's quite a conclusion for you to come to, Edith. You're not blaming your mother for it all, are you?'

'Someone's to blame. I can't blame me da. He was wonderful in every way; his only fault was loving me ma so much that he never refused her anything, even our last penny if she begged it so that she could get her drink. And it's that part of her that led to Albert . . .'

'Oh, my dear, you're not ready to try to analyse it all. Please don't . . . Look, now we've cleaned ourselves with the napkins, let's go for a walk.'

'Philip, I need to talk about it, please let me. It's like a painful cluster tightening me chest, making me want to scream as I did this morning. But no one listens to me; they talk about anything and everything to distract me and to change the subject. I know they are being kind, but that isn't what I need. I need to talk about what happened.'

'Oh, I didn't realise. I'm so sorry. Talk as much as you like while we walk, and I promise I will listen.'

Edith did just that as they walked around the village, then found another bench to sit on. She talked and talked and cried silent tears, until she was drained of emotion and felt so tired, and yet better – lightened of the heavy load that had burdened her.

'I'm so sorry, Edith, darling. I – I don't know what to say. I never knew your life was so bad.' Philip had a tear in his eye. It glistened in the sunshine, then escaped when he blinked and trickled down his cheek.

Edith put her hand up and wiped it away with her thumb, only to have Philip take hold of her hand and put it to his lips. 'You are so beautiful, Edith, from the inside out and the outside in. I love you.'

All pain dissolved. All heartbreak lessened as she felt herself wrapped in these words she so longed to hear.

'Oh, Philip, I love you too, so very much . . . but—'

Her protest went into his kiss. A gentle touching of lips that completed the putting together of her shattered world.

'There is no "but", darling. We will make it so there isn't any.'

'And your parents? Are they not a "but"?'

Philip took a deep breath. 'They are, well, a problem. But I will tackle them bit by bit so as not to hurt them – not that . . . well, they have such grand ideas of a wife for me. One from the upper classes, almost as if it would be the cherry on their cake for me to marry into a family that has a title, or someone from a family with a long history of wealth . . . Oh, it isn't the money – they have plenty – but the prestige it will give them, helping them to move from self-made to accepted.'

Edith didn't understand, except to know that she wasn't the kind of girl Philip's parents wanted for him. But then she already knew that from what he'd said before about them. 'So, what will you do?'

'I will try to make them see reason; remind them that they were nobody in the beginning. Just Mr and Mrs Bradshaw with a small business, and they thought it all right for them to prosper and move up in the world, so why isn't it acceptable for others to do the same?'

'Would it help if I tried to talk like you?'

'No, you mustn't do that. I love the way you speak, it is you. Don't change one thing about yourself. They will have to accept you as you are. Besides, Father has an accent. He tries hard not to slip in the odd word or he finds himself in real trouble with Mother but his natural way of speaking is not dissimilar to yours.'

Edith didn't say, but the more she heard, the more of an impression she gained that it was Philip's mother who was the problem. And she didn't feel strong enough to tackle any problems of any kind.

'Eeh, Philip, maybe we're not suited. I mean, we're so different – our backgrounds, our learning, our whole lives. I can't understand your world and you can't understand mine. By, I can see it all coming between us in the end.'

'No, Edith. It will work. We'll make it. If it comes to it, we could run away together, make a new life of our own. We'll find jobs and a cottage to rent. I have some money and can sell my car, we'll manage somehow.'

'No. You think you will, but you wouldn't last five minutes walking in my shoes.'

'I'm stronger than you think. And if it meant that was the only way, then I would do it to be with you.'

'Philip, talking about it is different to living it. I'm tired of having nothing and living hand to mouth. I want a better life for me and any children I might have in the future. I don't want to be like my parents; I want to be different and make them proud of me. Something's got to come out of me losing me family, and talking to you about the future – well, our future together – I know now that I want that to be in the kind of life you have, not the one I have.'

Philip looked shocked.

'I don't mean by marrying into your money, Philip. I mean by improving myself, by getting an education. I've realised that I have a chance now. I have no ties, Alice and Gerald have offered me a home – a room of me own and to live rent-free. If I go back to work and work hard, I'll be able to afford to go to the tutor who Jackie, Marg's sister, goes to, and then one day do something that gets me out of the rut I was born into.'

'Well, I don't know what to say . . . You mean, you won't marry me because you want to make your own way in life?'

'You never asked me to marry you. You talked of bringing your parents round to accepting me, and about running away together, but by, you never once asked me to marry you.'

With this, Philip went down on one knee in front of the bench and looked up into her face. To Edith, he looked beautiful with the lowering sun shining on him.

'Will you marry me, Edith?'

'Aye, I will, if you stop all this talk of making your parents accept me and start talking of how me and you can build a good future together, with or without them at first, but hoping they come to respect me for what I achieve in the future.'

'I promise. If you agree to marry me, we'll make a plan for us both to get a different future, separate from anyone else's influence.'

'Right, you're on. Under them terms, I'll marry you, in time. Just as soon as you prove to me that we can do this.'

'My, you're a hard woman.' Philip stood up. 'Well, as a man, I won't always bow down to you, but seeing as you are talking sense, I will this time. I've made my mind up, I am going to look into becoming a teacher, and no matter what the opposition, I am going to do it. I won't be able to marry you until then, but that day will come and we will marry with our heads held high.'

'Oh, I'm so glad, as you told me that was your ambition in the very beginning. If nothing else, I now know life is a gift and we have to follow our calling to be truly happy. I don't know what mine is yet, but when I find out what I am capable of, then I'll have options.'

'Is there anything you've ever admired? I mean, when you've seen something, you've had a desire to be doing it?'

'You'll think me daft now, but aye, and it's the same as yours. We had a teacher when I first started school – her name was Miss Clarke. I adored her and wanted to be like her and, well, one day, she said to me, "You're a very clever girl, Edith. Always pay attention to learning and life will change." I did for a while, but it became hopeless, and I just went the way of all the others of my standing. Not bothering with school, but looking for ways to earn money to help the family keep its head above water, then leaving school and going into the factory, solely to earn money, not because it was what I wanted to do.'

'I don't think that daft, I think it would be wonderful for us both to teach. We could sit and mark our pupils' work together, plan lessons for them together – even work at the same school!'

'But what if I'm not clever enough?'

'You are, I know you are. Would your pride allow me to help you fund extra lessons? I know you could afford one a week, but what if you had two?'

Edith's pride rose up, but she squashed it. Philip loved her, had faith in her, and so she wouldn't deny him the right to help her. 'Ta, Philip. With two lessons a week I'd soon catch up.'

'Well then, our future is set. Two years from now, I will be a teacher and you a trainee teacher, and we will marry. In the meantime, I am going to use some of the money I have to rent a small house, and to buy my teacher training course. I'll move out of my father and mother's as the atmosphere won't be worth living in, and certainly not conducive to me studying.'

Edith felt so happy. She thought Philip must have a fortune in his own right to be able to do all this and live without working for the time it would take, but she knew she wouldn't put obstacles in his way and would help him all she could.

A hope entered her, and a joy, which she never thought she would ever feel again – and with it came the knowledge that she had so much to live for and to look forward to . . . so very much.

THIRTY-FOUR

Alice

'Well, lass, tomorrow's the day.'

Alice felt a thrill go through her at these words from Marg. 'I can't believe it, but it's nice to have this evening with just the three of us.'

'Aye, the lads are happy with Jackie and Ma and Gran, so I'm able to be here at yours with no worries. So, where's that bottle of sherry you promised us, eh?'

When they had settled down with a glass of sherry each, Edith proposed a toast. 'To happiness.'

The toast done, Alice noticed Marg looked a little down. 'So, Marg, you've another walk with Clive arranged then?'

'Aye, I have, and I'm looking forward to it an' all. Talking to Clive's like nothing I've ever known. It's proper conversation, and I've found that I love walking. We did a whole circuit of the perimeter of Stanley Park and I hardly noticed it, and it was grand to get out of the house.'

'By, you learnt some big words an' all, by the sound of it.'

'Ha! Well, I'm being educated at the same time, as it happens – the names of flowers and bushes . . . oh, and trees an' all. And politics. I tell you, girls, there's a lot to why we should vote, you wouldn't believe it. And there's trouble brewing in the world an' all. But, hey, we won't talk about that.'

Alice was reminded of Gerald explaining things to her about what was happening in other countries and how it might affect them, but she didn't want to go down that road. 'So, you're falling for him, then?'

'Ha, Alice, you daft apeth! No, it's just that Clive listens to me. He'll let me rabbit on about my job, troubles at home . . . well, anything I choose to rabbit on about. I feel like a new person when I get home.'

'Eh, I have a good feeling about all of our futures. I mean, our Edith going back to school, that's something I never expected. Where did that come from, Edith?'

Marg laughed at Alice. 'Well, she was always the bright one when we were youngsters.'

'I know, but . . . I can't take it in. Not once have you ever expressed the wish to go back to taking lessons, Edith.'

'The desire was always there, but how could I, with my circumstances? Eeh, I'm not saying . . .'

'Don't be daft, we know what you're saying, and I for one am very proud of you.'

'Aye, me too, and excited that you're going to come to mine once a week and study with Jackie and bring Harry with you. By, I'll have a regular school going on in me front room.'

'Well, I thought it would be good to work with others. They can help me out. And then for me and you, Marg, to have a cocoa together before I go back to Alice's with Harry.'

'That'll be grand, though I'm not sure if you're coming to be with me or because you'll miss my cocoa!'

They all laughed at this. Then Alice said, 'Now you've mentioned cocoa, I think I'll come an' all. Me and you can have a natter while they're hard at it, Marg, and then the three of us can have our cocoa like we do now.'

Marg beamed. 'That'd be grand, lasses, just grand.'

The next morning was windy and cloudy, but it didn't dampen Alice's spirit. Today was going to be the happiest day of her life, whatever the weather.

The house smelt of bacon frying, and had the sound of a happy café as everyone busied themselves laying the table and making tea while Marg fried the bacon and eggs that Alice had bought in especially for this morning. The compensation that Clive had seen to it that Alice received, on top of what her da had been paid off with, paid for so many little extras, but most of it she'd used to open a savings account for each of the lads. Gerald had helped her with that.

The chatter was as loud as the clanging of plates, and the excitement had Alice trotting out the back to the loo a lot more often than she normally would.

She was so happy that even the strong Blackpool wind made her giggle. And despite it, she so looked forward to the special treat that Gerald had arranged for her.

Knowing her love of the Blackpool front, he'd organised that, after the service at St Kentigern's Church, a Rolls Royce would take them down to the seafront and along the promenade.

It felt to Alice that she was Cinderella, not Alice from a

poor family beaten by a sick da, used as a skivvy, and often hungry while fighting to make sure her brothers were looked after.

And she knew that the happiness she had found was gifted to Edith too, though it would take time – a long time – for Edith to fully be able to clutch that happiness and hold it as her right.

Marg still worried her, but there was hope, and she knew that from the allowance Gerald was going to give her, she could help Marg out whenever she needed it. So all in all, the three of them had made it through, and were stronger than they'd ever been. And that counted for a lot, didn't it?

THIRTY-FIVE

Marg

Marg's eyes filled with tears as she followed Alice up the aisle and as Gerald turned around to greet his beautiful bride. Alice looked like a princess in her cream satin gown.

She had to admit to feeling like one herself, and her heart swelled to see Jackie looking so grown-up and beautiful, and Edith ... oh, Edith, so regal-looking and graceful and, well, just stunning.

Each wore, just as Alice had dreamt of, a long straight gown in the same satin cream material as Alice's, but with a sash of different colours: royal blue, green and purple.

But it wasn't just the bridal party — the boys in smart suits and Gerald and Philip in tails — that made up the picture that touched her heart, it was seeing her gran too, dressed in a lovely blue frock, and her ma in a beige-coloured one, both of which they'd had for a long time but she'd never seen them wear. And Gran's hat, bonnet-type and brown with a felt bow on one side. Oh, how proud she looked.

As this thought went through her head, she heard her gran's voice. 'Eeh, Vera, I know that pretty girl there. The one with our Jackie. By, she's a bonny lass, and lovely with it an' all.'

A few sniggers went around as this resounded above the organ playing, but Marg didn't mind. Her gran was her gran, and she loved her.

During the service, Gran could be heard asking questions: 'Who's getting married, then, Vera? Eeh, I remember when I married me John. Handsome he was, just like the bridegroom at the altar is.'

Ma could be heard shushing Gran, but it made no difference.

'By, if I were a few years younger, that lass wouldn't stand a chance with him.'

Gerald burst out laughing at this, followed by the rest of the congregation. It was the priest who saved the day. 'Would the lovely lady with the commentary like to come up and sit at the front?'

Marg was astonished and a little embarrassed by this, but what happened next filled her with joy as Gerald's ma got up and went to Gran's pew. Taking Gran's arm, she guided her to the front to sit between her and her husband. Both of them took hold of one of Gran's hands and held them. Gran beamed. 'I had a lovely wedding last week. Me John'll be here in a mo.'

Mrs Melford's gentle voice could be heard saying, 'Oh, my dear, you must tell us about it and introduce us to your lovely John, but for a few moments, we have to be quiet to allow Alice and Gerald to get married, just like you did.'

'Aye, all right. I'll watch, eh?'

'Yes, dear.'

Marg saw that Jackie was bright red with embarrassment, so she winked at her and smiled. Jackie smiled back, reassuring Marg that she was all right.

When Alice and Gerald were declared man and wife, and the priest invited them to follow him to sign the register, and for Edith and Marg to come too to witness the signing, Gerald's parents came and brought Gran with them.

Marg could hear Mrs Melford explaining to Gran, 'This is an important part of the wedding, dear, as now they have to be married in the eyes of the law, too.'

'Aw, I knaw. And did you knaw that young lady, the prettiest of them all, is me granddaughter, Marg?'

Marg could hold her tears no longer, they spilt over. Gentle, loving tears that held the happiness of this moment for her.

Once the ceremony was over, she took Gran in her arms. 'Eeh, Gran, I love you.'

'Do you, lass? Well, that's nice of you. What's your name?'

Marg laughed out loud. 'Eeh, Gran, you're a one. Come on, we've to follow Alice and Gerald out of the church and see them off in that amazing car.'

Gran didn't protest at being led outside and waved in an excited manner as Alice and Gerald drove off. 'Eeh, I had a lovely wedding. Have you met me John?'

'I did when little, but tell me all about him, Gran.'

As she listened to the tale she'd heard so many times – often with naughty bits she didn't want to hear and was glad weren't included today – Marg looked at Jackie and Edith, and the thought passed through her head that this wasn't the end of life as she knew it, but the beginning of a new one.

For herself, she had a lot to worry about, but she knew she had the best friends and sister in the world to help her through it. Then something happened that lifted her back into hopefulness – she caught sight of Clive and gave him a little wave, but then blushed as he blew her a kiss.

He was nice. She liked Clive. Liked him a lot.

THIRTY-SIX

Alice

Alice had waved till they got out of sight and then snuggled up to Gerald – well, as close as her long veil would let her – and thrilled at his words.

'Darling, I love you, thank you for becoming my wife.'

'I love you an' all, Gerald, and I'm going to try to be the best wife any man has ever had.'

He planted a tender kiss on her lips.

The car rocked them gently, in a similar way to how she remembered the carriage of the big wheel doing when, aged around five, she'd sat in it with her da, waiting for others to load onto it.

The memory gave her a nice feeling as all memories of her da did now that the horrid ones were firmly in the back of her mind, to be rarely visited.

'Didn't Harry do a lovely job of giving me away? I was so proud of him.'

'I was proud of all my new family. As it feels as though Edith, Marg and Jackie are that too now. Oh, and after today, that includes Gran!'

They both laughed at this. 'She were a one, weren't she? Eeh, she reckoned she could give me a run for me money if she were young again.'

'Ha! I must admit to loving her wrinkly face and twinkly blue eyes, but no, she wouldn't have stood a chance, darling ... You know, joking aside, we have to admire Marg and Jackie for how they cope, and we'll have to help them all we can. How do you feel about having Gran to tea with us once a week, to give Marg a break?'

'That'd be grand, if she'd settle.'

'Yes, we must consider that, but we'll try it and see ... Oh, look, we're turning onto the prom.'

Alice looked out of the window at the churning sea as grey as the sky, and everything blowing in the wind – the skirts of the ladies, the flags still on the street lamps from the Coronation Day celebrations, and she giggled as a man lost his hat and went running after it.

On the other side she watched the stalls as they passed by. The rock stand with the lovely coloured sticks of rock she knew would have Blackpool written through them. The win-a-goldfish stall and the coconut shy. Here she waved and grinned out at Bendy, who lifted his hat and did a cartwheel, sending them both into a fit of giggles.

'I'll tell you about him one day, he's a card.'

Gerald smiled as they rested back again. 'I've still so much to learn about you, Alice, my darling wife. But I'm going to enjoy doing so.'

Alice didn't answer, just squeezed his hand. She didn't want anything to interrupt her from gazing out and enjoying the moment.

Above the silent engine she could hear the calls of the stall-holders, and drifting through her open window were the smells of Blackpool – the fish and chips, the hot tattie wagon and the salty sea air.

The smell of the food seemed to have got to Gerald as he said, 'Do you know, we should have ordered fish and chips for all our guests, darling. I think they would have gone down a treat.'

'No, they aren't for such occasions, they're really meant to be eaten out of the newspaper with your fingers – even how we had them was considered posh . . . Eeh, look!'

The car had stopped, as an elephant was led out of Blackpool Tower Circus to take a bath in the sea. 'Where else but Blackpool, eh?'

They laughed as the elephant looked their way and lifted his trunk to bellow at them. 'Eeh, this is the best treat ever. Ta, Gerald.'

'Well, you'll have a lifetime of treats now, my darling.'

Alice felt her body fill with happiness. Life had taken a surprising twist for her and for Edith. She hoped it would for Marg too.

As she leant back and Gerald put his arm around her, she knew she was blessed: to have Gerald, this wonderful chance in life, and the best friends anyone could wish for in Edith and Marg.

Suddenly, her ma came into her mind. She imagined her dancing with her da, just how she'd caught them doing one night when she was about eleven years old and she'd crept downstairs, drawn by the music.

Her ma's saying came to her: *Tomorrow's another day, lass.*

Aye, another day, Alice thought. *A new beginning for us all.*

406

ACKNOWLEDGEMENTS

My heartfelt thanks to Sphere, my publisher. And to all those involved in getting my book to the shelves; to Rebecca Farrell, my editor, and Thalia Proctor and her team of copy editing and proofreading editors, who make my work sing off the page whilst keeping my voice. Thank you.

Special thanks to my agent, Judith Murdoch, who is in my corner and works so hard for me and all her authors. A gem.

As always, to my beloved husband and rock, Roy, and to all my family. You all help me to climb my mountain and I love you all dearly.

A LETTER FROM MAGGIE

Hello everyone, from my little-bedroom office, where I sit for hours weaving my tales . . .

I hope you enjoyed what this one had to offer. If you did, may I share a little saying with you that authors have? 'A review is like a hug'.

So, if you are a member of Goodreads, Facebook, any book site, or Amazon, then you too can hug the author whose books you loved by leaving a review on these platforms. I hope I get mine. Thank you.

I hope, too, that you have all kept well and safe and have found lots to do during lockdown. For my part, I have been busy writing the second in the trilogy, *The Halfpenny Girls' Christmas*, so look out for that hitting the shelves later this year.

Set in 1939, this second book continues the girls' struggles to rebuild their lives. Happiness comes to them all, if peppered by devastation at times and the threat of war, which hovers like a black cloud above them. As the year goes on, their loved ones are called up and they wonder if they will be able to celebrate a family Christmas. But Marg, Edith and Alice stay strong throughout and their bond never breaks.

I loved writing it and cried, laughed and adored being in the girls' lives once more.

To research my books, I usually travel to the places they are set to get a feel for the area, but the only travelling I needed to do for this trilogy was to ride around my native, beloved Blackpool, looking for suitable streets to use, and refer to my wealth of history books on my town – see the reading list below for the main ones I used for this first in the trilogy.

And so, this book came mostly from my own knowledge and from my heart – as the dedication did too, as it honours people who meant so much to those who are special to me: my readers.

The golden couple and the selection of whose loved ones were chosen came about through my contact with readers on Facebook. We have an old saying up here: 'You come as a stranger, but leave as a friend'. And that is what happens on my Facebook page – though they stay, not leave!

I would love you to join me there too. I often run competitions and generally interact with all the followers, keeping everyone up to date with the latest news on my books and where I am holding book launches and book signings, etc, as well as what I am up to in my daily life.

The links to how to become part of all that, and to all the ways you can contact me direct, are listed below.

I look forward to hearing from you and making a friend of you too.

Much love, Maggie x

CONTACT ME

https://www.facebook.com/MaggieMasonAuthor

www.authormarywood.com

Twitter: @authormary

MY READING LIST

The Biscuit Girls – Hunter Davies
Lost Blackpool – Chris Bottomley and Allan W. Wood
A-Z of Blackpool: Places-People-History – Allen W. Wood and Chris Bottomley